ALGONQUINS

NATION IROQUOIS

Lac FRONTENAC

MER DES IROQUOIS

NOUV. ANGLETERRE

Nouv. Yorck

Sonnontouan Pensilvanie

IROQUOIS

u Chat

Les Calicuas

Tionontatecaga

VIRGINIE

Elan

Water R.

DE COLLIS

Port Royal

I. de Cumberland

Baye de S. Mathieu

Boston

Cap Henry

I. Pakach

I. Raonoik

C. Hatteras

Cap Lookout

Cap Fear

MER DE VIRGINIE DE LA NOUV. ANGLETERRE

GRANDE MER DU

Les Isles Bermudes

I. de S. Georges

LES ISLES LUCAYES

BAHAMA

Bahama

Bancde Bahama

DE BAHAMA

A Place
Called FREEDOM

A Place Called FREEDOM

KEN FOLLETT

CROWN PUBLISHERS, INC.
NEW YORK

Published by Crown Publishers, Inc., 201 East 50th Street, New York, New York 10022. Member of the Crown Publishing Group.

Random House, Inc. New York, Toronto, London, Sydney, Auckland

CROWN is a trademark of Crown Publishers, Inc.

Manufactured in the U.S.A.

Design by Nancy Kenmore

Endpaper and part title maps courtesy the Bettmann Archive

Library of Congress Cataloging-in-Publication Data
Follett, Ken.
    A place called freedom / Ken Follett.—1st ed.
      p. cm.
     I. Title.
  PR6056.045P58   1995
   823´.914—dc20   95-8404
                                                                        CIP

ISBN 0-517-70176-6

10 9 8 7 6 5 4 3 2 1

First Edition

Dedicated to
the memory of
JOHN SMITH

I did a lot of gardening when I first moved into High Glen House, and that's how I found the iron collar.

The house was falling down and the garden was overgrown. A crazy old lady had lived here for twenty years and never given it a lick of paint. She died and I bought it from her son, who owns the Toyota dealership in Kirkburn, the nearest town, fifty miles away.

You might wonder why a person would buy a dilapidated house fifty miles from nowhere. But I just love this valley. There are shy deer in the woods and an eagles' nest right at the top of the ridge. Out in the garden I would spend half the time leaning on my spade and staring at the blue-green mountainsides.

But I did some digging too. I decided to plant some shrubs around the outhouse. It's not a handsome building—clapboard walls with no windows—and I wanted to screen it with bushes. While I was digging the trench, I found a box.

It wasn't very big, about the size of those cases that contain twelve bottles of good wine. It wasn't fancy either: just plain unvarnished wood held together with rusty nails. I broke it open with the blade of my spade.

There were two things inside.

One was a big old book. I got quite excited at that: perhaps it was a family Bible, with an intriguing history written on the flyleaf—the births, marriages and deaths of people who had lived *in my house a hundred years ago. But I was disappointed. When I opened it I found that the pages had turned to pulp. Not a word could be read.*

The other item was an oilcloth bag. That, too, was rotten, and when I touched it with my gardening gloves it disintegrated. Inside was an iron ring about six inches across. It was tarnished, but the oilcloth bag had prevented it from rusting away.

It looked crudely made, probably by a village blacksmith, and at first I thought it might have been part of a cart or a plow. But why had someone wrapped it carefully in oilcloth to preserve it? There was a break in the ring and it had been bent. I began to think of it as a collar that some prisoner had been forced to wear. When the prisoner escaped the ring had been broken with a heavy blacksmith's tool, then bent to get it off.

I took it in the house and started to clean it up. It was slow work, so I steeped it in RustAway overnight then tried again in the morning. As I polished it with a rag, an inscription became visible.

It was engraved in old-fashioned curly writing, and it took me a while to figure it out, but this is what it said:

This man is the property of
Sir George Jamisson of Fife.

A.D. 1767.

It's here on my desk, beside the computer. I use it as a paperweight. I often pick it up and turn it in my hands, rereading that inscription. If the iron collar could talk, I think to myself, what kind of story would it tell?

I

Scotland

1

S NOW CROWNED THE RIDGES OF HIGH GLEN AND LAY ON THE WOODED slopes in pearly patches, like jewelry on the bosom of a green silk dress. In the valley bottom a hasty stream dodged between icy rocks. The bitter wind that howled inland from the North Sea brought flurries of sleet and hail.

Walking to church in the morning the McAsh twins, Malachi and Esther, followed a zigzag trail along the eastern slope of the glen. Malachi, known as Mack, wore a plaid cape and tweed breeches, but his legs were bare below the knee, and his feet, without stockings, froze in his wooden clogs. However, he was young and hot-blooded, and he hardly noticed the cold.

This was not the shortest way to church but High Glen always thrilled him. The high mountainsides, the quiet mysterious woods and the laughing water formed a landscape familiar to his soul. He had watched a pair of eagles raise three sets of nestlings here. Like the eagles, he had stolen the laird's salmon from the teeming stream. And, like the deer, he had hidden in the trees, silent and still, when the gamekeepers came.

The laird was a woman, Lady Hallim, a widow with a daughter. The land on the far side of the mountain belonged to Sir George Jamisson, and it was a different world. Engineers had torn great holes in the mountainsides; manmade hills of slag disfigured the valley; massive wagons loaded with coal plowed the muddy road; and the stream was black with dust. There the twins lived, in a village called Heugh, a long row of low stone houses marching uphill like a staircase.

They were male and female versions of the same image. Both had fair hair blackened by coal dust, and striking pale green eyes. Both were short and broad backed, with strongly muscled arms and legs. Both were opinionated and argumentative.

Arguments were a family tradition. Their father had been an all-round nonconformist, eager to disagree with the government, the church or any other authority. Their mother had worked for Lady Hallim before her marriage, and like many servants she identified with the upper class. One bitter winter, when the pit had closed for a month after an explosion, Father had died of the black spit, the cough that killed so many coal miners; and Mother got pneumonia and followed him within a few weeks. But the arguments went on, usually on Saturday nights in Mrs. Wheighel's parlor, the nearest thing to a tavern in the village of Heugh.

The estate workers and the crofters took Mother's view. They said the king was appointed by God, and that was why people had to obey him. The coal miners had heard newer ideas. John Locke and other philosophers said a government's authority could come only from the consent of the people. This theory appealed to Mack.

Few miners in Heugh could read, but Mack's mother could, and he had pestered her to teach him. She had taught both her children, ignoring the gibes of her husband, who said she had ideas above her station. At Mrs. Wheighel's Mack was called on to read aloud from the *Times*, the *Edinburgh Advertiser*, and political journals such as the radical *North Briton*. The papers were always weeks out of date, sometimes months, but the men and women of the village listened avidly to long speeches reported verbatim, satirical diatribes, and accounts of strikes, protests and riots.

It was after a Saturday night argument at Mrs. Wheighel's that Mack had written the letter.

None of the miners had ever written a letter before, and there had been long consultations about every word. It was addressed to Caspar Gordonson, a London lawyer who wrote articles in the journals ridiculing the government. The letter had been entrusted to Davey Patch, the one-eyed peddler, for posting; and Mack had wondered if it would ever reach its destination.

The reply had come yesterday, and it was the most exciting thing that had ever happened to Mack. It would change his life beyond recognition, he thought. It might set him free.

As far back as he could remember he had longed to be free. As a child he had envied Davey Patch, who roamed from village to village selling knives and string and ballads. What was so wonderful about Davey's life, to the child Mack, was that he could get up at sunrise and go to sleep when he felt tired. Mack, from the age of seven, had been shaken awake by his mother a few minutes before two o'clock in the morning and had worked down the mine for fifteen hours, finishing at five o'clock in the afternoon; then had staggered home, often to fall asleep over his evening porridge.

Mack no longer wanted to be a peddler, but he still yearned for a different life. He dreamed of building a house for himself, in a valley like High Glen, on a piece of land he could call his own; of working from dawn to dusk and resting all the hours of darkness; of the freedom to go fishing on a sunny day, in a place where the salmon belonged not to the laird but to whoever caught them. And the letter in his hand meant that his dreams might come true.

"I'm still not sure you should read it aloud in church," Esther said as they tramped across the frozen mountainside.

Mack was not sure either, but he said: "Why not?"

"There'll be trouble. Ratchett will be furious." Harry Ratchett was the viewer, the man who managed the mine on behalf of the owner. "He might even tell Sir George, and then what will they do to you?"

He knew she was right, and his heart was full of trepidation. But that did not stop him arguing with her. "If I keep the letter to myself, it's pointless," he said.

"Well, you could show it to Ratchett privately. He might let you leave quietly, without any fuss."

Mack glanced at his twin out of the corner of his eye. She was not in a dogmatic frame of mind, he could tell. She looked troubled rather than combative. He felt a surge of affection for her. Whatever happened, she would be on his side.

All the same he shook his head stubbornly. "I'm not the only one affected by this letter. There's at least five lads would want to get away from here, if they knew they could. And what about future generations?"

She gave him a shrewd look. "You may be right—but that's not the real reason. You want to stand up in church and prove the mine owner wrong."

"No, I don't!" Mack protested. Then he thought for a moment and grinned. "Well, there may be something in what you say. We've heard so many sermons about obeying the law and respecting our betters. Now we find that they've been lying to us, all along, about the one law that affects us most. Of course I want to stand up and shout it aloud."

"Don't give them reason to punish you," she said worriedly.

He tried to reassure her. "I'll be as polite and humble as can be," he said. "You'll hardly recognize me."

"Humble!" she said skeptically. "I'd like to see that."

"I'm just going to say what the law is—how can that be wrong?"

"It's incautious."

"Aye, that it is," he conceded. "But I'm going to do it anyway."

They crossed a ridge and dropped down the far side, back into Coalpit Glen. As they descended, the air became a little less cold. A few moments later the small stone church came into view, beside a bridge over the dirty river.

Near the churchyard clustered a few crofters' hovels. These were round huts with an open fire in the middle of the earth floor and a hole in the roof to let the smoke out, the one room shared by cattle and people all winter. The miners' houses, farther up the glen near the pits, were better: though they, too, had earth floors and turf roofs, every one had a fireplace and a proper chimney, and glass in the little window by the door; and miners were not obliged to share their space with cows. All the same the crofters considered themselves free and independent, and looked down on the miners.

However, it was not the peasants' huts that now arrested the attention of Mack and Esther and brought them up short. A closed carriage with a fine pair of grays in harness stood at the church porch. Several ladies in hooped skirts and fur wraps were getting out, helped by the pastor, holding on to their fashionable lacy hats.

Esther touched Mack's arm and pointed to the bridge. Riding across on a big chestnut hunter, his head bent into the cold wind, was the owner of the mine, the laird of the glen, Sir George Jamisson.

Jamisson had not been seen here for five years. He lived in London, which was a week's journey by ship, two weeks by stagecoach. He had once been a penny-pinching Edinburgh chandler, people said, selling candles and gin from a corner shop, and no more honest than he had to be. Then a relative had died young and childless, and George had inherited the castle and the mines. On that foundation he had built a business empire that stretched to such unimaginably distant places as Barbados and Virginia. And he was now starchily respectable: a baronet, a magistrate, and alderman of Wapping, responsible for law and order along London's waterfront.

He was obviously paying a visit to his Scottish estate, accompanied by family and guests.

"Well, that's that," Esther said with relief.

"What do you mean?" said Mack, although he could guess.

"You won't be able to read out your letter now."

"Why not?"

"Malachi McAsh, don't be a damn fool!" she exclaimed. "Not in front of the laird himself!"

"On the contrary," he said stubbornly. "This makes it all the better."

L IZZIE HALLIM REFUSED TO GO TO CHURCH IN THE CARRIAGE. IT WAS a silly idea. The road from Jamisson Castle was a rutted, potholed track, its muddy ridges frozen as hard as rock. The ride would be frightfully bumpy, the carriage would have to go at walking pace, and the passengers would arrive cold and bruised and probably late. She insisted on riding to church.

Such unladylike behavior made her mother despair. "How will you ever get a husband if you always act like a man?" Lady Hallim said.

"I can get a husband whenever I like," Lizzie replied. It was true: men fell in love with her all the time. "The problem is finding one I can put up with for more than half an hour."

"The problem is finding one that doesn't scare easily," her mother muttered.

Lizzie laughed. They were both right. Men fell in love with her at first sight, then found out what she was like and backed off hurriedly. Her comments had scandalized Edinburgh society for years. At her first ball, talking to a trio of old dowagers, she had remarked that the high sheriff had a fat backside, and her reputation had never recovered. Last year Mother had taken her to London in the spring and "launched" her into English society. It had been a disaster. Lizzie had talked too loud, laughed too much and openly mocked the elaborate manners and tight clothes of the dandified young men who tried to court her.

"It's because you grew up without a man in the house," her mother added. "It's made you too independent." With that she got into the carriage.

Lizzie walked across the flinty front of Jamisson Castle, heading for the stables on the east side. Her father had died when she was three, so she hardly remembered him. When she asked what killed him her mother said vaguely: "Liver." He had left them penniless. For years Mother had scraped by, mortgaging more and more of the Hallim estate, waiting for Lizzie to grow up and marry a wealthy man who would solve all their problems. Now Lizzie was twenty years old and it was time to fulfill her destiny.

That was undoubtedly why the Jamisson family were visiting their Scottish property again after all these years, and why their principal houseguests were their neighbors, Lizzie and her mother, who lived only ten miles away. The pretext for the party was the twenty-first birthday of the younger son, Jay; but the real reason was that they wanted Lizzie to marry the older son, Robert.

Mother was in favor, as Robert was the heir to a great fortune. Sir George was in favor because he wanted to add the Hallim estate to the Jamisson family's land. Robert seemed to be in favor, to judge by the way he had been paying attention to her ever since they arrived; although it was always hard to know what was in Robert's heart.

She saw him standing in the stable yard, waiting for the horses to be saddled. He resembled the portrait of his mother that hung in the castle hall—a grave, plain woman with fine hair and light eyes and a determined look about the mouth. There was nothing wrong with him: he was not especially ugly, neither thin nor fat, nor did he smell bad or drink too much or dress effeminately. He was a great catch, Lizzie told herself, and if he proposed marriage she would probably accept. She was not in love with him, but she knew her duty.

She decided to banter with him a little. "It really is most inconsiderate of you to live in London," she said.

"Inconsiderate?" He frowned. "Why?"

"You leave us without neighbors." Still he looked puzzled. It seemed he did not have much of a sense of humor. She explained: "With you away there isn't another soul between here and Edinburgh."

A voice behind her said: "Apart from a hundred families of coal miners and several villages of crofters."

"You know what I mean," she said, turning. The man who had spoken was a stranger to her. With her usual directness she said: "Anyway, who are you?"

"Jay Jamisson," he said with a bow. "Robert's cleverer brother. How could you forget?"

"Oh!" She had heard he had arrived late last night, but she had not recognized him. Five years ago he had been several inches shorter, with pimples on his forehead and a few soft blond hairs on his chin. He was handsomer now. But he had not been clever then and she doubted if he had changed in that respect. "I remember you," she said. "I recognize the conceit."

He grinned. "If only I'd had your example of humility and self-effacement to copy, Miss Hallim."

Robert said: "Hullo, Jay. Welcome to Castle Jamisson."

Jay looked suddenly sulky. "Drop the proprietorial air, Robert. You may be the elder son but you haven't inherited the place yet."

Lizzie intervened, saying: "Congratulations on your twenty-first birthday."

"Thank you."

"Is it today?"

"Yes."

Robert said impatiently: "Are you going to ride to church with us?"

Lizzie saw hatred in Jay's eyes, but his voice was neutral. "Yes. I've told them to saddle a horse for me."

"We'd better get going." Robert turned toward the stable and raised his voice. "Hurry up in there!"

"All set, sir," a groom called from within, and a moment later three horses were led out: a sturdy black pony, a light bay mare, and a gray gelding.

Jay said: "I suppose these beasts have been hired from some Edinburgh horse-dealer." His tone was critical, but he went to the gelding and patted its neck, letting it nuzzle his blue riding-coat. Lizzie saw that he was comfortable with horses and fond of them.

She mounted the black pony, riding sidesaddle, and trotted out of the yard. The brothers followed, Jay on the gelding and Robert on the mare. The wind blew sleet into Lizzie's eyes. Snow underfoot made the road treacherous, for it hid potholes a foot or more deep that caused the horses to stumble. Lizzie said: "Let's ride through the woods. It will be sheltered, and the ground is not so uneven." Without waiting for agreement she turned her horse off the road and into the ancient forest.

Underneath the tall pines the forest floor was clear of bushes. Streamlets and marshy patches were frozen hard, and the ground was dusted white. Lizzie urged her pony into a canter. After a moment the gray horse passed her. She glanced up and saw a challenging grin on Jay's face: he wanted to race. She gave a whoop and kicked the pony, who sprang forward eagerly.

They dashed through the trees, ducking under low boughs, jumping over fallen trunks, and splashing heedlessly through streams. Jay's horse was bigger and would have been faster in a gallop, but the pony's short legs and light frame were better adapted to this terrain, and gradually Lizzie pulled ahead. When she could no longer hear Jay's horse she slowed down and came to a standstill in a clearing.

Jay soon caught up, but there was no sign of Robert. Lizzie guessed he was too sensible to risk his neck in a pointless race. She and Jay walked on, side by side, catching their breath. Heat rose from the horses, keeping the riders warm. "I'd like to race you on the straight," Jay panted.

"Riding astride I'd beat you," she said.

He looked a little shocked. All well-bred women rode sidesaddle. For a woman to ride astride was considered vulgar. Lizzie thought that was a silly idea, and when she was alone she rode like a man.

She studied Jay out of the corner of her eye. His mother, Alicia, Sir George's second wife, was a fair-haired coquette, and Jay had her blue eyes and winning smile. "What do you do in London?" Lizzie asked him.

"I'm in the Third Regiment of Foot Guards." A note of pride came into his voice and he added: "I've just been made a captain."

"Well, Captain Jamisson, what do you brave soldiers have to do?"

she said mockingly. "Is there a war in London at the moment? Any enemies for you to kill?"

"There's plenty to do keeping the mob under control."

Lizzie suddenly remembered Jay as a mean, bullying child, and she wondered if he enjoyed his work. "And how do you control them?" she asked.

"For example, by escorting criminals to the gallows, and making sure they don't get rescued by their cronies before the hangman does his work."

"So you spend your time killing Englishmen, like a true Scots hero."

He did not seem to mind being teased. "One day I'd like to resign my commission and go abroad," he said.

"Oh—why?"

"No one takes any notice of a younger son in this country. Even servants stop and think about it when you give them an order."

"And you believe it will be different elsewhere?"

"Everything is different in the colonies. I've read books about it. People are more free and easy. You're taken for what you are."

"What would you do?"

"My family has a sugar plantation in Barbados. I'm hoping my father will give it to me for my twenty-first birthday, as my portion, so to speak."

Lizzie felt deeply envious. "Lucky you," she said. "There's nothing I'd like more than to go to a new country. How thrilling it would be."

"It's a rough life out there," he said. "You might miss the comforts of home—shops and operas and French fashions, and so on."

"I don't care for any of that," she said contemptuously. "I hate these clothes." She was wearing a hooped skirt and a tight-waisted corset. "I'd like to dress like a man, in breeches and shirt and riding boots."

He laughed. "That might be going a bit far, even in Barbados."

Lizzie was thinking: Now, if Robert would take me to Barbados, I'd marry him like a shot.

"And you have slaves to do all the work," Jay added.

They emerged from the forest a few yards upstream from the bridge.

On the other side of the water, the miners were filing into the little church.

Lizzie was still thinking about Barbados. "It must be very odd, to own slaves, and be able to do anything you like to them, as if they were beasts," she said. "Doesn't it make you feel strange?"

"Not in the least," Jay said with a smile.

T HE LITTLE CHURCH WAS FULL. THE JAMISSON FAMILY AND THEIR guests took up a great deal of room, the women with their wide skirts and the men with their swords and three-cornered hats. The miners and crofters who formed the usual Sunday congregation left a space around the newcomers, as if afraid they might touch the fine clothes and besmirch them with coal dust and cow dung.

Mack had spoken defiantly to Esther, but he was full of apprehension. Coal owners had the right to flog miners, and on top of that Sir George Jamisson was a magistrate, which meant he could order someone hanged, and there would be no one to contradict him. It was indeed foolhardy for Mack to risk the wrath of such a powerful man.

But right was right. Mack and the other miners were being treated unjustly, illegally, and every time he thought of it he felt so angry he wanted to shout it from the rooftops. He could not spread the news surreptitiously, as if it might not really be true. He had to be bold, or back out.

For a moment he considered backing out. Why make trouble? Then the hymn began, and the miners sang in harmony, filling the church with their thrilling voices. Behind him Mack heard the soaring tenor of Jimmy Lee, the finest singer in the village. The singing made him think of High Glen and the dream of freedom, and he steeled his nerve and resolved to go through with his plan.

The pastor, Reverend John York, was a mild-mannered forty-year-old with thinning hair. He spoke hesitantly, unnerved by the magnificence of the visitors. His sermon was about truth. How would he react to Mack's reading out the letter? His instinct would be to take the side of the mine owner. He was probably going to dine at the castle after the service. But he was a clergyman: he would be obliged to speak out for justice, regardless of what Sir George might say, wouldn't he?

The plain stone walls of the church were bare. There was no fire, of course, and Mack's breath clouded in the cold air. He studied the castle folk. He recognized most of the Jamisson family. When Mack was a boy they had spent much of their time here. Sir George was unmistakable, with his red face and fat belly. His wife was beside him, in a frilly pink dress that might have looked pretty on a younger woman. There was Robert, the elder son, hard eyed and humorless, twenty-six years old and just beginning to develop the round-bellied look of his father. Next to him was a handsome fair-haired man of about Mack's age: he had to be Jay, the younger son. The summer Mack was six years old he had played with Jay every day in the woods around Castle Jamisson, and both had thought they would be friends for life. But that winter Mack had started work in the pit, and then there was no more time for play.

He recognized some of the Jamissons' guests. Lady Hallim and her daughter, Lizzie, were familiar. Lizzie Hallim had long been a source of sensation and scandal in the glen. People said she roamed around in men's clothing, with a gun over her shoulder. She would give her boots to a barefoot child then berate its mother for not scrubbing her doorstep. Mack had not set eyes on her for years. The Hallim estate had its own church, so they did not come here every Sunday, but they visited when the Jamissons were in residence, and Mack recalled seeing Lizzie on the last occasion, when she had been about fifteen; dressed as a fine lady, but throwing stones at squirrels just like a boy.

Mack's mother had once been a ladies' maid at High Glen House, the Hallim mansion, and after she married she had sometimes gone back, on a Sunday afternoon, to see her old friends and show off her twin babies. Mack and Esther had played with Lizzie on those visits— probably without the knowledge of Lady Hallim. Lizzie had been a little minx: bossy, selfish and spoiled. Mack had kissed her once, and she had pulled his hair and made him cry. She looked as though she had not changed much. She had a small impish face, curly dark brown hair and very dark eyes that suggested mischief. Her mouth was like a pink bow. Staring at her, Mack thought *I'd like to kiss her now.* Just as the notion crossed his mind she caught his eye. He looked away, embarrassed, as if she might have read his mind.

The sermon came to an end. In addition to the usual Presbyterian service there was to be a christening today: Mack's cousin Jen had given birth to her fourth child. Her eldest, Wullie, was already working down the pit. Mack had decided that the most appropriate time for his announcement was during the christening. As the moment drew near he felt a watery sensation in his stomach. Then he told himself not to be foolish: he risked his life every day down a mine—why should he be nervous about defying a fat merchant?

Jen stood at the font, looking weary. She was only thirty but she had borne four children and worked down the pit for twenty-three years and she was worn out. Mr. York sprinkled water on her baby's head. Then her husband, Saul, repeated the form of words that made a slave of every Scottish miner's son. "I pledge this child to work in Sir George Jamisson's mines, boy and man, for as long as he is able, or until he die."

This was the moment Mack had decided on.

He stood up.

At this point in the ceremony the viewer, Harry Ratchett, would normally step up to the font and hand over to Saul the "arles," the traditional payment for pledging the child, a purse of ten pounds. However, to Mack's surprise, Sir George rose to perform this ritual personally.

As he stood up, he caught Mack's eye.

For a moment the two men stood staring at one another.

Then Sir George began to walk to the font.

Mack stepped into the central aisle of the little church and said loudly: "The payment of arles is meaningless."

Sir George froze in midstep and all heads turned to look at Mack.

There was a moment of shocked silence. Mack could hear his own heartbeat.

"This ceremony has no force," Mack declared. "The boy may not be pledged to the mine. A child cannot be enslaved."

Sir George said: "Sit down, you young fool, and shut your mouth."

The patronizing dismissal angered Mack so much that all his doubts vanished. "*You* sit down," he said recklessly, and the congregation gasped at his insolence. He pointed a finger at Mr. York. "You spoke about truth in your sermon, Pastor—will you stand up for truth now?"

The clergyman looked at Mack with a worried air. "What is this all about, McAsh?"

"Slavery!"

"Now, you know the law of Scotland," York said in a reasonable tone. "Coal miners are the property of the mine owner. As soon as a man has worked a year and a day, he loses his freedom."

"Aye," Mack said. "It's wicked, but it's the law. I'm saying the law does *not* enslave children, and I can prove it."

Saul spoke up. "We need the money, Mack!" he protested.

"Take the money," Mack said. "Your boy will work for Sir George until he's twenty-one, and that's worth ten pounds. But—" He raised his voice. "But when he's of age, *he will be free!*"

"I advise you to hold your tongue," Sir George said threateningly. "This is dangerous talk."

"It's true, though," Mack said stubbornly.

Sir George flushed purple: he was not used to being defied so persistently. "I will deal with you when the service is over," he said angrily. He handed the purse to Saul then turned to the pastor. "Carry on, please, Mr. York."

Mack was flummoxed. Surely they would not simply go on as if nothing had happened?

The pastor said: "Let us sing the final hymn."

Sir George returned to his seat. Mack remained standing, unable to believe it was all over.

The pastor said: "The Second Psalm: 'Why do the heathen rage, and the people imagine a vain thing?'"

A voice behind Mack said: "No, no—not yet."

He looked around. It was Jimmy Lee, the young miner with the wonderful singing voice. He had run away once already, and as a punishment he wore around his neck an iron collar stamped with the words *This man is the property of Sir George Jamisson of Fife*. Thank God for Jimmy, Mack thought.

"You can't stop now," Jimmy said. "I'm twenty-one next week. If I'm going to be free, I want to know about it."

Ma Lee, Jimmy's mother, said: "So do we all." She was a tough old woman with no teeth, much respected in the village, and her opinion was influential. Several other men and women voiced agreement.

"You're not going to be free," Sir George rasped, standing up again.

Esther tugged at Mack's sleeve. "The letter!" she hissed urgently. "Show them the letter!"

Mack had forgotten it in his excitement. "The law says differently, Sir George," he cried, waving the letter.

York said: "What is that paper, McAsh?"

"It's a letter from a London lawyer that I've consulted."

Sir George was so outraged he looked as if he might burst. Mack was glad they were separated by rows of pews; otherwise the laird might have got him by the throat. *"You* have consulted a *lawyer?"* he spluttered. That seemed to offend him more than anything else.

York said: "What does the letter say?"

"I'll read it," Mack said. " 'The ceremony of arles has no foundation in English or Scottish law.' " There was a rumble of surprised comment from the congregation: this contradicted everything they had been taught to believe. " 'The parents cannot sell what they do not own, namely the freedom of a grown man. They may compel their child to work in the mine until he reaches the age of twenty-one, but' "—Mack paused dramatically and read the next bit very slowly—" 'but then he will be free to leave!' "

All at once everyone wanted to say something. There was an uproar as a hundred people tried to speak, shout, begin a question or voice an exclamation. Probably half the men in the church had been pledged as children and had always considered themselves slaves in consequence.

Now they were being told they had been deceived, and they wanted to know the truth.

Mack held up a hand for quiet, and almost immediately they fell silent. For an instant he marveled at his power. "Let me read one more line," he said. " 'Once the man is adult, the law applies to him as it applies to everyone else in Scotland: when he has worked a year and a day *as an adult* he loses his freedom.' "

There were grunts of anger and disappointment. This was no revolution, the men realized; most of them were no more free than they had ever been. But their sons might escape.

York said: "Let me see that letter, McAsh."

Mack went up to the front and handed it to him.

Sir George, still flushed with anger, said: "Who is this so-called lawyer?"

Mack said: "His name is Caspar Gordonson."

York said: "Oh, yes, I've heard of him."

"So have I," said Sir George scornfully. "An out-and-out radical! He's an associate of John Wilkes." Everyone knew the name of Wilkes: he was the celebrated liberal leader, living in exile in Paris but constantly threatening to return and undermine the government. Sir George went on: "Gordonson will hang for this, if I have anything to do with it. That letter is treason."

The pastor was shocked at this talk of hanging. "I hardly think treason comes into it—"

"You'd better confine yourself to the kingdom of heaven," Sir George said sharply. "Leave it to men of this world to decide what is treason and what is not." With that he snatched the letter out of York's hand.

The congregation were shocked at this brutal rebuke to their pastor, and they went quiet, waiting to see how he would react. York held Jamisson's gaze, and Mack was sure the pastor would defy the laird; but then York dropped his eyes, and Jamisson looked triumphant. He sat down again, as if it were all over.

Mack was outraged by York's cowardice. The church was supposed to be the moral authority. A pastor who took orders from the laird was completely superfluous. Mack gave the man a look of frank contempt and said in a derisive voice: "Are we to respect the law, or not?"

Robert Jamisson stood up, flushed with anger like his father. "You'll respect the law, and your laird will tell you what the law is," he said.

"That's the same as having no law at all," Mack said.

"Which is just as well, as far as you're concerned," Robert said. "You're a coal miner: what have you to do with the law? As for writing to lawyers—" He took the letter from his father. "This is what I think of your lawyer." He tore the paper in half.

The miners gasped. Their future was written on those pages, and he was ripping them up.

Robert tore the letter again and again, then threw the pieces in the air. They fluttered over Saul and Jen like confetti at a wedding.

Mack felt as grief-stricken as if someone had died. The letter was the most important thing that had ever happened to him. He had planned to show it to everyone in the village. He had imagined taking it to other pits in other villages, until all Scotland knew about it. Yet Robert had destroyed it in a second.

Defeat must have shown in his face, for Robert looked triumphant. That enraged Mack. He would not be crushed so easily. Anger made him defiant. I'm not finished yet, he thought. The letter had gone but the law was still the same. "I see you're frightened enough to destroy that letter," he said, and he was surprised by the withering scorn in his own voice. "But you can't tear up the law of the land. That's written on a paper that's not so easily ripped."

Robert was startled. He hesitated, not sure how to respond to such eloquence. After a moment he said angrily: "Get out."

Mack looked at Mr. York, and the Jamissons did the same. No layman had the right to order a member of the congregation to leave a church. Would the pastor bow the knee, and let the laird's son throw out one of his flock? "Is this God's house, or Sir George Jamisson's?" Mack demanded.

It was a decisive moment, and York was not equal to it. He looked shamefaced and said: "You'd better leave, McAsh."

Mack could not resist a retort, though he knew it was foolhardy.

"Thank you for the sermon on truth, Pastor," he said. "I'll never forget it."

He turned away. Esther stood up with him. As they started down the aisle, Jimmy Lee got up and followed. One or two others stood, then Ma Lee got to her feet, and suddenly the exodus became general. There was a loud scraping of boots and rustling of dresses as the miners left their places, bringing their families with them. As Mack reached the door he knew that every miner in the place was following him out of the church, and he was seized by a feeling of fellowship and triumph that brought tears to his eyes.

They gathered around him in the churchyard. The wind had dropped but it was snowing, big flakes drifting lazily down onto the gravestones. "That was wrong, to tear up the letter," Jimmy said angrily.

Several others agreed. "We'll write again," said one.

Mack said: "It may not be so easy to get the letter posted a second time." His mind was not really on these details. He was breathing hard and he felt exhausted and exhilarated, as if he had run up the side of High Glen.

"The law is the law!" said another miner.

"Aye, but the laird is the laird," said a more cautious one.

As Mack calmed down he began to wonder realistically what he had achieved. He had stirred everyone up, of course, but that on its own would not change anything. The Jamissons had flatly refused to acknowledge the law. If they stuck to their guns what could the miners do? Was there ever any point in fighting for justice? Would it not be better to touch his forelock to the laird and hope one day to get Harry Ratchett's job as viewer?

A small figure in black fur shot out of the church porch like a deerhound unleashed. It was Lizzie Hallim. She made straight for Mack. The miners stepped out of her way with alacrity.

Mack stared at her. She had looked pretty enough in repose, but now that her face was alive with indignation she was ravishing. Her black eyes flashing fire, she said: "Who do you think you are?"

"I'm Malachi McAsh—"

"I know your name," she said. "How dare you talk to the laird and his son that way?"

"How dare they enslave us when the law says they may not?"

The miners murmured their agreement.

Lizzie looked around at them. Snowflakes clung to the fur of her coat. One landed on her nose and she brushed it off with an impatient gesture. "You're fortunate to have paid work," she said. "You should all be grateful to Sir George for developing his mines and providing your families with the means to live."

Mack said: "If we're so fortunate, why do they need laws forbidding us to leave the village and seek other work?"

"Because you're too foolish to know when you're well off!"

Mack realized he was enjoying this contest, and not just because it involved looking at a beautiful highborn woman. As an opponent she was more subtle than either Sir George or Robert.

He lowered his voice and adopted an inquiring tone. "Miss Hallim, have you ever been down a coal mine?"

Ma Lee cackled with laughter at the thought.

Lizzie said: "Don't be ridiculous."

"If one day you do, I guarantee that you'll never again call us lucky."

"I've heard enough of your insolence," she said. "You should be flogged."

"I probably will be," he said, but he did not believe it: no miner had been flogged here in his lifetime, though his father had seen it.

Her chest was heaving. He had to make an effort not to look at her bosom. She said: "You've an answer for everything, you always had."

"Aye, but you've never listened to any of them."

He felt an elbow dig painfully into his side: it was Esther, telling him to watch his step, reminding him that it never paid to outsmart the gentry. She said: "We'll think about what you've told us, Miss Hallim, and thank you for your advice."

Lizzie nodded condescendingly. "You're Esther, aren't you?"

"Aye, miss."

She turned to Mack. "You should listen to your sister, she's got more sense than you."

"That's the first true thing you've said to me today."

Esther hissed: "Mack—*shut your gob.*"

Lizzie grinned, and suddenly all her arrogance vanished. The smile lit up her face and she seemed another person, friendly and gay. "I haven't heard that phrase for a long time," she said, laughing. Mack could not help laughing with her.

She turned away, still chuckling.

Mack watched her walk back to the church porch and join the Jamissons, who were just emerging. "My God," he said, shaking his head. "What a woman."

4

JAY WAS ANGERED BY THE ROW IN THE CHURCH. IT INFURIATED HIM TO see people getting above their station. It was God's will and the law of the land that Malachi McAsh should spend his life hewing coal underground and Jay Jamisson should live a higher existence. To complain about the natural order was wicked. And McAsh had an infuriating way of speaking as if he were the equal of anyone, no matter how highborn.

In the colonies, now, a slave was a slave, and no nonsense about working a year and a day or being paid wages. That was the way to do things, in Jay's opinion. People would not work unless compelled to, and compulsion might as well be merciless—it was more efficient.

As he left the church some of the crofters offered congratulations on his twenty-first birthday, but not one of the miners spoke to him. They stood in a crowd to one side of the graveyard, arguing among themselves in low, angry voices. Jay was outraged by the blight they had cast on his celebratory day.

He hurried through the snow to where a groom held the horses. Robert was already there, but Lizzie was not. Jay looked around for her. He had been looking forward to riding home with Lizzie. "Where's Miss Elizabeth?" he said to the groom.

"Over by the porch, Mr. Jay."

Jay saw her talking animatedly to the pastor.

Robert tapped Jay on the chest with an aggressive finger. "Listen here, Jay—you leave Elizabeth Hallim alone, do you understand?"

Robert's face was set in belligerent lines. It was dangerous to cross him in this mood. But anger and disappointment gave Jay courage. "What the devil are you talking about?" he said.

"You're not going to marry her, I am."

"I don't want to marry her."

"Then don't flirt with her."

Jay knew that Lizzie had found him attractive, and he had enjoyed bantering with her, but he had no thought of capturing her heart. When he was fourteen and she thirteen he had thought she was the most beautiful girl in the world, and it had broken his heart that she was not interested in him (or, indeed, any other boy)—but that was a long time ago. Father's plan was for Robert to marry Lizzie, and neither Jay nor anyone else in the family would oppose the wishes of Sir George. So Jay was surprised Robert had been upset enough to complain. It showed he was insecure—and Robert, like his father, was not often unsure of himself.

Jay enjoyed the rare pleasure of seeing his brother worried. "What are you afraid of?" he said.

"You know damn well what I mean. You've been stealing my things since we were boys—my toys, my clothes, everything."

An old familiar resentment goaded Jay into saying: "Because you always got whatever you wanted, and I got nothing."

"Nonsense."

"Anyway, Miss Hallim is a guest at our house," Jay said in a more reasonable tone. "I can't ignore her, can I?"

Robert's mouth set in a stubborn line. "Do you want me to speak to Father about it?"

Those were the magic words that had ended so many childhood disputes. Both brothers knew that their father would always rule in favor of Robert. A long-familiar bitterness rose in Jay's throat. "All right, Robert," he conceded. "I'll try not to interfere with your courting."

He swung onto his horse and trotted away, leaving Robert to escort Lizzie to the castle.

Castle Jamisson was a dark gray stone fortress with turrets and a battlemented roofline, and it had the tall, overbearing look of so many Scottish country houses. It had been built seventy years ago, after the first coal pit in the glen began to bring wealth to the laird.

Sir George inherited the estate through a cousin of his first wife's. Throughout Jay's childhood his father had been obsessed with coal. He had spent all his time and money opening new pits, and no improvements had been made to the castle.

Although it was Jay's childhood home he did not like the place. The huge, drafty rooms on the ground floor—hall, dining room, drawing room, kitchen and servants' hall—were arranged around a central courtyard with a fountain that was frozen from October to May. The place was impossible to heat. Fires in every bedroom, burning the plentiful coal from the Jamisson pits, made little impression on the chill air of the big flagstoned chambers, and the corridors were so cold that you had to put on a cloak to go from one room to another.

Ten years ago the family had moved to London, leaving a skeleton staff to maintain the house and protect the game. For a while they would come back every year, bringing guests and servants with them, renting horses and a carriage from Edinburgh, hiring crofters' wives to mop the stone floors and keep the fires alight and empty the chamber-pots. But Father became more and more reluctant to leave his business, and the visits petered out. This year's revival of the old custom did not please Jay. However, the grown-up Lizzie Hallim was a pleasant surprise, and not merely because she gave him a means of tormenting his favored older brother.

He rode around to the stables and dismounted. He patted the gelding's neck. "He's no steeplechaser, but he's a well-behaved mount," he said to the groom, handing over the reins. "I'd be glad to have him in my regiment."

The groom looked pleased. "Thank you, sir," he said.

Jay went into the great hall. It was a big, gloomy chamber with dim shadowy corners into which the candlelight hardly penetrated. A sullen deerhound lay on an old fur rug in front of the coal fire. Jay gave it a nudge with the toe of his boot and made it get out of the way so that he could warm his hands.

Over the fireplace was the portrait of his father's first wife, Robert's mother, Olive. Jay hated that painting. There she was, solemn and saintly, looking down her long nose at all who came after her. When she caught a fever and died suddenly at the age of twenty-nine his father had remarried, but he never forgot his first love. He treated Jay's mother, Alicia, like a mistress, a plaything with no status and no rights; and he made Jay feel almost like an illegitimate son. Robert was the firstborn, the heir, the special one. Jay sometimes wanted to ask whether it had been an immaculate conception and a virgin birth.

He turned his back on the picture. A footman brought him a goblet of hot mulled wine and he sipped it gratefully. Perhaps it would settle the tension in his stomach. Today Father would announce what Jay's portion would be.

He knew he was not going to get half, or even a tenth, of his father's fortune. Robert would inherit this estate, with its rich mines, and the fleet of ships he already managed. Jay's mother had counseled him not to argue about that: she knew Father was implacable.

Robert was not merely the only son. He was Father all over again. Jay was different, and that was why his father spurned him. Like Father, Robert was clever, heartless, and mean with money. Jay was easygoing and spendthrift. Father hated people who were careless with money, especially his money. More than once he had shouted at Jay: "I sweat blood to make money that you throw away!"

Jay had made matters worse, just a few months ago, by running up a huge gambling debt, nine hundred pounds. He had got his mother to ask Father to pay. It was a small fortune, enough to buy Castle Jamisson, but Sir George could easily afford it. All the same he had acted as if he were losing a leg. Since then Jay had lost more money, although Father did not know about that.

Don't fight your father, Mother reasoned, but ask for something modest. Younger sons often went out to the colonies: there was a good chance his father would give him the sugar plantation in Barbados, with its estate house and African slaves. Both he and his mother had spoken to his father about it. Sir George had not said yes, but he had not said no, and Jay had high hopes.

His father came in a few minutes later, stamping snow off his riding boots. A footman helped him off with his cloak. "Send a message to

Ratchett," Father said to the man. "I want two men guarding the bridge twenty-four hours a day. If McAsh tries to leave the glen they should seize him."

There was only one bridge across the river, but there was another way out of the glen. Jay said: "What if McAsh goes over the mountain?"

"In this weather? He can try. As soon as we learn he's gone, we can send a party around by road and have the sheriff and a squad of troops waiting on the other side by the time he gets there. But I doubt he'd ever make it."

Jay was not so sure—these miners were as hardy as the deer, and McAsh was an obstinate wretch—but he did not argue with his father.

Lady Hallim arrived next. She was dark haired and dark eyed like her daughter, but she had none of Lizzie's spark and crackle. She was rather stout, and her fleshy face was marked with lines of disapproval. "Let me take your coat," Jay said, and helped her shrug off her heavy fur. "Come close to the fire, your hands are cold. Would you like some mulled wine?"

"What a nice boy you are, Jay," she said. "I'd love some."

The other churchgoers came in, rubbing their hands for warmth and dripping melted snow on the stone floor. Robert was doggedly making small talk to Lizzie, going from one trivial topic to another as if he had a list. Father began to discuss business with Henry Drome, a Glasgow merchant who was a relation of his first wife, Olive; and Jay's mother spoke to Lady Hallim. The pastor and his wife had not come: perhaps they were sulking about the row in the church. There was a handful of other guests, mostly relatives: Sir George's sister and her husband, Alicia's younger brother with his wife, and one or two neighbors. Most of the conversations were about Malachi McAsh and his stupid letter.

After a while Lizzie's raised voice was heard over the buzz of conversation, and one by one people turned to listen to her. "But why not?" she was saying. "I want to see for myself."

Robert said gravely: "A coal mine is no place for a lady, believe me."

"What's this?" Sir George asked. "Does Miss Hallim want to go down a pit?"

"I believe I should know what it's like," Lizzie explained.

Robert said: "Apart from any other considerations, female clothing would make it almost impossible."

"Then I'll disguise myself as a man," she shot back.

Sir George chuckled. "There are some girls I know who could manage that," he said. "But you, my dear, are much too pretty to get away with it." He obviously thought this a clever compliment and looked around for approval. The others laughed dutifully.

Jay's mother nudged his father and said something in a low voice. "Ah, yes," said Sir George. "Has everyone got a full cup?" Without waiting for an answer he went on: "Let us drink to my younger son, James Jamisson, known to us all as Jay, on his twenty-first birthday. To Jay!"

They drank the toast, then the women retired to prepare for dinner. The talk among the men turned to business. Henry Drome said: "I don't like the news from America. It could cost us a lot of money."

Jay knew what the man was talking about. The English government had imposed taxes on various commodities imported into the American colonies—tea, paper, glass, lead and painters' colors—and the colonists were outraged.

Sir George said indignantly: "They want the army to protect them from Frenchies and redskins, but they don't want to pay for it!"

"Nor will they, if they can help it," said Drome. "The Boston town meeting has announced a boycott of all British imports. They're giving up tea, and they've even agreed to save on black cloth by skimping on mourning clothes!"

Robert said: "If the other colonies follow the lead of Massachusetts, half our fleet of ships will have no cargoes."

Sir George said: "The colonists are a damned gang of bandits, that's all they are—and the Boston rum distillers are the worst." Jay was surprised at how riled his father was: the problem had to be costing him money, for him to get so worked up about it. "The law obliges them to buy molasses from British plantations, but they smuggle in French molasses and drive the price down."

"The Virginians are worse," said Drome. "The tobacco planters never pay their debts."

"Don't I know it," said Sir George. "I've just had a planter default—leaving me with a bankrupt plantation on my hands. A place called Mockjack Hall."

Robert said: "Thank God there's no import duty on convicts."

There was a general murmur of agreement. The most profitable part of the Jamisson shipping business was transporting convicted criminals to America. Every year the courts sentenced several hundred people to transportation—it was an alternative to hanging as punishment for crimes such as stealing—and the government paid five pounds per head to the shipper. Nine out of ten transportees crossed the Atlantic on a Jamisson vessel. But the government payment was not the only way money was made. On the other side the convicts were obliged to do seven years' unpaid labor, which meant they could be sold as seven-year slaves. Men fetched ten to fifteen pounds, women eight or nine, children less. With 130 or 140 convicts packed into the hold shoulder to shoulder like fish in a basket, Robert could show a profit of two thousand pounds—the purchase price of the ship—in a single voyage. It was a lucrative trade.

"Aye," said Father, and he drained his goblet. "But even that would stop if the colonists had their way."

The colonists complained about it constantly. Although they continued to buy the convicts—such was the shortage of cheap labor out there—they resented the mother country dumping its riffraff on them, and blamed the convicts for increasing crime.

"At least the coal mines are reliable," Sir George said. "They're the only thing we can count on these days. That's why McAsh has to be crushed."

Everyone had opinions about McAsh, and several different conversations broke out at once. Sir George seemed to have had enough of the subject, however. He turned to Robert. Adopting a jocular tone he said: "What about the Hallim girl, then, eh? A little jewel, if you ask me."

"Elizabeth is very spirited," Robert said dubiously.

"That's true," Father said with a laugh. "I remember when we shot the last wolf in this part of Scotland, eight or ten years ago, and she insisted on raising the cubs herself. She used to walk around with two little wolves on a leash. You've never seen anything like it in your life! The gamekeepers were outraged, said the cubs would escape and become a menace—but they died, fortunately."

"She may make a troublesome wife," Robert said.

"Nothing like a mettlesome mare," Sir George said. "Besides, a husband always has the upper hand, no matter what. You could do a lot worse." He lowered his voice. "Lady Hallim holds the estate in trust until Elizabeth marries. Since a woman's property belongs to her husband, the whole place will become her bridegroom's on her wedding day."

"I know," Robert said.

Jay had not known, but he was not surprised: few men would be happy to bequeath a sizable estate to a woman.

Sir George went on: "There must be a million tons of coal under High Glen—all the seams run in that direction. The girl is sitting on a fortune, pardon the vulgarity." He chortled.

Robert was characteristically dour. "I'm not sure how much she likes me."

"What is there to dislike? You're young, you're going to be rich, and when I die you'll be a baronet—what more could a girl want?"

"Romance?" Robert answered. He pronounced the word with distaste, as if it were an unfamiliar coin offered by a foreign merchant.

"Miss Hallim can't afford romance."

"I don't know," Robert said. "Lady Hallim has been living in debt since I can remember. Why should she not go on like that forever?"

"I'll tell you a secret," Sir George said. He glanced over his shoulder to make sure he was not overheard. "You know she has mortgaged the entire estate?"

"Everyone knows that."

"I happen to know that her creditor is not willing to renew."

Robert said: "But surely she could raise the money from another lender, and pay him off."

"Probably," Sir George said. "But she doesn't know it. And her financial adviser won't tell her—I've made sure of that."

Jay wondered what bribe or threat his father had used to suborn Lady Hallim's adviser.

Sir George chuckled. "So, you see, Robert, young Elizabeth can't afford to turn you down."

At that moment Henry Drome broke away from his conversation and came over to the three Jamisson men. "Before we go in to dinner, George, there's something I have to ask you. I may speak freely in front of your sons, I know."

"Of course."

"The American troubles have hit me quite hard—planters who can't pay their debts, and so on—and I fear I can't meet my obligations to you this quarter."

Sir George had obviously loaned money to Henry. Normally Father was brutally practical with debtors: they paid, or they went to jail. Now, however, he said: "I understand, Henry. Times are hard. Pay me when you can."

Jay's jaw dropped, but a moment later he realized why his father was being so soft. Drome was a relative of Robert's mother, Olive, and Father was being easy on Henry for her sake. Jay was so disgusted he walked away.

The ladies came back. Jay's mother wore a suppressed smile, as if she had an amusing secret. Before he could ask her what it was another guest arrived, a stranger in clerical gray. Alicia spoke to the man then took him to Sir George. "This is Mr. Cheshire," she said. "He's come in place of the pastor."

The newcomer was a pockmarked young man with spectacles and an old-fashioned curly wig. Although Sir George and the older men still wore wigs, younger men did so rarely, and Jay never did. "Reverend Mr. York sends his apologies," said Mr. Cheshire.

"Not at all, not at all," said Sir George, turning away: he was not interested in obscure young clergymen.

They went in to dinner. The smell of food mingled with a damp odor that came from the heavy old curtains. The long table was laid with an elaborate spread: joints of venison, beef, and ham; a whole roast salmon; and several different pies. But Jay could hardly eat. Would Father give him the Barbados property? If not, what else? It was hard to sit still and eat venison when your entire future was about to be decided.

In some ways he hardly knew his father. Although they lived together, at the family house in Grosvenor Square, Sir George was always at the warehouse with Robert. Jay spent the day with his regiment. They sometimes met briefly at breakfast, and occasionally at supper—but Sir George often ate supper in his study while looking over some papers. Jay could not guess what his father would do. So he toyed with his food and waited.

Mr. Cheshire proved mildly embarrassing. He belched loudly two or three times and spilled his claret, and Jay noticed him staring rather obviously into the cleavage of the woman sitting next to him.

They had sat down at three o'clock and, by the time the ladies withdrew, the winter afternoon was darkening into evening. As soon as they had gone Sir George shifted on his seat and farted volcanically. "That's better," he said.

A servant brought a bottle of port, a drum of tobacco and a box of clay pipes. The young clergyman filled a pipe and said: "Lady Jamisson's a damn fine woman, Sir George, if I may say so. Damn fine."

He seemed drunk, but even so such a remark could not be allowed to pass. Jay came to his mother's defense. "I'll thank you to say no more about Lady Jamisson, sir," he said frostily.

The clergyman put a taper to his pipe, inhaled, and began to cough. He had obviously never smoked before. Tears came to his eyes, and he gasped and spluttered and coughed again. The coughs shook him so hard that his wig and spectacles fell off—and Jay saw immediately that this was no clergyman.

He began to laugh. The others looked at him curiously. They had not seen it yet. "Look!" he said. "Don't you see who it is?"

Robert was the first to realize. "Good God, it's Miss Hallim in disguise!" he said.

There was a moment of startled silence. Then Sir George began to laugh. The other men, seeing that he was going to take it as a joke, laughed too.

Lizzie took a drink of water and coughed some more. As she

recovered, Jay admired her costume. The spectacles had hidden her flashing dark eyes, and the side-curls of the wig had partly obscured her pretty profile. A white linen stock thickened her neck and covered the smooth feminine skin of her throat. She had used charcoal or something to give her cheeks the pockmarked look, and she had drawn a few wispy hairs on her chin like the beard of a young man who did not yet shave every day. In the gloomy rooms of the castle, on a dull winter's afternoon in Scotland, no one had seen through her disguise.

"Well, you've proved you can pass for a man," said Sir George when she had stopped coughing. "But you still can't go down the pit. Go and fetch the other ladies, and we'll give Jay his birthday present."

For a few minutes Jay had forgotten his anxiety, but now it came back with a thump.

They met up with the women in the hall. Jay's mother and Lizzie were laughing fit to bust: Alicia had obviously been in on the plot, which accounted for her secretive grin before dinner. Lizzie's mother had not known about it, and she was looking frosty.

Sir George led the way out through the main doors. It was dusk. The snow had stopped. "Here," said Sir George. "This is your birthday present."

In front of the house a groom held the most beautiful horse Jay had ever seen. It was a white stallion about two years old, with the lean lines of an Arab. The crowd made it nervous, and it skipped sideways, forcing the groom to tug on its bridle to keep it still. There was a wild look in its eyes, and Jay knew instantly it would go like the wind.

He was lost in admiration, but his mother's voice cut through his thoughts like a knife. "Is that all?" she said.

Father said: "Now, Alicia, I hope you aren't going to be ungracious—"

"*Is that all?*" she repeated, and Jay saw that her face was twisted into a mask of rage.

"Yes," he admitted.

It had not occurred to Jay that this present was being given to him instead of the Barbados property. He stared at his parents as the news sank in. He felt so bitter that he could not speak.

His mother spoke for him. He had never seen her so angry. "This is your son!" she said, her voice shrill with fury. "He is twenty-one years old—he's entitled to his portion in life . . . and you give him a *horse?*"

The guests looked on, fascinated but horrified.

Sir George reddened. "Nobody gave me anything when I was twenty-one!" he said angrily. "I never inherited so much as a pair of shoes—"

"Oh, for heaven's sake," she said contemptuously. "We've all heard how your father died when you were fourteen and you worked in a mill to keep your sisters—that's no reason to inflict poverty on your own son, is it?"

"Poverty?" He spread his hands to indicate the castle, the estate, and the life that went with it. "What poverty?"

"He needs his independence—for God's sake give him the Barbados property."

Robert protested: "That's mine!"

Jay's jaw became unlocked, and at last he found his voice. "The plantation has never been properly administered," he said. "I thought I would run it more like a regiment, get the niggers working harder and so on, and make it more remunerative."

"Do you really think you could do that?" said his father.

Jay's heart leaped: perhaps Father would change his mind. "I do!" he said eagerly.

"Well, I don't," Father said harshly.

Jay felt as if he had been punched in the stomach.

"I don't believe you have an inkling how to run a plantation or any other enterprise," Sir George grated. "I think you're better off in the army where you're told what to do."

Jay was stunned. He looked at the beautiful white stallion. "I'll never ride that horse," he said. "Take it away."

Alicia spoke to Sir George. "Robert's getting the castle and the coal mines and the ships and everything else—does he have to have the plantation too?"

"He's the elder son."

"Jay is younger, but he's not *nothing*. Why does Robert have to get *everything?*"

"For the sake of his mother," Sir George said.

Alicia stared at Sir George, and Jay realized that she hated him. And I do too, he thought. I hate my father.

"Damn you, then," she said, to shocked gasps from the guests. "Damn you to hell." And she turned around and went back into the house.

5

THE McAsh TWINS LIVED IN A ONE-ROOM HOUSE FIFTEEN FEET square, with a fireplace on one side and two curtained alcoves for beds on the other. The front door opened onto a muddy track that ran downhill from the pit to the bottom of the glen where it met the road that led to the church, the castle and the outside world. The water supply was a mountain stream at the back of the row of houses.

All the way home Mack had been agonizing over what had happened in the church, but he said nothing, and Esther tactfully asked him no questions. Earlier that morning, before leaving for church, they had put a piece of bacon on the fire to boil, and when they returned home the smell of it filled the house and made Mack's mouth water, lifting his spirits. Esther shredded a cabbage into the pot while Mack went across the road to Mrs. Wheighel's for a jug of ale. The two of them ate with the gargantuan appetites of physical laborers. When the food and the beer were gone, Esther belched and said: "Well, what will you do?"

Mack sighed. Now that the question had been posed directly, he knew there was only one answer. "I've got to go away. I can't stay here, after all that. My pride won't let me. I'd be a constant reminder, to every young man in the glen, that the Jamissons cannot be defied. I must leave." He was trying to remain calm, but his voice was shaky with emotion.

"That's what I thought you'd say." Tears came to Esther's eyes. "You're pitting yourself against the most powerful people in the land."

"I'm right, though."

"Aye. But right and wrong don't count much in this world—only in the next."

"If I don't do it now, I never will—and I'll spend the rest of my life regretting it."

She nodded sadly. "That's for sure. But what if they try to stop you?"

"How?"

"They could post a guard on the bridge."

The only other way out of the glen was across the mountains, and that was too slow: the Jamissons could be waiting on the other side by the time Mack got there. "If they block the bridge, I'll swim the river," he said.

"The water's cold enough to kill you at this time of year."

"The river's about thirty yards wide. I reckon I can swim across in a minute or so."

"If they catch you they'll bring you back with an iron collar around your neck, like Jimmy Lee."

Mack winced. To wear a collar like a dog was a humiliation the miners all feared. "I'm cleverer than Jimmy," he said. "He ran out of money and tried to get work at a pit in Clackmannan, and the mine owner reported his name."

"That's the trouble. You've got to eat, and how will you earn your bread? Coal is all you know."

Mack had a little cash put aside but it would not last long. However, he had thought about this. "I'll go to Edinburgh," he said. He might get a ride on one of the heavy horse-drawn wagons that took the coal from the pithead—but he would be safer to walk. "Then I'll get on a ship—I hear they always want strong young men to work on the coalers. In three days I'll be out of Scotland. And they can't bring you back from outside the country—the laws don't run elsewhere."

"A ship," Esther said wonderingly. Neither of them had ever seen one, although they had looked at pictures in books. "Where will you go?"

"London, I expect." Most coal ships out of Edinburgh were destined for London. But some went to Amsterdam, Mack had been told. "Or Holland. Or Massachusetts, even."

"They're just names," Esther said. "We've never met anyone who's been to Massachusetts."

"I suppose people eat bread and live in houses and go to sleep at night, the same as everywhere else."

"I suppose so," she said dubiously.

"Anyway, I don't care," he said. "I'll go anywhere that's not Scotland—anywhere a man can be free. Think of it: to live where you like, not where you're told. To choose your work, free to leave your place and take another job that's better paid, or safer, or cleaner. To be your own man, and nobody's slave—won't that be grand?"

There were hot tears on her cheeks. "When will you go?"

"I'll stay another day or two, and hope the Jamissons relax their vigilance a bit. But Tuesday's my twenty-second birthday. If I'm at the pit on Wednesday I'll have worked my year-and-a-day, and I'll be a slave again."

"You're a slave anyway, in reality, whatever that letter said."

"But I like the thought that I've got the law on my side. I don't know why it should be important, but it is. It makes the Jamissons the criminals, whether they acknowledge it or not. So I'll be away Tuesday night."

In a small voice she said: "What about me?"

"You'd better work for Jimmy Lee, he's a good hewer and he's desperate for another bearer. And Annie—"

Esther interrupted him. "I want to go with you."

He was surprised. "You've never said anything about it!"

Her voice became louder. "Why do you think I've never married? Because if I get wed and have a child I'll never get out of here."

It was true she was the oldest single woman in Heugh. But Mack had assumed there was just no one good enough for her here. It had not occurred to him that all these years she had secretly wanted to escape. "I never knew!"

"I was afraid. I still am. But if you're going, I'll go with you."

He saw the desperation in her eyes, and it hurt him to refuse her, but he had to. "Women can't be sailors. We haven't the money for your passage, and they wouldn't let you work it. I'd have to leave you in Edinburgh."

"I won't stay here if you go!"

Mack loved his sister. They had always sided with one another in any conflict, from childhood scraps, through rows with their parents, to disputes with the pit management. Even when she had doubts about his wisdom she was as fierce as a lioness in his defense. He longed to take her with him, but it would be much harder for two to escape than one. "Stay a little while, Esther," he said. "When I get where I'm going, I'll write to you. As soon as I get work, I'll save money and send for you."

"Will you?"

"Aye, to be sure!"

"Spit and swear."

"Spit and swear?" It was something they had done as children, to seal a promise.

"I want you to!"

He could see she meant it. He spat on his palm, reached across the plank table, and took her hard hand in his own. "I swear I'll send for you."

"Thank you," she said.

6

A DEER HUNT HAD BEEN PLANNED FOR THE FOLLOWING MORNING, and Jay decided to go along. He felt like killing something.

He ate no breakfast but filled his pocket with whiskey butties, little balls of oatmeal steeped in whiskey, then stepped outside to look at the weather. It was just becoming light. The sky was gray but the cloud level was high, and there was no rain: they would be able to see to shoot.

He sat on the steps at the front of the castle and fitted a new wedge-shaped flint into the firing mechanism of his gun, fixing it firmly with a wad of soft leather. Perhaps slaughtering some stags would be an outlet for his rage, but he wished he could kill his brother Robert instead.

He was proud of his gun. A muzzle-loading flintlock rifle, it was made by Griffin of Bond Street and had a Spanish barrel with silver inlay. It was far superior to the crude "Brown Bess" issued to his men. He cocked the flintlock and aimed at a tree across the lawn. Sighting along the barrel, he imagined he saw a big stag with spreading antlers. He drew a bead on the chest just behind the shoulder, where the beast's big heart pumped. Then he changed the image and saw Robert in his sights: dour, dogged Robert, greedy and tireless, with his dark hair and well-fed face. Jay pulled the trigger. The flint struck steel and gave a satisfactory shower of sparks, but there was no gunpowder in the pan and no ball in the barrel.

He loaded his gun with steady hands. Using the measuring device in the nozzle of his gunpowder flask he poured exactly two and a half drams of black powder into the barrel. He took a ball from his pocket, wrapped it in a scrap of linen cloth, and pushed it into the barrel. Then he unclipped the ramrod from its housing under the barrel and used it to ram the ball into the gun as far as it would go. The ball was half an inch in diameter. It could kill a full-grown stag at a range of a hundred yards: it would smash Robert's ribs, tear through his lung, and rip open the muscle of his heart, killing him in seconds.

He heard his mother say: "Hello, Jay."

He stood up and kissed her good morning. He had not seen her since last night, when she had damned his father and stormed off. Now she looked weary and sad. "You slept badly, didn't you," he said sympathetically.

She nodded. "I've had better nights."

"Poor Mother."

"I shouldn't have cursed your father like that."

Hesitantly Jay said: "You must have loved him . . . once."

She sighed. "I don't know. He was handsome and rich and a baronet, and I wanted to be his wife."

"But now you hate him."

"Ever since he began to favor your brother over you."

Jay felt angry. "You'd think Robert would see the unfairness of it!"

"I'm sure he does, in his heart. But I'm afraid Robert is a very greedy young man. He wants it all."

"He always did." Jay was recalling Robert as a child, never happier than when he had grabbed Jay's share of the toy soldiers or the plum pudding. "Remember Robert's pony, Rob Roy?"

"Yes, why?"

"He was thirteen, and I was eight, when he got that pony. I longed for a pony—and I could ride better than he, even then. But he never once let me ride it. If he didn't want to ride it himself, he would make a groom exercise Rob Roy while I watched, rather than let me have a go."

"But you rode the other horses."

"By the time I was ten I had ridden everything else in the stable, including Father's hunters. But not Rob Roy."

"Let's take a turn up and down the drive." She was wearing a fur-lined coat with a hood, and Jay had his plaid cloak. They walked across the lawn, their feet crunching the frosted grass.

"What made my father like this?" Jay said. "Why does he hate me?"

She touched his cheek. "He doesn't hate you," she said, "although you could be forgiven for thinking otherwise."

"Then why does he treat me so badly?"

"Your father was a poor man when he married Olive Drome. He had nothing but a corner shop in a low-class district of Edinburgh. This place, that is now called Castle Jamisson, was owned by a distant cousin of Olive's, William Drome. William was a bachelor who lived alone, and when he fell ill Olive came here to look after him. He was so grateful that he changed his will, leaving everything to Olive; and then, despite her nursing, he died."

Jay nodded. "I've heard that story, more than once."

"The point is that your father feels this estate really belongs to Olive. And this estate is the foundation on which the whole of his business empire has been built. What's more, mining is still the most profitable of his enterprises."

"It's steady, he says," Jay put in, remembering yesterday's conversation. "Shipping is volatile and risky, but the coal just goes on and on."

"Anyway, your father feels he owes everything to Olive, and that it would be some kind of insult to her memory if he gave anything to you."

Jay shook his head. "There must be more to it than that. I feel we don't have the whole story."

"Perhaps you're right. I've told you all I know."

They reached the end of the drive and walked back in silence. Jay wondered whether his parents ever spent nights together. His guess was that they probably did. His father would feel that whether she loved him or not she was his wife, and therefore he was entitled to use her for relief. It was an unpleasant thought.

When they reached the castle entrance she said: "I've spent all night trying to think of a way to make things right for you, and so far I haven't succeeded. But don't despair. Something will come up."

Jay had always relied on his mother's strength. She could stand up to his father, make him do what she wanted. She had even persuaded Father to pay Jay's gambling debts. But this time Jay feared she might fail. "Father has decided that I shall get nothing. He must have known how it would make me feel. Yet he made the decision anyway. There's no point in pleading with him."

"I wasn't thinking of pleading," she said dryly.

"What, then?"

"I don't know, but I haven't given up. Good morning, Miss Hallim."

Lizzie was coming down the steps at the front of the castle, dressed for hunting, looking like a pretty pixie in a black fur cap and little leather boots. She smiled and seemed happy to see him. "Good morning!"

The sight of her cheered Jay up. "Are you coming out with us?" he inquired.

"I wouldn't miss it for the world."

It was unusual, though perfectly acceptable, for women to go hunting, and Jay, knowing Lizzie as he did, was not surprised that she planned to go out with the men. "Splendid!" he said. "You'll add a rare touch of refinement and style to what might otherwise be a coarsely masculine expedition."

"Don't bet on it," she said.

Mother said: "I'm going in. Good hunting, both of you."

When she had gone Lizzie said: "I'm so sorry your birthday was spoiled." She squeezed his arm sympathetically. "Perhaps you'll forget your troubles for an hour or so this morning."

He could not help smiling back. "I'll do my best."

She sniffed the air like a vixen. "A good strong southwest wind," she said. "Just right."

It was five years since Jay had last hunted red deer, but he remembered the lore. Hunters disliked a still day, when a sudden capricious breeze could blow the scent of men across the mountainside and send the deer running.

A gamekeeper walked around the corner of the castle with two dogs on a leash, and Lizzie went to pet them. Jay followed her, feeling cheered up. Glancing back, he saw his mother at the castle door, looking hard at Lizzie with an odd, speculative expression.

The dogs were the long-legged, gray-haired breed sometimes called Highland deerhounds and sometimes Irish wolfhounds. Lizzie crouched down and spoke to each of them in turn. "Is this Bran?" she asked the keeper.

"The son of Bran, Miss Elizabeth," he said. "Bran died a year ago. This one's Busker."

The dogs would be kept well to the rear of the hunt and released only after shots had been fired. Their role was to chase and bring down any deer wounded but not felled by the hunter's fire.

The rest of the party emerged from the castle: Robert, Sir George, and Henry. Jay stared at his brother, but Robert avoided his eye. Father nodded curtly, almost as if he had forgotten the events of last night.

On the east side of the castle the keepers had set up a target, a crude dummy deer made of wood and canvas. Each of the hunters would fire a few rounds at it to get his eye in. Jay wondered whether Lizzie could shoot. A lot of men said women could not shoot properly because their arms were too weak to hold the heavy gun, or because they lacked the killer instinct, or for some other reason. It would be interesting to see if it was true.

First they all shot from fifty yards. Lizzie went first and made a perfect hit, her shot striking the target in the killing spot just behind the shoulder. Jay and Sir George did the same. Robert and Henry struck farther back along the body, wounding shots that might allow the beast to get away and die slowly and painfully.

They shot again from seventy-five yards. Surprisingly, Lizzie hit perfectly again. So did Jay. Sir George hit the head and Henry the rump. Robert missed altogether, his ball striking sparks off the stone wall of the kitchen garden.

Finally they tried from a hundred yards, the outside limit for their weapons. To everyone's astonishment Lizzie scored another perfect hit. Robert, Sir George and Henry missed altogether. Jay, shooting last, was determined not to be beaten by a girl. He took his time, breathing evenly and sighting carefully, then he held his breath and squeezed the trigger gently—and broke the target's back leg.

So much for female inability to shoot: Lizzie had bested them all. Jay was full of admiration. "I don't suppose you'd like to join my regiment?" he joked. "Not many of my men can shoot like that."

The ponies were brought around by stable hands. Highland ponies were more surefooted than horses on rough ground. They mounted up and rode out of the courtyard.

As they jogged down the glen Henry Drome engaged Lizzie in conversation. With nothing to distract him, Jay found himself brooding over his father's rejection again. It burned in his stomach like an ulcer. He told himself that he should have expected refusal, for his father had always favored Robert. But he had fueled his foolish optimism by reminding himself that he was not a bastard, his mother was Lady Jamisson; and he had persuaded himself that this time his father would be fair. His father was never fair, though.

He wished he were the only son. He wished Robert were dead. If there were an accident today and Robert was killed, all Jay's troubles would be over.

He wished he had the nerve to kill him. He touched the barrel of the gun slung across his shoulder. He could make it look like an accident. With everyone shooting at the same time, it might be hard to tell who had fired the fatal ball. And even if they guessed the truth, the family would cover it up: nobody wanted scandal.

He felt a thrill of horror that he was even daydreaming about killing Robert. But I would never have had such an idea if Father had treated me fairly, he thought.

The Jamisson place was like most small Scottish estates. There was a little cultivable land in the valley bottoms, which the crofters farmed communally, using the medieval strip system and paying their rent to the laird in kind. Most of the land was forested mountains, good for nothing but hunting and fishing. A few landowners had cleared their forests and were experimenting with sheep. It was hard to get rich on a Scottish estate—unless you found coal, of course.

When they had ridden about three miles the gamekeepers saw a herd of twenty or thirty hinds half a mile farther on, above the tree line on a south-facing slope. The party halted and Jay took out his spyglass. The hinds were downwind of the hunters and, as they always grazed into the wind, they were facing away, showing the white flash of their rumps to Jay's glass.

Hinds made perfectly good eating but it was more usual to shoot the big stags with their spectacular antlers. Jay examined the mountainside above the hinds. He saw what he had hoped for, and he pointed. "Look—two stags . . . no, three . . . uphill from the females."

"I see them, just over the first ridge," Lizzie said. "And another, you can just see the antlers of the fourth."

Her face was flushed with excitement, making her even prettier. This was exactly the kind of thing she would like, of course: being out of doors, with horses and dogs and guns, doing something violently energetic and a little unsafe. He could not help smiling as he looked at her. He shifted uncomfortably in his saddle. The sight of her was enough to heat a man's blood.

He glanced at his brother. Robert looked ill at ease, out in the cold weather on a pony. He would rather be in a counting-house, Jay thought, calculating the quarterly interest on eighty-nine guineas at three and a half percent per annum. What a waste it would be for such a woman as Lizzie to marry Robert.

He turned away from them and tried to concentrate on the deer. He studied the mountainside with his spyglass, searching for a route by which the stags could be approached. The stalkers had to be downwind so that the beasts could not pick up the scent of humans. For preference they would come at the deer from higher up the hillside. As their target practice had confirmed, it was nearly impossible to shoot a deer from farther away than about a hundred yards, and fifty yards was ideal; so the whole skill of deer stalking lay in creeping up on them and getting close enough for a good shot.

Lizzie had already devised an approach. "There's a corrie a quarter of a mile back up the glen," she said animatedly. A corrie was the depression in the ground formed by a stream running down the mountainside, and it would hide the hunters as they climbed. "We can follow that to the high ridge then work our way along."

Sir George agreed. He did not often let anyone tell him what to do, but when he did it was usually a pretty girl.

They returned to the corrie then left the ponies and went up the mountainside on foot. The slope was steep and the ground both rocky and boggy, so that their feet either sank into mud or stumbled over stones. Before long Henry and Robert were puffing and blowing, although the keepers and Lizzie, who were used to such terrain, showed no signs of strain. Sir George was red in the face and panting, but he was surprisingly resilient and did not slow his pace. Jay was quite fit, because of his daily life in the Guards, but all the same he found himself breathing hard.

They crossed the ridge. In its lee, hidden from the deer, they worked their way across the mountainside. The wind was bitterly cold and there were flurries of sleet and swirls of freezing fog. Without the warmth of a horse beneath him Jay began to feel the cold. His fine kid gloves were soaked through, and the wet penetrated his riding boots and his costly Shetland wool stockings.

The keepers took the lead, knowing the ground. When they thought they were coming close to the stags they edged downhill. Suddenly they dropped to their knees, and the others followed suit. Jay forgot how cold and wet he was and began to feel exhilaration: it was the thrill of the hunt and the prospect of a kill.

He decided to risk a look. Still crawling, he veered uphill and peered over an outcrop of rock. As his eyes adjusted to the distance he saw the stags, four brown smears on the green slopes, ranged across the mountainside in a straggling line. It was unusual to see four together: they must have found a lush piece of grass. He looked through his glass. The farthest had the best head: he could not see the antlers clearly but it was big enough to have twelve points. He heard the caw of a raven and, glancing up, saw a pair of them circling over the hunters. They seemed to know that there might soon be offal for them to feed on.

Up ahead someone yelped and cursed: it was Robert, slipping into a muddy puddle. "Damn fool," Jay said under his breath. One of the dogs let out a low growl. A keeper held up a warning hand and they all froze, listening for the sound of fleeing hooves. But the deer did not run, and after a few moments the party crawled on.

Soon they had to sink to their bellies and wriggle. One of the keepers made the dogs lie down and covered their eyes with handkerchiefs, to keep them quiet. Sir George and the head keeper slid downhill to a ridge, raised their heads cautiously and peered over. When they came back to the main party, Sir George gave orders.

He spoke in a low voice. "There are four stags and five guns, so I shan't shoot this time, unless one of you should miss," he said. He could play the perfect host when he wanted to. "Henry, you take the beast on the right here. Robert, take the next one along—it's the nearest, and the easiest shot. Jay, you take the next. Miss Hallim, yours is the farthest, but it has the best head—and you're a pretty good shot. All set? Then let's get in position. We'll let Miss Hallim shoot first, shall we?"

The hunters spread out, slithering across the sloping mountainside, each looking for a lie from which to take aim. Jay followed Lizzie. She wore a short riding jacket and a loose skirt with no hoop, and he grinned as he watched her pert bottom wriggling in front of him. Not many girls would crawl around like that in front of a man—but Lizzie was not like other girls.

He worked his way uphill to a point where a stunted bush broke the skyline, giving him extra cover. Raising his head he looked down the mountain. He could see his stag, a youngish one with a small spread of antlers, about seventy yards away; and the other three ranged along the slope. He could also see the other hunters: Lizzie to his left, still crawling along; Henry to his far right; Sir George and the keepers with the dogs—and Robert, below and to Jay's right, twenty-five yards away, an easy target.

His heartbeat seemed to falter as he was struck, yet again, by the thought of killing his brother. The story of Cain and Abel came into his mind. Cain had said *My punishment is greater than I can bear*. But I feel like that already, Jay thought. I can't bear to be the superfluous second son, always overlooked, drifting through life with no portion, the poor son of a rich man, a nobody—I just can't bear it.

He tried to push the evil thought out of his mind. He primed his gun, pouring a little powder into the flashpan next to the touchhole, then closed the cover of the pan. Finally he cocked the firing mechanism. When he pulled the trigger, the lid of the flashpan would lift automatically at the same time as the flint struck sparks. The powder in the pan would light, and the flame would flash through the touchhole to ignite the larger quantity of powder behind the ball.

He rolled over and looked across the slope. The deer grazed in peaceful ignorance. All the hunters were in position except Lizzie, who was still moving. Jay sighted on his stag. Then he slowly swung the barrel around until it pointed at Robert's back.

He could say that his elbow slipped on a patch of ice at the crucial moment, causing him to drop his aim to one side and, with tragic ill fortune, shoot his brother in the back. His father might suspect the truth—but he would never be sure, and with only one son left, would he not bury his suspicions and give Jay everything he had previously reserved for Robert?

Lizzie's shot would be the signal for everyone to fire. Deer were surprisingly slow to react, Jay recalled. After the first gunshot they would all look up from their grazing and freeze, often for four or five heartbeats; then one of them would move and a moment later they would turn as one, like a flock of birds or a school of fish, and run away, their dainty hooves drumming on the hard turf, leaving the dead on the ground and the wounded limping behind.

Slowly Jay swung the rifle back until it was pointing at his stag again. Of course he would not kill his brother. It would be unthinkably wicked. He might be haunted all his life by guilty memories.

But if he refrained, might he not always regret it? Next time Father humiliated him by showing preference for Robert, would he not grind his teeth and wish with all his heart that he had solved the problem when he could and wiped his loathsome sibling off the face of the earth?

He swung the rifle back to Robert.

Father respected strength, decisiveness and ruthlessness. Even if he guessed that the fatal shot was deliberate, he would be forced to realize that Jay was a man, one who could not be ignored or overlooked without dreadful consequences.

That thought strengthened his resolve. In his heart Father would approve, Jay told himself. Sir George would never let himself be mistreated: his response to wrongdoing was brutal and savage. As a magistrate in London he had sent dozens of men, women and children to the Old Bailey. If a child could be hanged for stealing bread, what was wrong with killing Robert for stealing Jay's patrimony?

Lizzie was taking her time. Jay tried to breathe evenly but his heart was racing and his breath came in gasps. He was tempted to glance over at Lizzie, to see what the devil was holding her up, but he was afraid she would choose that instant to fire, and then he would miss his chance; so he kept his eyes and his gun barrel locked on Robert's back. His whole body was as taut as a harp string, and his muscles began to hurt with the tension, but he did not dare move.

No, he thought, this can't be happening, I'm not going to kill my brother. By God, I will, though, I swear it.

Hurry, Lizzie, please.

Out of the corner of his eye he saw something move near him. Before he could look up he heard the crack of Lizzie's gun. The stags froze. Holding his aim on Robert's spine, just between the shoulder blades, Jay squeezed his trigger gently. A bulky form loomed over him and he heard his father shout. There were two more bangs as Robert and Henry fired. Just as Jay's gun went off, a booted foot kicked the barrel. It jerked upward, and the ball went harmlessly up into the air. Fear and guilt possessed Jay's heart and he looked up into the enraged face of Sir George.

"You murdering little bastard," his father said.

7

THE DAY IN THE OPEN AIR MADE LIZZIE SLEEPY, AND SOON AFTER supper she announced that she was going to bed. Robert happened to be out of the room, and Jay politely sprang up to light her way upstairs with a candle. As they mounted the stone staircase he said quietly: "I'll take you down the mine, if you like."

Lizzie's sleepiness vanished. "Do you mean it?"

"Of course. I don't say things I don't mean." He grinned. "Do you dare to go?"

She was thrilled. "Yes!" she said. Here was a man after her own heart! "When can we go?" she said eagerly.

"Tonight. The hewers start work at midnight, the bearers an hour or two later."

"Really?" Lizzie was mystified. "Why do they work at night?"

"They work all day too. The bearers finish at the end of the afternoon."

"But they hardly have time to sleep!"

"It keeps them out of mischief."

She felt foolish. "I've spent most of my life in the next glen and I had no idea they worked such long hours." She wondered if McAsh would be proved right and the visit to the pit would turn her view of coal miners upside-down.

"Be ready at midnight," Jay said. "You'll have to dress as a man again—do you still have those clothes?"

"Yes."

"Go out by the kitchen door—I'll make sure it's open—and meet me in the stable yard. I'll saddle a couple of horses."

"This is so exciting!" she said.

He handed her the candle. "Until midnight," he whispered.

She went into her bedroom. Jay was happy again, she noted. Earlier today he had had another row of some kind with his father, up on the mountain. No one had seen exactly what happened—they had all been concentrating on the deer—but Jay missed his stag and Sir George had been white with rage. The quarrel, whatever it was, had been easily smoothed over in the excitement of the moment. Lizzie had killed her stag cleanly. Both Robert and Henry had wounded theirs. Robert's ran a few yards, then fell, and he finished it off with another shot; but Henry's got away, and the dogs went after it and brought it down after a chase. However, everyone knew something had happened, and Jay had been quiet for the rest of the day—until now, when he became animated and charming again.

She took off her dress, her petticoats and her shoes, then she wrapped herself in a blanket and sat in front of the blazing fire. Jay was such fun, she thought. He seemed to seek adventure, as she did. He was good-looking, too: tall, well dressed, and athletic, with a lot of wavy fair hair. She could hardly wait for midnight.

There was a tap at the door and her mother came in. Lizzie suffered a guilty pang. I hope Mother doesn't want a long chat, she thought anxiously. But it was not yet eleven: there was plenty of time.

Mother was wearing a cloak, as they all did to go from one room to another through the cold passages of Jamisson Castle. She took it off. Underneath she had on a wrap over her nightclothes. She unpinned Lizzie's hair and began to brush it.

Lizzie closed her eyes and relaxed. This always took her back to her childhood. "You must promise me not to dress as a man again," Mother said. Lizzie was startled. It was almost as if Mother had overheard her talking to Jay. She would have to be careful: Mother had a remarkable way of guessing when Lizzie was up to no good. "You're much too old for such games now," she added.

"Sir George was highly amused!" Lizzie protested.

"Perhaps, but it's no way to get a husband."

"Robert seems to want me."

"Yes—but you must give him a chance to pay court! Going to church yesterday you rode off with Jay and left Robert behind. Then again, tonight you chose to retire when Robert was out of the room, so that he lost the chance of escorting you upstairs."

Lizzie studied her mother in the looking-glass. The familiar lines of her face showed determination. Lizzie loved her mother and would have liked to please her. But she could not be the daughter her mother wanted: it was against her nature. "I'm sorry, Mother," she said. "I just don't think of these things."

"Do you . . . like Robert?"

"I'd take him if I were desperate."

Lady Hallim put down the hairbrush and sat opposite Lizzie. "My dear, we are desperate."

"But we've always been short of money, for as long as I can remember."

"That's true. And I've managed by borrowing, and mortgaging our land, and living most of the time up here where we can eat our own venison and wear our clothes until they have holes in them."

Once again Lizzie felt a pang of guilt. When Mother spent money it was almost always on Lizzie, not on herself. "Then let's just go on the same way. I don't mind having the cook serve at table, and sharing a maid with you. I like living here—I'd rather spend my days walking in High Glen than shopping in Bond Street."

"There's a limit to how much one can borrow, you know. They won't let us have any more."

"Then we'll live on the rents we get from the crofters. We must give up our trips to London. We won't even go to balls in Edinburgh. Nobody will come to dinner with us but the pastor. We'll live like nuns, and not see company from one year's end to the next."

"I'm afraid we can't even do that. They're threatening to take away Hallim House and the estate."

Lizzie was shocked. "They can't!"

"They can—that's what a mortgage means."

"Who are *they?*"

Mother looked vague. "Well, your father's lawyer is the one who arranged the loans for me, but I don't exactly know who has put up the money. But that doesn't matter. The point is that the lender wants his money back—or he will foreclose."

"Mother . . . are you really saying we're going to lose our home?"

"No, dear—not if you marry Robert."

"I see," Lizzie said solemnly.

The stable yard clock struck eleven. Mother stood up and kissed her. "Good night, dear. Sleep well."

"Good night, Mother."

Lizzie looked thoughtfully into the fire. She had known for years that it was her destiny to rescue their fortunes by marrying a wealthy man, and Robert had seemed as good as any other. She had not thought about it seriously until now: she did not think about things in advance, generally—she preferred to leave everything until the last moment, a habit that drove her mother crazy. But suddenly the prospect of marrying him appalled her. She felt a kind of physical disgust, as if she had swallowed something putrid.

But what could she do? She could not let her mother's creditors throw them out of their home! What would they do? Where would they go? How could they make a living? She felt a chill of fear as she pictured the two of them in cold rented rooms in an Edinburgh tenement, writing begging letters to distant relations and doing sewing for pennies. Better to marry dull Robert. Could she bring herself to, though? Whenever she vowed to do something unpleasant but necessary, like shooting a sick old hound or going to shop for petticoat material, she would eventually change her mind and wriggle out of it.

She pinned up her unruly hair, then dressed in the disguise she had worn yesterday: breeches, riding boots, a linen shirt and a topcoat, and a man's three-cornered hat which she secured with a hatpin. She darkened her cheeks with a dusting of soot from the chimney, but she decided against the curly wig this time. For warmth she added fur gloves, which also concealed her dainty hands, and a plaid blanket that made her shoulders seem broader.

When she heard midnight strike she took a candle and went downstairs.

She wondered nervously whether Jay would keep his word. Something might have happened to prevent him, or he could even have fallen asleep waiting. How disappointing that would be! But she found the kitchen door unlocked, as he had promised; and when she emerged into the stable yard he was waiting there, holding two ponies, murmuring softly to them to keep them quiet. She felt a glow of pleasure when he smiled at her in the moonlight. Without speaking, he handed her the reins of the smaller horse, then led the way out of the yard by the back path, avoiding the front drive which was overlooked by the principal bedrooms.

When they reached the road Jay unshrouded a lantern. They mounted their ponies and trotted away. "I was afraid you wouldn't come," Jay said.

"I was afraid you might fall asleep waiting," she replied, and they both laughed.

They rode up the glen toward the coal pits. "Did you have another row with your father this afternoon?" Lizzie asked him directly.

"Yes."

He did not offer details, but Lizzie's curiosity did not require encouragement. "What about?" she said.

She could not see his face but she sensed that he disliked her questioning. However, he answered mildly enough. "The same old thing, I'm afraid—my brother, Robert."

"I think you've been very badly treated, if that's any consolation."

"It is—thank you." He seemed to relax a bit.

As they approached the pits Lizzie's eagerness and curiosity heightened, and she began to speculate about what the mine would be like and why McAsh had implied it was some kind of hellhole. Would it be dreadfully hot or freezing cold? Did the men snarl at one another and fight, like caged wildcats? Would the pit be evil smelling, or infested with mice, or silent and ghostly? She began to feel apprehensive. But whatever happens, she thought, I'll know what it's like—and McAsh will no longer be able to taunt me with my ignorance.

After half an hour or so they passed a small mountain of coal for sale. "Who's there?" a voice barked, and a keeper with a deerhound straining at a leash entered the circle of Jay's lantern. The keepers traditionally looked after the deer and tried to catch poachers, but nowadays many of them enforced discipline at the pits and guarded against theft of coal.

Jay lifted his lantern to show his face.

"I beg your pardon, Mr. Jamisson, sir," the keeper said.

They rode on. The pithead itself was marked only by a horse trotting in a circle, turning a drum. As they got closer Lizzie saw that the drum wound a rope that pulled buckets of water out of the pit. "There's always water in a mine," Jay explained. "It seeps from the earth." The old wooden buckets leaked, making the ground around the pithead a treacherous mixture of mud and ice.

They tied up their horses and went to the edge of the pit. It was a shaft about six feet square with a steep wooden staircase descending its sides in a zigzag. Lizzie could not see the bottom.

There was no handrail.

Lizzie suffered a moment of panic. "How deep is it?" she asked in a shaky voice.

"If I remember rightly, this pit is two hundred and ten feet," Jay said.

Lizzie swallowed hard. If she called the whole thing off, Sir George and Robert might get to hear of it, then they would say: "I told you it was no place for a lady." She could not bear that—she would rather go down a two-hundred-foot staircase without a handrail.

Gritting her teeth, she said: "What are we waiting for?"

If Jay sensed her fear he made no comment. He went ahead, lighting the steps for her, and she followed with her heart in her mouth. However, after a few steps he said: "Why don't you put your hands on my shoulders, to steady yourself." She did so gratefully.

As they descended, the wooden buckets of water waltzed up the well in the middle of the shaft, banging against the empty ones going down, frequently splashing icy water on Lizzie. She had a scary vision of herself slipping off the stairs and tumbling crazily down the shaft, crashing into the buckets, overturning dozens of them before she hit the bottom of the shaft and died.

After a while Jay stopped to let her rest for a few moments. Although she thought of herself as fit and active, her legs ached and she was breathing hard. Wanting to give him the impression she was not tired, she made conversation. "You seem to know a lot about the mines— where the water comes from and how deep the pit is and so on."

"Coal is a constant topic of conversation in our family—it's where most of our money comes from. But I spent one summer with Harry Ratchett, the viewer, about six years ago. Mother had decided she wanted me to learn all about the business, in the hope that one day Father would want me to run it. Foolish aspiration."

Lizzie felt sorry for him.

They went on. A few minutes later the stairs ended in a deck that gave access to two tunnels. Below the level of the tunnels, the shaft was full of water. The pool was emptied by the buckets but constantly replenished by ditches that drained the tunnels. Lizzie stared into the darkness of the tunnels, her heart filled with mingled curiosity and fear.

Jay stepped off the deck into a tunnel, turned, and gave his hand to Lizzie. His grasp was firm and dry. As she entered the tunnel he drew her hand to his lips and kissed it. She was pleased by this little piece of gallantry.

As he turned to lead her on he kept hold of her hand. She was not sure what to make of this but she had no time to think about it. She had to concentrate on keeping her feet. She plowed through thick coal dust and she could taste it in the air. The roof was low in places and she had to stoop much of the time. She realized that she had a very unpleasant night ahead of her.

She tried to ignore her discomfort. On either side candlelight flickered in the gaps between broad columns, and she was reminded of a midnight service in a great cathedral. Jay said: "Each miner works a twelve-foot section of the coal face, called a 'room.' Between one room and another they leave a pillar of coal, sixteen feet square, to support the roof."

Lizzie suddenly realized that above her head there was two hundred and ten feet of earth and rock that could collapse on her if the miners had not done their work carefully; and she had to fight to suppress a feeling of panic. Involuntarily she gave Jay's hand a squeeze, and he squeezed back. From then on she was very conscious that they were holding hands. She found that she liked it.

The first rooms they passed were empty, presumably worked out, but after a while Jay stopped beside a room where a man was digging. To Lizzie's surprise the miner was not standing up: he lay on his side, attacking the coal face at floor level. A candle in a wooden holder near his head threw its inconstant light on his work. Despite his awkward position he swung his pick powerfully. With each swing he dug the point into the coal and prized out lumps. He was making an indentation two or three feet deep across the width of his room. Lizzie was shocked to realize that he was lying in running water, which seeped out of the coal face, flowed across the floor of his room, and drained into the ditch that ran along the tunnel. Lizzie dipped her fingers into the ditch. The water was freezing cold. She shivered. Yet the miner had taken off his coat and shirt and was working in his breeches and bare feet; and she could see the gleam of perspiration on his blackened shoulders.

The tunnel was not level, but rose and fell—with the seam of coal, Lizzie presumed. Now it began to go up more steeply. Jay stopped and pointed ahead to where a miner was doing something with a candle. "He's testing for firedamp," Jay said.

Lizzie let go of his hand and sat on a rock, to relieve her back from stooping.

"Are you all right?" Jay said.

"Fine. What's firedamp?"

"An inflammable gas."

"Inflammable?"

"Yes—it's what causes most explosions in coal mines."

This sounded mad. "If it's explosive, why is he using that candle?"

"It's the only way to detect the gas—you can't see it or smell it."

The miner was raising the candle slowly toward the roof, and seemed to be staring hard at the flame.

"The gas is lighter than air, so it concentrates at roof level," Jay went on. "A small amount will give a blue tinge to the candle flame."

"And what will a large amount do?"

"Blow us all to kingdom come."

Lizzie felt this was the last straw. She was filthy and exhausted and her mouth was full of coal dust, and now she was in danger of being blown up. She told herself to keep very calm. She had known, before she came here, that coal mining was a dangerous business, and she must just steel her nerve. Miners went underground every night: surely she had the courage to come here one time?

It would, however, be the last time: of that she had no doubt at all.

They watched the man for a few moments. He moved up the tunnel a few paces at a time, repeating his test. Lizzie was determined not to show her fear. Making her voice sound normal, she said: "And if he finds firedamp—what then? How do you get rid of it?"

"Set fire to it."

Lizzie swallowed. This was getting worse.

"One of the miners is designated fireman," Jay went on. "In this pit I believe it's McAsh, the young troublemaker. The job is generally handed down from father to son. The fireman is the pit's expert on gas. He knows what to do."

Lizzie wanted to run back down the tunnel to the shaft and all the way up the ladder to the outside world. She would have done so but for the humiliation of having Jay see her panic. In order to get away from this insanely dangerous test, she pointed to a side tunnel and said: "What's down there?"

Jay took her hand again. "Let's go and see."

There was a strange hush throughout the mine, Lizzie thought as they walked along. Nobody spoke much: a few of the men had boys helping them but most worked alone, and the bearers had not yet arrived. The clang of picks hitting the face and the rumble as the coal broke up were muffled by the walls and the thick dust underfoot. Every so often they passed through a door that was closed behind them by a small boy: the doors controlled the circulation of air in the tunnels, Jay explained.

They found themselves in a deserted section. Jay stopped. "This part seems to be worked out," he said, swinging his lantern in an arc. The feeble light was reflected in the tiny eyes of rats at the limit of the circle. No doubt they lived on leavings from the miners' dinner pails.

Lizzie noticed that Jay's face was smeared black, like the miners': the coal dust got everywhere. He looked funny, and she smiled.

"What is it?" he said.

"Your face is black!"

He grinned and touched her cheek with a fingertip. "And what do you think yours is like?"

She realized that she must look exactly the same. "Oh, no!" she said with a laugh.

"You're still beautiful, though," he said, and he kissed her.

She was surprised, but she did not flinch: she liked it. His lips were firm and dry, and she felt the slight roughness over his upper lip where he shaved. When he drew back she said the first thing that came into her head: "Is that what you brought me down here for?"

"Are you offended?"

It was certainly against the rules of polite society for a young gentleman to kiss a lady not his fiancée. She ought to be offended, she knew; but she had enjoyed it. She began to feel embarrassed. "Perhaps we should retrace our steps."

"May I keep holding your hand?"

"Yes."

He seemed satisfied with that, and he led her back. After a while she saw the rock she had sat on earlier. They stopped to watch a miner work. Lizzie thought about that kiss and felt a little shiver of excitement in her loins.

The miner had undercut the coal across the width of the room and was hammering wedges into the face higher up. Like most of them he was half naked, and the massive muscles of his back bunched and rolled as he swung his hammer. The coal, having nothing below to support it, eventually crumbled under its own weight and crashed to the floor in lumps. The miner stepped back quickly as the freshly exposed coal face creaked and shifted, spitting tiny fragments as it adjusted to the altered stresses.

At this point the bearers began to arrive, carrying their candles and wooden shovels, and Lizzie suffered her most horrifying shock yet.

They were nearly all women and girls.

She had never asked what miners' wives and daughters did with their time. It had not occurred to her that they spent their days, and half their nights, working underground.

The tunnels became noisy with their chatter, and the air rapidly warmed up, causing Lizzie to unfasten her coat. Because of the dark, most of the women did not notice the visitors, and their talk was uninhibited. Right in front of them an older man bumped into a woman who looked pregnant. "Out of the damn way, Sal," he said roughly.

"Out of the damn way yourself, you blind pizzle," she retorted.

Another woman said: "A pizzle's not blind, it's got one eye!" They all laughed coarsely.

Lizzie was startled. In her world women never said "damn," and as for "pizzle," she could only guess what it meant. She was also astonished that the women could laugh at anything at all, having got out of bed at two o'clock in the morning to work for fifteen hours underground.

She felt strange. Everything here was physical and sensory: the darkness, holding Jay's hand, the half-naked miners hewing coal, Jay's kiss, and the vulgar hilarity of the women—it was unnerving but at the same time stimulating. Her pulse beat faster, her skin was flushed and her heart was racing.

The chatter died down as the bearers got to work shoveling the coal into big baskets. "Why do women do this?" Lizzie asked Jay incredulously.

"A miner is paid by the weight of coal he delivers to the pithead," he replied. "If he has to pay a bearer, the money goes out of the family. So he gets his wife and children to do it, and that way they keep it all."

The big baskets were quickly filled. Lizzie watched as two women picked one up between them and heaved it onto the bent back of a third.

She grunted as she took the weight. The basket was secured by a strap around her forehead, then she headed slowly down the tunnel, bent double. Lizzie wondered how she could possibly carry it up two hundred feet of steps. "Is the basket as heavy as it looks?" she said.

One of the miners overheard her. "We call it a corf," he said to her. "It holds a hundred and fifty pounds of coal. Would you like to feel the weight, young sir?"

Jay answered before Lizzie could speak. "Certainly not," he said protectively.

The man persisted. "Or perhaps a half-corf, such as this wee one is carrying."

Approaching them was a girl of ten or eleven, wearing a shapeless wool dress and a head scarf. She was barefoot and carried on her back a corf half full of coal.

Lizzie saw Jay open his mouth to refuse, but she forestalled him. "Yes," she said. "Let me feel the weight."

The miner stopped the girl and one of his women lifted the corf. The child said nothing but seemed content to rest, breathing hard.

"Bend your back, master," the miner said. Lizzie obeyed. The woman swung the corf onto Lizzie's back.

Although she was braced for it, the weight was much more than she had anticipated, and she could not support it even for a second. Her legs buckled under her and she collapsed. The miner, seemingly expecting this, caught her, and she felt the weight lifted from her back as the woman removed the corf. They had known what would happen, Lizzie realized as she collapsed into the miner's arms.

The watching women all shrieked with laughter at the discomfiture of what they thought was a young gentleman. The miner caught Lizzie falling forward and easily supported her on his strong forearm. A callused hand as hard as a horse's hoof squashed her breast through the linen shirt. She heard the man grunt with surprise. The hand squeezed, as if double-checking; but her breasts were large—embarrassingly large, she often felt—and an instant later the hand slid away. The man lifted her upright. He held her by her shoulders, and astonished eyes stared at her out of his coal-blackened face.

"Miss Hallim!" he whispered.

She realized the miner was Malachi McAsh.

They looked at one another for a spellbound moment, while the women's laughter filled their ears. Lizzie found the sudden intimacy deeply arousing, after all that had gone before, and she could tell he felt it too. For a second she was closer to him than to Jay, even though Jay had kissed her and held her hand. Then another voice pierced the noise, and a woman said: "Mack—look at this!"

A black-faced woman was holding a candle up to the roof. McAsh looked at her, looked back at Lizzie, and then, seeming to resent leaving something unfinished, he released his hold on Lizzie and went over to the other woman.

He looked at the candle flame and said: "You're right, Esther." He turned back and addressed the others, ignoring Lizzie and Jay. "There's a little firedamp." Lizzie wanted to turn and run, but McAsh seemed calm. "It's not enough to sound the alarm—not yet, anyway. We'll check in different places and see how far it extends."

Lizzie found his equanimity incredible. What kind of people were these miners? Though their lives were brutally hard their spirits seemed unquenchable. By comparison her own life seemed pampered and purposeless.

Jay took Lizzie's arm. "I think we've seen enough, don't you?" he murmured.

Lizzie did not argue. Her curiosity had been satisfied long ago. Her back ached from bending constantly. She was tired and dirty and scared and she wanted to get out on the surface and feel the wind on her face.

They hurried along the tunnel toward the shaft. The mine was busy now and there were bearers in front of them and behind. The women hitched their skirts above their knees, for freedom of movement, and carried their candles in their teeth. They moved slowly under their enormous burdens. Lizzie saw a man relieving himself into the drainage ditch in full view of the women and girls. Can't he find somewhere private to do that? she thought, then she realized that down here there was nowhere private.

They reached the shaft and started up the stairs. The bearers went up on all fours, like small children: it suited their bent posture. They climbed at a steady pace. There was no chattering and joking now: the women and girls panted and groaned beneath the tremendous weights they were carrying. After a while Lizzie had to rest, but the bearers never stopped, and she felt humiliated and sick with guilt as she watched little girls pass her with their loads, some of them crying from pain and exhaustion. Now and again a child would slow down or stop for a moment, only to be hurried along by a curse or a brutal blow from its mother. Lizzie wanted to comfort them. All the emotions of the night came together and turned into anger. "I swear," she said vehemently, "I'll never allow coal to be mined on my land, as long as I live."

Before Jay could make any reply, a bell began to ring.

"The alarm," Jay said. "They must have found more firedamp."

Lizzie groaned and got to her feet. Her calves felt as if someone had stuck knives in them. Never again, she thought.

"I'll carry you," Jay said, and without more ado he slung her over his shoulder and began to climb the stairs.

8

THE FIREDAMP SPREAD WITH TERRIFYING SPEED.

At first the blue tinge had been visible only when the candle was at roof level, but a few minutes later it appeared a foot below the roof, and Mack had to stop testing for fear of setting fire to it before the pit was evacuated.

He was breathing in short, panicky gasps. He tried to be calm and think clearly.

Normally the gas seeped out gradually, but this was different. Something unusual must have happened. Most likely, firedamp had accumulated in a sealed-off area of exhausted workings, then an old wall had cracked and was rapidly leaking the dreaded gas into the occupied tunnels.

And every man, woman and child here carried a lighted candle.

A small trace would burn safely; a moderate amount would flash, scorching anyone in the vicinity; and a large quantity would explode, killing everyone and destroying the tunnels.

He took a deep breath. His first priority was to get everyone out of the pit as fast as possible. He rang the handbell vigorously while he counted to twelve. By the time he stopped, miners and bearers were hurrying along the tunnel toward the shaft, mothers urging their children to go faster.

While everyone else fled the pit, his two bearers stayed—his sister, Esther, calm and efficient, and his cousin Annie, who was strong and quick but also impulsive and clumsy. Using their coal shovels the two women began frantically to dig a shallow trench, the length and breadth of Mack, in the floor of the tunnel. Meanwhile Mack snatched an oilcloth bundle hanging from the roof of his room and ran for the mouth of the tunnel.

After his parents died there had been some muttering, among the men, about whether Mack was old enough to take over his father's role of fireman. Apart from the responsibility of the job, the fireman was regarded as a leader in the community. In truth Mack himself had shared their doubts. But no one else wanted the job—it was unpaid and dangerous. And when he dealt efficiently with the first crisis the muttering stopped. Now he was proud that older men trusted him, but his pride also forced him to appear calm and confident even when he was afraid.

He reached the mouth of the tunnel. The last stragglers were heading up the stairs. Now Mack had to get rid of the gas. Burning was the only way to do this. He had to set fire to it.

It was evilly bad luck that this should happen today. It was his birthday: he was leaving. Now he wished he had thrown caution to the winds and left the glen on Sunday night. He had told himself that a wait of a day or two might make the Jamissons think he was going to stay, and lull them into a false sense of security. He felt sick at heart that in his final hours as a coal miner he had to risk his life to save the pit he was about to quit forever.

If the firedamp were not burned off, the pit would close. And a pit closure in a mining village was like a failed harvest in a farming community: people starved. Mack would never forget the last time the pit closed, four winters ago. During the harrowing weeks that followed, the youngest and oldest villagers had died—including both his parents. The day after his mother died, Mack had dug up a nest of hibernating rabbits, and had broken their necks while they were still groggy; and that meat had saved him and Esther.

He stepped out onto the deck and tore the waterproof wrappings off his bundle. Inside was a big torch made of dry sticks and rags, a ball of string, and a large version of the hemispheric candle-holder the miners used, fixed to a flat wooden base so that it could not fall over. Mack stuck the torch firmly in the holder, tied the string to the base, and lit the torch with his candle. It blazed up immediately. Here it would burn safely, for the lighter-than-air gas could not gather at the bottom of the shaft. But his next task was to get the burning torch into the tunnel.

He took another moment to lower himself into the drainage pool at the bottom of the shaft, soaking his clothes and hair in the icy water to give him a little extra protection from burns. Then he hurried back along the tunnel unwinding the ball of string, at the same time scrutinizing the floor, removing large stones and other objects that might obstruct the movement of the blazing torch as it was drawn into the tunnel.

When he reached Esther and Annie, he saw by the light of the one candle on the floor that all was ready. The trench was dug. Esther was dipping a blanket into the drainage ditch, and now she quickly wrapped it around Mack. Shivering, he lay down in the trench, still holding the end of the string. Annie knelt beside him and, somewhat to his surprise, kissed him full on the lips. Then she covered the trench with a heavy board, closing him in.

There was a sloshing sound as they poured more water on the board, in a further attempt to protect him from the flames he was about to ignite. Then one of them tapped three times, the sign that they were leaving.

He counted to one hundred, to give them time to get out of the tunnel.

Then, with his heart full of dread, he started to pull on the string, drawing the blazing torch into the mine, toward where he lay, in a tunnel half full of explosive gas.

＊

Jay carried Lizzie to the top of the stairs and set her down on the icy mud at the pithead.

"Are you all right?" he said.

"I'm so glad to be above ground again," she said gratefully. "I can't thank you enough for carrying me. You must be exhausted."

"You weigh a good deal less than a corf full of coal," he said with a smile.

He talked as if her weight were nothing, but he looked a little unsteady on his legs as they walked away from the shaft. However, he had never faltered on the way up.

Daybreak was still hours away, and it had started to snow, not in gently drifting flakes but in driving icy pellets that blew into Lizzie's eyes. As the last of the miners and bearers came out of the shaft, Lizzie noticed the young woman whose child had been christened on Sunday—Jen, her name was. Although her child was only a week or so old, the poor woman was carrying a full corf. Surely she should have taken a rest after giving birth? She emptied the basket on the dump and handed the tallyman a wooden marker: Lizzie guessed the markers were used to calculate the wages at the end of the week. Perhaps Jen was too much in need of money to have time off.

Lizzie continued to watch because Jen looked distressed. With her candle raised above her head she darted among the crowd of seventy or eighty mine workers, peering through the falling snow, calling: "Wullie! Wullie!" It seemed she was searching for a child. She found her husband and had a rapid, frightened conversation with him. Then she screamed "No!" She ran to the pithead and started back down the stairs.

The husband went to the edge of the shaft then came back and looked around the crowd again, visibly distressed and bewildered. Lizzie said to him: "What's the matter?"

He replied in a shaky voice. "We can't find our laddie, and she thinks he's still down the pit."

"Oh, no!" Lizzie looked over the edge. She could see some kind of torch blazing at the bottom of the shaft. But as she looked it moved and disappeared into the tunnel.

✳

Mack had done this on three previous occasions, but this time it was much more frightening. Formerly the concentration of firedamp had been much lower, a slow seep rather than a sudden buildup. His father had dealt with major gas leaks, of course—and his father's body, as he washed himself in front of the fire on Saturday nights, had been covered with the marks of old burns.

Mack shivered in his blanket sodden with icy water. As he steadily wound in the string, pulling the blazing torch closer to himself and to the gas, he tried to calm his fear by thinking about Annie. They had grown up together and had always been fond of one another. Annie had a wild soul and a muscular body. She had never kissed him in public before, but she had often done it secretly. They had explored one another's bodies and taught each other how to give pleasure. They had tried all sorts of things together, only stopping short of what Annie called "making bairns." And they had almost done that. . . .

It was no use: he still felt terrified. To calm himself he tried to think in a detached way about how the gas moved and gathered. His trench was at a low point in the tunnel, so the concentration here should be less; but there was no accurate way of estimating it until it ignited. He was afraid of pain, and he knew that burns were torment. He was not really afraid to die. He did not think about religion much but he believed God must be merciful. However, he did not want to die now: he had done nothing, seen nothing, been nowhere. He had spent all his life so far as a slave. If I survive this night, he vowed, I will leave the glen today. I'll kiss Annie, and say good-bye to Esther, and defy the Jamissons, and walk away from here, so help me God.

The amount of string that had gathered in his hands told him the torch was now about halfway to him. It could light the firedamp at any moment. However, it might not catch fire at all: sometimes, his father had told him, the gas seemed to vanish, no one knew where.

He felt a slight resistance to his pull and knew that the torch was rubbing against the wall where the tunnel curved. If he looked out he would be able to see it. Surely the gas must blow now, he thought.

Then he heard a voice.

He was so shocked that at first he thought he was having a supernatural experience, an encounter with a ghost or a demon.

Then he realized that it was neither: he was hearing the voice of a terrified small child, crying and saying: "Where is everyone?"

Mack's heart stopped.

He knew instantly what had happened. As a small boy working in the mine he had often fallen asleep during his fifteen-hour day. This child had done the same, and had slept through the alarm. Then it had woken up, found the pit deserted, and panicked.

It took Mack only a split second to realize what he had to do.

He pushed aside the board and sprang out of his trench. The scene was illuminated by the burning torch and he could see the boy coming out of a side tunnel, rubbing his eyes and wailing. It was Wullie, the son of Mack's cousin Jen. "Uncle Mack!" he said joyfully.

Mack ran for the boy, unwrapping the sodden blanket from around him as he went. There was no room for two in the shallow trench: they would have to try to reach the shaft before the gas blew. Mack wrapped the boy in the wet blanket, saying: "There's firedamp, Wullie, we've got to get out!" He picked him up, tucked him under one arm, and ran on.

As he approached the burning torch he willed it not to ignite the gas, and heard himself shouting: "Not yet! Not yet!" Then they were past it.

The boy was light, but it was hard to run stooping, and the floor underfoot made it more difficult: muddy in places, thick with dust in others, and uneven everywhere, with outcroppings of rock to trip the hasty. Mack charged ahead regardless, stumbling sometimes but managing to keep his feet, listening for the bang that might be the last sound he ever heard.

As he rounded the curve in the tunnel, the light from the torch dimmed to nothing. He ran on into the darkness, but within seconds he crashed into the wall and fell headlong, dropping Wullie. He cursed and scrambled to his feet.

The boy began to cry. Mack located him by sound and picked him up again. He was forced to go on more slowly, feeling the tunnel wall with his free hand, cursing the dark. Then, mercifully, a candle flame appeared ahead, at the entrance to the tunnel, and Mack heard Jen's voice calling: "Wullie! Wullie!"

"I've got him here, Jen!" Mack shouted, breaking into a run. "Get yourself up the stair!"

She ignored his instruction and came toward him.

He was only a few yards from the end of the tunnel and safety.

"Go back!" he yelled, but she kept coming.

He crashed into her and swept her up in his free arm.

Then the gas blew.

For a split second there was an ear-piercing hiss, then there was a huge, deafening thump that shook the earth. A force that felt like a massive fist struck Mack's back and he was lifted off his feet, losing his grip on Wullie and Jen. He flew through the air. He felt a wave of scorching heat, and he was sure he was going to die; then he splashed headfirst into icy water, and realized he had been thrown into the drainage pool at the bottom of the mine shaft.

And he was still alive.

He broke the surface and dashed water from his eyes.

The wooden decking and staircase were burning in places, and the flames illuminated the scene fitfully. Mack located Jen, splashing about and choking. He grabbed her and heaved her out of the water.

Choking, she screamed: "Where's Wullie?"

He might have been knocked unconscious, Mack thought. He pushed himself from one side of the small pool to the other, bumping into the bucket chain, which had ceased to operate. At last he found a floating object that turned out to be Wullie. He shoved the boy onto the deck beside his mother and clambered out himself.

Wullie sat up and spewed water. "Thank God," Jen sobbed. "He's alive."

Mack looked into the tunnel. Stray wisps of gas burned sporadically like fiery spirits. "Away up the stairs with us," he said. "There might be a secondary blast." He pulled Jen and Wullie to their feet and pushed them up ahead of him. Jen lifted Wullie and slung him over her shoulder: his weight was nothing to a woman who could carry a full corf of coal up these stairs twenty times in a fifteen-hour shift.

Mack hesitated, looking at the small fires burning at the foot of the stairs. If the entire staircase burned, the pit might be out of commission for weeks while it was rebuilt. He took a few extra seconds to splash water from the pool over the flames and put them out. Then he followed Jen up.

When he reached the top he felt exhausted, bruised and dizzy. He was immediately surrounded by a crowd who shook his hand, slapped his back and congratulated him. The crowd parted for Jay Jamisson and his companion, whom Mack had recognized to be Lizzie Hallim dressed as a man. "Well done, McAsh," said Jay. "My family appreciates your courage."

You smug bastard, Mack thought.

Lizzie said: "Is there really no other way to deal with firedamp?"

"No," said Jay.

"Of course there is," Mack gasped.

"Really?" Lizzie said. "What?"

Mack caught his breath. "You sink ventilation shafts, which let the gas escape before ever it can accumulate." He took another deep breath. "The Jamissons have been told time and time again."

There was a murmur of agreement from the miners standing around.

Lizzie turned to Jay. "Then why don't you do it?"

"You don't understand business—why should you?" Jay said. "No man of business can pay for an expensive procedure when a cheaper one will achieve the same result. His rivals would undercut his price. It's political economy."

"Give it a fancy name if you like," Mack panted. "Ordinary folk call it wicked greed."

One or two of the miners shouted: "Aye! That's right!"

"Now, McAsh," Jay remonstrated. "Don't spoil everything by getting above your station again. You'll get into real trouble."

"I'm in no trouble," Mack said. "Today is my twenty-second birthday." He had not meant to say this, but now he could not stop himself. "I haven't worked here the full year-and-a-day, not quite—and I'm not going to." The crowd was suddenly quiet, and Mack was filled with an exhilarating sense of freedom. "I'm leaving, Mr. Jamisson," he said. "I quit. Good-bye." He turned his back on Jay and, in total silence, he walked away.

BY THE TIME JAY AND LIZZIE GOT BACK TO THE CASTLE, EIGHT OR ten servants were about, lighting fires and sweeping floors by candlelight. Lizzie, black with coal dust and almost helpless with fatigue, thanked Jay in a whisper and staggered upstairs. Jay ordered a tub and hot water to be brought to his room then took a bath, scrubbing the coal dust off his skin with a pumice stone.

In the last forty-eight hours, momentous events had happened in his life: his father had given him a derisory patrimony, his mother had cursed his father, and he had tried to murder his brother—but none of these things occupied his mind. As he lay there he thought about Lizzie. Her impish face appeared before him in the steam from his bath, smiling mischievously, the eyes crinkling in the corners, mocking him, tempting him, daring him. He recalled how she had felt in his arms as he had carried her up the mine shaft: she was soft and light, and he had pressed her small frame to himself as he climbed the stairs. He wondered if she was thinking about him. She must have called for hot water too: she could hardly go to bed as dirty as she was. He pictured her standing naked in front of her bedroom fire, soaping her body. He wished he could be with her, and take the sponge from her hand, and gently wipe the coal dust from the slopes of her breasts. The thought aroused him, and he sprang out of the bath and rubbed himself dry with a rough towel.

He did not feel sleepy. He wanted to talk to someone about the night's adventure, but Lizzie would probably sleep for hours. He thought about his mother. He could trust her. She sometimes pushed him into doing things against his inclination, but she was always on his side.

He shaved and put on fresh clothes then went along to her room. As he expected she was up, sipping chocolate at her dressing-table while her maid did her hair. She smiled at him. He kissed her and dropped onto a chair. She was pretty, even first thing in the morning, but there was steel in her soul.

She dismissed her maid. "Why are you up so early?" she asked Jay.

"I haven't been to bed. I went down the pit."

"With Lizzie Hallim?"

She was so clever, he thought fondly. She always knew what he was up to. But he did not mind, for she never condemned him. "How did you guess?"

"It wasn't difficult. She was itching to go, and she's the kind of girl who won't take no for an answer."

"We chose a bad day to go down. There was an explosion."

"Dear God, are you all right?"

"Yes—"

"I'll send for Dr. Stevenson anyway—"

"Mother, stop worrying! I was out of the pit by the time it blew. So was Lizzie. I'm just a bit weak in the knees from carrying her all the way up the shaft."

Mother calmed down. "What did Lizzie think of it?"

"She swore she would never allow mining on the Hallim estate."

Alicia laughed. "And your father is greedy for her coal. Well, I look forward to witnessing the battle. When Robert is her husband he will have the power to go against her wishes . . . in theory. We shall see. But how do you think the courtship is progressing?"

"Flirting isn't Robert's strong point, to say the least," Jay said scornfully.

"It's yours, though, isn't it?" she said indulgently.

Jay shrugged. "He's doing his clumsy best."

"Perhaps she won't marry him after all."

"I think she will have to."

Mother looked shrewdly at him. "Do you know something I don't?"

"Lady Hallim is having trouble renewing her mortgages—Father has made sure of it."

"Has he! How sly he is."

Jay sighed. "She's a wonderful girl. She'll be wasted on Robert."

Mother put a hand on his knee. "Jay, my sweet boy, she's not Robert's yet."

"I suppose she might marry someone else."

"She might marry you."

"Good God, Mother!" Although he had kissed Lizzie he had not got as far as thinking of marriage.

"You're in love with her. I can tell."

"Love? Is that what this is?"

"Of course—your eyes light up at the mention of her name, and when she's in the room you can't see anyone else."

She had described Jay's feelings exactly. He had no secrets from his mother. "But marry her?"

"If you're in love with her, ask her! You'd be the laird of High Glen."

"That would be one in the eye for Robert," Jay said with a grin. His heart was racing at the thought of having Lizzie as his wife, but he tried to concentrate on the practicalities. "I'd be penniless."

"You're penniless now. But you'd manage the estate better than Lady Hallim—she's no businesswoman. It's a big place—High Glen must be ten miles long, and she owns Craigie and Crook Glen too. You'd clear land for grazing, sell more venison, build a watermill. . . . You could make it produce a decent income, even without mining for coal."

"What about the mortgages?"

"You're a much more attractive borrower than she is—you're young and vigorous and you come from a wealthy family. You would find it easy enough to renew the loans. And then, in time . . ."

"What?"

"Well, Lizzie is an impulsive girl. Today she vows she will never allow mining on the Hallim estate. Tomorrow, God knows, she may decide that deer have feelings, and ban hunting. Next week she may have forgotten both edicts. If ever you do allow coal mining, you'll be able to pay off all your debts."

Jay grimaced. "I don't relish the prospect of going against Lizzie's wishes on something like that." He was also thinking that he wanted to be a Barbadian sugar grower, not a Scottish coal owner. But he wanted Lizzie, too.

With disconcerting suddenness Mother changed the subject. "What happened yesterday, when you were hunting?"

Jay was taken by surprise, and he found himself unable to tell a smooth lie. He flushed and stammered, and finally said: "I had another set-to with Father."

"I know that much," she said. "I could tell by your faces when you returned. But it wasn't just an argument. You did something that shook him. What was it?"

Jay had never been able to deceive her. "I tried to shoot Robert," he confessed miserably.

"Oh, Jay, that's dreadful," she said.

He bowed his head. It was all the worse that he had failed. If he had killed his brother, the guilt would have been appalling, but there would have been a certain savage sense of triumph. This way he had the guilt on its own.

Mother stood beside his chair and pulled his head to her bosom. "My poor boy," she said. "There was no need for that. We'll find another way, don't worry." And she rocked back and forth, stroking his hair and saying: "There, there."

*

"How could you do such a thing?" Lady Hallim wailed as she scrubbed Lizzie's back.

"I had to see for myself," Lizzie replied. "Not so hard!"

"I have to do it hard—the coal dust won't shift."

"Mack McAsh riled me when he said I didn't know what I was talking about," Lizzie went on.

"And why should you?" said her mother. "What business has a young lady to know about coal mining, may I ask?"

"I hate it when people dismiss me by saying that women don't understand about politics, or farming, or mining, or trade—it lets them get away with all kinds of nonsense."

Lady Hallim groaned. "I hope Robert doesn't mind your being so masculine."

"He'll have to take me as I am, or not at all."

Her mother gave an exasperated sigh. "My dear, this won't do. You must give him more encouragement. Of course a girl doesn't want to appear *eager,* but you go too far the other way. Now promise me you'll be nice to Robert today."

"Mother, what do you think of Jay?"

Mother smiled. "A charming boy, of course—" She stopped suddenly and stared hard at Lizzie. "Why do you ask?"

"He kissed me in the coal mine."

"No!" Lady Hallim stood upright and hurled the pumice stone across the room. "No, Elizabeth, I will not have this!" Lizzie was taken aback by her mother's sudden fury. "I have not lived twenty years in penury to see you grow up and marry a handsome pauper!"

"He's not a pauper—"

"Yes he is, you saw that awful scene with his father—his patrimony is a horse—Lizzie, you cannot do this!"

Mother was possessed by rage. Lizzie had never seen her like this and she could not understand it. "Mother, calm down, won't you?" she pleaded. She stood up and got out of the tub. "Pass me a towel, please?"

To her astonishment her mother put her hands to her face and began to cry. Lizzie put her arms around her and said: "Mother, dear, what is it?"

"Cover yourself, you wicked child," she said between sobs.

Lizzie wrapped a blanket around her wet body. "Sit down, Mother." She guided her to a chair.

After a while Mother spoke. "Your father was just like Jay, just like him," she said, and there was a bitter twist to the set of her mouth. "Tall, handsome, charming, and very keen on kissing in dark places— and weak, so weak. I gave in to my lower nature, and married him against my better judgment, even though I knew he was a will-o'-the-wisp. Within three years he had wasted my fortune, and a year after that he fell off his horse when drunk and broke his beautiful head and died."

"Oh, Mama." Lizzie was shocked by the hatred in her mother's voice. She normally spoke of Father in neutral tones: she had always told Lizzie that he was unlucky in business, that he had died tragically young, and that lawyers had made a mess of the estate's finances. Lizzie herself could hardly remember him, for she had been three years old when he died.

"And he scorned me for not giving him a son," Mother went on. "A son who would have been like him, faithless and feckless, and would have broken some girl's heart. But I knew how to prevent that."

Lizzie was shocked again. Was it true that women could prevent pregnancy? Could it be that her own mother had done such a thing in defiance of her husband's wishes?

Mother seized her hand. "Promise me you won't marry him, Lizzie. Promise me!"

Lizzie pulled her hand away. She felt disloyal, but she had to tell the truth. "I can't," she said. "I love him."

✳

When Jay left his mother's room, his feelings of guilt and shame seemed to dissipate, and suddenly he was hungry. He went down to the dining room. His father and Robert were there, eating thick slices of grilled ham with stewed apples and sugar, talking to Harry Ratchett. Ratchett, as manager of the pits, had come to report the firedamp blast. Father looked sternly at Jay and said: "I hear you went down Heugh pit last night."

Jay's appetite began to fade. "I did," he said. "There was an explosion." He poured a glass of ale from a jug.

"I know all about the explosion," Father said. "Who was your companion?"

Jay swallowed some beer. "Lizzie Hallim," he confessed.

Robert colored. "Damn you," he said. "You know Father did not wish her to be taken down the pit."

Jay was stung into a defiant response. "Well, Father, how will you punish me? Cut me off without a penny? You've already done that."

Father wagged a threatening finger. "I warn you not to disregard my orders."

"You should be worrying about McAsh, not me," Jay said, trying to turn his father's wrath onto another object. "He told everyone he was leaving today."

Robert said: "Insubordinate damned tyke." It was not clear whether he was referring to McAsh or Jay.

Harry Ratchett coughed. "You might just let McAsh go, Sir George," he said. "The man's a good worker, but he's a troublemaker, and we'd be well rid of him."

"I can't do that," Father replied. "McAsh has taken a public stand against me. If he gets away with it, every young miner will think he can leave too."

Robert put in: "It's not just us, either. This lawyer, Gordonson, could write to every pit in Scotland. If young miners are allowed to leave at the age of twenty-one, the entire industry could collapse."

"Exactly," Father agreed. "And then what would the British nation do for coal? I tell you, if I ever get Caspar Gordonson in front of me on a treason charge, I'll hang him quicker than you can say 'unconstitutional,' so help me."

Robert said: "In fact it's our patriotic duty to do something about McAsh."

They had forgotten about Jay's offense, to his relief. Keeping the conversation focused on McAsh he asked: "But what can be done?"

"I could jail him," said Sir George.

"No," Robert said. "When he came out he would still claim to be a free man."

There was a thoughtful silence.

"He could be flogged," Robert suggested.

"That might be the answer," said Sir George. "I have the right to whip them, in law."

Ratchett looked uneasy. "It's many years since that right was exercised by a coal owner, Sir George. And who would wield the lash?"

Robert said impatiently: "Well, what *do* we do with troublemakers?"

Sir George smiled. "We make them go the round," he said.

10

MACK WOULD HAVE LIKED TO START WALKING TO EDINBURGH RIGHT away, but he knew that would be foolish. Even though he had not worked a full shift he was exhausted, and the explosion had left him feeling slightly dazed. He needed time to think about what the Jamissons might do and how he could outwit them.

He went home, took off his wet clothes, lit the fire and got into bed. His immersion in the drainage pool had made him dirtier than usual, for the water was thick with coal dust, but the blankets on his bed were so black that a little more made no difference. Like most of the men, he bathed once a week, on Saturday night.

The other miners had gone back to work after the explosion. Esther had stayed at the pit, with Annie, to fetch the coal Mack had hewed and bring it up to the surface: she would not let hard work go to waste.

As he drifted off to sleep he wondered why men got weary more quickly than women. The hewers, all men, worked ten hours, from midnight until ten o'clock in the morning; the bearers, mostly women, worked from two A.M. until five P.M.—fifteen hours. The women's work was harder, climbing those stairs again and again with huge baskets of coal on their bent backs, yet they kept going long after their men had stumbled home and fallen into bed. Women sometimes became hewers, but it was rare: when wielding the pick or hammer most women could not hit hard enough, and it took them too long to win the coal from the face.

The men always took a nap when they came home. They would get up after an hour or so. Most would prepare dinner for their wives and children. Some spent the afternoon drinking at Mrs. Wheighel's: their wives were much pitied, for it was hard for a woman to come home, after fifteen hours of bearing coal, to find no fire, no food and a drunk husband. Life was hard for miners, but it was harder for their wives.

When Mack woke up he knew it was a momentous day but he could not remember why. Then it came back to him: he was leaving the glen.

He would not get far if he looked like an escaped coal miner, so the first thing he had to do was get clean. He built up the fire then made several trips to the stream with the water barrel. He heated the water on the fire and brought in the tin tub that hung outside the back door. The little room became steamy. He filled the bath then got in with a piece of soap and a stiff brush and scrubbed himself.

He began to feel good. This was the last time he would ever wash coal dust off his skin: he would never have to go down a mine again. Slavery was behind him. In front of him he had Edinburgh, London, the world. He would meet people who had never heard of Heugh pit. His destiny was a blank sheet of paper on which he could write anything he liked.

While he was in the bath, Annie came in.

She hesitated just inside the door, looking troubled and uncertain.

Mack smiled, offered her the brush, and said: "Would you do my back?"

She came forward and took it from him, but stood looking at him with the same unhappy expression.

"Go on," he said.

She began to scrub his back.

"They say a miner shouldn't wash his back," she said. "It's supposed to be weakening."

"I'm not a miner anymore."

She stopped. "Don't go, Mack," she pleaded. "Don't leave me here."

He had been afraid of something like this: that kiss on the lips had been a forewarning. He felt guilty. He was fond of his cousin, and he had enjoyed the fun and games they had had together last summer, rolling in the heather on warm Sunday afternoons; but he did not want to spend his life with her, especially if it meant staying in Heugh. Could he explain that without crucifying her? There were tears in her eyes, and he saw how she longed for him to promise he would stay. But he was determined to leave: he wanted it more than he had ever wanted anything. "I must go away," he said. "I'll miss you, Annie, but I have to go."

"You think you're better than the rest of us, don't you?" she said resentfully. "Your mother had ideas above her station and you're the same. You're too good for me, is that it? You're going to London to marry a fine lady, I suppose!"

His mother had certainly had ideas above her station, but he was not going to London to marry a fine lady. Was he better than the rest of them? Did he think he was too good for Annie? There was a grain of truth in what she said, and he felt embarrassed. "We're all too good for slavery," he said.

She knelt beside the tub and put her hand on his knee above the water. "Don't you love me, Mack?"

To his shame he began to feel aroused. He longed to embrace her and make her feel all right again, but he hardened his heart. "You're dear to me, Annie, but I never said 'I love you,' no more than you did."

She slipped her hand under the water and between his legs. She smiled when she felt how stiff he was.

He said: "Where's Esther?"

"Playing with Jen's new baby. She'll be away for a while."

Annie had asked her to stay away, Mack inferred: otherwise Esther would have hurried home to talk to him about his plans.

"Stay here and let's get married," Annie said, caressing him. The sensation was exquisite. He had taught her how to do it, last summer, and then he had made her show him how she pleasured herself. As he remembered that, he became more inflamed. "We could do anything we liked, all the time," she said.

"If I get married I'm stuck here for life," Mack said, but he felt his resistance weakening.

Annie stood up and pulled off her dress. She wore nothing else:

underwear was reserved for Sundays. Her body was lean and hard, with small, flat breasts and a mass of dense black hair at the groin. Her skin all over was gray with coal dust, like Mack's. To his astonishment she climbed into the tub with him, kneeling astride his legs. "It's your turn to wash me," she said, giving him the soap.

He rubbed the soap slowly, working up a lather, then he put his hands on her breasts. Her nipples were small and stiff. She moaned deep in her throat, then she grasped his wrists and pushed his hands down, across her hard, flat belly, to her groin. His soapy fingers slipped between her thighs and he felt the coarse curls of her thick pubic hair and the firm, soft flesh beneath it.

"Say you'll stay," she pleaded. "Let's do it. I want to feel you inside me."

He knew that if he gave in his fate was sealed. There was something dreamily unreal about the scene. "No," he said, but his voice was a whisper.

She came closer, pulling his face to her breasts, then lowered herself until she was poised over him, her sexual lips just touching the swollen end of his cock where it stuck up out of the water. "Say yes," she said.

He groaned and gave up the struggle. "Yes," he said. "Please. Quickly."

There was a terrific crash and the door flew open.

Annie screamed.

Four men burst in, filling the little room: Robert Jamisson, Harry Ratchett and two of the Jamissons' keepers. Robert wore a sword and a pair of pistols, and one of the keepers carried a musket.

Annie got off Mack and stepped out of the bath. Dazed and frightened, Mack stood up shakily.

The keeper with the musket looked at Annie. "Cozy cousins," he said with a leer. Mack knew the man: his name was McAlistair. He recognized the other one, a big bully called Tanner.

Robert laughed harshly. "Is that what she is—his cousin? I suppose incest is nothing to coal miners."

Mack's fear and bewilderment gave way to fury at this invasion of his home. He suppressed his anger and struggled to remain controlled.

He was in grave danger, and there was a chance Annie would suffer too. He had to keep his wits about him, not give in to outrage. He looked at Robert. "I'm a free man and I've broken no laws," he said. "What are you doing in my house?"

McAlistair was still staring at Annie's body, damp and steaming. "What a pretty sight," he said thickly.

Mack turned to him. In a low, even voice he said: "If you touch her I'll tear the head off your neck with my hands."

McAlistair looked at Mack's bare shoulders and realized he could do what he threatened. He paled and took a step back, even though he held a gun.

But Tanner was bigger and more reckless, and he reached out and grasped Annie's wet breast.

Mack acted without forethought. A second later he was out of the tub and grasping Tanner by the wrist. Before anyone else could move he had thrust Tanner's hand into the fire.

Tanner screamed and writhed, but he could not escape from Mack's grip. "Let me go!" he screeched. "Please, please!"

Mack held the man's hand in the burning coals and yelled: "Run, Annie!"

Annie snatched up her dress and flew out the back door.

The butt of a musket cracked into the back of Mack's head.

The blow enraged him, and with Annie gone he became heedless. He released Tanner, then grabbed McAlistair by the coat and butted him in the face, smashing the man's nose. Blood spurted and McAlistair roared with pain. Mack swung around and kicked Harry Ratchett in the groin with a bare foot as hard as a stone. Ratchett doubled up, groaning.

Every fight Mack had ever fought had taken place down the pit, so he was accustomed to combat in a confined space; but four opponents were too many. McAlistair hit him again with the butt of the musket, and for a moment Mack swayed, stunned. Then Ratchett grabbed him from behind, pinning his arms, and before he could release himself the point of Robert Jamisson's sword was at his throat.

After a moment Robert said: "Tie him up."

✳

They threw him across the back of a horse and covered his nakedness with a blanket, then they took him to Castle Jamisson and put him in the larder, still naked and tied hand and foot. He lay on the stone floor, shivering, surrounded by the dripping carcasses of deer, cattle and pigs. He tried to warm himself by moving as much as he could, but with his hands and feet tied he could not generate much heat. Eventually he managed to sit up with his back against the furry hide of a dead stag. For a while he sang to keep up his spirits—first the ballads they crooned at Mrs. Wheighel's on Saturday nights, then a few hymns, then some old Jacobite rebel ditties; but when he ran out of songs he felt worse than before.

His head hurt from the musket blows, but what pained him most was how easily the Jamissons had taken him. What a fool he was to have delayed his departure. He had given them time to take action. While they were planning his downfall he had been feeling his cousin's breasts.

It did not help to speculate about what they had in store for him. If he did not freeze to death here in the larder they would probably send him to Edinburgh and have him tried for assaulting the gamekeepers. Like most crimes, that was a hanging matter.

The light coming through the cracks around the door gradually faded as night fell. They came for him just as the stable yard clock struck eleven. There were six men this time, and he did not attempt to fight them.

Davy Taggart, the blacksmith who made the miners' tools, fitted an iron collar like Jimmy Lee's around Mack's neck. It was the ultimate humiliation: a sign for all the world to see, saying he was another man's property. He was less than a man, subhuman; he was livestock.

They untied his bonds and threw some clothes at him: a pair of breeches, a threadbare flannel shirt and a ripped waistcoat. He put them on hastily and still felt cold. The keepers tied his hands again and put him on a pony.

They rode to the pit.

The Wednesday shift would begin in a few minutes' time, at midnight. The ostler was putting a fresh horse in harness to drive the bucket chain. Mack realized they were going to make him go the round.

He groaned aloud. It was a crushing, humiliating torture. He would have given his life for a bowl of hot porridge and a few minutes in front of a blazing fire. Instead he was doomed to spend the night in the open air. He wanted to fall on his knees and beg for mercy; but the thought of how that would please the Jamissons stiffened his pride, and instead he roared: "You've no right to do this! No right!" The keepers laughed at him.

They stood him in the muddy circular track around which the pithead horses trotted day and night. He squared his shoulders and held his head high, although he felt like bursting into tears. They tied him to the harness, facing the horse, so that he could not get out of its way. Then the ostler whipped the horse into a trot.

Mack began to run backward.

He stumbled almost immediately, and the horse drew up. The ostler whipped it again, and Mack scrambled to his feet just in time. He began to get the knack of running backward. Then he became overconfident and slipped on the icy mud. This time the horse charged on. Mack slid to one side, writhing and twisting to get away from the hooves, and was dragged alongside the horse for a second or two, then he lost control and slipped under the horse's feet. The horse trod on his stomach and kicked his thigh, then stopped.

They made Mack stand up, then they lashed the horse again. The blow to the stomach had winded Mack, and his left leg felt weak, but he was forced into a limping backward run.

He gritted his teeth and tried to settle into a rhythm. He had seen others suffer this punishment—Jimmy Lee, for one. They had survived, although they bore the marks: Jimmy Lee had a scar over his left eye where the horse had kicked him, and the resentment that burned inside Jimmy was fueled by the memory of the humiliation. Mack, too, would survive. His mind dulled with pain and cold and defeat, he thought of nothing but staying on his feet and avoiding those deadly hooves.

As time went by he began to feel an affinity with the horse. They were both in harness and compelled to run in a circle. When the ostler cracked his whip, Mack went a little faster; and when Mack stumbled, the horse seemed to slacken its pace for a moment to allow him to recover.

He was aware of the hewers arriving at midnight to begin their shift. They came up the hill talking and shouting, ribbing one another and telling jokes as usual; then they fell silent as they approached the pithead and saw Mack. The keepers hefted their muskets menacingly whenever a miner seemed disposed to stop. Mack heard Jimmy Lee's voice raised in indignation and saw, from the corner of his eye, three or four other miners surround Jimmy, taking him by the arms and pushing and shoving him toward the pit to keep him out of trouble.

Gradually Mack lost all sense of time. The bearers arrived, women and children chattering on their way up the hill then falling silent, as the men had, when they passed Mack. He heard Annie cry: "Oh dear God, they've made Mack go the round!" She was kept away from him by the Jamissons' men, but she called out: "Esther's looking for you—I'll fetch her."

Esther appeared some time later, and before the keepers could prevent her she stopped the horse. She held a flagon of hot sweetened milk to Mack's lips. It tasted like the elixir of life, and he gulped it frantically, almost choking himself. He managed to drain the jug before they pulled Esther away.

The night wore on as slow as a year. The keepers put down their muskets and sat around the ostler's fire. Coal mining went on. The bearers came up from the pit, emptied their corves on the dump, and went down again in their endless round. When the ostler changed the horse Mack got a few minutes' rest, but the fresh horse trotted faster.

There came a moment when he realized it was daylight again. Now it could be only an hour or two until the hewers stopped work, but an hour was forever.

A pony came up the hill. Out of the corner of his eye Mack saw the rider get off and stand staring at him. Looking briefly in that direction he recognized Lizzie Hallim, in the same black fur coat she had worn to church. Was she here to mock him? he wondered. He felt humiliated, and wished she would go away. But when he looked again at her elfin face he saw no mockery there. Instead there was compassion, anger, and something else he could not read.

Another horse came up the hill and Robert got off. He spoke to Lizzie in an irate undertone. Lizzie's reply was clearly audible: "This is barbaric!" In his distress Mack felt profoundly grateful to her. Her indignation comforted him. It was some small consolation to know that there was one person among the gentry who felt human beings should not be treated this way.

Robert replied indignantly, but Mack could not make out his words. While they were arguing, the men began to come up from the pit. However, they did not return to their homes. Instead they stood around the horse-gin, watching without speaking. The women also began to gather: when they had emptied their corves they did not go back down the shaft but joined the silent crowd.

Robert ordered the ostler to stop the horse.

Mack at last stopped running. He tried to stand proud, but his legs would not support him, and he fell to his knees. The ostler came to untie him, but Robert stopped the man with a gesture.

Robert spoke loudly enough for everyone to hear. "Well, McAsh, you said yesterday that you were one day short of servitude. Now you have worked that extra day. Even by your own foolish rules you're my father's property now." He turned around to address the crowd.

But before he could speak again, Jimmy Lee started to sing.

Jimmy had a pure tenor voice, and the notes of a familiar hymn soared out across the glen:

> *Behold, a man in anguish bending*
> *Marked by pain and loss*
> *Yonder stony hill ascending*
> *Carrying a cross*

Robert flushed red and shouted: "Be quiet!"

Jimmy ignored him and began the second verse. The others joined in, some singing the harmonies, and a hundred voices swelled the melody.

> *He is now transfixed with sorrow*
> *In the eyes of men*
> *When we see the bright tomorrow*
> *He will rise again*

Robert turned away, helpless. He stamped across the mud to his horse, leaving Lizzie standing alone, a small figure of defiance. He mounted and rode off down the hill, looking furious, with the thrilling voices of the miners shaking the mountain air like a thunderstorm:

> *Look no more with eyes of pity*
> *See our victory*
> *When we build that heavenly city*
> *All men shall be free!*

11

JAY WOKE UP KNOWING HE WAS GOING TO PROPOSE MARRIAGE TO Lizzie.

It was only yesterday that his mother had put it into his mind, but the idea had taken root fast. It seemed natural, even inevitable. Now he was worried about whether she would have him.

She liked him well enough, he thought—most girls did. But she needed money and he had none. Mother said those problems could be solved but Lizzie might prefer the certainty of Robert's prospects. The idea of her marrying Robert was loathsome.

To his disappointment he found she had gone out early. He was tense, too tense to wait around the house for her to return. He went out to the stables and looked at the white stallion his father had given him for his birthday. The horse's name was Blizzard. Jay had vowed never to ride him, but he could not resist the temptation. He took Blizzard up to High Glen and galloped him along the springy turf beside the stream. It was worth breaking his vow. He felt as if he were on the back of an eagle, soaring through the air, borne up by the wind.

Blizzard was at his best when galloping. Walking or trotting he was skittish, unsure of his footing, discontented and bad tempered. But it was easy to forgive a horse for being a poor trotter when he could run like a bullet.

As Jay rode home he indulged himself in thoughts of Lizzie. She had always been exceptional, even as a girl: pretty and rebellious and beguiling. Now she was unique. She could shoot better than anyone Jay knew, she had beaten him in a horse race, she was not afraid to go down a coal mine, she could disguise herself and fool everyone at a dinner table—he had never met a woman like her.

She was difficult to deal with, of course: willful, opinionated and self-centered. She was more ready than most women to challenge what men said. But Jay and everyone else forgave her because she was so charming, tilting her pert little face this way and that, smiling and frowning even as she contradicted every word you said.

He reached the stable yard at the same time as his brother. Robert was in a bad mood. When angry he became even more like Father, red faced and pompous. Jay said: "What the devil is the matter with you?" but Robert threw his reins to a groom and stomped indoors.

While Jay was stabling Blizzard, Lizzie rode up. She, too, was upset, but the flush of anger on her cheeks and the glint in her eyes made her even prettier. Jay stared at her, enraptured. I want this girl, he thought; I want her for myself. He was ready to propose right then and there. But before he could speak she jumped off her horse and said: "I know that people who misbehave must be punished, but I don't believe in torture, do you?"

He saw nothing wrong in torturing criminals but he was not going to tell her that, not when she was in this mood. "Of course I don't," he said. "Have you come from the pithead?"

"It was awful. I told Robert to let the man go but he refused."

So she had quarreled with Robert. Jay concealed his delight. "You haven't seen a man go the round before? It's not so rare."

"No, I haven't. I don't know how I've remained so wretchedly ignorant about the lives of miners. I suppose people protected me from the grim truth because I was a girl."

"Robert seemed angry about something," Jay probed.

"All the miners sang a hymn and they wouldn't shut up when he ordered them to."

Jay was pleased. It sounded as if she had seen Robert at his worst. My chances of success are improving by the minute, he thought exultantly.

A groom took her horse and they walked across the yard into the castle. Robert was talking to Sir George in the hall. "It was a piece of brazen defiance," Robert was saying. "Whatever happens, we must make sure McAsh doesn't get away with this."

Lizzie made an exasperated noise and Jay saw a chance to score points with her. "I think we should consider letting McAsh go," he said to his father.

Robert said: "Don't be ridiculous."

Jay recalled Harry Ratchett's argument. "The man is a trouble-maker—we'd be better off without him."

"He has defied us openly," Robert protested. "He can't be allowed to get away with it."

"He hasn't got away with it!" Lizzie declared. "He's suffered the most savage punishment!"

Sir George said: "It's not savage, Elizabeth—you have to understand that they don't feel pain as we do." Before she could expostulate he turned to Robert. "But it's true that he hasn't got away with it. The miners now know they can't leave at the age of twenty-one: we've proved our point. I wonder if we shouldn't discreetly let him vanish."

Robert was not satisfied. "Jimmy Lee is a troublemaker but we brought him back."

"Different case," Father argued. "Lee is all heart and no brains—he'll never be a leader, we have nothing to fear from him. McAsh is made of finer material."

"I'm not afraid of McAsh," Robert said.

"He could be dangerous," Father said. "He can read and write. He's the fireman, which means they look up to him. And to judge by the scene you've just described to me, he's halfway to becoming a hero already. If we make him stay here, he'll cause trouble all his godforsaken life."

Reluctantly Robert nodded. "I still think it looks bad," he said.

"Then make it look better," Father said. "Leave the guard on the bridge. McAsh will go over the mountain, probably: we just won't chase him. I don't mind them thinking he's escaped—so long as they know he did not have the right to leave."

"Very well," said Robert.

Lizzie shot a triumphant look at Jay. Behind Robert's back she mouthed the words *Well done!*

"I must wash my hands before dinner," Robert said. He disappeared toward the back of the house, still looking grumpy.

Father went into his study. Lizzie threw her arms around Jay's neck. "You did it!" she said. "You set him free!" She gave him an exuberant kiss.

It was scandalously bold, and he was shocked, but he soon recovered. He put his arms around her waist and held her close. He leaned down and they kissed again. This was a different kiss, slow and sensual and exploring. Jay closed his eyes to concentrate on the sensations. He forgot they were in the most public room of his father's castle, where family and guests, neighbors and servants passed through constantly. By luck no one came in, and the kiss was not disturbed. When they broke apart, gasping for breath, they were still alone.

With a thrill of anxiety Jay realized that this was the moment to ask her to marry him.

"Lizzie . . ." Somehow he did not know just how to bring the subject up.

"What?"

"What I want to say . . . you can't marry Robert, now."

"I can do anything I like," she responded immediately.

Of course, that was the wrong tack to take with Lizzie. Never tell her what she could and couldn't do. "I didn't mean—"

"Robert might turn out to be even better at kissing than you," she said, and she grinned impishly.

Jay laughed.

Lizzie leaned her head on his chest. "Of course I can't marry him, not now."

"Because . . ."

She looked at him. "Because I'm going to marry you—am I not?"

He could hardly believe she had said that. "Well . . . yes!"

"Isn't that what you were about to ask me?"

"As a matter of fact—yes, it is."

"There you are, then. Now you can kiss me again."

Feeling a little dazed, he bent his head to hers. As soon as their lips met she opened her mouth, and he was shocked and delighted to feel the tip of her tongue hesitantly teasing its way through. It made him wonder how many other boys she had kissed, but this was not the time to ask. He responded the same way. He felt himself stiffen inside his breeches, and he was embarrassed in case she would notice. She leaned against him, and he was sure she must have felt it. She froze for a moment, as if unsure what to do, then she shocked him again by pressing up against him, as if eager to feel it. He had met knowing girls, in the taverns and coffeehouses of London, who would kiss and rub up against a man this way at the drop of a hat; but it felt different with Lizzie, as if she were doing it for the first time.

Jay did not hear the door open. Suddenly Robert was shouting in his ear: "What the devil is this?"

The lovers broke apart. "Calm down, Robert," said Jay.

Robert was furious. "Damn it, what do you think you're doing?" he spluttered.

"It's all right, brother," said Jay. "You see, we're engaged to be married."

"You swine!" Robert roared, and he lashed out with his fist.

It was a wild blow and Jay dodged it easily, but Robert came at him with fists flailing. Jay had not fought with his brother since they were boys, but he remembered Robert being strong, though slow moving. After ducking a rain of blows he rushed at Robert and grappled with him. To his astonishment Lizzie jumped on Robert's back, pummeling his head and screaming: "Leave him alone! Leave him alone!"

The sight made Jay laugh, and he could not go on fighting. He let Robert go. Robert swung at him with a punch that hit him right beside the eye. Jay stumbled back and fell on the floor. With his unhurt eye he saw Robert struggling to throw Lizzie off his back. Despite the pain in his face, Jay burst out laughing again.

Then Lizzie's mother came into the room, followed rapidly by Alicia and Sir George. After a shocked moment Lady Hallim said: "Elizabeth Hallim, get off that man at once!"

Jay got to his feet and Lizzie disentangled herself from Robert. The three parents were too bemused to speak. With one hand over his hurt eye, Jay bowed to Lizzie's mother and said: "Lady Hallim, I have the honor to ask for your daughter's hand in marriage."

✳

"You bloody fool, you'll have nothing to live on," Sir George said a few minutes later.

The families had separated to discuss the shocking news privately. Lady Hallim and Lizzie had gone upstairs. Sir George, Jay and Alicia were in the study. Robert had stomped off somewhere alone.

Jay bit back a hurt retort. Remembering what his mother had suggested, he said: "I'm sure I can manage High Glen better than Lady Hallim. There's a thousand acres or more—it should produce an income large enough for us to live on."

"Stupid boy, you won't have High Glen—it's mortgaged."

Jay was humiliated by his father's scornful dismissal, and he felt his cheeks flush red. His mother cut in: "Jay can raise new mortgages."

Father looked taken aback. "Are you on the boy's side in this, then?"

"You refused to give him anything. You want him to fight for everything, as you did. Well, he's fighting, and the first thing he's got is Lizzie Hallim. You can hardly complain."

"Has he got her—or have you done it for him?" Sir George said shrewdly.

"I didn't take her down the coal mine," Alicia said.

"Nor kiss her in the hall." Sir George's tone became resigned. "Oh, well. He's over twenty-one, so I don't suppose we can stop them." A crafty look came over his face. "At any rate the coal in High Glen will come into our family."

"Oh, no it won't," said Alicia.

Jay and Sir George both stared at her. Sir George said: "What the devil do you mean?"

"You're not going to dig pits on Jay's land—why should you?"

"Don't be a damn fool, Alicia—there's a fortune in coal under High Glen. It would be a sin to leave it there."

"Jay may lease the mining rights to someone else. There are several joint stock companies keen to open new pits—I've heard you say so."

"You wouldn't do business with my rivals!" Sir George exclaimed.

Mother was so strong, Jay was filled with admiration. But she seemed to have forgotten Lizzie's objections to coal mining. He said: "But Mother, remember that Lizzie—"

His mother threw him a warning look and cut him off, saying to Father: "Jay may prefer to do business with your rivals. After the way you insulted him on his twenty-first birthday, what does he owe you?"

"I'm his father, damn it!"

"Then start acting like his father. Congratulate him on his engagement. Welcome his fiancée like a daughter. Plan a lavish wedding celebration."

He stared at her for a moment. "Is that what you want?"

"It's not all."

"I might have guessed. What else?"

"His wedding present."

"What are you after, Alicia?"

"Barbados."

Jay almost jumped out of his chair. He had not expected this. How crafty Mother was!

"Out of the question!" his father roared.

Mother stood up. "Think about it," she said, almost as if she didn't care one way or the other. "Sugar is a problem, you've always said. Profits are high but there are always difficulties: the rains fail, slaves get sick and die, the French undercut your prices, ships are lost at sea. Whereas coal is easy. You dig it out of the ground and sell it. It's like finding money in the backyard, you told me once."

Jay was thrilled. He might get what he wanted, after all. But what about Lizzie?

His father said: "Barbados is promised to Robert."

"Let him down," Mother said. "You've let Jay down, God knows."

"The sugar plantation is Robert's patrimony."

Mother went to the door, and Jay followed her. "We've been through this before, George, and I know all your answers," she said. "But now the situation is different. If you want Jay's coal, you have to give him something for it. And what he wants is the plantation. If you don't give it to him, you won't have the coal. It's a simple choice, and you have plenty of time to think about it." She went out.

Jay went with her. In the hall he whispered: "You were marvelous! But Lizzie won't allow mining in High Glen."

"I know, I know," Mother said impatiently. "That's what she says now. She may change her mind."

"And if she doesn't?" Jay said worriedly.

"We'll cross that bridge when we come to it," Mother said.

12

LIZZIE CAME DOWN THE STAIRS WEARING A FUR CLOAK SO BIG THAT IT went around her twice and brushed the floor. She had to get outside for a while.

The house was full of tension: Robert and Jay hated one another, Mother was cross with her, Sir George was furious with Jay, and there was hostility between Alicia and Sir George too. Dinner had been nail-bitingly strained.

As she was crossing the hall, Robert stepped out of the shadows. She halted and looked at him.

"You bitch," he said.

It was a gross insult to a lady, but Lizzie was not easily offended by mere words, and anyway he had reason to be angry. "You must be like a brother to me now," she said in a conciliatory voice.

He grasped her arm, squeezing hard. "How could you prefer that smarmy little bastard to me?"

"I fell in love with him," she said. "Let go of my arm."

He squeezed harder, his face dark with fury. "I'll tell you something," he said. "Even if I can't have you, I'll still have High Glen."

"You won't," she said. "When I marry, High Glen will become my husband's property."

"You just wait and see."

He was hurting her. "Let go of my arm or I'll scream," she said in a dangerous voice.

He let go. "You're going to regret this for the rest of your life," he said, and he walked off.

Lizzie stepped out the castle door and pulled her furs more tightly around her. The clouds had partly cleared, and there was a moon: she could see well enough to pick her way across the drive and down the sloping lawn toward the river.

She felt no remorse about letting Robert down. He had never loved her. If he had, he would be sad, but he was not. Instead of being distraught about losing her, he was furious that his brother had got the better of him.

All the same, the encounter with Robert had shaken her. He had his father's ruthless determination. Of course he could not take High Glen from her. But what might he do instead?

She put him out of her mind. She had got what she wanted: Jay instead of Robert. Now she was eager to plan the wedding and set up house. She could hardly wait to live with him, and sleep in the same bed, and wake up every morning with his head on the pillow beside her.

She was thrilled and scared. She had known Jay all her life, but since he had become a man she had only spent a few days with him. She was leaping into the dark. But then, she thought, marriage must always be a leap into the dark: you could never really know another person until after you had lived together.

Mother was upset. Her dream was for Lizzie to marry a rich man and end the years of poverty. But she had to accept that Lizzie had her own dreams.

Lizzie was not worried about money. Sir George would probably give Jay something in the end, but if he did not they could live at High Glen House. Some Scottish landowners were clearing their deer forests and leasing the land to sheep farmers: Jay and Lizzie might try that, at first, to bring in more money.

Whatever happened it would be fun. What she liked best about Jay was his sense of adventure. He was willing to gallop through the woods and show her the coal mine and go to live in the colonies.

She wondered if that would ever happen. Jay still hoped he would get the Barbados property. The idea of going abroad excited Lizzie almost as much as the prospect of getting married. Life over there was said to be free and easy, lacking the stiff formalities that she found so irritating in British society. She imagined throwing away her petticoats and hooped skirts, cutting her hair short, and spending all day on horseback with a musket over her arm.

Did Jay have any faults? Mother said he was vain and self-absorbed, but Lizzie had never met a man who wasn't. At first she had thought he was weak for not standing up more to his brother and his father; but now she thought she must have been wrong about that, for in proposing to her he had defied them both.

She reached the bank of the river. This was no mountain stream, trickling down the glen. Thirty yards wide, it was a deep, fast-moving torrent. The moonlight gleamed off the troubled surface in patches of silver, like a smashed mosaic.

The air was so cold it hurt to breathe, but the fur kept her body warm. Lizzie leaned against the broad trunk of an old pine tree and stared at the restless water. As she looked over the river she saw movement on the far bank.

It was not opposite her, but some way upstream. At first she thought it must be a deer: they often moved at night. It did not look like a man, for its head was too large. Then she saw that it was a man with a bundle tied to his head. A moment later she understood. He stepped to the riverbank, ice cracking beneath his feet, and slipped into the water.

The bundle must be his clothes. But who would swim the river at this time of night in the middle of winter? She guessed it might be McAsh, sneaking past the guard on the bridge. Lizzie shivered inside her fur cloak when she thought how bitterly cold the water must be. It was hard to imagine how a man could swim in it and live.

She knew she ought to leave. Only trouble could result from her staying here and watching a naked man swim the river. Nevertheless her curiosity was too much for her, and she stood motionless, seeing his head move slantwise across the torrent at a steady speed. The strong current forced him into a diagonal course, but his pace did not falter: he seemed strong. He would reach the near bank at a point twenty or thirty yards upstream from where Lizzie stood.

But when he was halfway across he suffered a stroke of bad luck. Lizzie saw a dark shape rushing toward him on the surface of the water, and made it out to be a fallen tree. He seemed not to see it until it was upon him. A heavy branch struck his head, and his arms became entangled in the foliage. Lizzie gasped as he went under. She stared at the branches, looking for the man: she still did not know if it was McAsh. The tree came closer to her but he did not reappear. "Please don't drown," she whispered. The tree passed her and still there was no sign of him. She thought of running for help, but she was a quarter of a mile or more from the castle: by the time she got back he would be far downstream, dead or alive. But perhaps she should try anyway, she thought. As she stood there in an agony of indecision he surfaced, a yard behind the floating tree.

Miraculously, his bundle was still tied to his head. He was no longer able to swim with that steady stroke, though: he splashed about, waving and kicking, gasping air in great ragged gulps, spluttering and coughing. Lizzie went down to the river's edge. Icy water seeped through her silk shoes and froze her feet. "Over here!" she called. "I'll pull you out!" He seemed not to hear but continued to thrash about as if, having almost drowned, he could think of nothing but his breath. Then he appeared to calm himself with an effort, and look about him to get his bearings. Lizzie called to him again. "Over here! Let me help you!" He coughed and gasped more and his head went under, but it came up again almost immediately and he struck out toward her, thrashing and spluttering but moving in the right direction.

She knelt in the icy mud, careless of her silk dress and her furs. Her heart was in her mouth. As he came closer she reached out to him. His hands flailed the air randomly. She grabbed a wrist and pulled it to her. Grasping his arm with both hands, she heaved. He hit the side and collapsed, half on the bank and half in the water. She changed her grip, holding him under the arms, then dug her dainty slippers into the mud and heaved again. He pushed with his hands and feet and, at last, flopped out of the water onto the bank.

Lizzie stared at him, lying there naked and sodden and half dead like a sea monster caught by a giant fisherman. As she had guessed, the man whose life she had saved was Malachi McAsh.

She shook her head wonderingly. What kind of man was he? In the last two days he had been blasted by a gas explosion and subjected to a shattering torture, yet he had the stamina and guts to swim the freezing river to escape. He just never gave up.

He lay on his back, gasping raggedly and shivering uncontrollably. The iron collar had gone: she wondered how he had got it off. His wet skin gleamed silver in the moonlight. It was the first time she had looked at a naked man and, despite her concern for his life, she was fascinated to see his penis, a wrinkled tube nestling in a mass of dark curly hair at the fork of his muscular thighs.

If he lay there for long he might yet die of cold. She knelt beside him and untied the sodden bundle on his head. Then she put her hand on his shoulder. He felt as cold as the grave. "Stand up!" she said urgently. He did not move. She shook him, feeling the massive muscles under the skin. "Get up, or you'll die!" She grabbed him with both hands but without his volition she could not shift him at all: he felt made of rock. "Mack, please don't die," she said, and there was a sob in her voice.

Finally he moved. Slowly he got on all fours, then he reached up and took her hand. With a heave from her he struggled to his feet. "Thank God," she murmured. He leaned heavily on her but she just managed to support him without collapsing.

She had to warm him somehow. She opened her cloak and pressed her body up against his. Her breasts felt the terrible coldness of his flesh through the silk of her dress. He clung to her, his broad, hard body sucking the heat from hers. It was the second time they had embraced, and once again she felt a powerful sense of intimacy with him, almost as if they were lovers.

He could not get warm while he was wet. Somehow she had to dry him. She needed a rag, anything she could use as a towel. She was wearing several linen petticoats: she could spare him one. "Can you stand up alone now?" she said. He managed a nod between coughs. She let go of him and lifted her skirt. She felt his eyes on her, despite his condition, as she swiftly removed one petticoat. Then she began to rub him all over with it.

She wiped his face and rubbed his hair, then went behind him and dried his broad back and his hard, compact rear. She knelt to do his legs. She stood up again and turned him around to dry his chest, and she was shocked to see that his penis was sticking straight out.

She should have been disgusted and horrified, but she was not. She was fascinated and intrigued; she was foolishly proud that she was able to have that effect on a man; and she felt something else, an ache deep inside that made her swallow dryly. It was not the happy excitement she felt when she kissed Jay: this was nothing to do with teasing and petting. She was suddenly afraid McAsh would throw her to the ground and tear her clothes and ravish her, and the most frightening thing of all was that a tiny part of her wanted him to.

Her fears were groundless. "I'm sorry," he mumbled. He turned away, bent to his bundle and drew out a sodden pair of tweed breeches. He wrung most of the water out of them then pulled them on, and Lizzie's heartbeat began to return to normal.

As he started to wring out a shirt, Lizzie realized that if he put on wet clothes now he would probably die of pneumonia by daybreak. But he could not stay naked. "Let me get you some clothes from the castle," she said.

"No," he said. "They'll ask you what you're doing."

"I can sneak in and out—and I've got the men's clothes I wore down the mine."

He shook his head. "I'll not delay here. As soon as I start walking I'll get warmer." He started to squeeze water out of a plaid blanket.

On impulse she took off her fur cloak. Because it was so big it would fit Mack. It was costly, and she might never have another, but it would save his life. She refused to think about how she would explain its disappearance to her mother. "Wear this, then, and carry your plaid until you get a chance to dry it." Without waiting for his assent she put the fur over his shoulders. He hesitated, then drew it around him gratefully. It was big enough to cover him completely.

She picked up his bundle and took out his boots. He handed her the wet blanket and she stuffed it into the bag. As she did so she felt the iron collar. She took it out. The iron ring had been broken and the collar bent to get it off. "How did you do this?" she said.

He pulled on his boots. "Broke into the pithead smithy and used Taggart's tools."

He could not have done it alone, she thought. His sister must have helped him. "Why are you taking it with you?"

He stopped shivering and his eyes blazed with anger. "Never to forget," he said bitterly. "Never."

She put it back and felt a large book in the bottom of the bag. "What's this?" she said.

"*Robinson Crusoe.*"

"My favorite story!"

He took the bag from her. He was ready to go.

She remembered that Jay had persuaded Sir George to let McAsh go. "The keepers won't come after you," she said.

He looked hard at her. There was hope and skepticism in his expression. "How do you know?"

"Sir George decided you're such a troublemaker he'll be glad to be rid of you. He left the guard on the bridge, because he doesn't want the miners to know he's letting you go; but he expects you to sneak past them, and he's not going to try to get you back."

A look of relief came over his weary face. "So I needn't worry about the sheriff's men," he said. "Thank God."

Lizzie shivered without her cloak, but she felt warm inside. "Walk fast and don't pause to rest," she said. "If you stop before daybreak you'll die." She wondered where he would go, and what he would do with the rest of his life.

He nodded, then held out his hand. She shook it, but to her surprise he raised her hand to his white lips and kissed it. Then he walked away.

"Good luck," she said quietly.

∗

Mack's boots crunched the ice on the puddles in the road as he strode down the glen in the moonlight, but his body warmed quickly under Lizzie Hallim's fur cloak. Apart from his footsteps, the only sound was the rushing of the river that ran alongside the track. But his spirit was singing the song of freedom.

As he got farther from the castle he began to see the curious and even funny side of his encounter with Miss Hallim. There was she, in an embroidered dress and silk shoes and a hairdo that must have taken two maids half an hour to arrange, and he had come swimming across the river as naked as the day he was born. She must have had a shock!

Last Sunday at church she had acted like a typical arrogant Scottish aristocrat, purblind and self-satisfied. But she had had the guts to take up Mack's challenge and go down the pit. And tonight she had saved his life twice—once by pulling him out of the water, and again by giving him her cloak. She was a remarkable woman. She had pressed her body against his to warm him, then had knelt and dried him with her petticoat: was there another lady in Scotland who would have done that for a coal miner? He remembered her falling into his arms in the pit, and he recalled how her breast had felt, heavy and soft in his hand. He was sorry to think he might never see her again. He hoped she, too, would find a way to escape from this little place. Her sense of adventure deserved wider horizons.

A group of hinds, grazing beside the road under cover of darkness, scampered away when he approached, like a herd of ghosts; then he was all alone. He was very weary. "Going the round" had taken more out of him than he had imagined. It seemed a human body could not recover from that in a couple of days. Swimming the river should have been easy, but the encounter with the floating tree had exhausted him all over again. His head still hurt where the branch had hit him.

Happily he did not have far to go tonight. He would walk only to Craigie, a pit village six miles down the glen. There he would take refuge in the home of his mother's brother, Uncle Eb, and rest until tomorrow. He would sleep easily knowing the Jamissons were not intending to pursue him.

In the morning he would fill his belly with porridge and ham and set out for Edinburgh. Once there he would leave on the first ship that would hire him, no matter where it was going—any destination from Newcastle to Peking would serve his purpose.

He smiled at his own bravado. He had never ventured farther than the market town of Coats, twenty miles away—he had not even been to

Edinburgh—but he was telling himself he was willing to go to exotic destinations as if he knew what those places were like.

As he strode along the rutted mud track he began to feel solemn about his journey. He was leaving the only home he had ever known, the place where he had been born and his parents had died. He was leaving Esther, his friend and ally, although he hoped to rescue her from Heugh before too long. He was leaving Annie, the cousin who had taught him how to kiss and how to play her body like a musical instrument.

But he had always known this would happen. As long as he could remember he had dreamed of escape. He had envied the peddler, Davey Patch, and longed for that kind of freedom. Now he had it.

Now he had it. He was filled with elation as he thought of what he had done. He had got away.

He did not know what tomorrow would bring. There might be poverty and suffering and danger. But it would not be another day down the pit, another day of slavery, another day of being the property of Sir George Jamisson. Tomorrow he would be his own man.

He came to a bend in the road and looked back. He could still just see Castle Jamisson, its battlemented roofline lit by the moon. I'll never look at that again, he thought. It made him so happy that he began to dance a reel, there in the middle of the mud road, whistling the tune and jigging around in a circle.

Then he stopped, laughed softly at himself, and walked on down the glen.

II

London

13

SHYLOCK WORE WIDE TROUSERS, A LONG BLACK GOWN AND A RED three-cornered hat. The actor was bloodcurdlingly ugly, with a big nose, a long double chin, and a slitted mouth set in a permanent one-sided grimace. He came on stage with a slow, deliberate walk, the picture of evil. In a voluptuous growl he said: "Three thousand ducats." A shudder went through the audience.

Mack was spellbound. Even in the pit, where he stood with Dermot Riley, the crowd was still and silent. Shylock spoke every word in a husky voice between a grunt and a bark. His eyes stared brightly from under shaggy eyebrows. "Three thousand ducats for three months, and Antonio bound. . . ."

Dermot whispered in Mack's ear: "That's Charles Macklin—an Irishman. He killed a man and stood trial for murder, but he pleaded provocation and got off."

Mack hardly heard. He had known there were such things as theaters and plays, of course, but he had never imagined it would be like this: the heat, the smoky oil lamps, the fantastic costumes, the painted faces, and most of all the emotion—rage, passionate love, envy and hatred, portrayed so vividly that his heart beat as fast as if it were real.

When Shylock found out that his daughter had run away, he hurtled on stage with no hat, hair flying, hands clenched, in a perfect fury of grief, screaming "You knew!" like a man in the torment of hell. And when he said "Since I am a dog, beware my *fangs!*" he darted forward, as if to lunge across the footlights, and the entire audience flinched back.

Leaving the theater, Mack said to Dermot: "Is that what Jews are like?" He had never met a Jew, as far as he knew, but most people in the Bible were Jewish, and they were not portrayed that way.

"I've known Jews but never one like Shylock, thank God," Dermot replied. "Everyone hates a moneylender, though. They're all right when you need a loan, but it's the paying it back that causes the trouble."

London did not have many Jews but it was full of foreigners. There were dark-skinned Asian sailors called lascars; Huguenots from France; thousands of Africans with rich brown skin and tightly curled hair; and countless Irish like Dermot. For Mack this was part of the tingling excitement of the city. In Scotland everyone looked the same.

He loved London. He felt a thrill every morning when he woke up and remembered where he was. The city was full of sights and surprises, strange people and new experiences. He loved the enticing smell of coffee from the scores of coffeehouses, although he could not afford to drink it. He stared at the gorgeous colors of the clothes— bright yellow, purple, emerald green, scarlet, sky blue—worn by men and women. He heard the bellowing herds of terrified cattle being driven through the narrow streets to the city's slaughterhouses, and he dodged the swarms of nearly naked children, begging and stealing. He saw prostitutes and bishops, he went to bullfights and auctions, he tasted banana and ginger and red wine. Everything was exciting. Best of all, he was free to go where he would and do as he liked.

Of course he had to earn his living. It was not easy. London swarmed with starving families who had fled from country districts where there was no food, for there had been two years of bad harvests. There were also thousands of hand-loom silk weavers, put out of work by the new northern factories, so Dermot said. For every job there were five desperate applicants. The unlucky ones had to beg, steal, prostitute themselves or starve.

Dermot himself was a weaver. He had a wife and five children living in two rooms in Spitalfields. In order to get by they had to sublet Dermot's workroom, and Mack slept there, on the floor, beside the big silent loom that stood as a monument to the hazards of city life.

Mack and Dermot looked for work together. They sometimes got taken on as waiters in coffeehouses, but they lasted only a day or so: Mack was too big and clumsy to carry trays and pour drinks into little cups, and Dermot, being proud and touchy, always insulted a customer sooner or later. One day Mack was taken on as a footman in a big house in Clerkenwell, but he quit next morning after the master and mistress of the house asked him to get into bed with them. Today they had got portering work, carrying huge baskets of fish in the waterfront market at Billingsgate. At the end of the day Mack had been reluctant to waste his money on a theater ticket, but Dermot swore he would not regret it. Dermot had been right: it was worth twice the price to see such a marvel. All the same Mack worried about how long it could take him to save enough money to send for Esther.

Walking east from the theater, heading for Spitalfields, they passed through Covent Garden, where whores accosted them from doorways. Mack had been in London almost a month, and he was getting used to being offered sex at every corner. The women were of all kinds, young and old, ugly and beautiful, some dressed like fine ladies and others in rags. None of them tempted Mack, though there were many nights he thought wistfully of his lusty cousin Annie.

In the Strand was the Bear, a rambling whitewashed tavern with a coffee room and several bars around a courtyard. The heat of the theater had made them thirsty, and they went inside for a drink. The atmosphere was warm and smoky. They each bought a quart of ale.

Dermot said: "Let's take a look out the back."

The Bear was a sporting venue. Mack had been here before, and he knew that bearbaiting, dogfights, sword fights between women gladiators and all kinds of amusements were held in the backyard. When there was no organized entertainment the landlord would throw a cat into the duck pond and set four dogs on it, a game that generated uproarious laughter among the drinkers.

Tonight a prizefighting ring had been set up, lit by numerous oil lamps. A dwarf in a silk suit and buckled shoes was haranguing a crowd of drinkers. "A pound for anyone who can knock down the Bermondsey Bruiser! Come on, my lads, is there a brave one among you?" He turned three somersaults.

Dermot said to Mack: "You could knock him down, I'd say."

The Bermondsey Bruiser was a scarred man wearing nothing but breeches and heavy boots. He was shaved bald, and his face and head bore the marks of many fights. He was tall and heavy, but he looked stupid and slow. "I suppose I could," Mack said.

Dermot was enthusiastic. He grabbed the dwarf by the arm and said: "Hey, short-arse, here's a customer for you."

"A contender!" the dwarf bellowed, and the crowd cheered and clapped.

A pound was a lot of money, a week's wages for many people. Mack was tempted. "All right," he said.

The crowd cheered again.

"Watch out for his feet," said Dermot. "There'll be steel in the toes of his boots."

Mack nodded, taking off his coat.

Dermot added: "Be ready for him to jump you as soon as you get in the ring. There'll be no waiting for a signal to begin, mind you."

It was a common trick in fights between miners down the pit. The quickest way to win was to start before the other was ready. A man would say: "Come out and fight in the tunnel where there's more room," then hit his opponent as he stepped across the drainage ditch.

The ring was a rough circle of rope about waist height, supported by old wooden staves hammered into the mud. Mack approached, mindful of Dermot's warning. As he lifted his foot to step over the rope, the Bermondsey Bruiser rushed him.

Mack was ready for it, and he stepped back out of reach, catching a glancing blow to his forehead from the Bruiser's massive fist. The crowd gasped.

Mack acted without thinking, like a machine. He stepped quickly to the ring and kicked the Bruiser's shin under the rope, causing him to stumble. A cheer went up from the spectators, and Mack heard Dermot's voice yelling: "Kill him, Mack!"

Before the man could regain his balance, Mack hit him on each side of the head, left and right, then once more on the point of the chin with an uppercut that had all the force of his shoulders behind it. The Bruiser's legs wobbled and his eyes rolled up, then he staggered back two steps and fell flat on his back.

The crowd roared their enthusiasm.

The fight was over.

Mack looked at the man on the floor and saw a ruined hulk, damaged and good for nothing. He wished he had not taken him on. Feeling deflated, he turned away.

Dermot had the dwarf in an armlock. "The little devil tried to run away," he explained. "He wanted to cheat you of your prize. Pay up, long-legs. One pound."

With his free hand the dwarf took a gold sovereign from a pocket inside his shirt. Scowling, he handed it to Mack.

Mack took it, feeling like a thief.

Dermot released the dwarf.

A rough-faced man in expensive clothes appeared at Mack's side. "That was well done," he said. "Have you fought much?"

"Now and again, down the pit."

"I thought you might be a miner. Now listen, I'm putting on a prizefight at the Pelican in Shadwell next Saturday. If you want the chance of earning twenty pounds in a few minutes, I'll put you up against Rees Preece, the Welsh Mountain."

Dermot said: "Twenty pounds!"

"You won't knock him down as quickly as you did this lump of wood, but you'll have a chance."

Mack looked at the Bruiser, lying in a useless heap. "No," he said.

Dermot said: "Why the devil not?"

The promoter shrugged. "If you don't need the money . . ."

Mack thought of his twin, Esther, still carrying coal up the ladders of Heugh pit fifteen hours a day, waiting for the letter that would release her from a lifetime of slavery. Twenty pounds would pay her passage to London—and he could have the money in his hand on Saturday night.

"On second thought, yes," Mack said.

Dermot clapped him on the back. "That's me boy," he said.

14

L IZZIE HALLIM AND HER MOTHER RATTLED NORTHWARD THROUGH THE
city of London in a hackney carriage. Lizzie was excited and
happy: they were going to meet Jay and look at a house.

"Sir George has certainly changed his attitude," said Lady
Hallim. "Bringing us to London, planning a lavish wedding, and now
offering to pay the rent on a London house for the two of you to live
in."

"I think Lady Jamisson has talked him around," Lizzie said. "But
only in small matters. He still won't give Jay the Barbados property."

"Alicia is a clever woman," Lady Hallim mused. "All the same, I'm
surprised she can still persuade her husband, after that terrible row on
Jay's birthday."

"Perhaps Sir George is the type who forgets a quarrel."

"He never used to be—unless there was something in it for him. I
wonder what his motive might be. There isn't anything he wants from
you, is there?"

Lizzie laughed. "What could I give him? Perhaps he just wants me to
make his son happy."

"Which I'm sure you will. Here we are."

The carriage stopped in Chapel Street, a quietly elegant row of
houses in Holborn—not as fashionable as Mayfair or Westminster, but
less expensive. Lizzie got down from the carriage and looked at
number twelve. She liked it right away. There were four stories and a

basement, and the windows were tall and graceful. However, two of the windows were broken and the number *45* was crudely daubed on the gleaming black-painted front door. Lizzie was about to comment when another carriage drew up and Jay jumped out.

He was wearing a bright blue suit with gold buttons, and a blue bow in his fair hair: he looked good enough to eat. He kissed Lizzie's lips. It was a rather restrained kiss, as they were in a public street, but she relished it and hoped for more later. Jay handed his mother down from the carriage then knocked on the door of the house. "The owner is a brandy importer who has gone to France for a year," he said as they waited.

An elderly caretaker opened the door. "Who broke the windows?" Jay said immediately.

"The hatters, it was," the man said as they stepped inside. Lizzie had read in the newspaper that the people who made hats were on strike, as were the tailors and grinders.

Jay said: "I don't know what the damn fools think they'll achieve by smashing respectable people's windows."

Lizzie said: "Why are they on strike?"

The caretaker replied: "They want better wages, miss, and who can blame them, with the price of a fourpenny loaf gone up to eightpence farthing? How is a man to feed his family?"

"Not by painting '45' on every door in London," Jay said gruffly. "Show us the house, man."

Lizzie wondered about the significance of the number *45,* but she was more interested in the house. She went through the building excitedly throwing back curtains and opening windows. The furniture was new and expensive, and the drawing room was a wide, light room with three big windows at each end. The place had the musty smell of an uninhabited building, but it needed only a thorough cleaning, a lick of paint and a supply of linen to make it delightfully habitable.

She and Jay ran ahead of the two mothers and the old caretaker, and when they reached the attic floor they were alone. They stepped into one of several small bedrooms designed for servants. Lizzie put her arms around Jay and kissed him hungrily. They had only a minute or so.

She took his hands and placed them on her breasts. He stroked them gently. "Squeeze harder," she whispered between kisses. She wanted the pressure of his hands to linger after their embrace. Her nipples stiffened and his fingertips found them through the fabric of her dress. "Pinch them," she said, and as he did so the pang of mingled pain and pleasure made her gasp. Then she heard footsteps on the landing and they broke apart, panting.

Lizzie turned and looked out of a little dormer window, catching her breath. There was a long back garden. The caretaker was showing the two mothers all the little bedrooms. "What's the significance of the number forty-five?" she asked.

"It's all to do with that traitor John Wilkes," Jay replied. "He used to edit a journal called the *North Briton,* and the government charged him with seditious libel over issue number forty-five, in which he as good as called the king a liar. He ran away to Paris, but now he's come back to stir up more trouble among ignorant common people."

"Is it true they can't afford bread?"

"There's a shortage of grain all over Europe, so it's inevitable that the price of bread should go up. And the unemployment is caused by the American boycott of British goods."

She turned back to Jay. "I don't suppose that's much consolation to the hatters and tailors."

A frown crossed his face: he did not seem to like her sympathizing with the discontented. "I'm not sure you realize how dangerous all this talk of liberty is," he said.

"I'm not sure I do."

"For example, the rum distillers of Boston would like the freedom to buy their molasses anywhere. But the law says they must buy from British plantations, such as ours. Give them freedom and they'll buy cheaper, from the French—and then we won't be able to afford a house like this."

"I see." That did not make it right, she thought; but she decided not to say so.

"All sorts of riffraff might want freedom, from coal miners in Scotland to Negroes in Barbados. But God has set people like me in authority over common men."

That was true, of course. "But do you ever wonder why?" she said.

"What do you mean?"

"Why God should have set you in authority over coal miners and Negroes."

He shook his head irritably, and she realized she had overstepped the mark again. "I don't think women can understand these things," he said.

She took his arm. "I love this house, Jay," she said, trying to mollify him. She could still feel her nipples where he had pinched them. She lowered her voice. "I can't wait to move in here with you and sleep together every night."

He smiled. "Nor can I."

Lady Hallim and Lady Jamisson came into the room. Lizzie's mother's gaze dropped to Lizzie's bosom, and Lizzie realized her nipples were showing through her dress. Mother obviously guessed what had been going on. She frowned with disapproval. Lizzie did not care. She would be married soon.

Alicia said: "Well, Lizzie, do you like the house?"

"I adore it!"

"Then you shall have it."

Lizzie beamed and Jay squeezed her arm.

Lizzie's mother said: "Sir George is so kind, I don't know how to thank him."

"Thank my mother," Jay said. "She's the one who's made him behave decently."

Alicia gave him a reproving look, but Lizzie could tell she did not really mind. She and Jay were very fond of one another, it was obvious. Lizzie felt a pang of jealousy, and told herself it was silly: anyone would be fond of Jay.

They left the room. The caretaker was hovering outside. Jay said to him: "I'll see the owner's attorney tomorrow and have the lease drawn up."

"Very good, sir."

As they went down the stairs, Lizzie remembered something. "Oh, I must show you this!" she said to Jay. She had picked up a handbill in the street and saved it for him. She took it from her pocket and gave it to him to read. It read:

AT THE SIGN OF THE PELICAN
near SHAD-WELL
GENTLEMEN AND GAMESTERS TAKE NOTE
A GENERAL DAY OF SPORT
A MAD BULL TO BE LET LOOSE WITH FIREWORKS ALL OVER HIM,
AND DOGS AFTER HIM
A MATCH FOUGHT OUT BETWEEN TWO COCKS
OF WESTMINSTER,
AND TWO OF EAST CHEAP, FOR FIVE POUNDS
A GENERAL COMBAT WITH CUDGELS BETWEEN SEVEN WOMEN
AND
A FIST FIGHT—FOR TWENTY POUNDS!
REES PREECE, THE WELSH MOUNTAIN
VERSUS
MACK MCASH, THE KILLER COLLIER
SATURDAY NEXT
BEGINNING AT THREE A CLOCK

"What do you think?" she said impatiently. "It must be Malachi McAsh from Heugh, mustn't it?"

"So that's what's become of him," said Jay. "He's a prizefighter. He was better off working in my father's coal pit."

"I've never seen a prizefight," Lizzie said wistfully.

Jay laughed. "I should think not! It's no place for a lady."

"Nor is a coal mine, but you took me there."

"So I did, and you nearly got killed in an explosion."

"I thought you'd jump at the chance of taking me on another adventure."

Her mother overheard and said: "What's this? What adventure?"

"I want Jay to take me to a prizefight," Lizzie said.

"Don't be ridiculous," said her mother.

Lizzie was disappointed. Jay's daring seemed to have deserted him momentarily. However, she would not let that stand in her way. If he would not take her she would go alone.

*

Lizzie adjusted her wig and hat and looked in the mirror. A young man looked back at her. The secret lay in the light smear of chimney soot that darkened her cheeks, her throat, her chin and her upper lip, mimicking the look of a man who had shaved.

The body was easy. A heavy waistcoat flattened her bosom, the tail of her coat concealed the rounded curves of her womanly bottom, and knee boots covered her calves. The hat and wig of male pattern completed the illusion.

She opened her bedroom door. She and her mother were staying in a small house in the grounds of Sir George's mansion in Grosvenor Square. Mother was taking an afternoon nap. Lizzie listened for footsteps, in case any of Sir George's servants were about the house, but she heard nothing. She ran light-footed down the stairs and slipped out the door into the lane at the back of the property.

It was a cold, sunny day at the end of winter. When she reached the street she reminded herself to walk like a man, taking up a lot of space, swinging her arms and putting on a swagger, as if she owned the pavement and were ready to jostle anyone who disputed her claim.

She could not swagger all the way to Shadwell, which was across town on the east side of London. She waved down a sedan chair, remembering to hold her arm up in command instead of fluttering her hand beseechingly like a woman. As the chair men stopped and set down the conveyance she cleared her throat, spat in the gutter and said in a deep croak: "Take me to the Pelican tavern, and look sharp about it."

They carried her farther east than she had ever been in London, through streets of ever smaller and meaner houses, to a neighborhood of damp lanes and mud beaches, unsteady wharves and ramshackle boathouses, high-fenced timber yards and rickety warehouses with chained doors. They deposited her outside a big waterfront tavern with a crude painting of a pelican daubed on its wooden sign. The courtyard was full of noisy, excited people: workingmen in boots and neckerchiefs, waistcoated gentlemen, low-class women in shawls and clogs, and a few women with painted faces and exposed breasts who, Lizzie presumed, were prostitutes. There were no women of what her mother would have called "quality."

Lizzie paid her entrance fee and elbowed her way into the shouting, jeering crowd. There was a powerful smell of sweaty, unwashed people. She felt excited and wicked. The female gladiators were in the middle of their combat. Several women had already retired from the fray: one sitting on a bench holding her head, another trying to stanch a bleeding leg wound, a third flat on her back and unconscious despite the efforts of her friends to revive her. The remaining four milled about in a rope ring, attacking one another with roughly carved wooden clubs three feet long. They were all naked to the waist and barefoot, with ragged skirts. Their faces and bodies were bruised and scarred. The crowd of a hundred or more spectators cheered their favorites, and several men were taking bets on the outcome. The women swung the clubs with all their might, hitting one another bone-crunching blows. Every time one landed a well-aimed buffet the men roared their approval. Lizzie watched with horrid fascination. Soon another woman took a heavy blow to the head and fell unconscious. The sight of her half-naked body lying senseless on the muddy ground sickened Lizzie, and she turned away.

She went into the tavern, banged on the counter with a fist, and said to the barman: "A pint of strong ale, Jack." It was wonderful to address the world in such arrogant tones. If she did the same in women's clothing, every man she spoke to would feel entitled to reprove her, even tavern keepers and sedan chair men. But a pair of breeches was a license to command.

The bar smelled of tobacco ash and spilled beer. She sat in a corner and sipped her ale, wondering why she had come here. It was a place of violence and cruelty, and she was playing a dangerous game. What would these brutal people do if they realized she was an upper-class lady dressed as a man?

She was here partly because her curiosity was an irresistible passion. She had always been fascinated by whatever was forbidden, even as a child. The sentence "It's no place for a lady" was like a red rag to a bull. She could not help opening any door marked "No entry." Her curiosity was as urgent as her sexuality, and to repress it was as difficult as to stop kissing Jay.

But the main reason was McAsh. He had always been interesting. Even as a small boy he had been different: independent minded, disobedient, always questioning what he was told. In adulthood he was fulfilling his promise. He had defied the Jamissons, he had succeeded in escaping from Scotland—something few miners achieved—and he had made it all the way to London. Now he was a prizefighter. What would he do next?

Sir George had been clever to let him go, she thought. As Jay said, God intended some men to be masters of others, but McAsh would never accept that, and back in the village he would have made trouble for years. There was a magnetism about McAsh that made people follow his lead: the proud way he carried his powerful body, the confident tilt of his head, the intense look in his startling green eyes. She herself felt the attraction: it had drawn her here.

One of the painted women sat beside her and smiled intimately. Despite her rouge she looked old and tired. How flattering to her disguise it would be, Lizzie thought, if a whore propositioned her. But the woman was not so easily fooled. "I know what you are," she said.

Women had sharper eyes than men, Lizzie reflected. "Don't tell anyone," she said.

"You can play the man with me for a shilling," the woman said.

Lizzie did not know what she meant.

"I've done it before with your type," she went on. "Rich girls who like to play the man. I've got a fat candle at home that fits just right, do you know what I mean?"

Lizzie realized what she was getting at. "No, thank you," she said with a smile. "That's not what I'm here for." She reached into her pocket for a coin. "But here's a shilling for keeping my secret."

"God bless Your Ladyship," the prostitute said, and she went away.

You could learn a lot in disguise, Lizzie reflected. She would never have guessed that a prostitute would keep a special candle for women who liked to play the man. It was the kind of thing a lady might never find out unless she escaped from respectable society and went exploring the world outside her curtained windows.

A great cheer went up in the courtyard, and Lizzie guessed the cudgel fight had produced a victor—the last woman left standing, presumably. She went outside, carrying her beer like a man, her arm straight down at her side and her thumb hooked over the lip of the tankard.

The women gladiators were staggering away or being carried off, and the main event was about to begin. Lizzie saw McAsh right away. There was no doubt it was he: she could see the striking green eyes. He was no longer black with coal dust, and she saw to her surprise that his hair was quite fair. He stood close to the ring talking to another man. He glanced toward Lizzie several times, but he did not penetrate her disguise. He looked grimly determined.

His opponent, Rees Preece, deserved his nickname "the Welsh Mountain." He was the biggest man Lizzie had ever seen, at least a foot taller than Mack, heavy and red faced, with a crooked nose that had been broken more than once. There was a vicious look about the face, and Lizzie marveled at the courage, or foolhardiness, of anyone who would willingly go into a prizefighting ring with such an evil-looking animal. She felt frightened for McAsh. He could be maimed or even killed, she realized with a chill of dread. She did not want to see that. She was tempted to leave, but she could not drag herself away.

The fight was about to begin when Mack's friend got into an irate discussion with Preece's seconds. Voices were raised and Lizzie gathered it had to do with Preece's boots. Mack's second was insisting, in an Irish accent, that they fight barefoot. The crowd began a slow hand clap to express their impatience. Lizzie hoped the fight would be called off. But she was disappointed. After much vehement discussion, Preece took off his boots.

Then, suddenly, the fight was on. Lizzie saw no signal. The two men were at one another like cats, punching and kicking and butting in a frenzy, moving so fast she could hardly see who was doing what. The crowd roared and Lizzie realized she was screaming. She covered her mouth with her hand.

The initial flurry lasted only a few seconds: it was too energetic to be kept up. The men separated and began to circle one another, fists raised in front of their faces, protecting their bodies with their arms. Mack's lip was swelling and Preece's nose was bleeding. Lizzie bit her finger fearfully.

Preece rushed Mack again, but this time Mack jumped back, dodging, then suddenly stepped in and hit Preece once, very hard, on the side of the head. Lizzie winced to hear the thud of the blow: it sounded like a sledgehammer hitting a rock. The spectators cheered wildly. Preece seemed to hesitate, as if startled by the blow, and Lizzie guessed he was surprised by Mack's strength. She began to feel hopeful: perhaps Mack could defeat this huge man after all.

Mack danced back out of reach. Preece shook himself like a dog, then lowered his head and charged, punching wildly. Mack ducked and sidestepped and kicked Preece's legs with a hard bare foot, but somehow Preece managed to crowd him and land several mighty punches. Then Mack hit him hard on the side of the head again, and once more Preece was stopped in his tracks.

The same dance was repeated, and Lizzie heard the Irishman yell: "In for the kill, Mack, don't give him time to get over it!" She realized that after hitting a stopping punch Mack always backed off and let the other man recover. Preece, by contrast, always followed one punch with another and another until Mack fought him off.

After ten awful minutes someone rang a bell and the fighters took a rest. Lizzie felt as grateful as if she had been in the ring herself. The two boxers were given beer as they sat on crude stools on opposite sides of the ring. One of the seconds took an ordinary household needle and thread and began to stitch a rip in Preece's ear. Lizzie winced and looked away.

She tried to forget the damage being done to Mack's splendid body and think of the fight as a mere contest. Mack was more nimble and had the more powerful punch, but he did not possess the mindless savagery, the killer instinct that made one man want to destroy another. He needed to get angry.

When they began again both were moving more slowly, but the combat followed the same pattern: Preece chased the dancing Mack, crowded him, got in close, landed two or three solid blows, then was stopped by Mack's tremendous right-hand punch.

Soon Preece had one eye closed and was limping from Mack's repeated kicks, but Mack was bleeding from his mouth and from a cut over one eye. As the fight slowed down it became more brutal. Lacking the energy to dodge nimbly, the men seemed to accept the blows in mute suffering. How long could they stand there pounding one another into dead meat? Lizzie wondered why she cared so much about McAsh's body, and told herself that she would have felt the same about anyone.

There was another break. The Irishman knelt beside Mack's stool and spoke urgently to him, emphasizing his words with vigorous gestures of his fist. Lizzie guessed he was telling Mack to go in for the kill. Even she could see that in a crude trial of strength and stamina Preece would win, simply because he was bigger and more hardened to punishment. Could Mack not see that for himself?

It began again. As she watched them hammering at one another, Lizzie remembered Malachi McAsh as a six-year-old boy, playing on the lawn at High Glen House. She had been his opponent then, she remembered: she had pulled his hair and made him cry. The memory brought tears to her eyes. How sad that the little boy had come to this.

There was a flurry of activity in the ring. Mack hit Preece once, twice, and a third time, then kicked his thigh, making him stagger. Lizzie was seized by the hope that Preece would collapse and the fight would end. But then Mack backed off, waiting for his opponent to fall. The shouted advice of his seconds and the bloodthirsty cries of the crowd urged him to finish Preece off, but he took no notice.

To Lizzie's dismay Preece recovered yet again, rather suddenly, and hit Mack with a low punch in the pit of the belly. Mack involuntarily bent forward and gasped—and then, unexpectedly, Preece butted him, putting all the force of his broad back into it. Their heads met with a sickening crack. Everyone in the crowd drew breath.

Mack staggered, falling, and Preece kicked him in the side of the head. Mack's legs gave way and he fell to the ground. Preece kicked him in the head again as he lay prone. Mack did not move. Lizzie heard herself screaming: "Leave him alone!" Preece kicked Mack again and again, until the seconds from both sides jumped into the ring and pulled him away.

Preece looked dazed, as if he could not understand why the people who had been egging him on and screaming for blood now wanted him to stop; then he regained his senses and raised his hands in a gesture of victory, looking like a dog that has pleased its master.

Lizzie was afraid Mack might be dead. She pushed through the crowd and stepped into the ring. Mack's second knelt beside his prone body. Lizzie bent over Mack, her heart in her mouth. His eyes were closed, but she saw that he was breathing. "Thank God he's alive," she said.

The Irishman glanced briefly at her but did not speak. Lizzie prayed Mack was not permanently damaged. In the last half hour he had taken more heavy blows to the head than most people suffered in a lifetime. She was terrified that when he returned to consciousness he would be a drooling idiot.

He opened his eyes.

"How do you feel?" Lizzie said urgently.

He closed his eyes again without responding.

The Irishman stared at her and said: "Who are you, the boy soprano?" She realized she had forgotten to put on a man's voice.

"A friend," she replied. "Let's carry him inside—he shouldn't lie on the muddy ground."

After a moment's hesitation the man said: "All right." He grasped Mack under the arms. Two spectators took his legs and they lifted him.

Lizzie led the way into the tavern. In her most arrogant male voice she shouted: "Landlord—show me your best room, and quick about it!"

A woman came from behind the bar. "Who's paying?" she said guardedly.

Lizzie gave her a sovereign.

"This way," said the woman.

She led them up the stairs to a bedroom overlooking the courtyard. The room was clean and the four-poster bed was neatly made with a plain coarse blanket. The men laid Mack on the bed. Lizzie said to the woman: "Light the fire then bring us some French brandy. Do you know of a physician in the neighborhood who could dress this man's wounds?"

"I'll send for Dr. Samuels."

Lizzie sat on the edge of the bed. Mack's face was a mess, swollen and bloody. She undid his shirt and saw that his chest was covered with bruises and abrasions.

The helpers left. The Irishman said: "I'm Dermot Riley—Mack lodges in my house."

"My name is Elizabeth Hallim," she replied. "I've known him since we were children." She decided not to explain why she was dressed as a man: Riley could think what he liked.

"I don't think he's hurt bad," Riley said.

"We should bathe his wounds. Ask for some hot water in a bowl, will you?"

"All right." He went out, leaving her alone with the unconscious Mack.

Lizzie stared at Mack's still form. He was hardly breathing. Hesitantly, she put her hand on his chest. The skin was warm and the flesh beneath it was hard. She pressed down and felt the thump of his heartbeat, regular and strong.

She liked touching him. She put her other hand on her own bosom, feeling the difference between her soft breasts and his hard muscles. She touched his nipple, small and soft, and then her own, bigger and protruding.

He opened his eyes.

She snatched her hand away, feeling guilty. What in heaven's name am I doing? she thought.

He looked at her blankly. "Where am I? Who are you?"

"You were in a prizefight," she said. "You lost."

He stared at her for several seconds, then at last he grinned. "Lizzie Hallim, dressed as a man again," he said in a normal voice.

"Thank God you're all right!"

He gave her a peculiar look. "It's very . . . kind of you to care."

She felt embarrassed. "I can't think why I do," she said in a brittle tone. "You're only a coal miner who doesn't know his place." Then to her horror she felt tears running down her face. "It's very hard to watch a friend being beaten to a pulp," she said with a catch in her voice that she could not control.

He watched her cry. "Lizzie Hallim," he said wonderingly, "will I ever understand you?"

15

BRANDY EASED THE PAIN OF MACK'S WOUNDS THAT EVENING, BUT ON the following morning he woke up in agony. He hurt in every part of his body that he could identify, from his sore toes—injured by kicking Rees Preece so hard—to the top of his skull, where he had a headache that felt as if it would never go away. The face in the shard of mirror he used for shaving was all cuts and bruises, and too tender to be touched, let alone shaved.

All the same, his spirits were high. Lizzie Hallim never failed to stimulate him. Her irrepressible boldness made all things seem possible. Whatever would she do next? When he had recognized her, sitting on the edge of the bed, he had suffered a barely controllable urge to take her in his arms. He had resisted the temptation by reminding himself that such a move would be the end of their peculiar friendship. It was one thing for her to break the rules: she was a lady. She might play rough-and-tumble with a puppy dog, but if once it bit her she would put it out in the yard.

She had told him she was going to marry Jay Jamisson, and he had bitten his tongue instead of telling her she was a damn fool. It was none of his business and he did not want to offend her.

Dermot's wife, Bridget, made a breakfast of salt porridge and Mack ate it with the children. Bridget was a woman of about thirty who had once been beautiful but now just looked tired. When the food was all gone Mack and Dermot went out to look for work. "Bring home some money," Bridget called as they left.

It was not a lucky day. They toured the food markets of London, offering themselves as porters for the baskets of wet fish, barrels of wine, and bloody sides of beef the hungry city needed every day; but there were too many men and not enough work. At midday they gave up and walked to the West End to try the coffeehouses. By the end of the afternoon they were as weary as if they had worked all day, but they had nothing to show for it.

As they turned into the Strand a small figure shot out of an alley, like a bolting rabbit, and crashed into Dermot. It was a girl of about thirteen, ragged and thin and scared. Dermot made a noise like a punctured bladder. The child squealed in fright, stumbled, and regained her balance.

After her came a brawny young man in expensive but disheveled clothes. He came within an inch of grabbing her as she bounced off Dermot, but she ducked and dodged and ran on. Then she slipped and fell, and he was on her.

She screamed in terror. The man was mad with rage. He picked up the slight body and punched the side of her head, knocking her down again, then he kicked her puny chest with his booted foot.

Mack had become hardened to the violence on the streets of London. Men, women and children fought constantly, punching and scratching one another, their battles usually fueled by the cheap gin that was sold at every corner shop. But he had never seen a strong man beat a small child so mercilessly. It looked as if he might kill her. Mack was still in pain from his encounter with the Welsh Mountain, and the last thing he wanted was another fight, but he could not stand still and watch this. As the man was about to kick her again Mack grabbed him roughly and jerked him back.

He turned around. He was several inches taller than Mack. He put his hand in the center of Mack's chest and shoved him powerfully away. Mack staggered backward. The man turned again to the child. She was scrambling to her feet. He hit her a mighty slap to her face that sent her flying.

Mack saw red. He grabbed the man by the collar and the seat of the breeches and lifted him bodily off the ground. The man roared with surprise and anger, and began to writhe violently, but Mack held him and lifted him up over his head.

Dermot stared in surprise at the ease with which Mack held him up. "You're a strong boy, Mack, by gob," he said.

"Get your filthy hands off me!" the man shouted.

Mack set him on the ground but kept hold of one wrist. "Just leave the child alone."

Dermot helped the girl stand up and held her gently but firmly.

"She's a damned thief!" said the man aggressively; then he noticed Mack's ravaged face and decided not to make a fight of it.

"Is that all?" Mack said. "By the way you were kicking her I thought she'd murdered the king."

"What business of yours is it what she's done?" The man was calming down and catching his breath.

Mack let him go. "Whatever it was, I think you've punished her enough."

The man looked at him. "You're obviously just off the boat," he said. "You're a strong lad but, even so, you won't last long in London if you put your trust in the likes of her." With that he walked off.

The girl said: "Thanks, Jock—you saved my life."

People knew Mack was Scottish as soon as he spoke. He had not realized that he had an accent until he came to London. In Heugh everyone spoke the same: even the Jamissons had a softened version of the Scots dialect. Here it was like a badge.

Mack looked at the girl. She had dark hair roughly cropped and a pretty face already swelling with bruises from the beating. Her body was that of a child but there was a knowing, adult look in her eyes. She gazed warily at him, evidently wondering what he wanted from her. He said: "Are you all right?"

"I hurt," she said, holding her side. "I wish you'd killed that Christ-forsaken john."

"What did you do to him?"

"I tried to rob him while he was fucking Cora, but he cottoned to it."

Mack nodded. He had heard that prostitutes sometimes had accomplices who robbed their clients. "Would you like something to drink?"

"I'd kiss the pope's arse for a glass of gin."

Mack had never heard such talk from anyone, let alone a little girl. He did not know whether to be shocked or amused.

On the other side of the road was the Bear, the tavern where Mack had knocked down the Bermondsey Bruiser and won a pound from a dwarf. They crossed the street and went in. Mack bought three mugs of beer and they stood in a corner to drink them.

The girl tossed most of hers down in a few gulps and said: "You're a good man, Jock."

"My name is Mack," he said. "This is Dermot."

"I'm Peggy. They call me Quick Peg."

"On account of the way you drink, I suppose."

She grinned. "In this city, if you don't drink quick someone will steal your liquor. Where are you from, Jock?"

"A village called Heugh, about fifty miles from Edinburgh."

"Where's Edinburgh?"

"Scotland."

"How far away is that, then?"

"It took me a week on a ship, down the coast." It had been a long week. Mack was unnerved by the sea. After fifteen years working down a pit the endless ocean made him dizzy. But he had been obliged to climb the masts to tie ropes in all weathers. He would never be a sailor. "I believe the stagecoach takes thirteen days," he added.

"Why did you leave?"

"To be free. I ran away. In Scotland, coal miners are slaves."

"You mean like the blacks in Jamaicky?"

"You seem to know more about Jamaicky than Scotland."

She resented the implied criticism. "Why shouldn't I?"

"Scotland is nearer, that's all."

"I knew that." She was lying, Mack could tell. She was only a little girl, despite her bravado, and she touched his heart.

A woman's voice said breathlessly: "Peg, are you all right?"

Mack looked up to see a young woman wearing a dress the color of an orange.

Peg said: "Hello, Cora. I was rescued by a handsome prince. Meet Scotch Jock McKnock."

Cora smiled at Mack and said: "Thank you for helping Peg. I hope you didn't get those bruises in the process."

Mack shook his head. "That was another brute."

"Let me buy you a drink of gin."

Mack was about to refuse—he preferred beer—but Dermot said: "Very kind, we thank you."

Mack watched her as she went to the bar. She was about twenty years old, with an angelic face and a mass of flaming red hair. It was shocking to think someone so young and pretty was a whore. He said to Peg: "So she shagged that fellow who chased you, did she?"

"She doesn't usually have to go all the way with a man," Peg said knowledgeably. "She generally leaves him in some alley with his dick up and his breeches down."

"While you run off with his purse," Dermot said.

"Me? Get off. I'm a lady-in-waiting to Queen Charlotte."

Cora sat beside Mack. She wore a heavy, spicy perfume that had sandalwood and cinnamon in it. "What are you doing in London, Jock?"

He stared at her. She was very attractive. "Looking for work."

"Find any?"

"Not much."

She shook her head. "It's been a whore of a winter, cold as the grave, and the price of bread is shocking. There's too many men like you."

Peg put in: "That was what made my father turn to thieving, two years ago, only he didn't have the knack."

Mack reluctantly tore his gaze away from Cora and looked at Peg. "What happened to him?"

"He danced with the sheriff's collar on."

"What?"

Dermot explained. "It means he was hanged."

Mack said: "Oh, dear, I'm sorry."

"Don't feel sorry for me, you Scotch git, it makes me sick."

Peg was a real hard case. "All right, all right, I won't," Mack said mildly.

Cora said: "If you want work, I know someone who's looking for coal heavers, to unload the coal ships. The work is so heavy that only young men can do it, and they prefer out-of-towners who aren't so quick to complain."

"I'll do anything," Mack said, thinking of Esther.

"The coal heaving gangs are all run by tavern keepers down in Wapping. I know one of them, Sidney Lennox at the Sun."

"Is he a good man?"

Cora and Peg laughed. Cora said: "He's a lying, cheating, miserable-faced, evil-smelling festering drunken pig, but they're all the same, so what can you do?"

"Will you take us to the Sun?"

"Be it on your own head," said Cora.

*

A warm fog of sweat and coal dust filled the airless hold of the wooden ship. Mack stood on a mountain of coal, wielding a broad-bladed shovel, scooping up lumps of coal, working with a steady rhythm. The work was brutally hard; his arms ached and he was bathed in perspiration; but he felt good. He was young and strong, he was earning good money, and he was no one's slave.

He was one of a gang of sixteen coal heavers, bent over their shovels, grunting and swearing and making jokes. Most of the others were muscular young Irish farm boys: the work was too hard for stunted city-born men. Dermot was thirty and he was the oldest on the gang.

It seemed he could not escape from coal. But it made the world turn. As Mack worked he thought about where this coal was going: all the London drawing rooms it would heat, all the thousands of kitchen fires, all the bakery ovens and breweries it would fuel. The city had an appetite for coal that was never satisfied.

It was Saturday afternoon, and the gang had almost emptied this ship, the *Black Swan* from Newcastle. Mack enjoyed calculating how much he would be paid tonight. This was the second ship they had unloaded this week, and the gang got sixteen pence, a penny per man, for every score, or twenty sacks of coal. A strong man with a big shovel could move a sackful in two minutes. He reckoned each man had earned six pounds gross.

However, there were deductions. Sidney Lennox, the middleman or "undertaker," sent vast quantities of beer and gin on board for the men. They had to drink a lot to replace the gallons of fluid they lost by sweating, but Lennox gave them more than was necessary and most of the men drank it, gin too. Consequently there was generally at least one accident before the end of the day. And the liquor had to be paid for. So Mack was not sure how much he would receive when he lined up for his wages at the Sun tavern tonight. However, even if half of the money was lost in deductions—an estimate surely too high—the remainder would still be double what a coal miner would earn for a six-day week.

And at that rate he could send for Esther in a few weeks. Then he and his twin would be free of slavery. His heart leaped at the prospect.

He had written to Esther as soon as he had settled at Dermot's place, and she had replied. His escape was the talk of the glen, she said. Some of the young hewers were trying to get up a petition to the English Parliament protesting against slavery in the mines. And Annie had married Jimmy Lee. Mack felt a pang of regret about Annie. He would never again roll in the heather with her. But Jimmy Lee was a good man. Perhaps the petition would be the beginning of a change; perhaps the children of Jimmy and Annie would be free.

The last of the coal was shoveled into sacks and stacked on a barge, to be rowed to the shore and stored in a coal yard. Mack stretched his aching back and shouldered his shovel. Up on deck the cold air hit him like a blast, and he put on his shirt and the fur cloak Lizzie Hallim had given him. The coal heavers rode to shore with the last of the sacks, then walked to the Sun to get their wages.

The Sun was a rough place used by seamen and stevedores. Its earth floor was muddy, the benches and tables were battered and stained, and the smoky fire gave little heat. The landlord, Sidney Lennox, was a gambler, and there was always a game of some kind going on: cards, dice, or a complicated contest with a marked board and counters. The only good thing about the place was Black Mary, the African cook, who used shellfish and cheap cuts of meat to make spicy, hearty stews the customers loved.

Mack and Dermot were the first to arrive. They found Peg sitting in the bar with her legs crossed underneath her, smoking Virginia tobacco in a clay pipe. She lived at the Sun, sleeping on the floor in a corner of the bar. Lennox was a receiver as well as an undertaker, and Peg sold him the things she stole. When she saw Mack she spat into the fire and said cheerfully: "What ho, Jock—rescued any more maidens?"

"Not today." He grinned.

Black Mary put her smiling face around the kitchen door. "Oxtail soup, boys?" She had a Low Countries accent: people said she had once been the slave of a Dutch sea captain.

"No more than a couple of barrelfuls for me, please," Mack replied.

She smiled. "Hungry, eh? Been working hard?"

"Just taking a little exercise to give us an appetite," said Dermot.

Mack had no money to pay for his supper, but Lennox gave all the coal heavers credit against their earnings. After tonight, Mack resolved, he would pay cash on the nail for everything: he did not want to get into debt.

He sat beside Peg. "How's business?" he said facetiously.

She took his question seriously. "Me and Cora tumbled a rich old gent this afternoon so we're having the evening off."

Mack found it odd to be friends with a thief. He knew what drove her to it: she had no alternative but starvation. All the same something in him, some residue of his mother's attitudes, made him disapprove.

Peg was small and frail, with a bony frame and pretty blue eyes, but she had the callous air of a hardened criminal, and that was how people treated her. Mack suspected that her tough exterior was protective coloring: below the surface there was probably just a frightened little girl who had no one in the world to take care of her.

Black Mary brought him soup with oysters floating in it, a slab of bread and a tankard of dark beer, and he fell on it like a wolf.

The other coal heavers drifted in. There was no sign of Lennox, which was unusual: he was normally playing cards or dice with his customers. Mack wished he would hurry up. Mack was impatient to find out how much money he had made this week. He guessed Lennox was keeping the men waiting for their wages so that they would spend more at the bar.

Cora came in after an hour or so. She looked as striking as ever, in a mustard-colored outfit with black trimmings. All the men greeted her, but to Mack's surprise she came and sat with him. "I hear you had a profitable afternoon," he said.

"Easy money," she said. "A man old enough to know better."

"You'd better tell me how you do it, so I don't fall victim to someone like you."

She gave him a flirtatious look. "You'll never have to pay girls, Mack, I can promise you that."

"Tell me anyway—I'm curious."

"The simplest way is to pick up a wealthy drunk, get him amorous, take him down a dark alley then run off with his money."

"Is that what you did today?"

"No, this was better. We found an empty house and bribed the caretaker. I played the role of a bored housewife—Peg was my maid. We took him to the house, pretending I lived there. I got his clothes off and got him into bed, then Peg came rushing in to say my husband was back unexpectedly."

Peg laughed. "Poor old geezer, you should have seen his face, he was terrified. He hid in the wardrobe!"

"And we left, with his wallet, his watch and all his clothes."

"He's probably still in that wardrobe!" said Peg, and they both went off into gales of laughter.

The coal heavers' wives began to appear, many of them with babies in their arms and children clinging to their skirts. Some had the spirit and beauty of youth, but others looked weary and underfed, the beaten wives of violent and drunken men. Mack guessed they were all here in the hope of getting hold of some of the wages before all the money was drunk, gambled or stolen by whores. Bridget Riley came in with her five children and sat with Dermot and Mack.

Lennox finally showed up at midnight.

He carried a leather sack full of coins and a pair of pistols, presumably to protect him from robbery. The coal heavers, most of whom were drunk by this time, cheered him like a conquering hero when he came in, and Mack felt a momentary contempt toward his workmates: why did they show gratitude for what was no more than their due?

Lennox was a surly man of about thirty, wearing knee boots and a flannel waistcoat with no shirt. He was fit and muscular from carrying heavy kegs of beer and spirits. There was a cruel twist to his mouth. He had a distinctive odor, a sweet smell like rotting fruit. Mack noticed Peg flinch involuntarily as he went by: she was scared of the man.

Lennox pulled a table into a corner and put the sack down and the pistols next to it. The men and women crowded around, pushing and shoving, as if afraid Lennox would run out of cash before their turn came. Mack hung back: it was beneath his dignity to scramble for the wages he had earned.

He heard the harsh voice of Lennox raised over the hubbub. "Each man has earned a pound and eleven pence this week, before bar bills."

Mack was not sure he had heard right. They had unloaded two ships, some fifteen hundred score, or thirty thousand sacks of coal, giving each man a gross income of about six pounds. How could it have been reduced to little more than a pound each?

There was a groan of disappointment from the men, but none of them questioned the figure. As Lennox began to count out individual payments, Mack said: "Just a minute. How do you work that out?"

Lennox looked up with an angry scowl. "You've unloaded one thousand four hundred and forty-five score, which gives each man six pounds and five pence gross. Deduct fifteen shillings a day for drink—"

"What?" Mack interrupted. "Fifteen shillings a day?" That was three-quarters of their earnings!

Dermot Riley muttered his agreement. "Damned robbery, it is." He did not say it very loudly, but there were murmurs of agreement from some of the other men and women.

"My commission is sixteen pence per man per ship," Lennox went on. "There's another sixteen pence for the captain's tip, six pence per day for rent of a shovel—"

"Rent of a shovel?" Mack exploded.

"You're new here and you don't know the rules, McAsh," Lennox grated. "Why don't you shut your damned mouth and let me get on with it, or no one will get paid."

Mack was outraged, but reason told him Lennox had not invented this system tonight: it was obviously well established, and the men must have accepted it. Peg tugged at his sleeve and said in a low voice: "Don't cause trouble, Jock—Lennox will make it worse for you somehow."

Mack shrugged and kept quiet. However, his protest had struck a chord among the others, and Dermot Riley now raised his voice. "I didn't drink fifteen shillings' worth of liquor a day," he said.

His wife added: "For sure he didn't."

"Nor did I," said another man. "Who could? A man would burst with all that beer!"

Lennox replied angrily: "That's how much I sent on board for you— do you think I can keep a tally of what every man drinks every day?"

Mack said: "If not, you're the only innkeeper in London who can't!" The men laughed.

Lennox was infuriated by Mack's mockery and the laughter of the men. With a thunderous look he said: "The system is, you pay for fifteen shillings' worth of liquor, whether you drink it or not."

Mack stepped up to the table. "Well, I have a system too," he said. "I don't pay for liquor that I haven't asked for and haven't drunk. You may not have kept count but I have, and I can tell you exactly what I owe you."

"So can I," said another man. He was Charlie Smith, an English-born Negro with a flat Newcastle accent. "I've drunk eighty-three tankards of the small beer you sell in here for fourpence a pint. That's twenty-seven shillings and eightpence for the entire week, not fifteen shillings a day."

Lennox said: "You're lucky to be paid at all, you black villain, you ought to be a slave in chains."

Charlie's face darkened. "I'm an Englishman and a Christian, and I'm a better man than you because I'm honest," he said with controlled fury.

Dermot Riley said: "I can tell you exactly how much I've drunk, too."

Lennox was getting irate. "If you don't watch yourselves you'll get nothing at all, any of you," he said.

It crossed Mack's mind that he ought to cool things down. He tried to think of something conciliatory to say. Then he caught sight of Bridget Riley and her hungry children, and indignation got the better of him. He said to Lennox: "You'll not leave that table until you've paid what you owe."

Lennox's eyes fell to his pistols.

With a swift movement Mack swept the guns to the floor. "You'll not escape by shooting me either, you damn thief," he said angrily.

Lennox looked like a cornered mastiff. Mack wondered if he had gone too far: perhaps he should have left room for a face-saving compromise. But it was too late now. Lennox had to back down. He had made the coal heavers drunk and they would kill him unless he paid them.

He sat back on his chair, narrowed his eyes, gave Mack a look of pure hatred and said: "You'll suffer for this, McAsh, I swear by God you will."

Mack said mildly: "Come on, Lennox, the men are only asking you to pay them what they're due."

Lennox was not mollified, but he gave in. Scowling darkly, he began to count out money. He paid Charlie Smith first, then Dermot Riley, then Mack, taking their word for the amount of liquor they had consumed.

Mack stepped away from the table full of elation. He had three pounds and nine shillings in his hand: if he put half of it aside for Esther he would still be flush.

Other coal heavers made guesses at how much they had drunk, but Lennox did not argue, except in the case of Sam Potter, a huge fat boy from Cork, who claimed he had drunk only thirty quarts, causing uproarious laughter from the others: he eventually settled for three times that.

An air of jubilation spread among the men and their women as they pocketed their earnings. Several came up to Mack and slapped him on the back, and Bridget Riley kissed him. He realized he had done something remarkable, but he feared that the drama was not yet ended. Lennox had given in too easily.

As the last man was being paid, Mack picked up Lennox's guns from the floor. He blew the flintlocks clear of powder, so that they would not fire, then placed them on the table.

Lennox took his disarmed pistols and the nearly empty money bag and stood up. The room went quiet. He went to the door that led to his private rooms. Everyone watched him intently, as if they were afraid he might yet find a way to take the money back. He turned at the door. "Go home, all of you," he said malevolently. "And don't come back on Monday. There'll be no work for you. You're all dismissed."

✳

Mack lay awake most of the night, worrying. Some of the coal heavers said Lennox would have forgotten all about it by Monday morning, but Mack doubted that. Lennox did not seem the type of man to swallow defeat; and he could easily get another sixteen strong young men to form his gang.

It was Mack's fault. The coal heavers were like oxen, strong and stupid and easily led: they would not have rebelled against Lennox if Mack had not encouraged them. Now, he felt, it was up to him to set matters right.

He got up early on Sunday morning and went into the other room. Dermot and his wife lay on a mattress and the five children slept together in the opposite corner. Mack shook Dermot awake. "We've got to find work for our gang before tomorrow," Mack said.

Dermot got up. Bridget mumbled from the bed: "Wear something respectable, now, if you want to impress an undertaker." Dermot put on an old red waistcoat, and he loaned Mack the blue silk neckcloth he had bought for his wedding. They called for Charlie Smith on the way. Charlie had been a coal heaver for five years and he knew everyone. He put on his best blue coat and they went together to Wapping.

The muddy streets of the waterfront neighborhood were almost deserted. The bells of London's hundreds of churches called the devout to their prayers, but most of the sailors and stevedores and warehousemen were enjoying their day of rest, and they stayed at home. The brown river Thames lapped lazily at the deserted wharves, and rats sauntered boldly along the foreshore.

All the coal heaving undertakers were tavern keepers. The three men went first to the Frying Pan, a few yards from the Sun. They found the landlord boiling a ham in the yard. The smell made Mack's mouth water. "What ho, Harry," Charlie addressed him cheerfully.

He gave them a sour look. "What do you boys want, if it's not beer?"

"Work," Charlie replied. "Have you got a ship to uncoal tomorrow?"

"Yes, and a gang to do it, thanks all the same."

They left. Dermot said: "What was the matter with him? He looked at us like lepers."

"Too much gin last night," Charlie speculated.

Mack feared it might have been something more sinister, but he kept his thoughts to himself for the moment. "Let's go into the King's Head," he said.

Several coal heavers were drinking beer at the bar and greeted Charlie by name. "Are you busy, my lads?" Charlie said. "We're looking for a ship."

The landlord overheard. "You men been working for Sidney Lennox at the Sun?"

"Yes, but he doesn't need us next week," Charlie replied.

"Nor do I," said the landlord.

As they went out Charlie said: "We'll try Buck Delaney at the Swan. He runs two or three gangs at a time."

The Swan was a busy tavern with stables, a coffee room, a coal yard and several bars. They found the Irish landlord in his private room overlooking the courtyard. Delaney had been a coal heaver himself in his youth, though now he wore a wig and a lace cravat to take his breakfast of coffee and cold beef. "Let me give you a tip, me boys," he said. "Every undertaker in London has heard what happened at the Sun last night. There's not one will employ you, Sidney Lennox has made sure of that."

Mack's heart sank. He had been afraid of something like this.

"If I were you," Delaney went on, "I'd take ship and get out of town for a year or two. When you come back it will all be forgotten."

Dermot said angrily: "Are the coal heavers always to be robbed by you undertakers, then?"

If Delaney was offended he did not show it. "Look around you, me boy," he said mildly, indicating with a vague wave the silver coffee service, the carpeted room, and the bustling business that paid for it all. "I didn't get this by being fair to people."

Mack said: "What's to stop us going to the captains ourselves, and undertaking to unload ships?"

"Everything," said Delaney. "Now and again there comes along a coal heaver like you, McAsh, with a bit more gumption than the rest, and he wants to run his own gang, and cut out the undertaker and do away with liquor payments and all, and all. But there's too many people making too much money out of the present arrangement." He shook his head. "You're not the first to protest against the system, McAsh, and you won't be the last."

Mack was disgusted by Delaney's cynicism, but he felt the man was telling the truth. He could not think of anything else to say or do. Feeling defeated, he went to the door, and Dermot and Charlie followed.

"Take my advice, McAsh," Delaney said. "Be like me. Get yourself a little tavern and sell liquor to coal heavers. Stop trying to help them and start helping yourself. You could do well. You've got it in you, I can tell."

"Be like you?" Mack said. "You've made yourself rich by cheating your fellow men. By Christ, I wouldn't be like you for a kingdom."

As he went out he was gratified to see Delaney's face darken in anger at last.

But his satisfaction lasted no longer than it took to close the door. He had won an argument and lost everything else. If only he had swallowed his pride and accepted the undertakers' system, he would at least have work to do tomorrow morning. Now he had nothing— and he had put fifteen other men, and their families, in the same hopeless position. The prospect of bringing Esther to London was farther away than ever. He had handled everything wrong. He was a damn fool.

The three men sat in one of the bars and ordered beer and bread for their breakfast. Mack reflected that he had been arrogant to look down on the coal heavers for accepting their lot dumbly. In his mind he had called them oxen, but he was the ox.

He thought of Caspar Gordonson, the radical lawyer who had started all this by telling Mack his legal rights. If I could get hold of Gordonson, Mack thought, I'd let him know what legal rights are worth.

The law was useful only to those who had the power to enforce it, it seemed. Coal miners and coal heavers had no advocate at court. They were fools to talk of their rights. The smart people ignored right and wrong and took care of themselves, like Cora and Peg and Buck Delaney.

He picked up his tankard then froze with it halfway to his mouth. Caspar Gordonson lived in London, of course. Mack *could* get hold of him. He could let him know what legal rights were worth—but perhaps he could do better than that. Perhaps Gordonson would be the coal heavers' advocate. He was a lawyer, and he wrote constantly about English liberty: he ought to help.

It was worth a try.

✳

The fatal letter Mack received from Caspar Gordonson had come from an address in Fleet Street. The Fleet was a filthy stream running into the Thames at the foot of the hill upon which St. Paul's Cathedral stood. Gordonson lived in a three-story brick row house next to a large tavern.

"He must be a bachelor," said Dermot.

"How do you know?" Charlie Smith asked.

"Dirty windows, doorstep not polished—there's no lady in this house."

A manservant let them in, showing no surprise when they asked for Mr. Gordonson. As they entered, two well-dressed men were leaving, continuing as they went a heated discussion that involved William Pitt, the Lord Privy Seal, and Viscount Weymouth, a secretary of state. They did not pause in their argument but one nodded to Mack with absentminded politeness, which surprised him greatly, since gentlemen normally ignored low-class people.

Mack had imagined a lawyer's house to be a place of dusty documents and whispered secrets, in which the loudest noise was the slow scratching of pens. Gordonson's home was more like a printer's shop. Pamphlets and journals in string-tied bundles were stacked in the hall, the air smelled of cut paper and printing ink, and the sound of machinery from below stairs suggested that a press was being operated in the basement.

The servant stepped into a room off the hall. Mack wondered if he was wasting his time. People who wrote clever articles in journals probably did not dirty their hands by getting involved with workingmen. Gordonson's interest in liberty might be strictly theoretical. But Mack had to try everything. He had led his coal heaving gang into rebellion, and now they were all without work: he had to do something.

A loud and shrill voice came from within. "McAsh? Never heard of him! Who is he? You don't know? Then ask! Never mind—"

A moment later a balding man with no wig appeared in the doorway and peered at the three coal heavers through spectacles. "I don't think I know any of you," he said. "What do you want with me?"

It was a discouraging introduction, but Mack was not easily disheartened, and he said spiritedly: "You gave me some very bad advice recently but, despite that, I've come back for more."

There was a pause, and Mack thought he had given offense; then Gordonson laughed heartily. In a friendly voice he said: "Who are you, anyway?"

"Malachi McAsh, known as Mack. I was a coal miner at Heugh, near Edinburgh, until you wrote and told me I was a free man."

Understanding lit up Gordonson's expression. "You're the liberty-loving miner! Shake hands, man."

Mack introduced Dermot and Charlie.

"Come in, all of you. Have a glass of wine?"

They followed him into an untidy room furnished with a writing-table and walls of bookcases. More publications were piled on the floor, and printers' proofs were scattered across the table. A fat old dog lay on a stained rug in front of the fire. There was a ripe smell that must have come from the rug or the dog, or both. Mack lifted an open law book from a chair and sat down. "I won't take any wine, thank you," he said. He wanted his wits about him.

"A cup of coffee, perhaps? Wine sends you to sleep but coffee wakes you up." Without waiting for a reply he said to the servant: "Coffee for everyone." He turned back to Mack. "Now, McAsh, why was my advice to you so wrong?"

Mack told him the story of how he had left Heugh. Dermot and Charlie listened intently: they had never heard this. Gordonson lit a pipe and blew clouds of tobacco smoke, shaking his head in disgust from time to time. The coffee came as Mack was finishing.

"I know the Jamissons of old—they're greedy, heartless, brutal people," Gordonson said with feeling. "What did you do when you got to London?"

"I became a coal heaver." Mack related what had happened in the Sun tavern last night.

Gordonson said: "The liquor payments to coal heavers are a long-standing scandal."

Mack nodded. "I've been told I'm not the first to protest."

"Indeed not. Parliament actually passed a law against the practice ten years ago."

Mack was astonished. "Then how does it continue?"

"The law has never been enforced."

"Why not?"

"The government is afraid of disrupting the supply of coal. London runs on coal—nothing happens here without it: no bread is made, no beer brewed, no glass blown, no iron smelted, no horses shod, no nails manufactured—"

"I understand," Mack interrupted impatiently. "I ought not to be surprised that the law does nothing for men such as us."

"Now, you're wrong about that," Gordonson said in a pedantic tone. "The law makes no decisions. It has no will of its own. It's like a weapon, or a tool: it works for those who pick it up and use it."

"The rich."

"Usually," Gordonson conceded. "But it might work for you."

"How?" Mack said eagerly.

"Suppose you devised an alternative ganging system for unloading coal ships."

This was what Mack had been hoping for. "It wouldn't be difficult," he said. "The men could choose one of their number to be undertaker and deal with the captains. The money would be shared out as soon as it's received."

"I presume the coal heavers would prefer to work under the new system, and be free to spend their wages as they pleased."

"Yes," Mack said, suppressing his mounting excitement. "They could pay for their beer as they drink it, the way anyone does." But would Gordonson weigh in on the side of the coal heavers? If that happened everything could change.

Charlie Smith said lugubriously: "It's been tried before. It doesn't work."

Charlie had been a coal heaver for many years, Mack recalled. He asked: "Why doesn't it work?"

"What happens is, the undertakers bribe the ships' captains not to use the new gangs. Then there's trouble and fighting between the gangs. And it's the new gangs that get punished for the fights, because the magistrates are undertakers themselves, or friends of undertakers . . . and in the end all the coal heavers go back to the old ways."

"Damn fools," Mack said.

Charlie looked offended. "I suppose if they were clever they wouldn't be coal heavers."

Mack realized he had been supercilious, but it angered him when men were their own worst enemies. "They only need a little determination and solidarity," he said.

Gordonson put in: "There's more to it than that. It's a question of politics. I remember the last coal heavers' dispute. They were defeated because they had no champion. The undertakers were against them and no one was for them."

"Why should it be different this time?" said Mack.

"Because of John Wilkes."

Wilkes was the defender of liberty, but he was in exile. "He can't do much for us in Paris."

"He's not in Paris. He's back."

That was a surprise. "What's he going to do?"

"Stand for Parliament."

Mack could imagine how that would stir up trouble in London's political circles. "But I still don't see how it helps us."

"Wilkes will take the coal heavers' part, and the government will side with the undertakers. Such a dispute, with workingmen plainly in the right, and having the law on their side too, would do Wilkes nothing but good."

"How do you know what Wilkes will do?"

Gordonson smiled. "I'm his electoral agent."

Gordonson was more powerful than Mack had realized. This was a piece of luck.

Charlie Smith, still skeptical, said: "So you're planning to use the coal heavers to advance your own political purposes."

"Fair point," Gordonson said mildly. He put down his pipe. "But why do I support Wilkes? Let me explain. You came to me today complaining of injustice. This kind of thing happens all too often: ordinary men and women cruelly abused for the benefit of some greedy brute, a George Jamisson or a Sidney Lennox. It harms trade, because the bad enterprises undermine the good. And even if it were good for trade it would be wicked. I love my country and I hate the brutes who would destroy its people and ruin its prosperity. So I spend my life fighting for justice." He smiled and put his pipe back in his mouth. "I hope that doesn't sound too pompous."

"Not at all," said Mack. "I'm glad you're on our side."

16

J AY JAMISSON'S WEDDING DAY WAS COLD AND DAMP. FROM HIS bedroom in Grosvenor Square he could see Hyde Park, where his regiment was bivouacked. A low mist covered the ground, and the soldiers' tents looked like ships' sails on a swirling gray sea. Dull fires smoked here and there, adding to the fug. The men would be miserable, but soldiers were always miserable.

He turned from the window. Chip Marlborough, his brideman, was holding Jay's new coat. Jay shrugged into it with a grunt of thanks. Chip was a captain in the Third Foot Guards, like Jay. His father was Lord Arebury, who had business dealings with Jay's father. Jay was flattered that such an aristocratic scion had agreed to stand beside him on his wedding day.

"Have you seen to the horses?" Jay asked anxiously.

"Of course," said Chip.

Although the Third Foot was an infantry regiment, officers always went mounted, and Jay's responsibility was to supervise the men who looked after the horses. He was good with horses: he understood them instinctively. He had two days' leave for his wedding but he still worried whether the beasts were being looked after properly.

His leave was so short because the regiment was on active service. There was no war: the last war the British army had fought was the Seven Years' War, against the French in America, and that had ended while Jay and Chip were schoolboys. But the people of London were so restless and turbulent that the troops were standing by to suppress riots.

Every few days some group of angry craftsmen went on strike or marched on Parliament or ran through the streets breaking windows. Only this week silk weavers, outraged by a reduction in their rate of pay, had destroyed three of the new engine looms in Spitalfields.

"I hope the regiment isn't called out while I'm on leave," Jay said. "It would be just my luck to miss the action."

"Stop worrying!" Chip poured brandy from a decanter into two glasses. He was a great brandy drinker. "To love!" he said.

"To love," Jay repeated.

He did not know much about love, he reflected. He had lost his virginity five years ago with Arabella, one of his father's housemaids. He thought at the time that he was seducing her but, looking back, he could see that it had been the other way around. After he had shared her bed three times she said she was pregnant. He had paid her thirty pounds—which he had borrowed from a moneylender—to disappear. He now suspected she had never been pregnant and the whole thing was a deliberate swindle.

Since then he had flirted with dozens of girls, kissed many of them, and bedded a few. He found it easy to charm a girl: it was mainly a matter of pretending to be interested in everything she said, although good looks and good manners helped. He bowled them over without much effort. But now for the first time he had suffered the same treatment. When he was with Lizzie he always felt slightly breathless, and he knew that he stared at her as if she were the only person in the room, the way a girl stared at him when he was being fascinating. Was that love? He thought it must be.

His father had mellowed toward the marriage because of the possibility of getting at Lizzie's coal. That was why he was having Lizzie and her mother staying in the guest house, and paying the rent on the Chapel Street house where Jay and Lizzie would live after the wedding. They had not made any firm promises to Father, but neither had they told him that Lizzie was dead set against mining in High Glen. Jay just hoped it would work out all right in the end.

The door opened and a footman said: "Will you see a Mr. Lennox, sir?"

Jay's heart sank. He owed Sidney Lennox money: gambling losses. He would have sent the man away—he was only a tavern keeper—but then Lennox might turn nasty about the debt. "You'd better show him in," Jay said. "I'm sorry about this," he said to Chip.

"I know Lennox," Chip said. "I've lost money to him myself." Lennox walked in, and Jay noticed the distinctive sweet-sour smell of the man, like something fermenting. Chip greeted him. "How are you, you damned rogue?"

Lennox gave him a cool look. "You don't call me a damned rogue when you win, I notice."

Jay regarded him nervously. Lennox wore a yellow suit and silk stockings with buckled shoes, but he looked like a jackal dressed as a man: there was an air of menace about him that fancy clothes could not conceal. However, Jay could not quite bring himself to break with Lennox. He was a very useful acquaintance: he always knew where there was a cockfight, a gladiatorial combat or a horse race, and if all else failed he would start a card school or a dice game himself.

He was also willing to give credit to young officers who ran out of cash but wanted to continue gambling; and that was the trouble. Jay owed Lennox a hundred and fifty pounds. It would be embarrassing if Lennox insisted on collecting the debt now.

"You know I'm getting married today, Lennox," Jay said.

"Yes, I know that," Lennox said. "I came to drink your health."

"By all means, by all means. Chip—a tot for our friend."

Chip poured three generous measures of brandy.

Lennox said: "To you and your bride."

"Thank you," said Jay, and the three men drank.

Lennox addressed Chip. "There'll be a big faro game tomorrow night, at Lord Archer's coffeehouse, Captain Marlborough."

"It sounds good to me," said Chip.

"I'll hope to see you there. No doubt you'll be too busy, Captain Jamisson."

"I expect so," Jay replied. Anyway, I can't afford it, he thought to himself.

Lennox put down his glass. "I wish you a good day and hope the fog lifts." he said. and he went out.

Jay concealed his relief. Nothing had been said about the money. Lennox knew that Jay's father had paid the last debt, and perhaps he felt confident that Sir George would do the same again. Jay wondered why Lennox had come: surely not just to cadge a free glass of brandy? He had an unpleasant feeling that Lennox had been making some kind of point. There was an unspoken threat in the air. But what could a tavern keeper do to the son of a wealthy merchant, in the end?

From the street Jay heard the sound of carriages drawing up in front of the house. He put Lennox out of his mind. "Let's go downstairs," he said.

The drawing room was a grand space with expensive furniture made by Thomas Chippendale. It smelled of wax polish. Jay's mother, father and brother were there, all dressed for church. Alicia kissed Jay. Sir George and Robert greeted him awkwardly: they had never been an affectionate family, and the row over the twenty-first birthday gift was still fresh in their memories.

A footman was pouring coffee. Jay and Chip each took a cup. Before they could sip it the door flew open and Lizzie came in like a hurricane. "How dare you?" she stormed. "How dare you?"

Jay's heart missed a beat. What was the matter now? Lizzie was pink with indignation, her eyes flashing, her bosom heaving. She was wearing her bridal outfit, a simple white dress with a white cap, but she looked ravishing. "What have I done?" Jay asked plaintively.

"The wedding is off!" she replied.

"No!" Jay cried. Surely she was not to be snatched from him at the last moment? The thought was unbearable.

Lady Hallim hurried in after her, looking distraught. "Lizzie, please stop this," she said.

Jay's mother took charge. "Lizzie dear, what on earth is the trouble? Please tell us what has made you so distressed."

"This!" she said, and she fluttered a sheaf of papers.

Lady Hallim was wringing her hands. "It's a letter from my head keeper," she said.

Lizzie said: "It says that surveyors employed by the Jamissons have been sinking boreholes on the Hallim estate."

"Boreholes?" Jay said, mystified. He looked at Robert and saw a furtive expression on his face.

Lizzie said impatiently: "They're looking for coal, of course."

"Oh, no!" Jay protested. He understood what had happened. His impatient father had jumped the gun. He was so eager to get at Lizzie's coal that he had not been able to wait until the wedding.

But Father's impatience might have lost Jay his bride. That thought made Jay angry enough to shout at his father. "You damn fool!" he said recklessly. "Look what you've done!"

It was a shocking thing for a son to say, and Sir George was not used to opposition from anyone. He went red in the face and his eyes bulged. "Call off the damned wedding, then!" he roared. "What do I care?"

Alicia intervened. "Calm down, Jay, and you too, Lizzie," she said; and she meant Sir George as well, though she tactfully did not say so. "There has obviously been a mistake. No doubt Sir George's surveyors misunderstood some instructions. Lady Hallim, please take Lizzie back to the guest house and allow us to sort this out. I feel sure we do not need to do anything so drastic as to call off the wedding."

Chip Marlborough coughed. Jay had forgotten he was there. "If you'll excuse me . . . ," Chip said. He went to the door.

"Don't leave the house," Jay pleaded. "Wait upstairs."

"Certainly," Chip said, although his face showed that he would rather be anywhere else in the world.

Alicia gently ushered Lizzie and Lady Hallim toward the door behind Chip. "Please, just give me a few minutes and I will come and see you and everything will be all right."

As Lizzie went out she was looking more doubtful than angry, and Jay hoped she realized he had not known about the boreholes. His mother closed the door and turned around. Jay prayed she could do something to save the wedding. Did she have a plan? She was so clever. It was his only hope.

She did not remonstrate with his father. Instead she said: "If there's no wedding you won't get your coal."

"High Glen is bankrupt!" Sir George replied.

"But Lady Hallim could renew her mortgages with another lender."

"She doesn't know that."

"Someone will tell her."

There was a pause while that threat sank in. Jay was afraid his father would explode. But Mother was a good judge of how far he could be pushed, and in the end he said resignedly: "What do you want, Alicia?"

Jay breathed a sigh of relief. Perhaps his wedding might be saved after all.

Mother said: "First of all, Jay must speak to Lizzie and convince her that he did not know about the surveyors."

"It's true!" Jay interjected.

"Shut up and listen," his father said brutally.

Mother went on: "If he can do that, they can get married as planned."

"Then what?"

"Then be patient. In time, Jay and I can talk Lizzie around. She's against coal mining now, but she will change her mind, or at least become less passionate about it—especially when she has a home and a baby and begins to understand the importance of money."

Sir George shook his head. "It's not good enough, Alicia—I can't wait."

"Whyever not?"

He paused and looked at Robert, who shrugged. "I suppose I might as well tell you," Father said. "I've got debts of my own. You know we have always run on borrowed money—most of it from Lord Arebury. In the past we've made profits for ourselves and for him. But our trade with America has fallen very low since the trouble started in the colonies. And it's almost impossible to get paid for what little business we do—our biggest debtor has gone bust, leaving me with a tobacco plantation in Virginia that I can't sell."

Jay was stunned. It had never occurred to him that the family enterprises were risky and that the wealth he had always known might not last forever. He began to see why his father had been so enraged at having to pay his gambling debts.

Father went on: "The coal has been keeping us going, but it's not enough. Lord Arebury wants his money. So I have to have the Hallim estate. Otherwise I could lose my entire business."

There was a silence. Both Jay and his mother were too shocked to speak.

Eventually Alicia said: "Then there is only one solution. High Glen will have to be mined without Lizzie's knowledge."

Jay frowned anxiously. That proposal frightened him. But he decided not to say anything just yet.

"How could it be done?" said Sir George.

"Send her and Jay to another country."

Jay was startled. What a clever idea! "But Lady Hallim would know," he said. "And she'll be sure to tell Lizzie."

Alicia shook her head. "No, she won't. She'll do anything to make this marriage happen. She'll keep quiet if we tell her to."

Jay said: "But where would we go? What country?"

"Barbados," said his mother.

"No!" Robert interjected. "Jay can't have the sugar plantation."

Alicia said quietly: "I think your father will give it up if the survival of the entire family enterprise depends upon it."

Robert's face wore a triumphant look. "Father can't, even if he wants to. The plantation already belongs to me."

Alicia looked inquiringly at Sir George. "Is that true? Is it his?"

Sir George nodded. "I made it over to him."

"When?"

"Three years ago."

That was another shock. Jay had no idea. He felt wounded. "That's why you wouldn't give it to me for my birthday," he said sadly. "You had already given it to Robert."

Alicia said: "But, Robert, surely you'd give it back to save the entire business?"

"No!" Robert said hotly. "This is only the beginning—you'll start by stealing the plantation, and in the end you'll get everything! I know you've always wanted to take the business from me and give it to that little bastard."

"All I want for Jay is a fair share," she replied.

Sir George said: "Robert, if you don't do this it could mean bankruptcy for all of us."

"Not for me," he said triumphantly. "I'll still have a plantation."

"But you could have so much more," said Sir George.

Robert looked sly. "All right, I'll do it—on one condition: that you sign over the rest of the business to me, I mean everything. And you retire."

"No!" Sir George shouted. "I won't retire—I'm not yet fifty years old!"

They glared at one another, Robert and Sir George, and Jay thought how similar they were. Neither would give in over this, he knew, and his heart sank.

It was an impasse. The two stubborn men were deadlocked and between them they would ruin everything: the wedding, the business, and the family's future.

But Alicia was not ready to give up. "What's this Virginia property, George?"

"Mockjack Hall—it's a tobacco plantation, about a thousand acres and fifty slaves. . . . What are you thinking?"

"You could give that to Jay."

Jay's heart leaped. Virginia! It would be the fresh start he had longed for, away from his father and brother, with a place of his own to manage and cultivate. And Lizzie would jump at the chance.

Sir George's eyes narrowed. "I couldn't give him any money," he said. "He'd have to borrow what he needed to get the place going."

Jay said quickly: "I don't care about that."

Alicia put in: "But you'd have to pay the interest on Lady Hallim's mortgages—otherwise she could lose High Glen."

"I can do that out of the income from the coal." Father went on thinking out the details. "They'll have to leave for Virginia immediately, within a few weeks."

"They can't do that," Alicia protested. "They have to make preparations. Give them three months, at least."

He shook his head. "I need the coal sooner than that."

"That's all right. Lizzie won't want to make the journey back to Scotland—she'll be too busy preparing for her new life."

All this talk of deceiving Lizzie filled Jay with trepidation. He was the one who would suffer her wrath if she found out. "What if someone writes to her?" he said.

Alicia looked thoughtful. "We need to know which of the servants at High Glen House might do that—you can find that out, Jay."

"How will we stop them?"

"We'll send someone up there to dismiss them."

Sir George said: "That could work. All right—we'll do it."

Alicia turned to Jay and smiled triumphantly. She had got him his patrimony after all. She put her arms around him and kissed him. "Bless you, my dear son," she said. "Now go to her and tell her that you and your family are desperately sorry about this mistake, and that your father has given you Mockjack Hall as a wedding present."

Jay hugged her and whispered: "Well done, Mother—thank you."

He went out. As he walked across the garden he felt jubilant and apprehensive at the same time. He had got what he had always wanted. He wished it could have been done without deceiving his bride—but there was no other way. If he had refused he would have lost the property and he might have lost her as well.

He went into the little guest house adjoining the stables. Lady Hallim and Lizzie were in the modest drawing room sitting by a smoky coal fire. They had both been crying.

Jay felt a sudden dangerous impulse to tell Lizzie the truth. If he revealed the deception planned by the parents, and asked her to marry him and live in poverty, she might say yes.

But the risk scared him. And their dream of going to a new country would die. Sometimes, he told himself, a lie was kinder.

But would she believe it?

He knelt in front of her. Her wedding dress smelled of lavender. "My father is very sorry," he said. "He sent in the surveyors as a surprise for me—he thought we'd be pleased to know if there was coal on your land. He didn't know how strongly you felt about mining."

She looked skeptical. "Why didn't you tell him?"

He spread his hands in a gesture of helplessness. "He never asked." She still looked stubborn, but he had another card up his sleeve. "And there's something else. Our wedding present."

She frowned. "What is it?"

"Mockjack Hall—a tobacco plantation in Virginia. We can go there as soon as we like."

She stared at him in surprise.

"It's what we always wanted, isn't it?" he said. "A fresh start in a new country—an adventure!"

Slowly her face broke into a smile. "Really? Virginia? Can it really be true?"

He could hardly believe she would consent. "Will you accept it, then?" he said fearfully.

She smiled. Tears came to her eyes and she could not speak. She nodded dumbly.

Jay realized he had won. He had got everything he wanted. The feeling was like winning a big hand at cards. It was time to rake in his profits.

He stood up. He drew her out of her chair and gave her his arm. "Come with me, then," he said. "Let's get married."

17

A T NOON ON THE THIRD DAY, THE HOLD OF THE *DURHAM PRIMROSE* was empty of coal.

Mack looked around, hardly able to believe it had really happened. They had done it all without an undertaker.

They had watched the riverside and picked out a coal ship that arrived in the middle of the day, when the other gangs were already working. While the men waited on the riverbank, Mack and Charlie rowed out to the ship as it anchored and offered their services, starting immediately. The captain knew that if he held out for a regular gang he would have to wait until the following day, and time was money to ships' captains, so he hired them.

The men seemed to work faster knowing they would be paid in full. They still drank beer all day, but paying for it jar by jar they took only what they needed. And they uncoaled the ship in forty-eight hours.

Mack shouldered his shovel and went on deck. The weather was cold and misty, but Mack was hot from the hold. As the last sack of coal was thrown down onto the boat a great cheer went up from the coal heavers.

Mack conferred with the first mate. The boat carried five hundred sacks and they had both kept count of the number of round trips it had made. Now they counted the odd sacks left for the last trip and agreed on the total. Then they went to the captain's cabin.

Mack hoped there would be no last-minute snags. They had done the work: they had to be paid now, didn't they?

The captain was a thin, middle-aged man with a big red nose. He smelled of rum. "Finished?" he said. "You're quicker than the usual gangs. What's the tally?"

"Six hundred score, all but ninety-three," the first mate said, and Mack nodded. They counted in scores, or twenties, because each man was paid a penny per score.

He beckoned them inside and sat down with an abacus. "Six hundred score less ninety-three, at sixteen pence per score..." It was a complicated sum, but Mack was used to being paid by the weight of coal he produced, and he could do mental arithmetic when his wages depended on it.

The captain had a key on a chain attached to his belt. He used it to open a chest that stood in the corner. Mack stared as he took out a smaller box, put it on the table, and opened it. "If we call the odd seven sacks a half score, I owe you thirty-nine pounds fourteen shillings exactly." And he counted out the money.

The captain gave him a linen bag to carry it in and included plenty of pennies so that he could share it out exactly among the men. Mack felt a tremendous sense of triumph as he held the money in his hands. Each man had earned almost two pounds and ten shillings—more in two days than they got for two weeks with Lennox. But more important, they had proved they could stand up for their rights and win justice.

He sat cross-legged on the deck of the ship to pay the men out. The first in line, Amos Tipe, said: "Thank you, Mack, and God bless you, boy."

"Don't thank me, you earned it," Mack protested.

Despite his protest the next man thanked him in the same way, as if he were a prince dispensing favors.

"It's not just the money," Mack said as a third man, Slash Harley, stepped forward. "We've won our dignity, too."

"You can have the dignity, Mack," said Slash. "Just give me the money." The others laughed.

Mack felt a little angry with them as he continued to count out the coins. Why could they not see that this was more than a matter of today's wages? When they were so stupid about their own interests he felt they deserved to be abused by undertakers.

However, nothing could mar his victory. As they were all rowed to shore the men began lustily to sing a very obscene song called "The Mayor of Bayswater," and Mack joined in at the top of his voice.

He and Dermot walked to Spitalfields. The morning fog was lifting. Mack had a tune on his lips and a spring in his step. When he entered his room a pleasant surprise was waiting for him. Sitting on a three-legged stool, smelling of sandalwood and swinging a shapely leg, was Peg's red-haired friend Cora, in a chestnut-colored coat and a jaunty hat.

She had picked up his cloak, which normally lay on the straw mattress that was his bed, and she was stroking the fur. "Where did you get this?" she said.

"It was a gift from a fine lady," he said with a grin. "What are you doing here?"

"I came to see you," she said. "If you wash your face you can walk out with me—that is, if you don't have to go to tea with any fine ladies."

He must have appeared doubtful, for she added: "Don't look so startled. You probably think I'm a whore, but I'm not, except in desperation."

He took his sliver of soap and went down to the standpipe in the yard. Cora followed him and watched as he stripped to the waist and washed the coal dust from his skin and hair. He borrowed a clean shirt from Dermot, put on his coat and hat, and took Cora's arm.

They walked west, through the heart of the city. In London, Mack had learned, people walked the streets for recreation the way they walked the hills in Scotland. He enjoyed having Cora on his arm. He liked the way her hips swayed so that she touched him every now and again. Because of her striking coloring and her dashing clothes she attracted a lot of attention, and Mack got envious looks from other men.

They went into a tavern and ordered oysters, bread and the strong beer called porter. Cora ate with gusto, swallowing the oysters whole and washing them down with drafts of dark ale.

When they went out again the weather had changed. It was still cool, but there was a little weak sunshine. They strolled into the rich residential district called Mayfair.

In his first twenty-two years Mack had seen only two palatial homes, Jamisson Castle and High Glen House. In this neighborhood there were two such houses on every street, and another fifty only a little less magnificent. London's wealth never ceased to astonish him.

Outside one of the very grandest a series of carriages was drawing up and depositing guests as if for a party. On the pavement either side was a small crowd of passersby and servants from neighboring houses, and people were looking out from their doors and windows. The house was a blaze of light, although it was midafternoon, and the entrance was decorated with flowers. "It must be a wedding," Cora said.

As they watched, another carriage drew up and a familiar figure stepped out. Mack gave a start as he recognized Jay Jamisson. Jay handed his bride down from the carriage, and the bystanders cheered and clapped.

"She's pretty," Cora said.

Lizzie smiled and looked around, acknowledging the applause. Her eyes met Mack's, and for a moment she froze. He smiled and waved. She averted her eyes quickly and hurried inside.

It had taken only a fraction of a second, but the sharp-eyed Cora had not missed it. "Do you know her?"

"She's the one gave me the fur," Mack said.

"I hope her husband doesn't know she gives presents to coal heavers."

"She's throwing herself away on Jay Jamisson—he's a handsome weakling."

"I suppose you think she'd be better off marrying you," Cora said sarcastically.

"She would, too," Mack said seriously. "Shall we go to the theater?"

✳

Late that evening Lizzie and Jay sat up in bed in the bridal chamber, wearing their nightclothes, surrounded by giggling relations and friends, all more or less drunk. The older generation had long since left the room, but custom insisted that wedding guests should hang on, tormenting the couple, who were assumed to be in a desperate hurry to consummate their marriage.

The day had passed in a whirl. Lizzie had hardly thought about Jay's betrayal, his apology, her pardon, and their future in Virginia. There had been no time to ask herself whether she had made the right decision.

Chip Marlborough came in carrying a jug of posset. Pinned to his hat was one of Lizzie's garters. He proceeded to fill everyone's glasses. "A toast!" he said.

"A *final* toast!" said Jay, but they all laughed and jeered.

Lizzie sipped her drink, a mixture of wine, milk and egg yolk with sugar and cinnamon. She was exhausted. It had been a long day, from the morning's terrible quarrel and its surprisingly happy ending, through the church service, the wedding dinner, music and dancing, and now the final comic ritual.

Katie Drome, a Jamisson relation, sat on the end of the bed with one of Jay's white silk stockings in her hand and threw it backward over her head. If it hit Jay, the superstition said, then she would soon be married. She threw wildly but Jay good-humoredly reached out and caught the stocking and placed it on his head as if it had landed there, and everyone clapped.

A drunken man called Peter McKay sat on the bed beside Lizzie. "Virginia," he said. "Hamish Drome went to Virginia, you know, after he was cheated out of his inheritance by Robert's mother."

Lizzie was startled. The family legend was that Robert's mother, Olive, had nursed a bachelor cousin while he was dying, and he had changed his will in her favor out of gratitude.

Jay heard the remark. "Cheated?" he said.

"Olive forged that will, of course," McKay said. "But Hamish could never prove it, so he had to accept it. Went to Virginia and was never heard of again."

Jay laughed. "Ha! The saintly Olive—a forger!"

"Hush!" said McKay. "Sir George will kill us all if he hears!"

Lizzie was intrigued, but she had had enough of Jay's relations for one day. "Get these people out!" she hissed.

All the demands of custom had now been satisfied but one. "Right," said Jay. "If you won't go willingly . . ." He threw the blankets off his side of the bed and got out. As he advanced on the crowd he lifted his nightshirt to show his knees. All the girls screamed as if terrified—it was their role to pretend that the sight of a man in his nightshirt was more than a maiden could bear—and they rushed out of the room in a mob, chased by the men.

Jay shut the door and locked it. Then he moved a heavy chest of drawers across the doorway to make sure they would not be interrupted.

Suddenly Lizzie's mouth was dry. This was the moment she had been looking forward to ever since the day Jay had kissed her in the hall at Jamisson Castle and asked her to marry him. Since then their embraces, snatched in the few odd moments when they were left alone together, had become more and more passionate. From open-mouthed kissing they had progressed to ever more intimate caresses. They had done everything two people could do in an unlocked room with a mother or two liable to come in at any moment. Now, at last, they were allowed to lock the door.

Jay went around the room snuffing out candles. As he came to the last, Lizzie said: "Leave one burning."

He looked surprised. "Why?"

"I want to look at you." He seemed dubious, and she added: "Is that all right?"

"Yes, I suppose so," he said, and he climbed into bed.

As he began to kiss and caress her she wished they were both naked, but she decided not to suggest it. She would let him do it his way, this time.

The familiar excitement made her limbs tingle as his hands ran all over her body. In a moment he parted her legs and got on top of her. She lifted her face to kiss him as he entered her, but he was concentrating too hard and he did not see. She felt a sudden sharp pain, and she almost cried out, then it was gone.

He moved inside her, and she moved with him. She was not sure if it was the thing to do but it felt right. She was just starting to enjoy it when Jay stopped, gasped, thrust again, and collapsed on her, breathing hard.

She frowned. "Are you all right?" she said.

"Yes," he grunted.

Is that all, then? she thought, but she did not say it.

He rolled off her and lay looking at her. "Did you like it?" he said.

"It was a bit quick," she said. "Can we do it again in the morning?"

*

Wearing only her shift, Cora lay back on the fur cloak and pulled Mack down with her. When he put his tongue in her mouth she tasted of gin. He lifted her skirt. The fine, red-blond hair did not hide the folds of her sex. He stroked it, the way he had with Annie, and Cora gasped and said: "Who taught you to do that, my virgin boy?"

He pulled down his breeches. Cora reached for her purse and took out a small box. Inside was a tube made of something that looked like parchment. A pink ribbon was threaded through its open end.

"What's that?" said Mack.

"It's called a cundum," she said.

"What the hell is it for?"

By way of reply she slipped it over his erect penis and tied the ribbon tightly.

He said bemusedly: "Well, I know my dick isn't very pretty but I never thought a girl would want to cover it up."

She started to laugh. "You ignorant peasant, it's not for decoration, it's to stop me getting pregnant!"

He rolled over and entered her, and she stopped laughing. Ever since he was fourteen years old he had wondered what it would feel like, but he still felt he hardly knew, for this was neither one thing nor the other. He stopped and looked down at Cora's angelic face. She opened her eyes. "Don't stop," she said.

"After this, will I still be a virgin?" he said.

"If you are, I'll be a nun," she said. "Now stop talking. You're going to need all your breath."

And he did.

18

JAY AND LIZZIE MOVED INTO THE CHAPEL STREET HOUSE ON THE DAY after the wedding. For the first time they ate supper alone, with no one present but the servants. For the first time they went upstairs hand in hand, undressed together, and got into their own bed. For the first time they woke up together in their own house.

They were naked: Lizzie had persuaded Jay to take off his nightshirt last night. Now she pressed herself against him and stroked his body, arousing him; then she rolled on top of him.

She could tell he was surprised. "Do you mind?" she said.

He did not reply, but started to move inside her.

When it was over she said: "I shock you, don't I?"

After a pause he said: "Well, yes."

"Why?"

"It's not . . . normal for the woman to get on top."

"I've no idea what people think is normal—I've never been in bed with a man before."

"I should hope not!"

"But how do *you* know what's normal?"

"Never you mind."

He had probably seduced a few seamstresses and shopgirls who were overawed by him and let him take charge. Lizzie had no experience but she knew what she wanted and believed in taking it. She was not going to change her ways. She was enjoying it too much.

Jay was, too, even though he was shocked: she could tell by his vigorous movements and the pleased look on his face afterward.

She got up and went naked to the window. The weather was cold but sunny. The church bells were ringing muffled because it was a hanging day: one or more criminals would be executed this morning. Half the city's workingpeople would take an unofficial day off, and many of them would flock to Tyburn, the crossroads at the northwestern corner of London where the gallows stood, to see the spectacle. It was the kind of occasion when rioting could break out, so Jay's regiment would be on alert all day. However, Jay had one more day's leave.

She turned to face him and said: "Take me to the hanging."

He looked disapproving. "A gruesome request."

"Don't tell me it's no place for a lady."

He smiled. "I wouldn't dare."

"I know that rich and poor women and men go to see it."

"But why do you want to go?"

That was a good question. She had mixed feelings about it. It was shameful to make entertainment of death, and she knew she would be disgusted with herself afterward. But her curiosity was overwhelming. "I want to know what it's like," she said. "How do the condemned people behave? Do they weep, or pray, or gibber with fear? And what about the spectators? What is it like to watch a human life come to an end?"

She had always been this way. The first time she saw a deer shot, when she was only nine or ten years old, she had watched enthralled as the keeper gralloched it, taking out its entrails. She had been fascinated by the multiple stomachs and had insisted on touching the flesh to see what it felt like. It was warm and slimy. The beast was two or three months pregnant, and the keeper had shown her the tiny fetus in the transparent womb. None of it had revolted her: it was too interesting.

She understood perfectly why people flocked to see the spectacle. She also understood why others were revolted by the thought of watching it. But she was part of the inquisitive group.

Jay said: "Perhaps we could hire a room overlooking the gallows—that's what a lot of people do."

But Lizzie felt that would mute the experience. "Oh, no—I want to be in the crowd!" she protested.

"Women of our class don't do that."

"Then I'll dress as a man."

He looked doubtful.

"Jay, don't make faces at me! You were glad enough to take me down the coal mine dressed as a man."

"It is a bit different for a married woman."

"If you tell me that all adventures are over just because we're married, I shall run away to sea."

"Don't be ridiculous."

She grinned at him and jumped onto the bed. "Don't be an old curmudgeon." She bounced up and down. "Let's go to the hanging."

He could not help laughing. "All right," he said.

"Bravo!"

She performed her daily chores rapidly. She told the cook what to buy for dinner; decided which rooms the housemaids would clean; told the groom she would not be riding today; accepted an invitation for the two of them to dine with Captain Marlborough and his wife next Wednesday; postponed an appointment with a milliner; and took delivery of twelve brassbound trunks for the voyage to Virginia.

Then she put on her disguise.

*

The street known as Tyburn Street or Oxford Street was thronged with people. The gallows stood at the end of the street, outside Hyde Park. Houses with a view of the scaffold were crowded with wealthy spectators who had rented rooms for the day. People stood shoulder to shoulder on the stone wall of the park. Hawkers moved through the crowds selling hot sausages and tots of gin and printed copies of what they said were the dying speeches of the condemned.

Mack held Cora's hand and pushed through the crowd. He had no desire to watch people getting killed but Cora had insisted on going. Mack just wanted to spend all his free time with Cora. He liked holding her hand, kissing her lips whenever he wanted to, and touching her body in odd moments. He liked just to look at her. He enjoyed her devil-may-care attitude and her rough language and the wicked look in her eye. So he went with her to the hanging.

A friend of hers was going to be hanged. Her name was Dolly Macaroni, and she was a brothel keeper, but her crime was forgery. "What did she forge, anyway?" Mack said as they approached the gallows.

"A bank draft. She changed the amount from eleven pounds to eighty pounds."

"Where did she get a draft for eleven pounds?"

"From Lord Massey. She says he owed her more."

"She ought to have been transported, not hanged."

"They nearly always hang forgers."

They were as close as they could get, about twenty yards away. The gallows was a crude wooden structure, just three posts with crossbeams. Five ropes hung from the beams, their ends tied in nooses ready for the condemned. A chaplain stood nearby, with a handful of official-looking men who were presumably law officers. Soldiers with muskets kept the crowd at a distance.

Gradually Mack became aware of a roaring sound from farther down Tyburn Street. "What's that noise?" he asked Cora.

"They're coming."

First there was a squad of peace officers on horseback, led by a personage who was presumably the city marshal. Next were the constables, on foot and armed with clubs. Then came the tumbril, a high four-wheeled cart drawn by two plow horses. A company of javelin men brought up the rear, holding their pointed spears rigidly upright.

In the cart, sitting on what appeared to be coffins, their hands and arms bound with ropes, were five people: three men, a boy of about fifteen and a woman. "That's Dolly," Cora said, and she began to cry.

Mack stared in horrid fascination at the five who were to die. One of the men was drunk. The other two looked defiant. Dolly was praying aloud and the boy was crying.

The cart was driven under the scaffold. The drunk man waved to some friends, villainous-looking types, who stood at the front of the crowd. They shouted jokes and ribald comments: "Kind of the sheriff to invite you along!" and "I hope you've learned to dance!" and "Try that necklace on for size!" Dolly asked God's forgiveness in a loud, clear voice. The boy cried: "Save me, Mamma, save me, please!"

The two sober men were greeted by a group at the front of the crowd. After a moment Mack distinguished their accents as Irish. One of the condemned men shouted: "Don't let the surgeons have me, boys!" There was a roar of assent from his friends.

"What are they talking about?" Mack asked Cora.

"He must be a murderer. The bodies of murderers belong to the Company of Surgeons. They cut them up to see what's inside."

Mack shuddered.

The hangman climbed on the cart. One by one he placed the nooses around their necks and drew them tight. None of them struggled or protested or tried to escape. It would have been useless, surrounded as they were by guards, but Mack thought he would have tried anyway.

The priest, a bald man in stained robes, got up on the cart and spoke to each of them in turn: just for a few moments to the drunk, four or five minutes with the other two men, and longer with Dolly and the boy.

Mack had heard that sometimes executions went wrong, and he began to hope it would happen this time. Ropes could break; the crowd had been known to swarm the scaffold and release the prisoners; the hangman might cut people down before they were dead. It was too awful to think these five living human beings would in a few moments be dead.

The priest finished his work. The hangman blindfolded the five people with strips of rag then got down, leaving only the condemned on the cart. The drunk man could not keep his balance and he stumbled and fell; and the noose began to strangle him. Dolly continued to pray loudly.

The hangman whipped the horses.

*

Lizzie heard herself scream: "No!"

The cart jerked and moved off.

The hangman lashed the horses again and they struggled to a trot. The cart was drawn from under the condemned people and, one by one, they fell to the extent of the ropes: first the drunk, already half dead; then the two Irishmen; then the weeping boy; and at last the woman, whose prayer was cut off in midsentence.

Lizzie stared at the five bodies dangling from the ropes, and she was filled with loathing for herself and the crowd around her.

They were not all dead. The boy, mercifully, seemed to have broken his neck instantly, as did the two Irishmen; but the drunk was still moving, and the woman, whose blindfold had slipped, stared out of open, terrified eyes as she slowly choked.

Lizzie buried her face in Jay's shoulder.

She would have been glad to leave, but she forced herself to stay. She had wanted to see this and now she should stick it out until the end.

She opened her eyes again.

The drunk had expired, but the woman's face worked in agony. The rowdy onlookers had fallen silent, stilled by the horror in front of them. Several minutes went by.

At last her eyes closed.

The sheriff stepped up to cut down the bodies, and that was when the trouble started.

The Irish group surged forward, trying to get past the guards to the scaffold. The constables fought back, and the javelin men joined in, stabbing at the Irish. Blood began to flow.

"I was afraid of this," Jay said. "They want to keep their friends' bodies out of the hands of the surgeons. Let's get clear as fast as we can."

Many around them had the same idea, but those at the back were trying to get closer and see what was happening. As some surged one way and some the other, fistfights broke out. Jay tried to force a way through. Lizzie stuck close to him. They found themselves up against an unbroken wave of people going the other way. Everyone was shouting or screaming. They were forced back toward the gallows. The scaffold was now swarming with Irish, some of whom were beating off the guards and dodging the lunges of the javelin men while others tried to cut down the bodies of their friends.

For no apparent reason the crush around Lizzie and Jay eased suddenly. She turned around and saw a gap between two big, rough-looking men. "Jay, come on!" she shouted, and darted between them. She turned to make sure Jay was behind her. Then the gap closed. Jay stepped forward to push his way through, but one of the men raised a hand threateningly. Jay flinched and stepped back, momentarily afraid. The hesitation was fatal: he was cut off from her. She saw his blond head above the crowd and fought to get back to him but she was stopped by a wall of people. "Jay!" she screamed. "Jay!" He shouted back but the crowd forced them farther apart. He was pushed in the direction of Tyburn Street while the crowd took her the opposite way, toward the park. A moment later he was lost from sight.

She was on her own. She gritted her teeth and turned her back on the scaffold. She faced a solid pack of people. She tried to push herself between a small man and a big-bosomed matron. "Keep your hands to yourself, young man," the woman said. Lizzie persisted in pushing and managed to squeeze through. She repeated the process. She trod on the toes of a sour-faced man and he punched her in the ribs. She gasped with pain and pressed on.

She saw a familiar face and recognized Mack McAsh. He, too, was fighting his way through the crowd. "Mack!" she yelled gratefully. He was with the red-haired woman who had been at his side in Grosvenor Square. "Over here!" Lizzie cried. "Help me!" He saw her and recognized her. Then a tall man's elbow jabbed her eye and for a few moments she could hardly see. When her vision returned to normal Mack and the woman had vanished.

Grimly she pressed on. Inch by inch she was getting away from the fracas at the gallows. With each step she found it a little easier to move. Within five minutes she was no longer squeezing between tightly packed people but passing through gaps several inches wide. Eventually she came up against the front wall of a house. She worked her way along to the corner of the building and stepped into an alley two or three feet wide.

She leaned against the house wall, catching her breath. The alley was foul and stank of human waste. Her ribs ached where she had been punched. She touched her face gingerly and found that the flesh around her eye was swelling.

She hoped Jay was all right. She turned around to look for him, and was startled to see two men staring at her.

One was middle-aged and unshaven with a fat belly, the other a youth of about eighteen. Something about their stares frightened her, but before she could move away they pounced. They grabbed her by the arms and threw her to the ground. They snatched her hat and the man's wig she wore, pulled off her silver-buckled shoes, and went through her pockets with bewildering speed, taking her purse, her pocket watch and a handkerchief.

The older man shoved the spoils into a sack, stared at her for a moment, then said: "That's a good coat—nearly new."

They both bent over her again and began to pull off her coat and matching waistcoat. She struggled but all she achieved was to rip her shirt. They stuffed her garments into a sack. She realized her breasts were exposed. Hastily she covered herself with the shreds of her clothes but she was too late. "Hey, it's a girl!" cried the younger man.

She scrambled to her feet but he grabbed her and held her.

The fat one stared at her. "And a pretty girl, too, by God," he said. He licked his lips. "I'm going to fuck her," he said decisively.

Seized with horror, Lizzie struggled violently, but she could not shake off the young man's grip.

The youth looked back along the alley to the crowd in the street. "What, here?"

"Nobody's looking this way, you young fool." He stroked himself between the legs. "Get those breeches off her and let's have a look."

The boy threw her to the ground, sat on her heavily and started to pull off her breeches while the other man watched. Fear flooded Lizzie and she screamed at the top of her voice, but there was so much noise in the street she doubted whether anyone would hear her.

Then, suddenly, Mack McAsh appeared.

She glimpsed his face and a raised fist, then he struck the older one on the side of the head. The thief rocked sideways and staggered. Mack hit him again, and the man's eyes rolled up into his head. Mack hit him a third time, and the man slumped and lay still.

The boy scrambled off Lizzie and tried to run away but she grabbed his ankle and tripped him. He measured his length on the ground. Mack picked him up and threw him against the house wall, then hit him on the chin with a punch that came up from below with all his weight behind it, and the boy fell unconscious on top of his partner-in-crime.

Lizzie got to her feet. "Thank God you were here!" she said fervently. Tears of relief filled her eyes. She threw her arms around him and said: "You saved me—thank you, thank you!"

He hugged her closely. "You saved me, once—when you pulled me out of the river."

She held him tight and tried to stop shaking. She felt his hand behind her head, stroking her hair. In her breeches and shirt, with no petticoats to get in the way, she could feel the entire length of his body pressed against hers. He felt completely different from her husband. Jay was tall and supple, Mack short and massive and hard.

He shifted and looked at her. His green eyes were mesmerizing. The rest of his face seemed to blur. "You saved me, and I saved you," he said with a wry smile. "I'm your guardian angel, and you're mine."

She began to calm down. She remembered that her shirt was torn and her breasts were bare. "If I were an angel, I wouldn't be in your arms," she said, and she made to detach herself from his embrace.

He looked into her eyes for a moment, then gave that wry smile again and nodded, as if agreeing with her. He turned away.

He bent and took the sack from the older thief's limp hand. He took out her waistcoat and she put it on, buttoning it hastily to cover her nakedness. As soon as she felt safe again she began to worry about Jay. "I have to look for my husband," she said as Mack helped her put her coat on. "Will you help me?"

"Of course." He handed her the wig and hat, purse and watch and handkerchief.

"What about your red-haired friend?" she asked.

"Cora. I made sure she was safe before I came after you."

"Did you?" Lizzie felt unreasonably irritated. "Are you and Cora lovers?" she said rudely.

Mack smiled. "Yes," he said. "Since the day before yesterday."

"My wedding day."

"I'm having a wonderful time. Are you?"

A sharp retort came to her lips then, despite herself, she laughed. "Thank you for rescuing me," she said, and she leaned forward and kissed him briefly on the lips.

"I'd do it all over again for a kiss like that."

She grinned at him then turned toward the street.

Jay stood there watching.

She felt terribly guilty. Had he seen her kiss McAsh? She guessed he had, by the thunderous look on his face. "Oh, Jay!" she said. "Thank heaven you're all right!"

"What happened here?" he said.

"Those two men robbed me."

"I knew we shouldn't have come." He took her by the arm to lead her out of the alley.

"McAsh knocked them down and rescued me," she said.

"That's no reason to kiss him," said her husband.

19

J AY'S REGIMENT WAS ON DUTY IN PALACE YARD ON THE DAY OF JOHN
Wilkes's trial.

The liberal hero had been convicted of criminal libel years ago
and had fled to Paris. On his return, earlier this year, he was
accused of being an outlaw. But while the legal action against him
dragged on he won the Middlesex by-election handsomely. However,
he had not yet taken his seat in Parliament, and the government hoped
to prevent him doing so by having him convicted in court.

Jay steadied his horse and looked nervously over the crowd of
several hundred Wilkes supporters milling around outside Westminster
Hall, where the trial was taking place. Many of them wore pinned to
their hats the blue cockade that identified them as Wilkesites. Tories
such as Jay's father wanted Wilkes silenced, but everyone was worried
about what his supporters would do.

If violence broke out, Jay's regiment was supposed to keep order.
There was a small detachment of guards—too damn small, in Jay's
opinion: just forty men and a few officers under Colonel Cranbrough,
Jay's commanding officer. They formed a thin red-and-white line
between the court building and the mob.

Cranbrough took orders from the Westminster magistrates,
represented by Sir John Fielding. Fielding was blind, but that did not
seem to hinder him in his work. He was a famous reforming justice,
although Jay thought him too soft. He had been known to say that crime

was caused by poverty. That was like saying adultery was caused by marriage.

The young officers were always hoping to see action, and Jay said he felt the same, but he was also scared. He had never actually used his sword or gun in a real fight.

It was a long day, and the captains took turns to break off from patrolling and drink a glass of wine. Toward the end of the afternoon, while Jay was giving his horse an apple, he was approached by Sidney Lennox.

His heart sank. Lennox wanted his money. No doubt he had intended to ask for it when he called at Grosvenor Square but had postponed the request because of the wedding.

Jay did not have the money. But he was terrified that Lennox would go to his father.

He put on a show of bravado. "What are you doing here, Lennox? I didn't know you were a Wilkesite."

"John Wilkes can go to the devil," Lennox replied. "I've come about the hundred and fifty pounds you lost at Lord Archer's faro game."

Jay blanched at the reminder of the amount. His father gave him thirty pounds a month, but it was never enough, and he did not know when he could lay his hands on a hundred and fifty. The thought that his father might find out he had lost more money gambling made his legs feel weak. He would do anything to avoid that. "I may have to ask you to wait a little longer," he said with a feeble attempt at an air of superior indifference.

Lennox did not reply directly. "I believe you know a man called Mack McAsh."

"Unfortunately I do."

"He's started his own coal heaving gang, with the help of Caspar Gordonson. The two of them are causing a lot of trouble."

"It doesn't surprise me. He was a damned nuisance in my father's coal mine."

"The problem is not just McAsh," Lennox went on. "His two cronies, Dermot Riley and Charlie Smith, have gangs of their own now, and there'll be more by the end of the week."

"That will cost you undertakers a fortune."

"It will ruin the trade unless it's stopped."

"All the same, it's not my problem."

"But you could help me with it."

"I doubt it." Jay did not want to get involved with Lennox's business.

"It would be worth money to me."

"How much?" Jay said warily.

"A hundred and fifty pounds."

Jay's heart leaped. The prospect of wiping out his debt was a godsend.

But Lennox would not readily give away so much. He must want a heavyweight favor. "What would I have to do?" Jay said suspiciously.

"I want the ship owners to refuse to hire McAsh's gangs. Now, some of the coal shippers are undertakers themselves, so they will cooperate. But most are independent. The biggest owner in London is your father. If he gave a lead, the others would follow."

"But why should he? He doesn't care about undertakers and coal heavers."

"He's alderman of Wapping, and the undertakers have a lot of votes. He ought to defend our interests. Besides, the coal heavers are a troublesome crowd, and we keep them under control."

Jay frowned. It was a tall order. He had no influence at all with his father. Few people did: Sir George could not be influenced into coming in out of the rain. But Jay had to try.

A roar from the crowd signaled that Wilkes was coming out. Jay mounted his horse hastily. "I'll see what I can do," he called to Lennox as he trotted away.

Jay found Chip Marlborough and said: "What's happening?"

"Wilkes has been refused bail and committed to the King's Bench Prison."

The colonel was mustering his officers. He said to Jay: "Pass the word—no one is to fire unless Sir John gives the order. Tell your men."

Jay suppressed an anxious protest. How were soldiers to control the mob if their hands were tied? But he rode around and relayed the instruction.

A carriage emerged from the gateway. The crowd gave a bloodcurdling roar, and Jay felt a stab of fear. The soldiers made a path for the carriage by beating the mob with their muskets. Wilkes's supporters ran across Westminster Bridge, and Jay realized that the carriage would have to cross the river into Surrey to get to the prison. He spurred his horse toward the bridge, but Colonel Cranbrough waved him down. "Don't cross the bridge," he commanded. "Our orders are to keep the peace here, outside the court."

Jay reined in. Surrey was a separate district, and the Surrey magistrates had not asked for army support. This was ridiculous. He watched, helpless, as the carriage crossed the river Thames. Before it reached the Surrey side the crowd stopped it and detached the horses.

Sir John Fielding was in the heart of the throng, following the carriage with two assistants to guide him and tell him what was happening. As Jay watched, a dozen strong men got between the traces and began to pull the carriage themselves. They turned it around and headed back toward Westminster, and the mob roared its approval.

Jay's heart beat faster. What would happen when the mob reached Palace Yard? Colonel Cranbrough was holding up a cautionary hand, indicating that they should do nothing.

Jay said to Chip: "Do you think we could take the carriage away from the mob?"

"The magistrates don't want any bloodshed," Chip said.

One of Sir John's clerks darted through the crowd and conferred with Cranbrough.

Once across the bridge the mob turned the carriage east. Cranbrough shouted to his men: "Follow at a distance—don't take action!"

The detachment of guards fell in behind the mob. Jay ground his teeth. This was humiliating. A few rounds of musket fire would disperse the crowd in a minute. He could see that Wilkes would make political capital out of being fired on by the troops, but so what?

The carriage was drawn along the Strand and into the heart of the city. The mob sang and danced and shouted "Wilkes and liberty!" and "Number forty-five!" They did not stop until they reached Spitalfields. There the carriage drew up outside the church. Wilkes got out and went into the Three Tuns tavern, followed hastily by Sir John Fielding.

Some of his supporters went in after them, but they could not all get through the door. They milled about in the street for a while, and then Wilkes appeared at an upstairs window, to tumultuous applause. He began to speak. Jay was too far away to hear everything, but he caught the general drift: Wilkes was appealing for order.

During the speech Fielding's clerk came out and spoke to Colonel Cranbrough again. Cranbrough whispered the news to his captains. A deal had been done: Wilkes would slip out of a back door and surrender himself at the King's Bench Prison tonight.

Wilkes finished his speech, waved and bowed, and vanished. As it became clear that he was not going to reappear, the crowd began to get bored and drift away. Sir John came out of the Three Tuns and shook Cranbrough's hand. "A splendid job, Colonel, and my thanks to your men. Bloodshed was avoided and the law was satisfied." He was putting a brave face on it, Jay thought, but the truth was that the law had been laughed at by the mob.

As the guard marched back to Hyde Park, Jay felt depressed. He had been keyed up for a fight all day, and the letdown was hard to bear. But the government could not go on appeasing the mob forever. Sooner or later they would try to clamp down. Then there would be action.

*

When he had dismissed his men and checked that the horses were taken care of, Jay remembered Lennox's proposition. Jay was reluctant to put Lennox's plan to his father, but it would be easier than asking for a hundred and fifty pounds to pay another gambling debt. So he decided to call in at Grosvenor Square on his way home.

It was late. The family had eaten supper, the footman said, and Sir George was in the small study at the back of the house. Jay hesitated in the cold, marble-floored hall. He hated to ask his father for anything.

He would either be scorned for wanting the wrong thing, or reprimanded for demanding more than his due. But he had to go through with it. He knocked on the door and went in.

Sir George was drinking wine and yawning over a list of molasses prices. Jay sat down and said: "Wilkes was refused bail."

"So I heard."

Perhaps his father would like to hear how Jay's regiment had kept the peace. "The mob drew his carriage to Spitalfields, and we followed, but he promised to surrender himself tonight."

"Good. What brings you here so late?"

Jay gave up trying to interest his father in what he had done today. "Did you know that Malachi McAsh has surfaced here in London?"

His father shook his head. "I don't think it matters," he said dismissively.

"He's stirring up trouble among the coal heavers."

"That doesn't take much doing—they're a quarrelsome lot."

"I've been asked to approach you on behalf of the undertakers."

Sir George raised his eyebrows. "Why you?" he said in a tone that implied no one with any sense would employ Jay as an ambassador.

Jay shrugged. "I happen to be acquainted with one particular undertaker, and he asked me to come to you."

"Tavern keepers are a powerful voting group," Sir George said thoughtfully. "What's the proposition?"

"McAsh and his friends have started independent gangs who don't work through the undertakers. The undertakers are asking ship owners to be loyal to them and turn away the new gangs. They feel that if you give a lead the other shippers will follow."

"I'm not sure I should interfere. It's not our battle."

Jay was disappointed. He thought he had put the proposition well. He pretended indifference. "It's nothing to me, but I'm surprised— you're always saying we've got to take a firm line with seditious laboring men who get ideas above their station."

At that moment there was a terrific hammering at the front door. Sir George frowned and Jay stepped into the hall to have a look. A footman hurried past and opened the door. There stood a burly workingman with clogs on his feet and a blue cockade in his greasy cap. "Light up!" he ordered the footman. "Illuminate for Wilkes!"

Sir George emerged from the study and stood with Jay, watching. Jay said: "They do this—make people put candles in all their windows in support of Wilkes."

Sir George said: "What's that on the door?"

They walked forward. The number *45* was chalked on the door. Outside in the square a small mob was going from house to house.

Sir George confronted the man on the doorstep. "Do you know what you've done?" he said. "That number is a code. It means: 'The king is a liar.' Your precious Wilkes has gone to jail for it, and you could too."

"Will you light up for Wilkes?" the man said, ignoring Sir George's speech.

Sir George reddened. It infuriated him when the lower orders failed to treat him with deference. "Go to the devil!" he said, and he slammed the door in the man's face.

He went back to the study and Jay followed him. As they sat down they heard the sound of breaking glass. They both jumped up again and rushed into the dining room at the front of the house. There was a broken pane in one of the two windows and a stone on the polished wood floor. "That's Best Crown Glass!" Sir George said furiously. "Two shillings a square foot!" As they stood staring, another stone crashed through the other window.

Sir George stepped into the hall and spoke to the footman. "Tell everyone to move to the back of the house, out of harm's way," he said.

The footman, looking scared, said: "Wouldn't it be better just to put candles in the windows like they said, sir?"

"Shut your damned mouth and do as you're told," Sir George replied.

There was a third smash somewhere upstairs, and Jay heard his mother scream in fright. He ran up the stairs, his heart pounding, and met her coming out of the drawing room. "Are you all right, Mamma?"

She was pale but calm. "I'm fine—what's happening?"

Sir George came up the stairs saying with suppressed fury: "Nothing to be afraid of, just a damned Wilkesite mob. We'll stay out of the way until they've gone."

As more windows were smashed they all hurried into the small sitting-room at the rear of the house. Jay could see his father was boiling with rage. Being forced to retreat was guaranteed to madden him. This might be the moment to bring up Lennox's request again. Throwing caution to the winds he said: "You know, Father, we really have to start dealing more decisively with these troublemakers."

"What the devil are you talking about?"

"I was thinking of McAsh and the coal heavers. If they're allowed to defy authority once, they'll do it again." It was not like him to speak this way, and he caught a curious glance from his mother. He plowed on. "Better to nip these things in the bud. Teach them to know their place."

Sir George looked as if he were about to make another angry rejoinder; then he hesitated, scowled and said: "You're absolutely right. We'll do it tomorrow."

Jay smiled.

20

A S MACK WALKED DOWN THE MUDDY LANE KNOWN AS WAPPING High Street he felt he knew what it must be like to be king. From every tavern doorway, from windows and yards and rooftops, men waved at him, called out his name and pointed him out to their friends. Everyone wanted to shake his hand. But the men's appreciation was nothing compared with that of their wives. The men were not only bringing home three or four times as much money, they were also ending the day much soberer. The women embraced him in the street and kissed his hands and called to their neighbors, saying: "It's Mack McAsh, the man who defied the undertakers, come quick and see!"

He reached the waterfront and looked over the broad gray river. The tide was high and there were several new ships at anchor. He looked for a boatman to row him out. The traditional undertakers waited at their taverns until the captains came to them and asked for a gang to uncoal their ships: Mack and his gangs went to the captains, saving them time and making sure of the work.

He went out to the *Prince of Denmark* and climbed aboard. The crew had gone ashore, leaving one old sailor smoking a pipe on deck. He directed Mack to the captain's cabin. The skipper was at the table, writing laboriously in the ship's log with a quill pen. "Good day to you, Captain," Mack said with a friendly smile. "I'm Mack McAsh."

"What is it?" the man said gruffly. He did not ask Mack to take a seat.

Mack ignored his rudeness: captains were never very polite. "Would you like your ship uncoaled quickly and efficiently tomorrow?" he said pleasantly.

"No."

Mack was surprised. Had someone got here before him? "Who's going to do it for you, then?"

"None of your damn business."

"It certainly is my business; but if you don't want to tell me, no matter—someone else will."

"Good day to you, then."

Mack frowned. He was reluctant to leave without finding out what was wrong. "What the devil is the trouble with you, Captain—have I done something to offend you?"

"I've nothing more to say to you, young man, and you'll oblige me by taking your leave."

Mack had a bad feeling about this but he could not think of anything else to say, so he left. Ships' captains were a notoriously bad-tempered lot—perhaps because they were away from their wives so much.

He looked along the river. Another new ship, *Whitehaven Jack,* was anchored next to the *Prince.* Her crew were still furling sails and winding ropes into neat coils on the deck. Mack decided to try her next, and got his boatman to take him there.

He found the captain on the poop deck with a young gentleman in sword and wig. He greeted them with the relaxed courtesy which, he had found, was the fastest way to win people's confidence. "Captain, sir, good day to you both."

This captain was polite. "Good day to you. This is Mr. Tallow, the owner's son. What's your business?"

Mack replied: "Would you like your ship uncoaled tomorrow by a fast and sober gang?"

The captain and the gentleman spoke together.

"Yes," said the captain.

"No," said Tallow.

The captain showed surprise and looked questioningly at Tallow. The young man addressed Mack, saying: "You're McAsh, aren't you?"

"Yes. I believe shippers are beginning to take my name as a guarantee of good work—"

"We don't want you," said Tallow.

This second rejection riled Mack. "Why not?" he said challengingly.

"We've done business with Harry Nipper at the Frying Pan for years and never had any trouble."

The captain interjected: "I wouldn't exactly say we've had no trouble."

Tallow glared at him.

Mack said: "And it's not fair that men should be forced to drink their wages, is it?"

Tallow looked piqued. "I'm not going to argue with the likes of you—there's no work for you here, so be off."

Mack persisted. "But why would you want your ship uncoaled in three days by a drunken and rowdy gang when you could have it done faster by my men?"

The captain, who was clearly not overawed by the owner's son, added: "Yes, I'd like to know that."

"Don't you dare to question me, either of you," Tallow said. He was trying to stand on his dignity but he was a little too young to succeed.

A suspicion crossed Mack's mind. "Has someone told you not to hire my gang?" The look on Tallow's face told him he had guessed right.

"You'll find that nobody on the river will hire your gang, or Riley's or Charlie Smith's," Tallow said petulantly. "The word has gone out that you're a troublemaker."

Mack realized this was very serious, and a cold chill settled on his heart. He had known that Lennox and the undertakers would move against him sooner or later, but he had not expected them to be supported by the ship owners.

It was a little puzzling. The old system was not particularly good for the owners. However, they had worked with the undertakers for years, and perhaps sheer conservatism led them to side with people they knew, regardless of justice.

It would be no use to show anger, so he spoke mildly to Tallow. "I'm sorry you've made that decision. It's bad for the men and bad for the owners. I hope you'll reconsider, and I bid you good day."

Tallow made no reply, and Jay had himself rowed ashore. He felt dashed. He held his head in his hands and looked at the filthy brown water of the Thames. What had made him think he could defeat a group of men as wealthy and ruthless as the undertakers? They had connections and support. Who was he? Mack McAsh from Heugh.

He should have foreseen this.

He jumped ashore and made his way to St. Luke's Coffee House, which had become his unofficial headquarters. There were now at least five gangs working the new system. Next Saturday night, when the remaining old-style gangs received their decimated wages from the rapacious tavern keepers, most of them would change over. But the shippers' boycott would ruin that prospect.

The coffeehouse was next to St. Luke's Church. It served beer and spirits as well as coffee, and food too, but everyone sat down to eat and drink, whereas most stood up in a tavern.

Cora was there, eating bread and butter. Although it was midafternoon, this was her breakfast: she was often up half the night. Mack asked for a plate of hashed mutton and a tankard of beer and sat down with her. Straightaway she said: "What's the matter?"

He told her. As he talked he watched her innocent face. She was ready for work, dressed in the orange gown she had worn the first time he had met her and scented with her spicy perfume. She looked like a picture of the Virgin Mary, but she smelled like a sultan's harem. It was no wonder that drunks with gold in their purses were willing to follow her down dark alleys, he thought.

He had spent three of the last six nights with her. She wanted to buy him a new coat. He wanted her to give up the life she led. She was his first real lover.

As he was finishing his story, Dermot and Charlie came in. He had been cherishing a faint hope that they might have had better luck than he, but their expressions told him they had not. Charlie's black face was a picture of despondency, and Dermot said in his Irish brogue: "The owners have conspired against us. There's not a captain on the river that will give us work."

"Damn their eyes," Mack said. The boycott was working and he was in trouble.

He suffered a moment of righteous indignation. All he wanted was to work hard and earn enough money to buy his sister's freedom, but he was constantly thwarted by people who had money in bagfuls.

Dermot said: "We're finished, Mack."

His readiness to give up angered Mack more than the boycott itself. "Finished?" he said scornfully. "Are you a man or what?"

"But what can we do?" said Dermot. "If the owners won't hire our gangs, the men will go back to the old system. They've got to live."

Without thinking, Mack said: "We could organize a strike."

The other men were silent.

Cora said: "Strike?"

Mack had blurted out his suggestion as soon as it came into his mind but, as he thought more, it seemed the only thing to do. "All the coal heavers want to change to our system," he said. "We could persuade them to stop working for the old undertakers. Then the shippers would have to hire the new gangs."

Dermot was skeptical. "Suppose they still refuse to hire us?"

This pessimism angered Mack. Why did men always expect the worst? "If they do that, no coal will come ashore."

"What will the men live on?"

"They can afford to take a few days off. It happens all the time—when there are no coal ships in port none of us work."

"That's true. But we couldn't hold out forever."

Mack wanted to scream with frustration. "Nor can the shippers—London must have coal!"

Dermot still looked dubious. Cora said: "But what else can you do, Dermot?"

Dermot frowned, and he thought for a moment, then his face cleared. "I'd hate to go back to the old ways. I'll give it a try, by gob."

"Good!" said Mack, relieved.

"I was in a strike once," Charlie said lugubriously. "It's the wives that suffer."

"When were you in a strike?" Mack asked. He had no experience: it was something he had read about in the newspapers.

"Three years ago, on Tyneside. I was a coal miner."

"I didn't know you'd been a miner." It had never occurred to Mack, or anyone in Heugh, that miners could strike. "How did it end?"

"The coal owners gave in," Charlie admitted.

"There you are!" Mack said triumphantly.

Cora said anxiously: "You're not up against northern landowners here, Mack. You're talking about London tavern keepers, the scum of the earth. They might just send someone to cut your throat while you sleep."

Mack looked into her eyes and saw that she was genuinely frightened for him. "I'll take precautions," he said.

She gave him a skeptical look but said no more.

Dermot said: "It's the men that will have to be persuaded."

"That's right," Mack said decisively. "There's no point in the four of us discussing it as if we had the power to make the decision. We'll call a meeting. What o'clock is it?"

They all glanced outside. It was becoming evening. Cora said: "It must be six."

Mack went on: "The gangs that are working today will finish as soon as it gets dark. You two go around all the taverns along the High Street and spread the word."

They both nodded. Charlie said: "We can't meet here—it's too small. There are about fifty gangs altogether."

"The Jolly Sailor's got a big courtyard," said Dermot. "And the landlord's not an undertaker."

"Right," Mack agreed. "Tell them to be there an hour after nightfall."

"They won't all get there," said Charlie.

"Most will, though."

Dermot said: "We'll round up as many as we can." He and Charlie went out.

Mack looked at Cora. "Are you taking an evening off?" he said hopefully.

She shook her head. "Just waiting for my accomplice."

It troubled Mack that Peg was a thief and Cora was responsible. "I wish we could find a way for that child to make a living without stealing," he said.

"Why?"

The question flummoxed him. "Well, obviously . . ."

"Obviously what?"

"It would be better if she grew up honest."

"How would it be better?"

Mack heard the undertone of anger in Cora's questions, but he could not back off now. "What she does now is dangerous. She could end up hanging at Tyburn."

"Would she be better off scrubbing the kitchen floor in some rich house, beaten by the cook and raped by the master?"

"I don't think every kitchen skivvy gets raped—"

"Every pretty one does. And how would I make a living without her?"

"You could do anything, you're shrewd and beautiful—"

"I don't want to do *anything,* Mack, I want to do this."

"Why?"

"I like it. I like dressing up and drinking gin and flirting. I steal from stupid men who have more money than they deserve. It's exciting and it's easy and I make ten times as much as I'd get dressmaking or running a little shop or serving customers in a coffeehouse."

He was shocked. He had thought she would say she stole because she had to. The notion that she liked it overturned his expectations. "I really don't know you," he said.

"You're clever, Mack, but you don't know a damn thing."

Peg arrived. She was pale and thin and tired, as always. Mack said: "Have you had some breakfast?"

"No," she said, sitting down. "I'd love a glass of gin."

Mack waved at a waiter. "A bowl of porridge with cream, please."

Peg made a face, but when the food came she tucked in with relish.

While she was eating, Caspar Gordonson came in. Mack was glad to see him: he had been thinking of calling at the Fleet Street house to discuss the shippers' boycott and the idea of a strike. Now he swiftly ran over the day's events while the untidy lawyer sipped brandy.

As Mack talked, Gordonson looked more and more worried. When he had done, the lawyer began to speak in his high-pitched voice. "You have to understand that our rulers are frightened. Not just the royal court and the government, but the entire top layer: dukes and earls, aldermen, judges, merchants, landowners. All this talk of liberty unnerves them, and the food riots last year and the year before showed them what the people can do when they're angry."

"Good!" said Mack. "Then they should give us what we want."

"Not necessarily. They're afraid that if they do that you'll only ask for more. What they really want is an excuse to call out the troops and shoot people."

Mack could see that behind Gordonson's cool analysis lay real fear. "Do they need an excuse?"

"Oh, yes. That's because of John Wilkes. He's a real thorn in their flesh. He accuses the government of being despotic. And as soon as troops are used against citizens, then thousands of people of the middling sort will say: 'There, Wilkes was right, this government is a tyranny.' And all those shopkeepers and silversmiths and bakers have votes."

"So what kind of excuse does the government need?"

"They want you to scare those middling people by violence and rioting. That will get people worrying about the need to maintain order, and stop them thinking about freedom of speech. Then, when the army marches in, there will be a collective sigh of relief instead of a roar of outrage."

Mack was fascinated and unnerved. He had never thought about politics this way. He had discussed high-flown theories out of books, and he had been the helpless victim of unjust laws, but this was halfway between the two. This was the zone where contending forces struggled and swayed, and tactics could alter the result. This, he felt, was the real thing—and it was dangerous.

The enchantment was lost on Gordonson: he just looked worried. "I got you into this, Mack, and if you get killed it will be on my conscience."

His fear began to infect Mack. Four months ago I was just a coal miner, he thought; now I'm an enemy of the government, someone they want to kill. Did I ask for this? But he was under a powerful obligation. Just as Gordonson felt responsible for him, he was responsible for the coal heavers. He could not run away and hide. It would be shameful and cowardly. He had led the men into trouble and now he had to lead them out of it.

"What do you think we should do?" he asked Gordonson.

"If the men agree to strike, your job will be to keep them under control. You'll have to stop them setting fire to ships and murdering strikebreakers and laying siege to undertakers' taverns. These men aren't parsons, as you well know—they're young and strong and angry, and if they run riot they'll burn London."

"I think I might be able to do that," Mack said. "They listen to me. They seem to respect me."

"They worship you," Gordonson said. "And that puts you in even greater danger. You're a ringleader, and the government may break the strike by hanging you. From the moment the men say yes, you'll be in terrible danger."

Mack was beginning to wish he had never mentioned the word "strike." He said: "What should I do?"

"Leave the place where you're lodging and move somewhere else. Keep your address secret from all but a few trusted people."

Cora said: "Come and live with me."

Mack managed a smile. That part would not be difficult.

Gordonson went on: "Don't show yourself on the streets in daylight. Appear at meetings, then vanish. Become a ghost."

It was faintly ridiculous, Mack felt, but his fear made him accept it. "All right."

Cora got up to leave. To Mack's surprise, Peg put her arms around his waist and hugged him. "Be careful, Scotch Jock," she said. "Don't get knifed."

Mack was surprised and touched by how much they all cared for him. Three months ago he had never met Peg, Cora or Gordonson.

Cora kissed him on the lips and then sauntered out, already swaying her hips seductively. Peg followed.

A few moments later Mack and Gordonson left for the Jolly Sailor. It was dark, but Wapping High Street was busy, and candlelight gleamed from tavern doorways, house windows and handheld lanterns. The tide was out, and a strong smell of rottenness wafted up from the foreshore.

Mack was surprised to see the tavern's courtyard packed with men. There were about eight hundred coal heavers in London, and at least half of them were here. Someone had hastily erected a crude platform and placed four blazing torches around it for illumination. Mack pushed through the crowd. Every man recognized him and spoke a word or clapped him on the back. The news of his arrival spread quickly and they started to cheer. By the time he reached the platform they were roaring. He stepped up and gazed at them. Hundreds of coal-smeared faces looked back at him in the torchlight. He fought back tears of gratitude for their trust in him. He could not speak: they were shouting too loudly. He held up his hands for quiet, but it did no good. Some cried his name, others yelled "Wilkes and liberty!" and other slogans. Gradually one chant emerged and came to dominate the rest, until they were all bellowing the same:

"Strike! Strike! Strike!"

Mack stood and stared at them, thinking: What have I done?

21

J AY JAMISSON RECEIVED A NOTE FROM HIS FATHER AT BREAKFAST
time. It was characteristically curt.

> *Grosvenor Square*
>
> *8 o'clock a.m.*

Meet me at my place of business at noon.

> *—G.J.*

His first guilty thought was that Father had found out about the deal
he had made with Lennox.

It had gone off perfectly. The shippers had boycotted the new coal
heaving gangs, as Lennox had wanted; and Lennox had returned Jay's
IOUs, as agreed. But now the coal heavers were on strike and no coal
had been landed in London for a week. Had Father discovered that all
that might not have happened but for Jay's gambling debts? The
thought was dreadful.

He went to the Hyde Park encampment as usual and got permission
from Colonel Cranbrough to be absent in the middle of the day. He
spent the morning worrying. His bad temper made his men surly and
his horses skittish.

The church bells were striking twelve as he entered the Jamissons'
riverside warehouse. The dusty air was laden with spicy smells—coffee

and cinnamon, rum and port, pepper and oranges. It always made Jay think of his childhood, when the barrels and tea-chests had seemed so much bigger. Now he felt as he had as a boy, when he had done something naughty and was about to be carpeted. He crossed the floor, acknowledging the deferential greetings of the men, and climbed a rickety wooden staircase to the counting-house. After passing through a lobby occupied by clerks he went into his father's office, a corner room full of maps and bills and pictures of ships.

"Good morning, Father," he said. "Where's Robert?" His brother was almost always at Father's side.

"He had to go to Rochester. But this concerns you more than him. Sir Philip Armstrong wants to see me."

Armstrong was the right-hand man of Secretary of State Viscount Weymouth. Jay felt even more nervous. Was he in trouble with the government as well as with his father? "What does Armstrong want?"

"He wants this coal strike brought to an end and he knows we started it."

This did not seem to have anything to do with gambling debts, Jay inferred. But he was still anxious.

"He'll be here any moment now," Father added.

"Why is he coming here?" Such an important personage would normally summon people to his office in Whitehall.

"Secrecy, I imagine."

Before he could ask any more questions the door opened and Armstrong came in. Both Jay and Sir George stood up. Armstrong was a middle-aged man formally dressed with wig and sword. He walked with his nose a little high, as if to show that he did not usually descend into the mire of commercial activity. Sir George did not like him—Jay could tell by his father's expression as he shook hands and asked Armstrong to sit down.

Armstrong refused a glass of wine. "This strike has to end," he said. "The coal heavers have closed down half of London's industry."

Sir George said: "We tried to get the sailors to uncoal the ships. It worked for a day or two."

"What went wrong?"

"They were persuaded, or intimidated, or both, and now they are on strike too."

"And the watermen," Armstrong said with exasperation. "And even before the coal dispute started, there was trouble with tailors, silk weavers, hatters, sawyers. . . . This cannot go on."

"But why have you come to me, Sir Philip?"

"Because I understand you were influential in starting the shippers' boycott which provoked the coal heavers."

"It's true."

"May I ask why?"

Sir George looked at Jay, who swallowed nervously and said: "I was approached by the undertakers who organize the coal heaving gangs. My father and I did not want the established order on the waterfront to be disturbed."

"Quite right, I'm sure," Armstrong said, and Jay thought: Get to the point. "Do you know who the ringleaders are?"

"I certainly do," Jay said. "The most important is a man called Malachi McAsh, known as Mack. As it happens, he used to be a coal hewer in my father's mines."

"I'd like to see McAsh arrested and charged with a capital offense under the Riot Act. But it would have to be plausible: no trumped-up charges or bribed witnesses. There would have to be a real riot, unmistakably led by striking workmen, with firearms used against officers of the Crown, and numerous people killed and injured."

Jay was confused. Was Armstrong telling the Jamissons to organize such a riot?

His father showed no sign of puzzlement. "You make yourself very clear, Sir Philip." He looked at Jay. "Do you know where McAsh can be found?"

"No," he said. Then, seeing the expression of scorn on his father's face, he added hastily: "But I'm sure I can find out."

＊

At daybreak Mack woke Cora and made love to her. She had come to bed in the small hours, smelling of tobacco smoke, and he had kissed her and gone back to sleep. Now he was wide awake and she was the sleepy one. Her body was warm and relaxed, her skin soft, her red hair tangled. She wrapped her arms around him loosely and moaned quietly, and at the end she gave a small cry of delight. Then she went back to sleep.

He watched her for a while. Her face was perfect, small and pink and regular. But her way of life troubled him more and more. It seemed hard-hearted to use a child as her accomplice. If he talked to her about it, she got angry and told him that he was guilty too, for he was living here rent free and eating the food she bought with her ill-gotten gains.

He sighed and got up.

Cora's home was the upstairs floor of a tumbledown building in a coal yard. The yard owner had once lived here, but when he prospered he had moved. Now he used the ground floor as an office and rented the upper floor to Cora.

There were two rooms, a big bed in one and a table and chairs in the other. The bedroom was full of what Cora spent all her money on: clothes. Both Esther and Annie had owned two dresses, one for work and one for Sundays, but Cora had eight or ten different outfits, all in striking colors: yellow, red, bright green and rich brown. She had shoes to match each one, and as many stockings and gloves and handkerchiefs as a fine lady.

He washed his face, dressed quickly and left. A few minutes later he was at Dermot's house. The family were eating their breakfast porridge. Mack smiled at the children. Every time he used Cora's "cundum" he wondered if he would have children of his own someday. At times he thought he would like Cora to have his baby; then he remembered how she lived and changed his mind.

Mack refused a bowl of porridge, for he knew they could not spare it. Dermot, like Mack, was living off a woman: his wife washed pots in a coffeehouse in the evenings while he took care of the children.

"You've got a letter," Dermot said, and handed Mack a sealed note.

Mack recognized the handwriting. It was almost identical with his own. The letter was from Esther. He felt a stab of guilt. He was supposed to be saving money for her, but he was on strike and penniless.

"Where's it to be today?" Dermot said. Every day Mack met his lieutenants at a different location.

"The back bar of the Queen's Head tavern," Mack replied.

"I'll spread the word." Dermot put his hat on and went out.

Mack opened his letter and began to read.

It was full of news. Annie was pregnant, and if the child turned out to be a boy they would call him Mack. For some reason that brought tears to Mack's eyes. The Jamissons were sinking a new coal pit in High Glen, on the Hallim estate: they had dug fast and Esther would be working there as a bearer within a few days. That news was surprising: Mack had heard Lizzie say she would never allow coal mining in High Glen. The Reverend Mr. York's wife had taken a fever and died: no shock there, she had always been sickly. And Esther was still determined to leave Heugh as soon as Mack could save the money.

He folded the letter and pocketed it. He must not let anything undermine his determination. He would win the strike, then he would be able to save.

He kissed Dermot's children and went along to the Queen's Head.

His men were already arriving, and he got down to business right away.

One-Eye Wilson, a coal heaver who had been sent to check on new ships anchoring in the river, reported two coal carriers arrived on the morning tide. "From Sunderland, both of them," he said. "I spoke to a sailor who came ashore for bread."

Mack turned to Charlie Smith. "Go on board the ships and talk to the captains, Charlie. Explain why we're on strike and ask them to wait patiently. Say we hope the shippers will soon give in and allow the new gangs to uncoal the ships."

One-Eye interjected: "Why send a nigger? They might listen better to an Englishman."

"I am an Englishman," Charlie said indignantly.

Mack said: "Most of these captains were born in the northeast coal field, and Charlie speaks with their accent. Anyway, he's done this sort of thing before and he's proved himself a good ambassador."

"No offense, Charlie," said One-Eye.

Charlie shrugged and left to do his assigned task. A woman rushed in, pushing past him, and approached Mack's table, breathless and flustered. Mack recognized Sairey, the wife of a bellicose coal heaver called Buster McBride. "Mack, they've caught a sailor bringing a sack of coal ashore and I'm afraid Buster will kill him."

"Where are they?"

"They've put him in the outhouse at the Swan and locked him in, but Buster's drinking and he wants to hang him upside-down from the clock tower, and some of the others are egging him on."

This kind of thing happened constantly. The coal heavers were always on the edge of violence. So far Mack had been able to rein them in. He picked a big, affable boy called Pigskin Pollard. "Go along there and calm the boys down, Pigskin. The last thing we want is a murder."

"I'm on my way," he said.

Caspar Gordonson arrived with egg yolk on his shirt and a note in his hand. "There's a barge train bringing coal to London along the river Lea. It should arrive at Enfield Lock this afternoon."

"Enfield," Mack said. "How far away is that?"

"Twelve miles," Gordonson replied. "We can get there by midday, even if we walk."

"Good. We must get control of the lock and prevent the barges passing. I'd like to go myself. I'll take twelve steady men."

Another coal heaver came in. "Fat Sam Barrows, the landlord of the Green Man, is trying to recruit a gang to uncoal the *Spirit of Jarrow*," he said.

"He'd be lucky," Mack commented. "Nobody likes Fat Sam: he's never paid honest wages in his life. Still, we'd better keep an eye on the tavern, just in case. Will Trimble, go along there and snoop about. Let me know if there's any danger of Sam getting sixteen men."

✳

"He's gone to ground," said Sidney Lennox. "He's left his lodgings and no one knows where he went."

Jay felt awful. He had told his father, in front of Sir Philip

Armstrong, that he could locate McAsh. He wished he had said nothing. If he failed to deliver on his promise, his father's scorn would be blistering.

He had been counting on Lennox to know where to find McAsh. "But if he's in hiding, how does he run the strike?" he said.

"He appears every morning at a different coffeehouse. Somehow his henchmen know where to go. He gives his orders and vanishes until the next day."

"Someone must know where he lays his head," Jay said plaintively. "If we can find him, we can smash this strike."

Lennox nodded. He more than anyone wanted to see the coal heavers defeated. "Well, Caspar Gordonson must know."

Jay shook his head. "That's no use to us. Does McAsh have a woman?"

"Yes—Cora. But she's as tough as a boot. She won't tell."

"There must be someone else."

"There's the kid," Lennox said thoughtfully.

"Kid?"

"Quick Peg. She goes robbing with Cora. I wonder . . ."

✳

At midnight Lord Archer's coffeehouse was packed with officers, gentlemen and whores. The air was full of tobacco smoke and the smell of spilled wine. A fiddler was playing in a corner but he could hardly be heard over the roar of a hundred shouted conversations.

Several card games were in progress, but Jay was not playing. He was drinking. The idea was for him to pretend to be drunk, and at first he had tipped most of his brandy down the front of his waistcoat; but as the evening wore on he drank more, and now he did not have to make much effort to appear unsteady on his feet. Chip Marlborough had been drinking seriously from the start of the evening, but he never seemed to get drunk.

Jay was too worried to enjoy himself. His father would never listen to excuses. Jay had to produce an address for McAsh. He had toyed with the idea of making one up, then claiming McAsh must have moved again; but he felt his father would know he was lying.

So he was drinking in Archer's and hoping to meet Cora. During the course of the evening numerous girls had approached him, but none fitted the description of Cora: pretty face, flaming red hair, age about nineteen or twenty. Each time, he and Chip would flirt for a while, until the girl realized they were not serious and moved on. Sidney Lennox was a watchful presence on the far side of the room, smoking a pipe and playing faro for low stakes.

Jay was beginning to think they would be unlucky tonight. There were a hundred girls like Cora in Covent Garden. He might have to repeat this performance tomorrow, and even the day after, before running into her. And he had a wife waiting at home who did not understand why he needed to spend the evening in a place where respectable ladies were not seen.

Just as he was thinking wistfully of climbing into a warm bed and finding Lizzie there, eager and waiting, Cora came in.

Jay was sure it was she. She was easily the prettiest girl in the room, and her hair really was the color of the flames in the fireplace. She was dressed like a whore in a red silk dress with a low neckline and red shoes with bows, and she scanned the room with a professional gaze.

Jay looked over at Lennox and saw him nod slowly twice.

Thank God, he thought.

He looked away, caught Cora's eye and smiled.

He saw a faint flash of recognition in her expression, as if she knew who he was; then she smiled back and came over.

Jay felt nervous and told himself that he only had to be charming. He had charmed a hundred women. He kissed her hand. She wore a heady perfume with sandalwood in it. "I thought I knew every beautiful woman in London, but I was wrong," he said gallantly. "I'm Captain Jonathan and this is Captain Chip." Jay had decided not to use his real name in case Mack had mentioned him to Cora. If she found out who he was she would be sure to smell a rat.

"I'm Cora," she said, giving them a once-over look. "What a handsome pair. I can't decide which captain I like best."

Chip said: "My family is nobler than Jay's."

"But mine's richer," said Jay, and for some reason that made them both giggle.

"If you're so rich, buy me a measure of brandy," she said.

Jay waved at a waiter and offered her a seat.

She squeezed in between him and Chip on the bench. He smelled gin on her breath. He looked down at her shoulders and the swell of her breasts. He could not help comparing her with his wife. Lizzie was short but voluptuous, with wide hips and a deep bosom. Cora was taller and more slender, and her breasts looked to him like two apples lying side by side in a bowl.

Giving him a quizzical look she said: "Do I know you?"

He felt a stab of anxiety. Surely they had never met? "I don't think so," he said. If she recognized him the game would be up.

"You look familiar. I know I've never spoken to you, but I've seen you."

"Now's our chance to get to know one another," he said with a desperate smile. He put his arm over the back of the seat and stroked her neck. She closed her eyes as if she were enjoying it, and Jay began to relax.

She was so convincing that he almost forgot she was pretending. She put a hand on his thigh, close to his crotch. He told himself not to enjoy this too much: he was supposed to be playacting. He wished he had not drunk so much. He might need his wits about him.

Her brandy came and she drank it in a gulp. "Come on, big boy," she said. "We'd better get some air before you burst out of those breeches."

Jay realized he had a visible erection, and he blushed.

Cora stood up and headed for the door, and Jay followed.

When they were outside she put her arm around his waist and led him along the colonnaded sidewalk of the Covent Garden piazza. He draped an arm over her shoulder, then worked his hand into the bosom of her dress and played with her nipple. She giggled and turned into an alley.

They embraced and kissed, and he squeezed both her breasts. He forgot all about Lennox and the plot: Cora was warm and willing and he wanted her. Her hands were all over him, undoing his waistcoat, rubbing his chest, and diving into his breeches. He pushed his tongue into her mouth and tried to lift her skirts up at the same time. He felt cold air on his belly.

From behind him there came a childish scream. Cora gave a start and pushed Jay away. She looked over his shoulder then turned as if to run, but Chip Marlborough appeared and grabbed her before she took the first step.

Jay turned around and saw Lennox struggling to keep hold of a screaming, scratching, wriggling child. As they struggled the child dropped several objects. In the starlight Jay recognized his own wallet and pocket watch, silk handkerchief and silver seal. She had been picking his pockets while he was kissing Cora. Even though he was expecting it he had felt nothing. But he had entered very fully into the part he was playing.

The child stopped struggling and Lennox said: "We're taking you two before a magistrate. Picking pockets is a hanging offense."

Jay looked around, half expecting Cora's friends to come rushing to her defense; but no one had seen the scuffle in the alley.

Chip glanced at Jay's crotch and said: "You can put your weapon away, Captain Jamisson—the battle is over."

*

Most wealthy and powerful men were magistrates and Sir George Jamisson was no exception. Although he never held open court, he had the right to try cases at home. He could order offenders to be flogged, branded or imprisoned, and he had the power to commit more serious offenders to the Old Bailey for trial.

He was expecting Jay, so he had not gone to bed, but all the same he was irritable at having been kept up so late. "I expected you around ten o'clock," he said grumpily when they all trooped into the drawing room of the Grosvenor Square house.

Cora, dragged in by Chip Marlborough with her hands tied, said: "So you were expecting us! This was all planned—you evil pigs."

Sir George said: "Shut your mouth or I'll have you flogged around the square before we begin."

Cora seemed to believe him, for she said no more.

He drew paper toward him and dipped a pen in an inkwell. "Jay Jamisson, Esquire, is the prosecutor. He complains that his pocket was picked by . . ."

Lennox said: "She's called Quick Peg, sir."

"I can't write that down," Sir George snapped. "What is your real name, child?"

"Peggy Knapp, sir."

"And the woman's name?"

"Cora Higgins," said Cora.

"Pocket picked by Peggy Knapp, accomplice Cora Higgins. The crime witnessed by . . ."

"Sidney Lennox, keeper of the Sun tavern in Wapping."

"And Captain Marlborough?"

Chip raised his hands in a defensive gesture. "I'd rather not get involved, if Mr. Lennox's evidence will suffice."

"It surely will, Captain," said Sir George. He was always polite to Chip because he owed Chip's father money. "Very good of you to assist in the apprehension of these thieves. Now, have the accused anything to say?"

Cora said: "I'm not her accomplice—I've never seen her before in my life." Peg gasped and stared at Cora in disbelief, but Cora carried on. "I went for a walk with a handsome young man, that's all. I never knew she was picking his pockets."

Lennox said: "The two are known associates, Sir George—I've seen them together many times."

"I've heard enough," Sir George said. "You are both committed to Newgate Prison on charges of pickpocketing."

Peg began to cry. Cora was white with fear. "Why are you all doing this?" she said. She pointed an accusing finger at Jay. "You were waiting for me in Archer's." She pointed at Lennox. "You followed us out. And you, Sir George Jamisson, stayed up late, when you should be in bed, to commit us. What's the point of it all? What have Peg and me ever done to you?"

Sir George ignored her. "Captain Marlborough, oblige me by taking the woman outside and guarding her for a few moments." They all waited while Chip led Cora out and closed the door. Then Sir George turned to Peg. "Now, child, what is the punishment for picking pockets—do you know?"

She was pale and trembling. "The sheriff's collar," she whispered.

"If you mean hanging, you're right. But did you know that some people are not hanged, but sent to America instead?"

The child nodded.

"They are people who have influential friends to plead for them, and beg the judge to be merciful. Do you have influential friends?"

She shook her head.

"Well, now, what if I tell you that I will be your influential friend and intercede for you?"

She looked up at him, and hope gleamed in her little face.

"But you have to do something for me."

"What?" she said.

"I will save you from hanging if you tell us where Mack McAsh is living."

The room was silent for a long moment.

"In the attic over the coal yard in Wapping High Street," she said, and she burst into tears.

22

MACK WAS SURPRISED TO WAKE UP ALONE.

Cora had never before stayed out until daybreak. He had been living with her for only two weeks and he did not know all her habits, but all the same he was worried.

He got up and followed his usual routine. He spent the morning at St. Luke's Coffee House, sending messages and receiving reports. He asked everyone if they had seen or heard of Cora, but no one had. He sent someone to the Sun tavern to speak to Quick Peg, but she too had been out all night and had not returned.

In the afternoon he walked to Covent Garden and went around the taverns and coffeehouses, questioning the whores and waiters. Several people had seen Cora last night. A waiter at Lord Archer's had noticed her leaving with a rich young drunk. After that there was no trace.

He went to Dermot's lodgings in Spitalfields, hoping for news. Dermot was feeding his children a broth made of bones for their supper. He had been asking after Cora all day and had heard nothing.

Mack walked home in the dark, hoping that when he arrived at Cora's apartment over the coal yard she would be there, lying on the bed in her underwear, waiting for him. But the place was cold and dark and empty.

He lit a candle and sat brooding. Outside on Wapping High Street the taverns were filling up. Although the coal heavers were on strike they still found money for beer. Mack would have liked to join them, but for safety he did not show his face in the taverns at night.

He ate some bread and cheese and read a book Gordonson had loaned him, a novel called *Tristram Shandy*, but he could not concentrate. Late in the evening, when he was beginning to wonder if Cora was dead, there was a commotion in the street outside.

He heard men shouting and the noise of running feet and what sounded like several horses and carts. Fearing that the coal heavers might start some kind of fracas he went to the window.

The sky was clear and there was a half-moon, so Mack could see all along the High Street. Ten or twelve horse-drawn carts were lumbering down the uneven dirt road in the moonlight, evidently headed for the coal yard. A crowd of men followed the carts, jeering and shouting, and more spilled out of the taverns and joined them at every corner.

The scene had all the makings of a riot.

Mack cursed. It was the last thing he wanted.

He turned from the window and rushed down the stairs. If he could talk to the men with the carts and persuade them not to unload, he might avert violence.

When he reached the street the first cart was turning into the coal yard. As he ran forward the men jumped off the carts and, without warning, began to throw lumps of coal at the crowd. Some of the heavers were hit; others picked up the lumps of coal and threw them back. Mack heard a woman scream and saw children being herded indoors.

"Stop!" he yelled. He ran between the coal heavers and the carts with his hands held up. "Stop!" The men recognized him and for a moment there was quiet. He was grateful to see Charlie Smith's face in the crowd. "Try to keep order here, Charlie, for God's sake," he said. "I'll talk to these people."

"Everybody stay calm," Charlie called out. "Leave it to Mack."

Mack turned his back on the heavers. On either side of the narrow street, people were standing on house doorsteps, curious to see what was happening but ready to duck quickly inside. There were at least five men on each coal cart. In the unnatural silence Mack approached the lead cart. "Who's in charge here?" he said.

A figure stepped forward in the moonlight. "I am."

Mack recognized Sidney Lennox.

He was shocked and puzzled. What was going on here? Why was Lennox trying to deliver coal to a yard? He had a cold premonition of disaster.

He spotted the owner of the yard, Jack Cooper, known as Black Jack because he was always covered in black dust like a miner. "Jack, close up the gates of your yard, for God's sake," he pleaded. "There'll be murder done if you let this go on."

Cooper looked sulky. "I've got to make a living."

"You will, as soon as the strike is over. You don't want to see bloodshed on Wapping High Street, do you?"

"I've set my hand to the plow and I'll not look back now."

Mack gave him a hard look. "Who asked you to do this, Jack? Is there someone else involved?"

"I'm my own man—no one tells me what to do."

Mack began to see what was happening, and it made him angry. He turned to Lennox. "You've paid him off. But why?"

They were interrupted by the sound of a handbell being rung loudly. Mack turned to see three people standing at the upstairs window of the Frying Pan tavern. One was ringing the bell, another holding a lantern. The third man, in the middle, wore the wig and sword that marked him as someone of importance.

When the bell stopped ringing, the third man announced himself. "I am Roland MacPherson, a justice of the peace in Wapping, and I hereby declare a riot." He went on to read the key section of the Riot Act.

Once a riot had been declared, everyone had to disperse within an hour. Defiance was punishable by death.

The magistrate had got here quickly, Mack thought. Clearly he had been expecting this and waiting in the tavern for his cue. This whole episode had been carefully planned.

But to what end? It seemed to him they wanted to provoke a riot that would discredit the coal heavers and give them a pretext to hang the ringleaders. And that meant him.

His first reaction was aggressive. He wanted to yell, "If they're asking for a riot, by God we'll give them one they'll never forget—

we'll burn London before we're done!" He wanted to get his hands around Lennox's throat. But he forced himself to be calm and think clearly. How could he frustrate Lennox's plan?

His only hope was to give in and let the coal be delivered.

He turned to the coal heavers, gathered in an angry crowd around the open gates of the yard. "Listen to me," he began. "This is a plot to provoke us into a riot. If we all go home peacefully we will outwit our enemies. If we stay and fight, we're lost."

There was a rumble of discontent.

Dear God, Mack thought, these men are stupid. "Don't you understand?" he said. "They want an excuse to hang some of us. Why give them what they want? Let's go home tonight and fight on tomorrow!"

"He's right," Charlie piped up. "Look who's here—Sidney Lennox. He's up to no good, we can be sure of that."

Some of the coal heavers were nodding agreement now, and Mack began to think he might persuade them. Then he heard Lennox's voice yell: "Get him!"

Several men came at Mack at once. He turned to run, but one tackled him and he crashed to the muddy ground. As he struggled he heard the coal heavers roar, and he knew that what he had dreaded was about to begin: a pitched battle.

He was kicked and punched but he hardly felt the blows as he struggled to get up. Then the men attacking him were thrown aside by coal heavers and he regained his feet.

He looked around swiftly. Lennox had vanished. The rival gangs filled the narrow street. He saw fierce hand-to-hand fighting on all sides. The horses bucked and strained in their traces, neighing in terror. His instincts made him want to join in the fray and start knocking people down, but he held himself back. What was the quickest way to end this? He tried to think fast. The coal heavers would not retreat: it was against their nature. The best bet might be to get them into a defensive position and hope for a standoff.

He grabbed Charlie. "We'll try to get inside the coal yard and close the gates on them," he said. "Tell the men!"

Charlie ran from man to man spreading the order, shouting at the top of his voice to be heard over the noise of the battle: "Inside the yard and close the gates! Keep them out of the yard!" Then, to his horror, Mack heard the bang of a musket.

"What the hell is going on?" he said, although no one was listening. Since when did coal drivers carry firearms? Who were these people?

He saw a blunderbuss, a musket with a shortened barrel, pointed at him. Before he could move, Charlie snatched the gun, turned it on the man who held it, and shot him at point-blank range. The man fell dead.

Mack cursed. Charlie could hang for that.

Someone rushed him. Mack sidestepped and swung a fist. His blow landed on the point of the chin and the man fell down.

Mack backed away and tried to think. The whole thing was taking place right outside Mack's window. That must have been intentional. They had found out his address somehow. Who had betrayed him?

The first shots were followed by a ragged tattoo of gunfire. Flashes lit up the night and the smell of gunpowder mingled with the coal dust in the air. Mack cried out in protest as several coal heavers fell dead or wounded: their wives and widows would blame him, and they would be right. He had started something he could not control.

Most of the coal heavers got into the yard where there was a supply of coal to throw. They fought frenziedly to keep the coal drivers out. The yard walls gave them cover from the musket fire that rattled intermittently.

The hand-to-hand fighting was fiercest at the yard entrance, and Mack saw that if he could get the high wooden gates closed the entire battle might peter out. He fought his way through the melee, got behind one of the heavy timber gates, and started to push. Some of the coal heavers saw what he was attempting and joined in. The big gate swept several scuffling men out of the way, and Mack thought they would get it shut in a moment; then it was blocked by a cart.

Gasping for breath, Mack shouted: "Move the cart, move the cart!"

His plan was already having some effect, he saw with an access of hope. The angled gate made a partial barrier between the two sides. Furthermore, the first excitement of the battle had passed, and the men's zest for fighting had been tempered by injuries and bruises and the sight of some of their comrades lying dead or wounded. The instinct of self-preservation was reasserting itself, and they were looking for ways to disengage with dignity.

Mack began to think he might end the fighting soon. If the confrontation could be stalled before someone called out the troops, the whole thing might be perceived as a minor skirmish and the strike could continue to be seen as a mainly peaceful protest.

A dozen coal heavers began to drag the cart out of the yard while others pushed the gates. Someone cut the horse's traces, and the frightened beast ran around in a panic, neighing and kicking. "Keep pushing, don't stop!" Mack yelled as huge lumps of coal rained down on them. The cart inched out and the gates closed the gap with maddening slowness.

Then Mack heard a noise that wiped out all his hopes at a stroke: the sound of marching feet.

✴

The guards marched down Wapping High Street, their white-and-red uniforms gleaming in the moonlight. Jay rode at the head of the column, keeping his horse close-reined at a brisk walk. He was about to get what he had said he wanted: action.

He kept his face expressionless but his heart was pounding. He could hear the roar of the battle Lennox had started: men shouting, horses neighing, muskets banging. Jay had never yet used a sword or gun in anger: tonight would be his first engagement. He told himself that a rabble of coal heavers would be terrified of a disciplined and trained troop of guards, but he found it hard to be confident.

Colonel Cranbrough had given him this assignment and sent him out without a superior officer. Normally Cranbrough would have commanded the detachment himself, but he knew this was a special situation, with heavy political interference, and he wanted to keep out of it. Jay had been pleased at first, but now he wished he had an experienced superior to help him.

Lennox's plan had sounded foolproof in theory, but as he rode to battle Jay found it full of holes. What if McAsh were somewhere else tonight? What if he escaped before Jay could arrest him?

As they approached the coal yard the pace of the march seemed to slow, until Jay felt they were creeping forward by inches. Seeing the soldiers, many of the rioters fled and others took cover; but some threw coal, and a rain of lumps came down on Jay and his men. Without flinching they marched up to the coal yard gates and, as prearranged, took up their firing positions.

There would be only one volley. They were so close to the enemy that they would not have time to reload.

Jay raised his sword. The coal heavers were trapped in the yard. They had been trying to close the yard gates but now they gave up and the gates swung fully open. Some scrambled over the walls, others tried pathetically to find cover among the heaps of coal or behind the wheels of a cart. It was like shooting chickens in a coop.

Suddenly McAsh appeared on top of the wall, a broad-shouldered figure, his face lit by the moon. "Stop!" he yelled. "Don't shoot!"

Go to hell, Jay thought.

He swept his sword down and shouted: "Fire!"

The muskets cracked like thunder. A pall of smoke appeared and hid the soldiers for a moment. Ten or twelve coal heavers fell, some shouting in pain, others deathly silent. McAsh jumped down from the wall and knelt by the motionless, blood-soaked body of a Negro. He looked up and met Jay's eye, and the rage in his face chilled Jay's blood.

Jay shouted: "Charge!"

The coal heavers engaged the guards aggressively, surprising Jay. He had expected them to flee, but they dodged swords and muskets to grapple hand-to-hand, fighting with sticks and lumps of coal and fists and feet. Jay was dismayed to see several uniforms fall.

He looked around for McAsh and could not see him.

Jay cursed. The whole purpose of this was to arrest McAsh. That was what Sir Philip had asked for, and Jay had promised to deliver. Surely he had not slipped away?

Then, suddenly, McAsh was in front of him.

Instead of running away the man was coming after Jay.

McAsh grabbed Jay's bridle. Jay lifted his sword, and McAsh ducked around to Jay's left side. Jay struck awkwardly and missed. McAsh jumped up, grabbed Jay's sleeve and pulled. Jay tried to jerk his arm back but McAsh would not let go. With dreadful inevitability Jay slid sideways in his saddle. McAsh gave a mighty heave and pulled him off his horse.

Suddenly Jay feared for his life.

He managed to land on his feet. McAsh's hands were around his throat in an instant. He drew back his sword but, before he could strike, McAsh lowered his head and butted Jay's face brutally. Jay went blind for a moment and felt hot blood on his face. He swung his sword wildly. It connected with something and he thought he had wounded McAsh, but the grip on his throat did not slacken. His vision returned and he looked into McAsh's eyes and saw murder there. He was terrified, and if he could have spoken he would have begged for mercy.

One of his men saw him in trouble and swung the butt of a musket. The blow hit McAsh on the ear. For a moment his grip slackened, then it became tighter than ever. The soldier swung again. McAsh tried to duck, but he was not quick enough, and the heavy wooden stock of the gun connected with a crack that could be heard over the roar of the battle. For a split second McAsh's stranglehold increased, and Jay struggled for air like a drowning man; then McAsh's eyes rolled up in his head, his hands slipped from Jay's neck, and he slumped to the ground, unconscious.

Jay drew breath raggedly and leaned on his sword. Slowly his terror eased. His face hurt like fire: he was sure his nose must be broken. But as he looked at the man crumpled on the ground at his feet he felt nothing but satisfaction.

23

L IZZIE DID NOT SLEEP THAT NIGHT.

Jay had told her there might be trouble, and she sat in their bedroom waiting for him, with a novel open but unread on her knee. He came home in the early hours with blood and dirt all over him and a bandage on his nose. She was so pleased to see him alive that she threw her arms around him and hugged him, ruining her white silk robe.

She woke the servants and ordered hot water, and he told her the story of the riot bit by bit as she helped him out of his filthy uniform and washed his bruised body and got him a clean nightshirt.

Later, when they were lying side by side in the big four-poster bed, she said tentatively: "Do you think McAsh will be hanged?"

"I certainly hope so," Jay said, touching his bandage with a careful finger. "We have witnesses to say he incited the crowd to riot and personally attacked officers. I can't imagine a judge giving him a light sentence in the present climate. If he had influential friends to plead for him it would be a different matter."

She frowned. "I never thought of him as a particularly violent man. Insubordinate, disobedient, insolent, arrogant—but not savage."

Jay looked smug. "You may be right. But things were arranged so that he had no choice."

"What do you mean?"

"Sir Philip Armstrong paid a clandestine visit to the warehouse to speak to me and Father. He told us he wanted McAsh arrested for rioting. He practically told us to make it happen. So Lennox and I arranged a riot."

Lizzie was shocked. It made her feel even worse to think that Mack had been deliberately provoked. "And is Sir Philip pleased with what you've done?"

"He is. And Colonel Cranbrough was impressed by the way I handled the riot. I can resign my commission and leave the army with an unimpeachable reputation."

Jay made love to her then, but she was too troubled to enjoy his caresses. Normally she liked to romp around the bed, rolling him over and getting on top sometimes, changing positions, kissing and talking and laughing; and naturally he noticed that she was different. When it was over he said: "You're very quiet."

She thought of an excuse. "I was afraid of hurting you."

He accepted that and a few moments later he was asleep. Lizzie lay awake. It was the second time she had been shocked by her husband's attitude to justice—and both occasions had involved Lennox. Jay was not vicious, she was sure; but he could be led into evil by others, particularly strong-minded men such as Lennox. She was glad they were leaving England in a month's time. Once they set sail, they would never see Lennox again.

Still she could not sleep. There was a cold, leaden feeling in the pit of her stomach. Mack McAsh was going to be hanged. She had been revolted to watch the hanging of total strangers the morning she had gone to Tyburn Cross in disguise. The thought of the same thing happening to her childhood friend was unbearable.

Mack was not her problem, she told herself. He had run away, broken the law, gone on strike and taken part in a riot. He had done all he could to get into trouble: it was not her responsibility to rescue him now. Her duty was to the husband she had married.

It was all true, but still she could not sleep.

When the light of dawn began to show around the edges of the curtains, she got up. She decided to begin packing for the voyage, and when the servants appeared she told them to fetch the waterproof trunks she had bought and start filling them with her wedding presents: table linen, cutlery, china and glassware, cooking pots and kitchen knives.

Jay woke up aching and bad tempered. He drank a shot of brandy for breakfast and went off to his regiment. Lizzie's mother, who was still living at the Jamissons' house, called on Lizzie soon after Jay left, and the two of them went to the bedroom and began folding Lizzie's stockings and petticoats and handkerchiefs.

"What ship will you travel on?" Mother asked.

"The *Rosebud.* She's a Jamisson vessel."

"And when you reach Virginia—how will you get to the plantation?"

"Oceangoing ships can sail up the Rappahannock River all the way to Fredericksburg, which is only ten miles from Mockjack Hall." Lizzie could see that her mother was anxious about her undertaking a long sea voyage. "Don't worry, Mother, there are no pirates anymore."

"You must take your own fresh water and keep the barrel in your cabin—don't share with the crew. I'll make up a medicine chest for you in case of sickness."

"Thank you, Mother." Because of the cramped quarters, contaminated food and stale water Lizzie was much more likely to die of some shipboard illness than be attacked by pirates.

"How long will it take?"

"Six or seven weeks." Lizzie knew that was a minimum: if the ship was blown off course the voyage could stretch to three months. Then the chance of sickness was much greater. However, she and Jay were young and strong and healthy, and they would survive. And it would be an adventure!

She could hardly wait to see America. It was a whole new continent and everything would be different: the birds, the trees, the food, the air, the people. She tingled whenever she thought about it.

She had been living in London for four months, and she disliked it more every day. Polite society bored her to death. She and Jay often dined with other officers and their wives, but the officers talked of card games and incompetent generals and the women were interested only in hats and servants. Lizzie found it impossible to make small talk, but if she spoke her mind she always shocked them.

Once or twice a week she and Jay dined at Grosvenor Square. There at least the conversation was about something real: business, politics, and the wave of strikes and disturbances that had washed over London this spring. But the Jamissons' view of events was completely one-sided. Sir George would rail against the workingmen, Robert would forecast disaster, and Jay would propose a clampdown by the military. No one, not even Alicia, had the imagination to see the conflict from the point of view of the other side. Lizzie did not think the workingmen were right to strike, of course, but she believed they had reasons that seemed strong to them. That possibility was never admitted around the highly polished dining table at Grosvenor Square.

"I expect you'll be glad to go back to Hallim House," Lizzie said to her mother.

Mother nodded. "The Jamissons are very kind, but I miss my home, humble though it is."

Lizzie was putting her favorite books into a trunk: *Robinson Crusoe, Tom Jones, Roderick Random*—all stories of adventure— when a footman knocked and said that Caspar Gordonson was downstairs.

She asked the man to repeat the visitor's name, because she could hardly believe Gordonson would dare to call on any member of the Jamisson family. She should have refused to see him, she knew: he had encouraged and supported the strike that was damaging her father-in-law's business. But curiosity got the better of her, as ever, and she told the footman to show him into the drawing room.

However, she had no intention of making him welcome. "You've caused a great deal of trouble," she said as she walked in.

To her surprise he was not the aggressive know-it-all bully she had expected, but an untidy, shortsighted man with a high-pitched voice and the manner of an absentminded schoolteacher. "I'm sure I didn't mean to," he said. "That is . . . I did, of course . . . but not to you personally."

"Why have you come here? If my husband were at home he would throw you out on your ear."

"Mack McAsh has been charged under the Riot Act and committed to Newgate Prison. He will be tried at the Old Bailey in three weeks' time. It's a hanging offense."

The reminder struck Lizzie like a blow, but she hid her feelings. "I know," she said coldly. "Such a tragedy—a strong young man with his life in front of him."

"You must feel guilty," Gordonson said.

"You insolent fool!" she blazed. "Who encouraged McAsh to think he was a free man? Who told him he had rights? You! You're the one who should feel guilty!"

"I do," he said quietly.

She was surprised: she had expected a hot denial. His humility calmed her. Tears came to her eyes but she fought them back. "He should have stayed in Scotland."

"You realize that many people who are convicted of capital offenses don't hang, in the end."

"Yes." There was still hope, of course. Her spirits lifted a little. "Do you think Mack will get a royal pardon?"

"It depends who is willing to speak for him. Influential friends are everything in our legal system. I will plead for his life, but my words won't count for much. Most judges hate me. However, if *you* would plead for him—"

"I can't do that!" she protested. "My husband is prosecuting McAsh. It would be dreadfully disloyal of me."

"You could save his life."

"But it would make Jay look such a fool!"

"Don't you think he might understand—"

"No! I know he wouldn't. No husband would."

"Think about it—"

"I won't! I'll do something else. I'll . . ." She cast about for ideas. "I'll write to Mr. York, the pastor of the church in Heugh. I'll ask him to come to London and plead for Mack's life at the trial."

Gordonson said: "A country parson from Scotland? I don't think he'll have much influence. The only way to be certain is for you to do it yourself."

"It's out of the question."

"I won't argue with you—it will only make you more determined," Gordonson said shrewdly. He went to the door. "You can change your mind at any time. Just come to the Old Bailey three weeks from tomorrow. Remember that his life may depend on it."

He went out, and Lizzie let herself cry.

*

Mack was in one of the common wards of Newgate Prison.

He could not remember all that had happened to him the night before. He had a dazed recollection of being tied up and thrown across the back of a horse and carried through London. There was a tall building with barred windows, a cobbled courtyard, a staircase and a studded door. Then he had been led in here. It had been dark, and he had not been able to see much. Battered and fatigued, he had fallen asleep.

He woke to find himself in a room about the size of Cora's apartment. It was cold: there was no glass in the windows and no fire in the fireplace. The place smelled foul. At least thirty other people were crammed in with him: men, women and children, plus a dog and a pig. Everyone slept on the floor and shared a large chamber-pot.

There was constant coming and going. Some of the women left early in the morning, and Mack learned they were not prisoners but prisoners' wives who bribed the jailers and spent nights here. The warders brought in food, beer, gin and newspapers for those who could pay their grossly inflated prices. People went to see friends in other wards. One prisoner was visited by a clergyman, another by a barber. Anything was permitted, it seemed, but everything had to be paid for.

People laughed about their plight and joked about their crimes. There was an air of jollity that annoyed Mack. He was hardly awake before he was offered a swallow of gin from someone's bottle and a puff on a pipe of tobacco, as if they were all at a wedding.

Mack hurt all over, but his head was the worst. There was a lump at the back that was crusted with blood. He felt hopelessly gloomy. He had failed in every way. He had run away from Heugh to be free, yet he was in jail. He had fought for the coal heavers' rights and had got some of them killed. He had lost Cora. He would be put on trial for treason, or riot, or murder. And he would probably die on the gallows. Many of the people around him had as much reason to grieve, but perhaps they were too stupid to grasp their fate.

Poor Esther would never get out of the village now. He wished he had brought her with him. She could have dressed as a man, the way Lizzie Hallim did. She would have managed sailors' work more easily than Mack himself, for she was nimbler. And her common sense might even have kept Mack out of trouble.

He hoped Annie's baby would be a boy. At least there would still be a Mack. Perhaps Mack Lee would have a luckier life, and a longer one, than Mack McAsh.

He was at a low point when a warder opened the door and Cora walked in.

Her face was dirty and her red dress was torn but she still looked ravishing, and everyone turned to stare.

Mack sprang to his feet and embraced her, to cheers from the other prisoners.

"What happened to you?" he said.

"I was done for picking pockets—but it was all on account of you," she said.

"What do you mean?"

"It was a trap. He looked like any other rich young drunk, but he was Jay Jamisson. They nabbed us and took us in front of his father. It's a hanging offense, picking pockets. But they offered Peg a pardon—if she would tell them where you lived."

Mack suffered a moment of anger with Peg for betraying him; but she was just a child, she could not be blamed. "So that was how they found out."

"What happened to you?"

He told her the story of the riot.

When he had done she said: "By Christ, McAsh, you're an unlucky man to know."

It was true, he thought. Everyone he met got into some kind of trouble. "Charlie Smith is dead," he said.

"You must talk to Peg," she said. "She thinks you must hate her."

"I hate myself for getting her into this."

Cora shrugged. "You didn't tell her to thieve. Come on."

She banged on the door and a warder opened it. She gave him a coin, jerked a thumb at Mack and said: "He's with me." The warder nodded and let them out.

She led him along a corridor to another door and they entered a room very like the one they had left. Peg was sitting on the floor in a corner. When she saw Mack she stood up, looking scared. "I'm sorry," she said. "They made me do it, I'm sorry!"

"It wasn't your fault," he said.

Her eyes filled with tears. "I let you down," she whispered.

"Don't be silly." He took her in his arms, and her tiny frame shook as she sobbed and sobbed.

*

Caspar Gordonson arrived with a banquet: fish soup in a big tureen, a joint of beef, new bread, several jugs of ale, and a custard. He paid the jailer for a private room with table and chairs. Mack, Cora and Peg were brought from their ward and they all sat down to eat.

Mack was hungry, but he found he had little appetite. He was too worried. He wanted to know what Gordonson thought of his chances at the trial. He forced himself to be patient and drank some beer.

When they had finished eating, Gordonson's servant cleared away and brought pipes and tobacco. Gordonson took a pipe, and so did Peg, who was addicted to this adult vice.

Gordonson began by talking about Peg and Cora's case. "I've spoken with the Jamisson family lawyer about the pickpocketing charge," he began. "Sir George will stand by his promise to ask for mercy for Peg."

"That surprises me," said Mack. "It's not like the Jamissons to keep their word."

"Ah, well, they want something," Gordonson said. "You see, it will be embarrassing for them if Jay tells the court he picked Cora up thinking she was a prostitute. So they want to pretend she just met him in the street and got him talking while Peg picked his pocket."

Peg said scornfully: "And we're supposed to go along with this fairy tale, and protect Jay's reputation."

"If you want Sir George to plead for your life, yes."

Cora said: "We have no choice. Of course we'll do it."

"Good." Gordonson turned to Mack. "I wish your case was so easy."

Mack protested: "But I didn't riot!"

"You didn't go away after the Riot Act was read."

"For God's sake—I tried to get everyone to go, but Lennox's ruffians attacked."

"Let's look at this step by step."

Mack took a deep breath and suppressed his exasperation. "All right."

"The prosecutor will say simply that the Riot Act was read, and you did not go away, so you are guilty and should be hanged."

"Yes, but everyone knows there's more to it than that!"

"There: that's your defense. You simply say that the prosecutor has told half the story. Can you bring witnesses to say that you pleaded with everyone to disperse?"

"I'm sure I can. Dermot Riley can get any number of coal heavers to testify. But we should ask the Jamissons why the coal was being delivered to that yard, of all places, and at that time of night!"

"Well—"

Mack banged the table impatiently. "The whole riot was prearranged, we have to say that."

"It would be hard to prove."

Mack was infuriated by Gordonson's dismissive attitude. "The riot was caused by a conspiracy—surely you're not going to leave that out? If the facts don't come out in court, where will they?"

Peg said: "Will you be at the trial, Mr. Gordonson?"

"Yes—but the judge may not let me speak."

"For God's sake, why not?" Mack said indignantly.

"The theory is that if you're innocent you don't need legal expertise to prove it. But sometimes judges make exceptions."

"I hope we get a friendly judge," Mack said anxiously.

"The judge ought to help the accused. It's his duty to make sure the defense case is clear to the jury. But don't rely on it. Place your faith in the plain truth. It's the only thing that can save you from the hangman."

24

O
N THE DAY OF THE TRIAL THE PRISONERS WERE AWAKENED AT FIVE
o'clock in the morning.

Dermot Riley arrived a few minutes later with a suit for Mack
to borrow: it was the outfit Dermot had got married in, and Mack
was touched. He also brought a razor and a sliver of soap. Half an hour
later Mack looked respectable and felt ready to face the judge.

With Cora and Peg and fifteen or twenty others he was tied up and
marched out of the prison, along Newgate Street, down a side street
called Old Bailey and up an alley to the Sessions House.

Caspar Gordonson met him there and explained who was who. The
yard in front of the building was already full of people: prosecutors,
witnesses, jurors, lawyers, friends and relatives, idle spectators, and
probably whores and thieves looking for business. The prisoners were
led across the yard and through a gate to the bail dock. It was already
half full of defendants, presumably from other prisons: the Fleet Prison,
the Bridewell and Ludgate Prison. From there Mack could see
the imposing Sessions House. Stone steps led up to its ground floor,
which was open on one side except for a row of columns. Inside was
the judges' bench on a high platform. On either side were railed-off
spaces for jurors, and balconies for court officers and privileged
spectators.

It reminded Mack of a theater—but he was the villain of the piece.

He watched with grim fascination as the court began its long day of trials. The first defendant was a woman accused of stealing fifteen yards of linsey-woolsey—cheap cloth made of a mixture of linen and wool—from a shop. The shopkeeper was the prosecutor, and he valued the cloth at fifteen shillings. The witness, an employee, swore that the woman picked up the bolt of cloth and went to the door then, realizing she was observed, dropped the material and ran away. The woman claimed she had only been looking at the cloth and had never intended to make off with it.

The jurors went into a huddle. They came from the social class known as "the middling sort": they were small traders, well-to-do craftsmen and shopkeepers. They hated disorder and theft but they mistrusted the government and jealously defended liberty—their own, at least.

They found her guilty but valued the cloth at four shillings, a lot less than it was worth. Gordonson explained that she could be hanged for stealing goods worth more than five shillings from a shop. The verdict was intended to prevent the judge from sentencing the woman to death.

She was not sentenced immediately, however: the sentences would all be read out at the end of the day.

The whole thing had taken no more than a quarter of an hour. The following cases were dealt with equally rapidly, few taking more than half an hour. Cora and Peg were tried together at about midafternoon. Mack knew that the course of the trial was preordained, but still he crossed his fingers and hoped it would go according to plan.

Jay Jamisson testified that Cora had engaged him in conversation in the street while Peg picked his pockets. He called Sidney Lennox as the witness who had seen what was happening and warned him. Neither Cora nor Peg challenged this version of events.

Their reward was the appearance of Sir George, who testified that they had been helpful in the apprehension of another criminal and asked the judge to sentence them to transportation rather than hanging.

The judge nodded sympathetically, but the sentence would not be pronounced until the end of the day.

Mack's case was called a few minutes later.

✳

Lizzie could think of nothing but the trial.

She had dinner at three o'clock and, as Jay was at the court all day, her mother came to dine and keep her company.

"You're looking quite plump, my dear," Lady Hallim said. "Have you been eating a lot?"

"On the contrary," Lizzie said. "Sometimes food makes me feel ill. It's all the excitement of going to Virginia, I suppose. And now this dreadful trial."

"It's not your concern," Lady Hallim said briskly. "Dozens of people are hanged every year for much less dreadful crimes. He can't be reprieved just because you knew him as a child."

"How do you know he committed a crime at all?"

"If he did not, he will be found not guilty. I'm sure he is being treated the same as anyone foolish enough to get involved in a riot."

"But he isn't," Lizzie protested. "Jay and Sir George deliberately provoked that riot so that they could arrest Mack and finish the coal heavers' strike—Jay told me."

"Then I'm sure they had good reason."

Tears came to Lizzie's eyes. "Mother, don't you think it's *wrong?*"

"I'm quite sure it's none of my business or yours, Lizzie," she said firmly.

Wanting to hide her distress from her mother, Lizzie ate a spoonful of dessert—apples mashed with sugar—but it made her feel sick and she put down her spoon. "Caspar Gordonson said I could save Mack's life if I would speak for him in court."

"Heaven forbid!" Mother was shocked. "That you should go against your own husband in a public courtroom—don't even speak of it!"

"But it's a man's life! Think of his poor sister—how she will grieve when she finds out he has been hanged."

"My dear, they are miners, they aren't like us. Life is cheap, they don't grieve as we do. His sister will just get drunk on gin and go back down the pit."

"You don't really believe that, Mother, I know."

"Perhaps I'm exaggerating. But I'm quite sure it does no good to worry about such things."

"I just can't help it. He's a brave young man who only wanted to be free, and I can't bear the thought of him hanging from that rope."

"You could pray for him."

"I do," Lizzie said. "I do."

*

The prosecutor was a lawyer, Augustus Pym.

"He does a lot of work for the government," Gordonson whispered to Mack. "They must be paying him to prosecute this case."

So the government wanted Mack hanged. That made him feel low.

Gordonson approached the bench and addressed the judge. "My lord, as the prosecution is to be done by a professional lawyer, will you allow me to speak for Mr. McAsh?"

"Certainly not," said the judge. "If McAsh cannot convince the jury unless he has outside help, he can't have much of a case."

Mack's throat was dry and he could hear his heartbeat. He was going to have to fight for his life alone. Well, he would fight every inch of the way.

Pym began. "On the day in question a delivery of coal was being made to the yard of Mr. John Cooper, known as Black Jack, in Wapping High Street."

Mack said: "It wasn't day—it was night."

The judge said: "Don't make foolish remarks."

"It's not foolish," Mack said. "Whoever heard of coal being delivered at eleven o'clock at night?"

"Be quiet. Carry on, Mr. Pym."

"The delivery men were attacked by a group of striking coal heavers, and the Wapping magistrates were alerted."

"Who by?" said Mack.

Pym answered: "By the landlord of the Frying Pan tavern, Mr. Harold Nipper."

"An undertaker," said Mack.

The judge said: "And a respectable tradesman, I believe."

Pym went on: "Mr. Roland MacPherson, justice of the peace, arrived and declared a riot. The coal heavers refused to disperse."

"We were attacked!" Mack said.

They ignored him. "Mr. MacPherson then summoned the troops, as was his right and duty. A detachment of the Third Foot Guards arrived under the command of Captain Jamisson. The prisoner was among those arrested. The Crown's first witness is John Cooper."

Black Jack testified that he went downriver to Rochester to buy coal that had been unloaded there. He had it driven to London in carts.

Mack asked: "Who did the ship belong to?"

"I don't know—I dealt with the captain."

"Where was the ship from?"

"Edinburgh."

"Could it have belonged to Sir George Jamisson?"

"I don't know."

"Who suggested to you that you might be able to buy coal in Rochester?"

"Sidney Lennox."

"A friend of the Jamissons'."

"I don't know about that."

Pym's next witness was Roland MacPherson, who swore that he had read the Riot Act at a quarter past eleven in the evening, and the crowd had refused to disperse.

Mack said: "You were on the scene very quickly."

"Yes."

"Who summoned you?"

"Harold Nipper."

"The landlord of the Frying Pan."

"Yes."

"Did he have far to go?"

"I don't know what you mean."

"Where were you when he summoned you?"

"In the back parlor of his tavern."

"That was handy! Was it planned?"

"I knew there was going to be a coal delivery and I feared there might be trouble."

"Who forewarned you?"

"Sidney Lennox."

One of the jurors said: "Ho!"

Mack looked at him. He was a youngish man with a skeptical expression, and Mack marked him down as a potential ally in the jury.

Finally Pym called Jay Jamisson. Jay talked easily, and the judge looked faintly bored, as if they were friends discussing a matter of no importance. Mack wanted to shout: "Don't be so casual—my life is at stake!"

Jay said he had been in command of a detachment of Guards at the Tower of London.

The skeptical juror interrupted: "What were you doing there?"

Jay looked as if the question had taken him by surprise. He said nothing.

"Answer the question," said the juror.

Jay looked at the judge, who seemed annoyed with the juror and said with obvious reluctance: "You must answer the jury's questions, Captain."

"We were there in readiness," Jay said.

"For what?" said the juror.

"In case our assistance was needed in keeping the peace in the eastern part of the city."

"Is that your usual barracks?" said the juror.

"No."

"Where, then?"

"Hyde Park, at the moment."

"On the other side of London."

"Yes."

"How many nights have you made this special trip to the Tower?"

"Just one."

"How did you come to be there that particular night?"

"I assume my commanding officers feared trouble."

"Sidney Lennox warned them, I suppose," the juror said, and there was a ripple of laughter.

Pym continued to question Jay, who said that when he and his men arrived at the coal yard there was a riot in full progress, which was true. He told how Mack had attacked him—also true—and had been knocked out by another soldier.

Mack asked him: "What do you think of coal heavers who riot?"

"They are breaking the law and should be punished."

"Do you believe most folk agree with you, by and large?"

"Yes."

"Do you think the riot will turn folk against the coal heavers?"

"I'm sure of it."

"So the riot makes it more likely that the authorities will take drastic action to end the strike?"

"I certainly hope so."

Beside Mack, Caspar Gordonson was muttering: "Brilliant, brilliant, he fell right into your trap."

"And when the strike is over, the Jamisson family's coal ships will be unloaded and you will be able to sell your coal again."

Jay began to see where he was being led, but it was too late. "Yes."

"An end to the strike is worth a lot of money to you."

"Yes."

"So the coal heavers' riot will make money for you."

"It might stop my family losing money."

"Is that why you cooperated with Sidney Lennox in provoking the riot?" Mack turned away.

"I did no such thing!" said Jay, but he was speaking to the back of Mack's head.

Gordonson said: "You should be a lawyer, Mack. Where did you learn to argue like that?"

"Mrs. Wheighel's parlor," he replied.

Gordonson was mystified.

Pym had no more witnesses. The skeptical juror said: "Aren't we going to hear from this Lennox character?"

"The Crown has no more witnesses," Pym repeated.

"Well, I think we should hear from him. He seems to be behind it all."

"Jurors cannot call witnesses," the judge said.

Mack called his first, an Irish coal heaver known as Red Michael for the color of his hair. Red told how Mack had been on the point of persuading the coal heavers to go home when they were attacked.

When he had finished, the judge said: "And what work do you do, young man?"

"I'm a coal heaver, sir," Red replied.

The judge said: "The jury will take that into account when considering whether to believe you or not."

Mack's heart sank. The judge was doing all he could to prejudice the jury against him. He called his next witness, but he was another coal heaver and suffered the same fate. The third and last was also a coal heaver. That was because they had been in the thick of things and had seen exactly what happened.

His witnesses had been destroyed. Now there was only himself and his own character and eloquence.

"Coal heaving is hard work, cruelly hard," he began. "Only strong young men can do it. But it's highly paid—in my first week I earned six pounds. I *earned* it, but I did not receive it: most was stolen from me by an undertaker."

The judge interrupted him. "This has nothing to do with the case," he said. "The charge is riot."

"I didn't riot," Mack said. He took a deep breath and gathered his thoughts, then went on. "I simply refused to let undertakers steal my wages. That's my crime. Undertakers get rich by stealing from coal heavers. But when the coal heavers decided to do their own undertaking, what happened? They were boycotted by the shippers. And who are the shippers, gentlemen? The Jamisson family which is so inextricably involved in this trial today."

The judge said irritably: "Can you prove that you did not riot?"

The skeptical juror interjected: "The point is that the fighting was instigated by others."

Mack was not put off by the interruption. He simply continued with what he wanted to say. "Gentlemen of the jury, ask yourselves some questions." He turned away from the jurors and looked straight at Jay. "Who ordered that wagons of coal should be brought down Wapping

High Street at an hour when the taverns are full of coal heavers? Who sent them to the very coal yard where I live? Who paid the men who escorted the wagons?" The judge was trying to break in again but Mack raised his voice and plowed on. "Who gave them muskets and ammunition? Who made sure the troops were standing by in the immediate neighborhood? Who orchestrated the entire riot?" He swung around swiftly and looked at the jury. "You know the answer, don't you?" He held their gaze a moment longer, then turned away.

He felt shaky. He had done his best, and now his life was in the hands of others.

Gordonson got to his feet. "We were expecting a character witness to appear on McAsh's behalf—the Reverend Mr. York, pastor of the church in the village of his birth—but he has not yet arrived."

Mack was not very disappointed about York, for he did not expect York's testimony to have much effect, and neither did Gordonson.

The judge said: "If he arrives he may speak before sentencing." Gordonson raised his eyebrows and the judge added: "That is, unless the jury finds the defendant not guilty, in which case further testimony would be superfluous, needless to say. Gentlemen, consider your verdict."

Mack studied the jurors fearfully as they conferred. He thought, to his dismay, that they looked unsympathetic. Perhaps he had come on too strong. "What do you think?" he said to Gordonson.

The lawyer shook his head. "They'll find it hard to believe that the Jamisson family entered into a shabby conspiracy with Sidney Lennox. You might have done better to present the coal heavers as well intentioned but misguided."

"I told the truth," Mack said. "I can't help it."

Gordonson smiled sadly. "If you weren't that kind of man, you might not be in so much trouble."

The jurors were arguing. "What the devil are they talking about?" Mack said. "I wish we could hear." He could see the skeptical one making a point forcefully, wagging his finger. Were the others listening attentively, or ranged against him?

"Be grateful," Gordonson said. "The longer they talk, the better for you."

"Why?"

"If they're arguing, there must be doubt; and if there is doubt, they have to find you not guilty."

Mack watched fearfully. The skeptical one shrugged and half turned away, and Mack feared he had lost the argument. The foreman said something to him, and he nodded.

The foreman approached the bench.

The judge said: "Have you reached a verdict?"

"We have."

Mack held his breath.

"And how do you find the prisoner?"

"We find him guilty as charged."

＊

Lady Hallim said: "Your feeling for this miner is rather strange, my dear. A husband might find it objectionable."

"Oh, Mother, don't be so ridiculous."

There was a knock at the dining room door and a footman came in. "The Reverend Mr. York, madam," he said.

"What a lovely surprise!" said Mother. She had always been fond of York. In a low voice she added: "His wife died, Lizzie—did I tell you?—leaving him with three children."

"But what's he doing here?" Lizzie said anxiously. "He's supposed to be at the Old Bailey. Show him in, quickly."

The pastor came in, looking as if he had dressed hastily. Before Lizzie could ask him why he was not at the trial he said something that momentarily took her mind off Mack.

"Lady Hallim, Mrs. Jamisson, I arrived in London a few hours ago, and I've called on you at the earliest posssible moment to offer you both my sympathies. What a dreadful—"

Lizzie's mother said, *"No—"* then clamped her lips tight.

"—blow to you."

Lizzie shot a puzzled look at her mother and said: "What are you talking about, Mr. York?"

"The pit disaster, of course."

"I don't know anything about it—although I see my mother does. . . ."

"My goodness, I'm terribly sorry to have shocked you. There was a roof collapse at your pit, and twenty people were killed."

Lizzie gasped. "How absolutely dreadful." In her mind she saw twenty new graves in the little churchyard by the bridge. There would be so much grief: everyone in the neighborhood would be mourning someone. But something else worried her. "What do you mean when you say 'your' pit?"

"High Glen."

Lizzie went cold. *"There is no pit at High Glen."*

"Only the new one, of course—the one that was begun when you married Mr. Jamisson."

Lizzie felt frozen with rage. She rounded on her mother. "You knew, didn't you?"

Lady Hallim had the grace to look ashamed. "My dear, it was the only thing to do. That's why Sir George gave you the Virginia property—"

"You betrayed me!" Lizzie cried. "You all deceived me. Even my husband. How could you? How could you lie to me?"

Her mother began to cry. "We thought you'd never know. You're going to America—"

Her tears did nothing to blunt Lizzie's outrage. "You thought I'd never know? I can hardly believe my ears!"

"Don't do anything rash, I beg you."

An awful thought struck Lizzie. She turned to the pastor. "Mack's twin sister . . ."

"I'm afraid Esther McAsh was among the dead," he said.

"Oh, no." Mack and Esther were the first twins Lizzie had ever seen, and she had been fascinated by them. As children they were hard to tell apart until you got to know them. In later life Esther looked like a female Mack, with the same striking green eyes and the miner's squat muscularity. Lizzie remembered them a few short months ago, standing side by side outside the church. Esther had told Mack to shut his gob, and that had made Lizzie laugh. Now Esther was dead and Mack was about to be condemned to death—

Remembering Mack, she said: "The trial is today!"

York said: "Oh, my goodness, I didn't know it was so soon—am I too late?"

"Perhaps not, if you go now."

"I will. How far is it?"

"Fifteen minutes' walk, five minutes in a sedan chair. I'm coming with you."

Mother said: "No, please—"

Lizzie made her voice harsh. "Don't try to stop me, Mother. I'm going to plead for Mack's life myself. We killed the sister—perhaps we can save the brother."

"I'm coming with you," said Lady Hallim.

＊

The Sessions Yard was crammed with people. Lizzie was confused and lost, and neither York nor her mother was any help. She pushed through the crowd, searching for Gordonson or Mack. She came to a low wall that enclosed an inner yard and at last saw Mack and Caspar Gordonson through the railings. When she called, Gordonson came out through a gate.

At the same time Sir George and Jay appeared.

Jay said in a reproving tone: "Lizzie, why are you here?"

She ignored him and spoke to Gordonson: "This is the Reverend Mr. York, from our village in Scotland. He's come to plead for Mack's life."

Sir George wagged a finger at York. "If you've got any sense you'll turn around and go straight back to Scotland."

Lizzie said: "And I'm going to plead for his life, too."

"Thank you," Gordonson said fervently. "It's the best thing you could possibly do."

Lady Hallim said: "I tried to stop her, Sir George."

Jay flushed with anger and grabbed Lizzie by the arm, squeezing hard. "How dare you humiliate me like this?" he spat. "I absolutely forbid you to speak!"

"Are you intimidating this witness?" said Gordonson.

Jay looked cowed and let go. A lawyer with a bundle of papers pushed through the middle of their little group. Jay said: "Do we have to have this discussion here where the whole world can see?"

"Yes," said Gordonson. "We can't leave the court."

Sir George said to Lizzie: "What the devil do you mean by this, my girl?"

The arrogant tone maddened Lizzie. "You know damn well what I mean by it," she said. The men were all startled to hear her swear, and two or three people standing nearby turned and looked at her. She ignored their reactions. "You all planned this riot to trap McAsh. I'm not going to stand by and see you hang him."

Sir George reddened. "Remember that you're my daughter-in-law and—"

"Shut up, George," she interrupted. "I won't be bullied."

He was thunderstruck. No one ever told him to shut up, she was sure.

Jay took up the cudgels. "You can't go against your own husband," he stormed. "It's disloyal!"

"Disloyal?" she repeated scornfully. "Who the hell are you to talk to me about loyalty? You swore to me that you would not mine coal on my land—then went ahead and did exactly that. You betrayed me on our wedding day!"

They all went quiet, and for a moment Lizzie could hear a witness giving evidence loudly on the other side of the wall. "You know about the accident, then," said Jay.

She took a deep breath. "I might as well say now that Jay and I will be leading separate lives from today. We'll be married in name only. I shall return to my house in Scotland, and none of the Jamisson family will be welcomed there. As for my speaking up for McAsh: I'm not going to help you hang my friend, and you can both—both—kiss my arse."

Sir George was too stupefied to say anything. No one had spoken to him this way for years. He was beetroot red, his eyes bulged, and he spluttered, but no words came out.

Caspar Gordonson addressed Jay. "May I make a suggestion?"

Jay gave him a hostile glare but said curtly: "Go on, go on."

"Mrs. Jamisson might be persuaded not to testify—on one condition."

"What?"

"You, Jay, should plead for Mack's life."

"Absolutely not," said Jay.

Gordonson went on: "It would be just as effective. But it would save the family the embarrassment of a wife going against her husband in open court." He suddenly looked sly. "Instead, you would look magnanimous. You could say that Mack was a miner in the Jamisson pits and for that reason the family wishes to be merciful."

Lizzie's heart leaped with hope. A plea for mercy from Jay, the officer who had quelled the riot, would be much more effective.

She could see hesitation flicker across Jay's face as he weighed the consequences. Then he said sulkily: "I suppose I have to accept this."

Before Lizzie had time to feel exultant, Sir George intervened. "There's one condition, which I know Jay will insist upon."

Lizzie had a bad feeling that she knew what was coming.

Sir George looked at her. "You must forget all this nonsense about separate lives. You are to be a proper wife to Jay in every way."

"No!" she cried. "He has betrayed me—how can I trust him? I won't do it."

Sir George said: "Then Jay will not plead for McAsh's life."

Gordonson said: "I must tell you, Lizzie, that Jay's plea will be more effective than yours, because he's the prosecutor."

Lizzie felt bewildered. It was not fair—she was being forced to choose between Mack's life and her own. How could she decide such a thing? She was pulled both ways, and it hurt.

They were all staring at her: Jay, Sir George, Gordonson, her mother, and York. She knew she should give in, but something inside would not let her. "No," she said defiantly. "I will not trade my own life for Mack's."

Gordonson said: "Think again."

Then her mother said: "You have to."

Lizzie looked at her. Of course her mother would urge her to do the conventional thing. But Mother was on the verge of tears. "What is it?"

She began to cry. "You have to be a proper wife to Jay."

"Why?"

"Because you're going to have a baby."

Lizzie stared at her. "What? What are you talking about?"

"You're pregnant," her mother said.

"How would you know?"

Mother spoke through sobs. "Your bosom has got bigger and food makes you feel sick. You've been married for two months: it's not exactly unexpected."

"Oh, my God." Lizzie was dumbfounded. Everything was turned upside-down. A baby! Could it be? She thought back and realized she had not had the curse since her wedding day. So it was true. She was trapped by her own body. Jay was the father of her child. And Mother had realized this was the one thing that could change Lizzie's mind.

She looked at her husband. On his face she saw anger mixed with a pleading look. "Why did you lie to me?" she said.

"I didn't want to, but I had to," he said.

She felt bitter. Her love for him would never be quite the same, she knew. But he was still her husband.

"All right," she said. "I accept."

Caspar Gordonson said: "Then we're all in agreement."

It sounded to Lizzie like a life sentence.

*

"Oh yes! Oh yes! Oh yes!" shouted the court crier. "My lords, the king's justices, strictly command all manner of persons to keep silence while the sentence of death is passing on the prisoners at the bar, on pain of imprisonment."

The judge put on his black cap and stood up.

Mack shuddered with loathing. Nineteen cases had been tried on the same day, and twelve people had been found guilty. Mack suffered a wave of terror. Lizzie had forced Jay to plead for mercy, which meant that his death sentence should be reprieved, but what if the judge decided to discount Jay's plea or just made a mistake?

Lizzie was at the back of the court. Mack caught her eye. She looked pale and shaken. He had not had a chance to speak to her. She tried to give him an encouraging smile, but it turned into a grimace of fear.

The judge looked at the twelve prisoners, standing in a line, and after a moment he spoke. "The law is that thou shalt return from hence, to the place whence thou camest, and from thence to the place of execution, where thou shalt hang by the neck, till the body be dead! dead! dead! and the Lord have mercy on thy soul."

There was an awful pause. Cora held Mack's arm, and he felt her fingers digging into his flesh as she suffered the same dreadful anxiety. The other prisoners had little hope of pardon. As they heard their death sentences some screamed abuse, some wept, and one prayed loudly.

"Peg Knapp is reprieved and recommended for transportation," the judge intoned. "Cora Higgins is reprieved and recommended for transportation. Malachi McAsh is reprieved and recommended for transportation. The rest are left to hang."

Mack put his arms around Cora and Peg, and the three of them stood in a mutual embrace. Their lives had been spared.

Caspar Gordonson joined in the embrace, then he took Mack's arm and said solemnly: "I have to give you some dreadful news."

Mack was scared again: would their reprieves somehow be overturned?

"There has been a roof collapse in one of the Jamisson pits," he went on. Mack's heart missed a beat: he dreaded what was coming. "Twenty people were killed," Gordonson said.

"Esther . . . ?"

"I'm sorry, Mack. Your sister was among the dead."

"Dead?" It was hard to take in. Life and death had been dealt out like cards today. Esther, dead? How could he not have a twin? He had always had her, since he was born.

"I should have let her come with me," he said as his eyes filled with tears. "Why did I leave her behind?"

Peg stared at him wide-eyed. Cora held his hand and said: "A life saved, and a life lost."

Mack put his hands over his face and wept.

25

THE DAY OF DEPARTURE CAME QUICKLY.

One morning without warning all the prisoners who had been sentenced to transportation were told to pick up their possessions and herded into the courtyard.

Mack had few possessions. Other than his clothes, there was just his *Robinson Crusoe,* the broken iron collar he had brought from Heugh, and the fur cloak Lizzie had given him.

In the courtyard a blacksmith shackled them in pairs with heavy leg irons. Mack was humiliated by the fetters. The feel of the cold iron on his ankle brought him very low. He had fought for his freedom and lost the battle, and once again he was in chains like an animal. He hoped the ship would sink and he would drown.

Males and females were not allowed to be chained together. Mack was paired with a filthy old drunk called Mad Barney. Cora made eyes at the blacksmith and got herself paired with Peg.

"I don't believe Caspar knows we're leaving today," Mack said worriedly. "Perhaps they don't have to notify anyone."

He looked up and down the line of convicts. There were more than a hundred, he reckoned; around a quarter of them were female, with a sprinkling of children from about nine years upward. Among the men was Sidney Lennox.

Lennox's fall had caused much glee. No one would trust him since he gave evidence against Peg. The thieves who had disposed of their stolen goods at the Sun tavern now went elsewhere. And although the coal heavers' strike had been broken, and most of the men were back at work, no one would work for Lennox at any price. He had tried to coerce a woman called Gwen Sixpence into stealing for him, but she and two friends had informed against him for receiving stolen property, and he had duly been convicted. The Jamissons had intervened and saved him from the gallows, but they could not prevent his being transported.

The great wooden doors of the prison swung wide. A squad of eight guards stood outside to escort them. A jailer gave a violent shove to the pair at the front of the line, and slowly they moved out into the busy city street.

"We're not far from Fleet Street," Mack said. "It's possible Caspar may get to know of this."

"What difference does it make?" said Cora.

"He can bribe the ship's captain to give us special treatment."

Mack had learned a little about crossing the Atlantic by questioning prisoners, guards and visitors in Newgate. The one indubitable fact he had learned was that the voyage killed many people. Whether the passengers were slaves, convicts or indentured servants, conditions below decks were lethally unhealthy. Shippers were motivated by money: they crammed as many people as possible into their holds. But captains were mercenary too, and a prisoner with cash for bribes could travel in a cabin.

Londoners stopped what they were doing to watch the convicts make their last, shameful progress through the heart of the city. Some shouted condolences, some jeered and mocked, and a few threw stones or rubbish. Mack asked a friendly-looking woman to take a message to Caspar Gordonson, but she refused. He tried again, twice, with the same result.

The irons slowed them down, and it took more than an hour to shuffle to the waterfront. The river was busy with ships, barges, ferries and rafts, for the strikes were over, crushed by the troops. It was a warm spring morning. Sunlight glinted off the muddy Thames. A boat was waiting to take them out to their ship, which was anchored in midstream. Mack read its name: "The *Rosebud.*"

"Is it a Jamisson ship?" said Cora.

"I think most of the convict ships are."

As he stepped from the muddy foreshore into the boat, Mack realized this would be the last time he stood on British soil for many years, perhaps forever. He had mixed feelings: fear and apprehension mingled with a certain reckless excitement at the prospect of a new country and a new life.

Boarding the ship was difficult: they had to climb the ladder in pairs with the leg irons on. Peg and Cora managed easily enough, being young and nimble, but Mack had to carry Barney. One pair of men fell into the river. Neither the guards nor the sailors did anything to help them, and they would have drowned if the other prisoners had not reached out and pulled them back into the boat.

The ship was about forty feet long by fifteen wide. Peg commented: "I've burgled drawing rooms that were bigger than this, by Christ." On deck were hens in a coop, a small pigsty, and a tethered goat. On the other side of the ship a magnificent white horse was being hoisted out of a boat with the help of the yardarm used as a crane. A scrawny cat bared its fangs at Mack. He had an impression of coiled ropes and furled sails, a smell of varnish, and a rocking motion underfoot; then they were shoved across the lip of a hatch and down a ladder.

There seemed to be three lower decks. On the first, four sailors were eating their midday meal, sitting cross-legged on the floor, surrounded by sacks and chests that presumably contained supplies for the voyage. On the third, all the way down at the foot of the ladder, two men were stacking barrels, hammering wedges between them so that they could not move during the voyage. At the level of the middle deck, which was obviously for the convicts, a sailor roughly pulled Mack and Barney off the ladder and shoved them through a doorway.

There was an odor of tar and vinegar. Mack peered at his surroundings in the gloom. The ceiling was an inch or two above his head: a tall man would have to stoop. It was pierced by two gratings that admitted a little light and air, not from outside but from the enclosed deck above, which itself was lit by open hatches. Along both sides of the hold were wooden racks, six feet wide, one at waist height and one a few inches off the floor.

With horror Mack realized the racks were for the convicts to lie on. They would be spending the voyage on these bare shelves.

They shuffled along the narrow walkway between the rows. The first few berths were already occupied by convicts lying flat, still chained in pairs. They were quiet, stunned by what was happening to them. A sailor directed Peg and Cora to lie next to Mack and Barney, like knives in a drawer. They took their positions, and the sailor roughly shoved them closer together, so that they were touching. Peg was able to sit upright but the grown-ups were not, for there was not enough headroom. The best Mack could do was to prop himself on one elbow.

At the end of the row Mack spotted a large earthenware jar, about two feet high, cone shaped with a broad flat base and a rim about nine inches across. There were three others around the hold. They were the only items of furniture visible, and he realized they were the toilets.

"How long will it take to get to Virginia?" said Peg.

"Seven weeks," he said. "If we're lucky."

*

Lizzie watched as her trunk was carried into the large cabin at the rear of the *Rosebud*. She and Jay had the owner's quarters, a bedroom and a day room, and there was more space than she had expected. Everyone talked of the horrors of the transatlantic voyage, but she was determined to make the best of it and try to enjoy the novel experience.

Making the best of things was now her philosophy of life. She could not forget Jay's betrayal—she still clenched her fists and bit her lip every time she thought of the hollow promise he had made on their wedding day—but she tried always to push it to the back of her mind.

Only a few weeks ago she would have been thrilled by this trip. Going to America was her great ambition: it was one of the reasons she had married Jay. She had anticipated a new life in the colonies, a more free-and-easy, outdoor existence, without petticoats or calling cards, where a woman could get dirt under her fingernails and speak her mind like a man. But the dream had lost some of its glow when she learned of the deal Jay had made. They ought to call the plantation "Twenty Graves," she thought moodily.

She tried to pretend that Jay was as dear to her as ever, but her body told the truth. When he touched her at night she did not respond as she once had. She would kiss and caress him, but his fingers did not scorch her skin, and his tongue no longer seemed to reach all the way inside to touch her soul. Once upon a time the mere sight of him had made her moist between the legs; now she surreptitiously oiled herself with cold cream before getting into bed, otherwise intercourse hurt her. He always ended up groaning and gasping with pleasure as he spilled his seed inside her, but there was no such culmination for her. Instead she was left with an unfulfilled feeling. Later, when she heard him snoring, she would console herself with her fingers, and then her head would fill with strange images, men wrestling and whores with exposed breasts.

But her life was dominated by thoughts of the baby. Her pregnancy made her disappointments seem less important. She would love her baby without reservation. The child would become her life's work. And he, or she, would grow up a Virginian.

As she was taking off her hat there was a tap at the cabin door. A wiry man in a blue coat and a three-cornered hat stepped inside and bowed. "Silas Bone, first mate, at your service, Mrs. Jamisson, Mr. Jamisson," he said.

"Good day to you, Bone," Jay said stiffly, assuming the dignity of the owner's son.

"Captain's compliments to you both," Bone said. They had already met Captain Parridge, a dour, aloof Kentishman from Rochester. "We'll get under way at the turn of the tide," Bone went on. He gave Lizzie a patronizing smile. "However, we'll be within the Thames estuary for the first day or two, so madam need not worry about bumpy weather just yet."

Jay said: "Are my horses on board?"

"Yes sir."

"Let's have a look at their accommodation."

"Certainly. Perhaps Mrs. J. will stay and unpack her little bits and pieces."

Lizzie said: "I'll come with you. I'd like to take a look around."

Bone said: "You'll find it best to stay in your cabin as much as possible on the voyage, Mrs. J. Sailors are rough folk and the weather is rougher."

Lizzie bridled. "I have no intention of spending the next seven weeks cooped up in this little room," she snapped. "Lead the way, Mr. Bone."

"Aye-aye, Mrs. J."

They stepped out of the cabin and walked along the deck to an open hatch. The mate scampered down a ladder, agile as a monkey. Jay went after him and Lizzie followed. They went to the second of the lower decks. Daylight filtered down from the open hatch, and it was augmented a little by a single lamp on a hook.

Jay's favorite horses, the two grays, and the birthday present, Blizzard, stood in narrow stalls. Each had a sling under its belly, attached to a beam overhead, so that if it lost its footing in heavy seas it could not fall. There was hay in a manger at the horses' heads, and the deck below them was sanded to protect their hooves. They were valuable beasts and would be hard to replace in America. They were nervous and Jay petted them for a while, speaking to them soothingly.

Lizzie became impatient and wandered along the deck to where a heavy door stood open. Bone followed her. "I wouldn't wander around, if I were you, Mrs. J.," he said. "You might see things that would distress you."

She ignored him and went forward. She was not squeamish.

"That's the convict hold ahead," he said. "It's no place for a lady."

He had said the magic words that guaranteed she would persist. She turned around and fixed him with a look. "Mr. Bone, this ship belongs to my father-in-law and I will go where I like. Is that clear?"

"Aye-aye, Mrs. J."

"And you can call me Mrs. Jamisson."

"Aye-aye, Mrs. Jamisson."

She was keen to see the convict hold because McAsh might be there:

this was the first convict ship to leave London since his trial. She went forward a couple of paces, ducked her head under a beam, pushed open a door and found herself in the main hold.

It was warm, and there was an oppressive stink of crowded humanity. She stared into the gloom. At first she could see nobody, although she heard the murmur of many voices. She was in a big space filled with what looked like storage racks for barrels. Something moved on the shelf beside her, with a clank like a chain, and she jumped. Then she saw to her horror that what had moved was a human foot in an iron clamp. Someone was lying on the shelf, she saw; no, two people, fettered together at their ankles. As her eyes adjusted she saw another couple lying shoulder to shoulder with the first, then another, and she realized there were dozens of them, packed together on these racks like herrings in a fishmonger's tray.

Surely, she thought, this was just temporary accommodation, and they would be given proper bunks, at least, for the voyage? Then she realized what a foolish notion that was. Where could such bunks be? This was the main hold, occupying most of the space below deck. There was nowhere else for these wretched people to go. They would spend at least seven weeks lying here in the airless gloom.

"Lizzie Jamisson!" said a voice.

She gave a start. She recognized the Scots accent: it was Mack. She peered into the dark, saying: "Mack—where are you?"

"Here."

She took a few paces along the narrow walkway between the racks. An arm was stretched out to her, ghostly gray in the twilight. She squeezed Mack's hard hand. "This is dreadful," she said. "What can I do?"

"Nothing, now," he said.

She saw Cora lying beside him and the child, Peg, next to her. At least they were all together. Something in Cora's expression made Lizzie let go of Mack's hand. "Perhaps I can make sure you get enough food and water," she said.

"That would be kind."

Lizzie could not think of anything else to say. She stood there in silence for a few moments. "I'll come back down here every day, if I can," she said at last.

"Thank you."

She turned and hurried out.

She retraced her steps with an indignant protest on her lips, but when she caught the eye of Silas Bone she saw such a look of scorn on his face that she bit back her words. The convicts were on board and the ship was about to set sail, and nothing she could say would change matters now. A protest would only vindicate Bone's warning that women should not go below decks.

"The horses are comfortably settled," Jay said with an air of satisfaction.

Lizzie could not resist a retort. "They're better off than the human beings!"

"Ah, that reminds me," said Jay. "Bone, there's a convict in the hold called Sidney Lennox. Have his irons struck and put him in a cabin, please."

"Aye-aye, sir."

"Why is Lennox with us?" Lizzie said, aghast.

"He was convicted of receiving stolen goods. But the family has made use of him in the past and we can't abandon him. He might die in the hold."

"Oh, Jay!" Lizzie cried in dismay. "He's such a bad man!"

"On the contrary, he's quite useful."

Lizzie turned away. She had rejoiced to be leaving Lennox behind in England. What bad luck that he too had been transported. Would Jay never escape from his malign influence?

Bone said: "The tide's on the turn, Mr. Jamisson. Captain will be impatient to weigh anchor."

"My compliments to the captain, and tell him to carry on."

They all climbed the ladder.

A few minutes later Lizzie and Jay stood in the bows as the ship began to move downriver on the tide. A fresh evening breeze buffeted Lizzie's cheeks. As the dome of St. Paul slipped below the skyline of warehouses she said: "I wonder if we'll ever see London again.

III

Virginia

26

MACK LAY IN THE HOLD OF THE *ROSEBUD*, SHAKING WITH FEVER. He felt like an animal: filthy, nearly naked, chained and helpless. He could hardly stand upright but his mind was clear enough. He vowed he would never again allow anyone to put iron fetters on him. He would fight, try to escape, and hope they killed him rather than suffer this degradation again.

An excited cry from on deck penetrated the hold: "Soundings at thirty-five fathoms, Captain—sand and reeds!"

A cheer went up from the crew. Peg said: "What's a fathom?"

"Six feet of water," Mack said with weary relief. "It means we're approaching land."

He had often felt he would not make it. Twenty-five of the prisoners had died at sea. They had not starved: it seemed that Lizzie, who had not reappeared below decks, had nevertheless kept her promise and ensured they had enough to eat and drink. But the drinking water had been foul and the diet of salt meat and bread unhealthily monotonous, and all the convicts had been violently ill with the type of sickness that was called sometimes hospital fever and sometimes jail fever. Mad Barney had been the first to die of it: the old went quickest.

Disease was not the only cause of death. Five people had been killed in one dreadful storm, when the prisoners had been tossed around the hold, helplessly injuring themselves and others with their iron chains.

Peg had always been thin but now she looked as if she were made of sticks. Cora had aged. Even in the half dark of the hold Mack could see that her hair was falling out, her face was drawn, and her once voluptuous body was scraggy and disfigured with sores. Mack was just glad they were still alive.

Some time later he heard another sounding: "Eighteen fathoms and white sand." Next time it was thirteen fathoms and shells; and then, at last, the cry: "Land ho!"

Despite his weakness Mack longed to go on deck. This is America, he thought. I've crossed the world to the far side, and I'm still alive; I wish I could see America.

That night the *Rosebud* anchored in calm waters. The seaman who brought the prisoners' rations of salt pork and foul water was one of the more friendly crew members. His name was Ezekiel Bell. He was disfigured—he had lost one ear, he was completely bald and he had a huge goiter like a hen's egg on his neck—and he was ironically known as Beau Bell. He told them they were off Cape Henry, near the town of Hampton in Virginia.

Next day the ship remained at anchor. Mack wondered angrily what was prolonging their voyage. Someone must have gone ashore for supplies, because that night there came from the galley a mouthwatering smell of fresh meat roasting. It tortured the prisoners and gave Mack stomach cramps.

"Mack, what happens when we get to Virginia?" Peg asked.

"We'll be sold, and have to work for whoever buys us," he replied.

"Will we be sold together?"

He knew there was little chance of it, but he did not say so. "We might be," he said. "Let's hope for the best."

There was a silence while Peg took that in. When she spoke again her voice was frightened. "Who will buy us?"

"Farmers, planters, housewives . . . anyone who needs workers and wants them cheap."

"Someone might want all three of us."

Who would want a coal miner and two thieves? Mack said: "Or perhaps we might be bought by people who live close together."

"What work will we do?"

"Anything we're told to, I suppose: farm work, cleaning, building . . ."

"We'll be just like slaves."

"But only for seven years."

"Seven years," she said dismally. "I'll be grown-up!"

"And I'll be almost thirty," Mack said. It seemed middle-aged.

"Will they beat us?"

Mack knew that the answer was yes, but he lied. "Not if we work hard and keep our mouths shut."

"Who gets the money when we're bought?"

"Sir George Jamisson." The fever had tired him, and he added impatiently: "I'm sure you've asked me half these damn questions before."

Peg turned away, hurt. Cora said: "She's worried, Mack—that's why she keeps asking the same questions."

I'm worried too, Mack thought wretchedly.

"I don't want to reach Virginia," Peg said. "I want the voyage to go on forever."

Cora laughed bitterly. "You enjoy living this way?"

"It's like having a mother and father," Peg said.

Cora put her arm around the child and hugged her.

They weighed anchor the following morning, and Mack could feel the ship bowling along in front of a strong favorable wind. In the evening he learned they were almost at the mouth of the Rappahannock River. Then contrary winds kept them at anchor for two wasted days before they could head upriver.

Mack's fever abated and he was strong enough to go up on deck for one of the intermittent exercise periods; and as the ship tacked upriver he got his first sight of America.

Thick woods and cultivated fields lined both banks. At intervals there would be a jetty, a cleared stretch of bank, and a lawn rising up to a grand house. Here and there around the jetties he saw the huge barrels known as hogsheads, used for transporting tobacco: he had watched them being unloaded in the port of London, and it now struck him as remarkable that every one had survived the hazardous and violent transatlantic voyage to get there from here. Most of the people in the fields were black, he noticed. The horses and dogs looked the same as any others, but the birds perching on the ship's rail were unfamiliar. There were lots of other vessels on the river, a few merchantmen like the *Rosebud* and many smaller craft.

That brief survey was all he saw for the next four days, but he kept the picture in his mind like a treasured souvenir as he lay in the hold: the sunshine, the people walking around in the fresh air, the woods and the lawns and the houses. The longing he felt, to get off the *Rosebud* and walk around in the open air, was so strong it was like a pain.

When at last they anchored he learned they were at Fredericksburg, their destination. The voyage had taken eight weeks.

That night the convicts got cooked food: a broth of fresh pork with Indian corn and potatoes in it, a slab of new bread, and a quart of ale. The unaccustomed rich food and strong ale made Mack feel dizzy and sick all night.

Next morning they were brought up on deck in groups of ten, and they saw Fredericksburg.

They were anchored in a muddy river with midstream islands. There was a narrow sandy beach, a strip of wooded waterfront, then a short, sharp rise to the town itself, which was built around a bluff. It looked as though a couple of hundred people might live there: it was not much bigger than Heugh, the village where Mack had been born, but it seemed a cheerful, prosperous place, with houses of wood painted white and green. On the opposite bank, a little upstream, was another town, which Mack learned was called Falmouth.

The river was crowded, with two more ships as big as the *Rosebud,* several smaller coasters, some flatboats, and a ferry crossing between the two towns. Men worked busily all along the waterfront unloading ships, rolling barrels and carrying chests in and out of warehouses.

The prisoners were given soap and made to wash, and a barber came on board to shave the men and cut their hair. Those whose clothes were so ragged as to be indecent were given replacement garments, but their gratitude was diminished when they recognized them as having been taken from those who had died on the voyage. Mack got Mad Barney's verminous coat: he draped it over a rail and beat it with a stick until no more lice fell out.

The captain made a list of the surviving prisoners and asked each what his trade had been at home. Some had been casual laborers or, like Cora and Peg, had never earned an honest living: they were encouraged to exaggerate or invent something. Peg was put down as a dressmaker's apprentice, Cora as a barmaid. Mack realized it was all a belated effort to make them look attractive to buyers.

They were returned to the hold, and that afternoon two men were brought down to inspect them. They were an odd-looking pair: one wore the red coat of a British soldier over homespun breeches, the other a once fashionable yellow waistcoat with crudely sewn buckskin trousers. Despite their odd clothes they looked well fed and had the red noses of men who could afford all the liquor they wanted. Beau Bell whispered to Mack that they were "soul drivers" and explained what that meant: they would buy up groups of slaves, convicts and indentured servants and herd them up-country like sheep, to sell to remote farmers and mountain men. Mack did not like the look of them. They went away without making a purchase. Tomorrow was Race Day, Bell said: the gentry came into town from all around for the horse races. Most of the convicts would be sold by the end of the day. Then the soul drivers would offer a knockdown price for all those who remained. Mack hoped Cora and Peg did not end up in their hands.

That night there was another good meal. Mack ate it slowly and slept soundly. In the morning everyone was looking a little better: they seemed bright eyed and able to smile. Throughout the voyage their only meal had been dinner, but today they got a breakfast of porridge and molasses and a ration of rum and water.

Consequently, despite the uncertain future that faced them, it was a cheerful group that mounted the ladder out of the hold and hobbled, still chained, on deck. There was more activity on the waterfront today, with several small boats landing, numerous carts passing along the main street, and small knots of smartly dressed people lounging around, obviously taking a day off.

A fat-bellied man in a straw hat came on board accompanied by a tall, gray-haired Negro. The two of them looked over the convicts, picking out some and rejecting others. Mack soon figured that they were selecting the youngest and strongest men, and inevitably he was among the fourteen or fifteen chosen. No women or children were picked.

When the selection was finished the captain said: "Right, you lot, go with these men."

"Where are we going?" Mack asked. They ignored him.

Peg began to cry.

Mack embraced her. He had known this was going to happen, and it broke his heart. Every adult Peg trusted had been taken from her: her mother killed by sickness, her father hanged, and now Mack sold away from her. He hugged her hard and she clung to him. "Take me with you!" she wailed.

He detached himself from her. "Try and stay with Cora, if you can," he said.

Cora kissed him on the lips with desperate passion. It was hard to believe that he might never see her again, never again lie in bed with her and touch her body and make her gasp with pleasure. Hot tears ran down her face and into his mouth as they kissed. "Try and find us, Mack, for God's sake," she pleaded.

"I'll do my best—"

"Promise me!" she insisted.

"I promise, I'll find you."

The fat-bellied man said: "Come on, lover boy," and jerked Mack away from her.

He looked back over his shoulder as he was pushed down the gangway onto the wharf. Cora and Peg stood watching with their arms around one another, crying. Mack thought of his parting from Esther. I won't fail Cora and Peg the way I failed Esther, he vowed. Then they were lost from sight.

It felt strange to put his feet on solid ground after eight weeks of having the never-ceasing movement of the sea beneath him. As he hobbled down the unpaved main street in his chains he stared about him, looking at America. The town center had a church, a market house, a pillory and a gallows. Brick and wood houses stood widely spaced along either side of the street. Sheep and chickens foraged in the muddy road. Some buildings seemed old-established but there was a raw, new look to many.

The town was thronged with people, horses, carts, and carriages, most of which must have come from the countryside all around. The women had new bonnets and ribbons, and the men wore polished boots and clean gloves. Many people's clothes had a homemade look, even though the fabrics were costly. He overheard several people talking of races and betting odds. Virginians seemed keen on gambling.

The townspeople looked at the convicts with mild curiosity, the way they might have watched a horse canter along the street, a sight they had seen before but which continued to interest them.

The town petered out after half a mile. They waded across the river at a ford, then set off along a rough track through wooded countryside. Mack put himself next to the middle-aged Negro. "My name is Malachi McAsh," he said. "They call me Mack."

The man kept his eyes straight ahead but spoke in a friendly enough way. "I'm Kobe," he said, pronouncing it to rhyme with Toby. "Kobe Tambala."

"The fat man in the straw hat—does he own us now?"

"No. Bill Sowerby's just the overseer. Him and me was told to go aboard the *Rosebud* and pick out the best field hands."

"Who has bought us?"

"You ain't exactly been *bought.*"

"What, then?"

"Mr. Jay Jamisson decided to keep you for hisself, to work on his own place, Mockjack Hall."

"Jamisson!"

"That's right."

Mack was once again owned by the Jamisson family. The thought made him angry. Damn them to hell, I'll run away again, he vowed. I will be my own man.

Kobe said: "What work did you do, before?"

"I used to be a coal miner."

"Coal? I've heard tell of it. A rock that burns like wood, but hotter?"

"Aye. Trouble is, you have to go deep underground to find it. What about yourself?"

"My people were farmers in Africa. My father had a big piece of land, more than Mr. Jamisson."

Mack was surprised: he had never thought of slaves as coming from rich families. "What kind of farm?"

"Mixed—wheat, some cattle—but no tobacco. We have a root called the yam grows out there. Never seen it here, though."

"You speak English well."

"I've been here nearly forty years." A look of bitterness came over his face. "I was just a boy when they stole me."

Peg and Cora were on Mack's mind. "There were two people on the ship with me, a woman and a girl," he said. "Will I be able to find out who bought them?"

Kobe gave a humorless laugh. "Everybody's trying to find someone they were sold apart from. People ask around all the time. When slaves meet up, on the road or in the woods, that's all they talk about."

"The child's name is Peg," Mack persisted. "She's only thirteen. She doesn't have a mother or father."

"When you've been bought, nobody has a mother or father."

Kobe had given up, Mack realized. He had grown accustomed to his slavery and learned to live with it. He was bitter, but he had abandoned all hope of freedom. I swear I'll never do that, Mack thought.

They walked about ten miles. It was slow, because the convicts were fettered. Some were still chained in pairs. Those whose partners had died on the voyage were hobbled, their ankles chained together so that they could walk but not run. None of them could go fast and they might have collapsed if they had tried, so weak were they from lying flat for eight weeks. The overseer, Sowerby, was on horseback, but he seemed in no hurry, and as he rode he sipped some kind of liquor from a flask.

The countryside was more like England than Scotland, and not as alien as Mack had anticipated. The road followed the rocky river, which wound through a lush forest. Mack wished he could lie in the shade of those big trees for a while.

He wondered how soon he would see the amazing Lizzie. He felt bitter about being the property of a Jamisson again, but her presence would be some consolation. Unlike her father-in-law she was not cruel, though she could be thoughtless. Her unorthodox ways and her vivacious personality delighted Mack. And she had a sense of justice that had saved his life in the past and might do so again.

It was noon when they arrived at the Jamisson plantation. A path led through an orchard where cattle grazed to a muddy compound with a dozen or so cabins. Two elderly black women were cooking over open fires, and four or five naked children played in the dirt. The cabins were crudely built with rough-hewn planks, and their shuttered windows had no glass.

Sowerby exchanged a few words with Kobe and disappeared.

Kobe said to the convicts: "These are your quarters."

Someone said: "Do we have to live with the blackies?"

Mack laughed. After eight weeks in the hellhole of the *Rosebud* it was a miracle they could complain about their accommodation.

Kobe said: "White and black live in separate cabins. There's no law about it, but it always seems to work out that way. Each cabin takes six people. Before we rest we have one more chore. Follow me."

They walked along a footpath that wound between fields of green wheat, tall Indian corn growing out of hillocks, and the fragrant tobacco plant. Men and women were at work in every field, weeding between the rows and picking grubs off the tobacco leaves.

They emerged onto a wide lawn and went up a rise toward a sprawling, dilapidated clapboard house with drab peeling paint and closed shutters: Mockjack Hall, presumably. Skirting the house, they came to a group of outbuildings at the back. One of the buildings was a smithy. Working there was a Negro whom Kobe addressed as Cass. He began to strike the fetters from the convicts' legs.

Mack watched as the convicts were unchained one by one. He felt a sense of liberation, though he knew it was false. These chains had been put on him in Newgate Prison, on the far side of the world. He had resented them every minute of the eight degrading weeks he had worn them.

From the high point where the house stood he could see the glint of the Rappahannock River, about half a mile away, winding through woodland. When my chains are struck I could just run away, down to the river, he thought, and I could jump in and swim across and make a bid for freedom.

He would have to restrain himself. He was still so weak that he probably could not run half a mile. Besides, he had promised to search for Peg and Cora, and he would have to find them before he escaped, for he might not be able to afterward. And he had to plan carefully. He knew nothing of the geography of this land. He needed to know where he was going and how he would get there.

All the same, when at last he felt the irons fall from his legs he had to make an effort not to run away.

While he was still fighting the impulse, Kobe began to speak. "Now you've lost your chains, some of you are already figuring how far you can get by sundown. Before you run away, there's something important you need to know, so listen up and pay attention."

He paused for effect, then went on: "People who run away are generally caught, and they get punished. First they're flogged, but that's the easy part. Then they have to wear the iron collar, which some find shameful. But the worst is, your time is made longer. If you're away for a week, you have to serve two weeks extra. We got people here run away so many times they won't be free until they're a hundred years old." He looked around and caught Mack's eye. "If you're willing to chance that much," he finished, "all I can say is, I wish you luck."

*

In the morning the old women cooked a boiled corn dish called hominy for breakfast. The convicts and slaves ate it with their fingers out of wooden bowls.

There were about forty field hands altogether. Apart from the new intake of convicts, most were black slaves. There were four indentured servants, people who had sold four years' labor in advance to pay for their transatlantic ticket. They kept apart from the others and evidently considered themselves superior. There were only three regular waged employees, two free blacks and a white woman, all past fifty years old. Some of the blacks spoke good English, but many talked in their own African languages and communicated with the whites in a childish kind of pidgin. At first Mack was inclined to treat them as children, then it struck him that they were superior to him in speaking one and a half languages, for he had only one.

They were marched a mile or two across broad fields to where the tobacco was ready to harvest. The tobacco plants stood in neat rows about three feet apart and a quarter of a mile long. They were about as tall as Mack, each with a dozen or so broad green leaves.

The hands were given their orders by Bill Sowerby and Kobe. They were divided into three groups. The first were given sharp knives and set to cutting down the ripe plants. The next group went into a field that had been cut the previous day. The plants lay on the ground, their big leaves wilted after a day drying in the sun. Newcomers were shown how to split the stalks of the cut plants and spear them on long wooden spikes. Mack was in the third group, which had the job of carrying the loaded spikes across the fields to the tobacco house, where they were hung from the high ceiling to cure in the air.

It was a long, hot summer day. The men from the *Rosebud* were not able to work as hard as the others. Mack found himself constantly overtaken by women and children. He had been weakened by disease, malnutrition and inactivity. Bill Sowerby carried a whip but Mack did not see him use it.

At noon they got a meal of coarse cornbread that the slaves called pone. While they were eating Mack was dismayed, but not completely surprised, to see the familiar figure of Sidney Lennox, dressed in new clothes, being shown around the plantation by Sowerby. No doubt Jay felt that Lennox had been useful to him in the past and might be so again.

At sundown, feeling exhausted, they left the fields; but instead of returning to their cabins they were marched to the tobacco house, now lit up by dozens of candles. After a hasty meal they worked on, stripping the leaves from cured plants, removing the thick central spine, and pressing the leaves into bundles. As the night wore on some of the children and older people fell asleep at their work, and an elaborate warning system came into play, whereby the stronger ones covered for the weak and woke them when Sowerby approached.

It must have been past midnight, Mack guessed, when at last the candles were snuffed and the hands were allowed to return to their cabins and lie down on their wooden bunks. Mack fell asleep immediately.

It seemed only seconds later that he was being shaken awake to go back to work. Wearily he got to his feet and staggered outside. Leaning against the cabin wall he ate his bowl of hominy. No sooner had he stuffed the last handful into his mouth than they were marched off again.

As they entered the field in the dawn light, he saw Lizzie.

He had not set eyes on her since the day they had boarded the *Rosebud*. She was on a white horse, crossing the field at a walk. She wore a loose linen dress and a big hat. The sun was about to rise and there was a clear, watery light. She looked well: rested, comfortable, the lady of the manor riding about her estate. She had put on some weight, Mack noticed, while he had wasted away from starvation. But he could not resent her, for she stood up for what was right and had thereby saved his life more than once.

He recalled the time he had embraced her, in the alley off Tyburn Street, after he had saved her from the two ruffians. He had held that soft body close to his own and inhaled the fragrance of soap and feminine perspiration; and for a mad moment he had thought that Lizzie, rather than Cora, might be the woman for him. Then sanity had returned.

Looking at her rounded body he realized she was not getting fat, she was pregnant. She would have a son and he would grow up a Jamisson, cruel and greedy and heartless, Mack thought. He would own this plantation and buy human beings and treat them like cattle, and he would be rich.

Lizzie caught his eye. He felt guilty that he had been thinking such harsh thoughts of her unborn child. She stared at first, unsure who he was; then she seemed to recognize him with a jolt. Perhaps she was shocked by the change in his appearance caused by the voyage.

He held her eye for a long time, hoping she would come over to him; but then she turned away without speaking and kicked her horse into a trot, and a moment later she disappeared into the woods.

27

A WEEK AFTER ARRIVING AT MOCKJACK HALL JAY JAMISSON SAT watching two slaves unpack a trunk of glassware. Belle was middle-aged and heavy, and she had ballooning breasts and a vast rear; but Mildred was about eighteen years old, with perfect tobacco-colored skin and lazy eyes. When she reached up to the shelves of the cabinet he could see her breasts move under the drab homespun shift she wore. His stare made both women uneasy, and they unwrapped the delicate crystal with shaky hands. If they broke anything they would have to be punished. Jay wondered if he should beat them.

The thought made him restless, and he got up and went outside. Mockjack Hall was a big, long-fronted house with a pillared portico facing down a sloping lawn to the muddy Rappahannock River. Any house of its size in England would have been made of stone or brick, but this was a wood-frame building. It had been painted white with green shutters many years ago, but now the paint was peeling and the colors had faded to a uniform drab. At the back and sides were numerous outhouses containing the kitchen, laundry, and stables. The main house had grand reception rooms—drawing room, dining room, and even a ballroom—and spacious bedrooms upstairs, but the whole interior needed redecoration. There was much once fashionable imported furniture, and faded silk hangings and worn rugs. The air of lost grandeur about the place was like a smell of drains.

Nevertheless Jay felt good as he surveyed his estate from the portico. It was a thousand acres of cultivated fields, wooded hillsides, bright streams and broad ponds, with forty hands and three house servants; and the land and the people belonged to him. Not to his family, not to his father, but to him. At last he was a gentleman in his own right.

And this was just the start. He planned to cut a dash in Virginia society. He did not know just how colonial government worked, but he understood they had local leaders called vestrymen, and the assembly in Williamsburg was composed of burgesses, the equivalent of members of Parliament. Given his status he thought he might skip the local stage and stand for election to the House of Burgesses at the earliest opportunity. He wanted everyone to know that Jay Jamisson was a man of importance.

Lizzie came across the lawn, riding Blizzard, who had survived the voyage unscathed. She was riding him well, Jay thought, almost like a man—and then he realized, to his irritation, that she was riding astride. It was so vulgar for a woman to go up and down like that with her legs apart. When she reined in he said: "You shouldn't ride like that."

She put a hand on her rounded waist. "I've been going very slowly, just walking and trotting."

"I wasn't thinking of the baby. I hope nobody saw you riding astride."

Her face fell, but her rejoinder was defiant, as always: "I don't intend to ride sidesaddle out here."

"Out here?" he repeated. "What does it matter where we are?"

"But there's nobody here to see me."

"I can see you. So can the servants. And we might have visitors. You wouldn't walk around naked 'out here,' would you?"

"I'll ride sidesaddle to church, and when we're with company, but not on my own."

There was no arguing with her in this mood. "Anyway, quite soon you'll have to stop riding altogether, for the sake of the baby," he said sulkily.

"But not just yet," she said brightly. She was five months pregnant: she planned to stop riding at six. She changed the subject. "I've been looking around. The land is in better condition than the house. Sowerby is a drunk, but he has kept the place going. We probably should be grateful, considering he hasn't been paid his wages for almost a year."

"He may have to wait a little longer—cash is short."

"Your father said there were fifty hands, but in fact there are only twenty-five. It's a good thing we have the fifteen convicts from the *Rosebud.*" She frowned. "Is McAsh among them?"

"Yes."

"I thought I saw him across the fields."

"I told Sowerby to pick out the youngest and strongest." Jay had not realized that McAsh was on the ship. If he had thought about it, he might have guessed and told Sowerby to be sure to leave the troublemaker behind. But now that he was here Jay was reluctant to send him away: he did not want to appear intimidated by a mere convict.

Lizzie said: "I presume we didn't pay for the new men."

"Certainly not—why should I pay for something that belongs to my family?"

"Your father may find out."

"He certainly will. Captain Parridge demanded a receipt for fifteen convicts, and naturally I obliged him. He will hand that to Father."

"And then?"

Jay shrugged. "Father will probably send me a bill, which I will pay—when I can." He was rather pleased with this little piece of business. He had got fifteen strong men to work for seven years, and it had cost him nothing.

"How will your father take it?"

Jay grinned. "He'll be furious, but what can he do at this distance?"

"I suppose it's all right," Lizzie said dubiously.

He did not like her questioning his judgment. "These things are best left to men."

That annoyed her, as always. She went on the attack. "I'm sorry to see Lennox here—I can't understand your attachment to that man."

Jay had mixed feelings about Lennox. He might be as useful here as he had been in London—but he was an uncomfortable presence.

However, once he had been rescued from the hold of the *Rosebud,* the man had assumed he would be living on the Jamisson plantation, and Jay had never summoned the nerve to discuss the matter. "I thought it would be useful to have a white man to do my bidding," he said airily.

"But what will he do?"

"Sowerby needs an assistant."

"Lennox knows nothing about tobacco, except how to smoke the stuff."

"He can learn. Besides, it's mainly a matter of making the Negroes work."

"He'll be good at that," Lizzie said caustically.

Jay did not want to discuss Lennox. "I may go into public life here," he said. "I'd like to get elected to the House of Burgesses. I wonder how soon it could be arranged."

"You'd better meet our neighbors and talk to them about it."

He nodded. "In a month or so, when the house is ready, we'll give a big party and invite everyone of importance from round about Fredericksburg. That will give me a chance to get the measure of the local gentry."

"A party," Lizzie said dubiously. "Can we afford it?"

Once again she was questioning his judgment. "Leave the finances to me," he snapped. "I'm sure we can get supplies on credit—the family has been trading in these parts for at least ten years, my name must be worth quite a lot."

She persisted with her questions. "Wouldn't it be better to concentrate on running the plantation, at least for a year or two? Then you could be sure you had a solid foundation for your public career."

"Don't be stupid," he said. "I didn't come here to be a farmer."

*

The ballroom was small, but it had a good floor and a little balcony for the musicians. Twenty or thirty couples were dancing in their bright satin clothes, the men wearing wigs and the women in lacy hats. Two fiddlers, a drummer and a French horn player were giving a minuet.

Dozens of candles lit up the fresh paintwork and floral decorations. In the other rooms of the house, guests played cards, smoked, drank and flirted.

Jay and Lizzie moved from the ballroom to the dining room, smiling and nodding at their guests. Jay was wearing a new apple green silk suit he had bought in London just before they left; Lizzie was in purple, her favorite color. Jay had thought their clothes might outshine those of the guests, but to his surprise he found that Virginians were as fashionable as Londoners.

He had drunk plenty of wine and was feeling good. They had served dinner earlier, but refreshments were now on the table: wine, jellies, cheesecakes, syllabubs and fruit. The party had cost a small fortune, but it was a success: everyone who was anyone had come.

The only sour note had been struck by the overseer, Sowerby, who had chosen today to ask for his back pay. When Jay told him it was not possible to pay him until the first tobacco crop was sold, Sowerby had insolently asked how Jay could afford to give a party for fifty guests. The truth was that Jay could not afford it—everything had been bought on credit—but he was too proud to say that to his overseer. So he had told him to hold his tongue. Sowerby had looked disappointed and worried, and Jay had wondered if he had some specific money problem. However, he did not inquire.

In the dining room the Jamissons' nearest neighbors were standing at the fire, eating cake. There were three couples: Colonel and Mrs. Thumson, Bill and Suzy Delahaye, and the Armstead brothers, two bachelors. The Thumsons were very elevated: the colonel was a burgess, a member of the general assembly, grave and self-important. He had distinguished himself in the British army and the Virginia militia, then had retired to grow tobacco and help rule the colony. Jay felt he could model himself on Thumson.

They were talking politics, and Thumson explained: "The governor of Virginia died last March, and we're waiting for his replacement."

Jay assumed the air of an insider in the London court. "The king has appointed Norborne Berkeley, the baron de Botetourt."

John Armstead, who was drunk, laughed coarsely. "What a name!"

Jay gave him a frosty look. "I believe the baron was hoping to leave London soon after I did."

Thumson said: "The president of the council is acting as his deputy in the interim."

Jay was keen to show that he knew a lot about local affairs. He said: "I assume that's why the burgesses were so unwise as to support the Massachusetts Letter." The letter in question was a protest against customs duties. It had been sent by the Massachusetts Legislature to King George. Then the Virginia Legislature had passed a resolution approving of the letter. Jay and most London Tories considered both the letter and the Virginia resolution disloyal.

Thumson seemed to disagree. He said stiffly: "I trust the burgesses were not unwise."

"His Majesty certainly thought so," Jay rejoined. He did not explain how he knew what the king thought, but left room for them to suppose the king had told him personally.

"Well, I'm sorry to hear that," said Thumson, not sounding sorry at all.

Jay felt that he might be on dangerous ground, but he wanted to impress these people with his acumen, so he went on. "I'm quite sure the new governor will demand that the resolution be withdrawn." He had learned this before leaving London.

Bill Delahaye, younger than Thumson, said hotly: "The burgesses will refuse." His pretty wife, Suzy, put a restraining hand on his arm, but he felt strongly, and he added: "It's their duty to tell the king the truth, not mouth empty phrases that will please his Tory sycophants."

Thumson said tactfully: "Not that all Tories are sycophants, of course."

Jay said: "If the burgesses refuse to withdraw their resolution, the governor will have to dissolve the assembly."

Roderick Armstead, soberer than his brother, said: "It's curious how little difference that makes, nowadays."

Jay was mystified. "How so?"

"Colonial parliaments are constantly being dissolved for one reason or another. They simply reassemble informally, in a tavern or a private house, and carry on their business."

"But in those circumstances they have no legal status!" Jay protested.

Colonel Thumson answered him. "Still, they have the consent of the people they govern, and that seems to be enough."

Jay had heard this sort of thing before, from men who read too much philosophy. The idea that governments got their authority from the consent of the people was dangerous nonsense. The implication was that kings had no right to rule. It was the kind of thing John Wilkes was saying back at home. Jay began to get angry with Thumson. "In London a man could be jailed for talking that way, Colonel," he said.

"Quite," Thumson said enigmatically.

Lizzie intervened. "Have you tried the syllabub, Mrs. Thumson?"

The colonel's wife responded with exaggerated enthusiasm. "Yes, it's very good, quite delicious."

"I'm so glad. Syllabub can so easily go wrong."

Jay knew that Lizzie could not care less about syllabub; she was trying to move the conversation away from politics. But he had not finished. "I must say I'm surprised by some of your attitudes, Colonel," he said.

"Ah, I see Dr. Finch—I must have a word with him," Thumson said, and moved smoothly, with his wife, to another group.

Bill Delahaye said: "You've only just arrived, Jamisson. You may find that living here for a while gives you a different perspective."

His tone was not unkind, but he was saying Jay did not yet know enough to have a view of his own. Jay was offended. "I trust, sir, that my loyalty to my sovereign will be unshaken, no matter where I may choose to live."

Delahaye's face darkened. "No doubt," he said, and he too moved away, taking his wife with him.

Roderick Armstead said, "I must try this syllabub," and turned to the table, leaving Jay and Lizzie with his drunk brother.

"Politics and religion," said John Armstead. "Never talk about politics and religion at a party." And with that he leaned backward, closed his eyes and fell flat.

*

Jay came down to breakfast at midday. He had a headache.

He had not seen Lizzie: they had adjoining bedrooms, a luxury they had not been able to afford in London. However, he found her eating grilled ham while the house slaves cleaned up after the ball.

There was a letter for him. He sat down and opened it, but before he could read it Lizzie glared at him and said: "Why on earth did you start that quarrel last night?"

"What quarrel?"

"With Thumson and Delahaye, of course."

"It wasn't a quarrel, it was a discussion."

"You've offended our nearest neighbors."

"Then they're too easily offended."

"You practically called Colonel Thumson a traitor!"

"It seems to me he probably is a traitor."

"He's a landowner, a member of the House of Burgesses, and a retired officer—how in the name of heaven can he be a traitor?"

"You heard him talk."

"That's obviously normal here."

"Well, it's never going to be normal in my house."

Sarah, the cook, came in, interrupting the argument. Jay ordered tea and toast.

Lizzie got the last word, as always. "After spending all that money to get to know our neighbors you succeeded in making them dislike you." She resumed eating.

Jay looked at his letter. It was from a lawyer in Williamsburg.

Duke of Gloucester Street
Williamsburg
29 August 1768

I am commanded to write to you, dear Mr Jamisson, by your father, Sir George. I welcome you to Virginia and hope that we shall soon have the pleasure of seeing you here in the colonial capital.

Jay was surprised. This was uncharacteristically thoughtful of his father. Would he start to be kind, now that Jay was half a world away?

> *Until then, please let me know if I may be of any assistance. I know that you have taken over a plantation in difficulties, and that you may choose to seek financial help. Allow me to offer my services should you require a mortgage. I am sure a lender could be found without difficulty. I remain, Sir,*
>
> > *your most humble and obedient servant—*
> > *Matthew Murchman.*

Jay smiled. This was just what he needed. The repair and redecoration of the house, and the lavish party, had already put him up to his neck in debt with local merchants; and Sowerby kept asking for supplies: seed, new tools, clothes for the slaves, rope, paint, the list was endless. "Well, you needn't worry about money any longer," he said to Lizzie as he put down the letter.

She looked skeptical.

"I'm going to Williamsburg," he said.

28

WHILE JAY WAS IN WILLIAMSBURG LIZZIE GOT A LETTER FROM her mother. The first thing that struck her about it was the return address:

> *The Manse*
> *St John's Church*
> *Aberdeen*
> *August 15th, 1768*

What was Mother doing in a vicarage in Aberdeen? She read on:

> *I have so much to tell you, my dear daughter! But I must take care to write it step by step, as it happened.*
>
> *Soon after I returned to High Glen your brother-in-law, Robert Jamisson, took over the management of the estate. Sir George is now paying the interest on my mortgages so I am in no position to argue. Robert asked me to leave the big house and live in the old hunting lodge, for the sake of economy. I confess I was not best pleased with the arrangement but he insisted, and I have to tell you he was not as pleasant or affectionate as a family member might be.*

A surge of impotent anger possessed Lizzie. How dare Robert evict Lizzie's mother from her home? She recalled his words after she had rejected him and accepted Jay: "Even if I can't have you, I'll still have High Glen." It had seemed impossible at the time, but now it had come true.

Gritting her teeth, she continued to read.

> *Then the Reverend Mr York announced that he was leaving us. He has been pastor at Heugh for fifteen years and he is my oldest friend. I understood that after the tragic early death of his wife he felt the need to go and live in a new place. But you may imagine how distraught I was that he was leaving just when I needed friends.*
>
> *Then the most astonishing thing happened. My dear, I blush to tell you that he asked me to marry him!! And I accepted!!!*

"Good God!" Lizzie said aloud.

> *So you see we are wed, and have moved to Aberdeen, from where I write.*
>
> *Many will say I married beneath myself, being the widow of Lord Hallim; but I know how worthless a title is, and John cares nothing for what society people think. We live quietly, and I am known as Mrs York, and I am happier now than I ever have been.*

There was more—about her three stepchildren, the servants at the manse, Mr. York's first sermon, and the ladies in the congregation—but Lizzie was too shocked to take it in.

She had never thought of her mother remarrying. There was no reason why not, of course: Mother was only forty. She might even have more children; it was not impossible.

What shocked Lizzie was a sense of being cast adrift. High Glen had always been her home. Although her life was here in Virginia with her husband and her baby, she had thought of High Glen House as a place she could always return to, if she really needed sanctuary. But now it was in the hands of Robert.

Lizzie had always been the center of her mother's life. It had never occurred to her that this would change. But now her mother was a minister's wife living in Aberdeen, with three stepchildren to love and care for, and she might even be expecting a new baby of her own.

It meant Lizzie had no home but this plantation, no family but Jay.

Well, she was determined to make a good life for herself here.

She had privileges many women would envy: a big house, an estate of a thousand acres, a handsome husband, and slaves to do her bidding. The house slaves had taken her to their hearts. Sarah was the cook, fat Belle did most of the cleaning, and Mildred was her personal maid and also served at table sometimes. Belle had a twelve-year-old son, Jimmy, who was the stable boy: his father had been sold away years ago. Lizzie had not yet got to know many of the field hands, apart from Mack, but she liked Kobe, the supervisor, and the blacksmith, Cass, whose workshop was at the back of the house.

The house was spacious and grand, but it had an empty, abandoned feel. It was too big. It would suit a family with six growing children and a few aunts and grandparents, and troops of slaves to light fires in every room and serve vast communal dinners. For Lizzie and Jay it was a mausoleum. But the plantation was beautiful: thick woodlands, broad sloping fields, and a hundred little streams.

She knew Jay was not quite the man she had taken him for. He was not the daring free spirit he had seemed to be when he took her down the coal mine. And his lying to her over mining in High Glen had shaken her: after that she could never feel the same about him. They no longer romped in bed in the mornings. They spent most of the day apart. They ate dinner and supper together, but they never sat in front of the fire, holding hands and talking of nothing in particular, the way they once had. But perhaps Jay was disappointed, too. He might have similar feelings about her: that she was not as perfect as she had once seemed. There was no point in regrets. They had to love one another as they were today.

All the same she often felt a powerful urge to run away. But whenever she did, she remembered the child growing inside her. She could no longer think only of herself. Her baby needed its father.

Jay did not talk about the baby much. He seemed uninterested. But he would change when it was born, especially if it was a boy.

She put her letter in a drawer.

When she had given the day's orders to the house slaves she got her coat and went outside.

The air was cool. It was now mid-October; they had been here two months. She headed across the lawn and down toward the river. She went on foot: she was past six months now, and she could feel the baby kick—sometimes painfully. She was afraid she might harm the baby if she rode.

Still she walked around the estate almost every day. It took her several hours. She was usually accompanied by Roy and Rex, two deerhounds Jay had bought. She kept a close eye on the work of the plantation, for Jay took no interest at all. She watched the processing of the tobacco and kept count of the bales; she saw the men cutting trees and making barrels; she looked at the cows and horses in the meadows and the chickens and geese in the yard. Today was Sunday, the hands' day of rest, and it gave her a special opportunity to poke around while Sowerby and Lennox were somewhere else. Roy followed her, but Rex lazily remained on the porch.

The tobacco harvest was in. There was still a lot of work to do processing the crop: sweating, stemming, stripping and pressing the leaves before they could be packed into hogsheads for the voyage to London or Glasgow. They were sowing winter wheat in the field they called Stream Quarter, and barley, rye and clover in Lower Oak. But they had come to the end of the period of most intensive activity, the time when they worked in the fields from dawn to dusk and then labored on by candlelight in the tobacco sheds until midnight.

The hands should have some reward, she thought, for all their effort. Even slaves and convicts needed encouragement. It occurred to her that she might give them a party.

The more she thought about it, the more she liked the idea. Jay might be against it, but he would not be home for a couple of weeks—

Williamsburg was three days away—so it could be over and done with by the time he returned.

She walked along the bank of the Rappahannock River, turning the idea over in her mind. The river was shallow and rocky here, upstream from Fredericksburg, which marked the fall line, the limit of navigation. She skirted a clump of half-submerged bushes and stopped suddenly. A man was standing waist deep in the water, washing, his broad back to her. It was McAsh.

Roy bristled, then recognized Mack.

Lizzie had seen him naked in a river once before, almost a year ago. She remembered drying his skin with her petticoat. At the time it had seemed natural but, looking back, she felt the scene had a strange quality, like a dream: the moonlight, the rushing water, the strong man looking so vulnerable, and the way she had embraced him and warmed him with her body.

She held back now, watching him, as he came out of the river. He was completely naked, as he had been that night.

She remembered another moment from the past. One afternoon in High Glen she had surprised a young deer drinking in a burn. The sight came back to her like a picture. She had emerged from the trees and found herself a few feet away from a buck two or three years old. It had lifted its head and stared at her. The far bank of the stream had been steep, so the deer had been forced to move toward her. As it came out of the stream the water glistened on its muscular flanks. Her rifle was in her hand, loaded and primed, but she could not shoot: being so close seemed to make her too intimate with the beast.

As she watched the water roll off Mack's skin she thought that, despite all he had been through, he still had the powerful grace of a young animal. As he pulled on his breeches Roy loped up to him. Mack looked up, saw Lizzie and froze, startled. Then he said: "You might turn your back."

"You might turn yours!" she replied.

"I was here first."

"I own the place!" she snapped. It was astonishing how quickly he could irritate her. He obviously felt he was every bit as good as she. He was a convict farmhand and she was a fine lady, but to him that was no reason to show respect: it was the act of an arbitrary providence, and it did her no credit and brought him no shame. His audacity was annoying, but at least it was honest. McAsh was never sly. Jay, by contrast, often mystified her. She did not know what was going on in his mind, and when she questioned him he became defensive, as if he were being accused of something.

McAsh seemed amused now as he tied the string that held up his breeches. "You own me, too," he said.

She was looking at his chest. He was getting his muscles back. "And I've seen you naked before."

Suddenly the tension was gone and they were laughing, just as they had outside the church when Esther had told Mack to shut his gob.

"I'm going to give a party for the field hands," she said.

He pulled on his shirt. "What kind of party?"

Lizzie found herself wishing he had left the shirt off a little longer; she liked looking at his body. "What kind would you like?"

He looked thoughtful. "You could have a bonfire in the backyard. What the hands would like most of all would be a good meal, with plenty of meat. They never get enough to eat."

"What food would they like?"

"Hmm." He licked his lips. "The smell of fried ham coming from the kitchen is so good it hurts. Everyone loves those sweet potatoes. And wheat bread—the field hands never get anything but that coarse cornbread they call pone."

She was glad she had thought to talk to Mack about this: it was helpful. "What do they like to drink?"

"Rum. But some of the men get in a fighting mood when they drink. If I were you I'd give them apple cider, or beer."

"Good idea."

"How about some music? The Negroes love to dance and sing."

Lizzie was enjoying herself. It was fun planning a party with Mack. "All right—but who would play?"

"There's a free black called Pepper Jones who performs in the ordinaries in Fredericksburg. You could hire him. He plays the banjo."

Lizzie knew that "ordinary" was the local term for a tavern, but she had never heard of a banjo. "What's that?" she said.

"I think it's an African instrument. Not as sweet as a fiddle but more rhythmic."

"How do you know about this man? When have you been to Fredericksburg?"

A shadow crossed his face. "I went once on a Sunday."

"What for?"

"To look for Cora."

"Did you find her?"

"No."

"I'm sorry."

He shrugged. "Everyone has lost somebody." He turned his face away, looking sad.

She wanted to put her arms around him and comfort him, but she restrained herself. Pregnant though she was, she could not embrace anyone other than her husband. She made her voice cheerful again. "Do you think Pepper Jones could be persuaded to come here and perform?"

"I'm sure of it. I've seen him play in the slave quarters at the Thumson plantation."

Lizzie was intrigued. "What were you doing there?"

"Visiting."

"I never thought about slaves doing that kind of thing."

"We have to have something in our lives other than work."

"What do you do?"

"The young men love cockfights—they'll walk ten miles to see one. The young women love the young men. The older ones just want to look at one another's babies and talk about brothers and sisters they've lost. And they sing. The Africans have these sad songs that they sing in harmony. You can't understand the words, but the tunes make your hair stand on end."

"The coal miners used to sing."

He was silent for a moment. "Aye, we did."

She saw that she had made him sad. "Do you think you will ever go back to High Glen?"

"No. Do you?"

Tears came to her eyes. "No," she said. "I don't think you or I will ever go back."

The baby kicked her, and she said: "Ouch!"

"What?" said Mack.

She put a hand on her bulge. "The baby is kicking. He doesn't want me to yearn for High Glen. He's going to be a Virginian. Ow! He just did it again."

"Does it really hurt?"

"Yes—feel." She took his hand and placed it on her belly. His fingers were hard and rough skinned, but his touch was gentle.

The baby was still. Mack said: "When is it due?"

"Ten weeks."

"What will you call it?"

"My husband has decided on Jonathan for a boy, Alicia for a girl."

The baby kicked again. "That's hard!" Mack said, laughing. "I'm not surprised you wince." He took his hand away.

She wished he had left it there a little longer. To hide her feelings she changed the subject. "I'd better talk to Bill Sowerby about this party."

"You haven't heard?"

"What?"

"Ah. Bill Sowerby has left."

"Left? What do you mean?"

"He disappeared."

"When?"

"Two nights ago."

Lizzie realized she had not seen Sowerby for a couple of days. She had not been alarmed because she did not necessarily see him every day. "Did he say when he was coming back?"

"I don't know that he talked to anyone, directly. But I'd say he isn't coming back at all."

"Why?"

"He owes money to Sidney Lennox, a lot of money, and he can't pay."

Lizzie felt indignant. "And I suppose Lennox has been acting as overseer ever since."

"It's only been one working day . . . but yes, he has."

"I don't want that brute taking over the plantation!" she said hotly.

"Amen to that," Mack said with feeling. "None of the hands want it either."

Lizzie frowned suspiciously. Sowerby was owed a lot in wages. Jay had told him he would be paid when the first tobacco crop was sold. Why had he not simply waited? He could have paid his debts eventually. He must have been frightened. Lennox had threatened him, she felt sure. The more she thought about it, the angrier she got. "I believe Lennox has forced Sowerby out," she said.

Mack nodded. "I don't know much about it but that's my guess too. I've done battle with Lennox, and look what happened to me."

There was no self-pity in his tone, just a bitter practicality, but her heart went out to him. She touched his arm and said: "You should be proud. You're brave and honorable."

"And Lennox is corrupt and savage, and what happens? He'll become overseer here, then he'll steal enough from you, one way and another, to open a tavern in Fredericksburg; and soon he'll be living much as he did in London."

"Not if I can help it," Lizzie said determinedly. "I'm going to speak to him right away." Lennox had a small two-room house down by the tobacco sheds, near Sowerby's house. "I hope he's at home."

"He's not there now. At this time on a Sunday he'll be at the Ferry House—that's an ordinary three or four miles upriver from here. He'll stay there until late tonight."

Lizzie could not wait until tomorrow: she had no patience when there was something like this on her mind. "I'll go to the Ferry House. I can't ride—I'll take the pony trap."

Mack frowned. "Wouldn't it be better to have it out with him here, where you're the mistress of the house? He's a rough man."

Lizzie felt a pang of fear. Mack was right. Lennox was dangerous. But she could not bear to postpone the confrontation. Mack could protect her. "Will you come with me?" she said. "I'd feel safe if you were there."

"Of course."

"You can drive the trap."

"You'll have to teach me."

"There's nothing to it."

They walked up from the river to the house. The stable boy, Jimmy, was watering the horses. Mack and he got the trap out and put a pony in the traces while Lizzie went into the house to put on a hat.

They drove out of the estate onto the riverside road and followed it upstream to the ferry crossing. The Ferry House was a wood-frame building not much bigger than the two-room houses lived in by Sowerby and Lennox. Lizzie let Mack help her down from the trap and hold open the door of the tavern for her.

It was gloomy and smoky inside. Ten or twelve people sat on benches and wooden chairs drinking from tankards and pottery cups. Some were playing cards and dice, others smoking pipes. The click of billiard balls came from the back room.

There were no women and no blacks.

Mack followed her in but stood back, by the door, his face in shadow.

A man came through a doorway from the back room, wiping his hands on a towel, and said: "What can I bring you, sir— Oh! A lady!"

"Nothing, thank you," Lizzie said in a clear voice, and the room went quiet.

She looked around at the upturned faces. Lennox was in the corner, bent over a shaker and a pair of dice. The little table in front of him had several piles of small coins. His face showed resentment at being interrupted.

He carefully scooped up his coins, taking his time, before he stood up and took off his hat. "What are you doing here, Mrs. Jamisson?"

"I didn't come to play dice, obviously," she said crisply. "Where is Mr. Sowerby?"

She heard one or two approving murmurs, as if others in the place would like to know what had happened to Sowerby; and she saw a gray-haired man turn in his chair and look at her.

"He's run off, it seems," Lennox answered.

"Why haven't you reported this to me?"

Lennox shrugged. "Because there's nothing you can do about it."

"I want to know about such things, all the same. Don't do it again. Is that clear?"

Lennox made no reply.

"Why did Sowerby leave?"

"How should I know?"

The gray-haired man piped up: "He owed money."

Lizzie turned to him. "Who to?"

The man jerked a thumb. "Lennox, that's who."

She turned back to Lennox. "Is this true?"

"Yes."

"For what?"

"I don't know what you mean."

"Why did he borrow money from you?"

"He didn't, exactly. He lost it to me."

"Gambling."

"Yes."

"And did you threaten him?"

The gray-haired man gave a sarcastic laugh. "Did he? I'll swear."

"I asked for my money," Lennox said coolly.

"And that drove him away."

"I tell you I don't know why he left."

"I believe he was frightened of you."

A nasty smile crossed Lennox's face. "Many people are," he said, and the threat in his voice was hardly veiled.

Lizzie felt scared as well as angry. "Let's get something clear," she said. There was a tremor in her voice and she swallowed to get it under control. "I am the mistress of the plantation and you will do what I say. I shall now take charge of the place until my husband returns. Then he will decide how to replace Mr. Sowerby."

Lennox shook his head. "Oh, no," he said. "I'm Sowerby's deputy. Mr. Jamisson has told me quite particularly that I'm in charge if Sowerby should fall ill or anything. Besides, what do you know about tobacco growing?"

"As much as a London tavern keeper, at least."

"Well, that's not how Mr. Jamisson sees it, and I take my orders from him."

Lizzie could have screamed with frustration. She would not let this man give orders on her plantation! "I'm warning you, Lennox, you'd better obey me!"

"And if I don't?" He took a step toward her, grinning, and she smelled his characteristic ripe odor. She was forced to step backward. The other customers in the tavern sat frozen to their seats. "What will you do, Mrs. Jamisson?" he said, still coming toward her. "Knock me down?" As he said this he lifted his hand over his head, in a gesture that might have been an illustration of what he was saying but could just as easily have been a threat.

Lizzie gave a cry of fear and jumped back. Her legs came up against the seat of a chair and she sat down with a bump.

Suddenly Mack was there, standing between Lennox and her. "You've raised your hand to a woman, Lennox," he said. "Now let's see you raise it to a man."

"You!" Lennox said. "I didn't know it was you, standing in the corner like a nigger."

"And now that you know, what are you going to do?"

"You're a damn fool, McAsh. You always take the losing side."

"You've just insulted the wife of the man who owns you—I don't call that clever."

"I didn't come here to argue. I came to play dice." Lennox turned and went back to his table.

Lizzie felt as angry and frustrated as she had when she arrived. She stood up. "Let's go," she said to Mack.

He opened the door and she went out.

*

She had to know more about tobacco growing, she decided when she had calmed down. Lennox was going to try to take over, and the only way she could defeat him was by persuading Jay that she would do a better job. She already knew a good deal about the running of the plantation but she did not really understand the plant itself.

Next day she got out the pony and trap again and went over to Colonel Thumson's place, with Jimmy driving her.

In the weeks since the party, the neighbors had been cool to Lizzie and Jay, particularly to Jay. They had been invited to big social occasions, a ball and a grand wedding reception, but no one had asked them to a small celebration or an intimate dinner. However, when Jay left for Williamsburg they seemed to know, for since then Mrs. Thumson had called and Suzy Delahaye had invited Lizzie to tea. It distressed her that they preferred her on her own, but Jay had offended everyone with his opinions.

As she drove through the Thumson plantation she was struck by how prosperous it looked. There were rows of hogsheads on the jetty; the slaves looked active and fit; the sheds were painted and the fields were neat. She saw the colonel across a meadow, talking to a small group of hands, pointing to show them something. Jay never stood in the fields giving instructions.

Mrs. Thumson was a fat and kindly woman past fifty. The Thumson children, two boys, were both grown-up and living elsewhere. She poured tea and asked about the pregnancy. Lizzie confessed that she had occasional backache and constant heartburn, and was relieved to hear that Mrs. Thumson had suffered exactly the same. She had also noticed slight bleeding once or twice, and Mrs. Thumson frowned and said that had not happened to her, but it was not uncommon, and she should rest more.

But she had not come to talk about pregnancy, and she was glad when the colonel came in for tea. He was in his fifties, tall and white haired, and vigorous for his age. He shook her hand stiffly but she softened him with a smile and a compliment. "Why does your plantation look so much more impressive than anyone else's?"

"Well, it's kind of you to say so," he replied. "I'd say the main factor is that I'm here. You see, Bill Delahaye is always going away to horse races and cockfights. John Armstead would rather drink than work, and his brother spends every afternoon playing billiards and throwing dice at the Ferry House." He said nothing about Mockjack Hall.

"Why do your slaves look so energetic?"

"Now, that depends what you feed them." He was obviously

enjoying sharing his expertise with this attractive young woman. "They can live on hominy and corn pone, but they'll work better if you give them salt fish every day and meat once a week. It's expensive, but not as bad as buying new slaves every few years."

"Why have so many plantations gone bankrupt recently?"

"You have to understand the tobacco plant. It exhausts the soil. After four or five years the quality deteriorates. You have to switch the field to wheat or Indian corn and find new land for your tobacco."

"Why, you must be constantly clearing ground."

"Indeed. Every winter I clear woodland and open up new fields for cultivation."

"But you're fortunate—you have so much land."

"There's woodland aplenty on your place. And when that runs out you should buy or rent more. The only way to grow tobacco is to keep moving."

"Does everyone do that?"

"No. Some get credit from merchants, and hope the price of tobacco will go up to save them. Dick Richards, the previous owner of your place, followed that road, which is how come your father-in-law ended up owning the place."

Lizzie did not tell him that Jay had gone to Williamsburg to borrow money. "We could clear Stafford Park in time for next spring." Stafford Park was a piece of rough land separate from the main estate, ten miles upriver. Because of the distance it was neglected, and Jay had tried to lease or sell it, but there had been no takers.

"Why not start with Pond Copse?" said the colonel. "It's close to your curing sheds and the soil is right. Which reminds me." He glanced at the clock on the mantelpiece. "I have to visit my sheds before it gets dark."

Lizzie stood up. "I must get back and speak to my overseer."

Mrs. Thumson said: "Don't do too much, Mrs. Jamisson—remember your baby."

Lizzie smiled. "I'm going to take plenty of rest too, I promise."

Colonel Thumson kissed his wife then walked out with Lizzie. He helped her onto the seat of the trap, then rode with her as far as his sheds. "If you'll forgive my making a personal comment, you're a remarkable young lady, Mrs. Jamisson."

"Why, thank you," she said.

"I hope we'll see more of you." He smiled, and his blue eyes twinkled. He took her hand, and as he lifted it to kiss it his arm brushed her breast, as if by accident. "Please send for me any time I can help you in *any* way."

She drove off. I do believe I have just received my first adulterous proposition, she thought. And me six months pregnant. The wicked old man! She supposed she ought to be outraged, but in fact she was pleased. Of course she would never take him up on his offer. Indeed, she would be careful to avoid the colonel from now on. But it was flattering to be thought desirable.

"Let's go faster, Jimmy," she said. "I want my supper."

＊

Next morning she sent Jimmy to summon Lennox to her drawing room. She had not spoken to him since the incident in the Ferry House. She was more than a little afraid of him, and she considered sending for Mack as protection. But she refused to believe she needed a bodyguard in her own house.

She sat in a big carved chair that must have been brought from Britain a century ago. Lennox arrived two hours later, with mud on his boots. She knew the delay was his way of showing he was not obliged to jump when she whistled. If she challenged him he was sure to have some excuse, so she decided to act as if he had come immediately.

"We're going to clear Pond Copse ready for tobacco planting next spring," she said. "I want you to begin today."

For once he was taken by surprise. "Why?" he said.

"Tobacco farmers must clear new land every winter. It's the only way to maintain high yields. I've looked around, and Pond Copse seems the most promising. Colonel Thumson agrees with me."

"Bill Sowerby never did that."

"Bill Sowerby never made any money."

"There's nothing wrong with the old fields."

"Tobacco cultivation exhausts the land."

"Ah, yes," he said. "But we manure heavily."

She frowned. Thumson had not mentioned manuring. "I don't know. . . ."

Her hesitation was fatal. "These things are best left to men," he said.

"Never mind the homilies," she snapped. "Tell me about the manuring."

"We pen the cattle in the tobacco fields at night, for the manure. It refreshes the land for the next season."

"It can't be as good as new land," she said, but she was not sure.

"It's just the same," he insisted. "But if you want to change you'll have to speak to Mr. Jamisson."

She hated to let Lennox win, even temporarily, but she would have to wait until Jay returned. Feeling irritated, she said: "You can go now."

He gave a little smile of victory and went out without another word.

＊

She forced herself to rest for the remainder of the day, but on the following morning she made her usual tour of the plantation.

In the sheds, the bundles of drying tobacco plants were being taken down from their hooks so that the leaves could be separated from the stems and the heavy fibers stripped out. Next they would be bundled up again and covered with cloth to "sweat."

Some of the hands were in the woods, cutting wood to make barrels. Others were sowing winter wheat in Stream Quarter. Lizzie spotted Mack there, working alongside a young black woman. They crossed the plowed field in a line, distributing the seed from heavy baskets. Lennox followed, hurrying the slower workers with a kick or a touch of the whip. It was a short whip with a hard handle and a lash two or three feet long made of some flexible wood. After he noticed Lizzie watching, he began to use it more freely, as if challenging her to try to stop him.

She turned away and started back toward the house. But before she was out of earshot she heard a cry and turned back.

The hand working next to Mack had collapsed. It was Bess, an adolescent girl about fifteen years old, tall and thin: Lizzie's mother would have said she had outgrown her strength.

Lizzie hurried toward the prone figure, but Mack was nearer. He put down his basket and knelt beside Bess. He touched her forehead and her hands. "I think she's just fainted," he said.

Lennox came up and kicked the girl in the ribs with a heavily booted foot.

Her body jerked with the impact but her eyes did not open.

Lizzie cried out: "Stop it, don't kick her!"

"Lazy black bitch, I'll teach her a lesson," Lennox said, and he drew back the arm that held the whip.

"Don't you dare!" Lizzie said furiously.

He brought the whip down on the back of the unconscious girl.

Mack sprang to his feet.

"Stop!" Lizzie cried.

Lennox lifted the whip again.

Mack stood between Lennox and Bess.

"Your mistress told you to stop," Mack said.

Lennox changed his grip and slashed Mack across the face.

Mack staggered sideways and his hand flew to his face. A purplish weal appeared immediately on his cheek and blood trickled between his lips.

Lennox raised his whip hand again, but the blow never fell.

Lizzie hardly saw what happened, it was so quick, but in a moment Lennox was flat on the ground, groaning, and Mack had the whip. He took it in both hands and snapped it over his knee, then contemptuously threw it at Lennox.

Lizzie felt a surge of triumph. The bully was broken.

Everyone stood around staring for a long moment.

Then Lizzie said: "Get on with your work, everyone!"

The hands turned away and recommenced sowing seed. Lennox got to his feet, staring at Mack evilly.

"Can you carry Bess to the house?" Lizzie asked Mack.

"Of course." He picked her up in his arms.

They walked back across the fields to the house and took her into the kitchen, which was an outbuilding at the back. By the time Mack put her in a chair she had recovered consciousness.

Sarah, the cook, was a middle-aged black woman always in a sweat. Lizzie sent her to fetch some of Jay's brandy. After a sip Bess declared she felt all right except for bruised ribs, and she could not understand why she had fainted. Lizzie told her to have something to eat and rest until tomorrow.

Leaving the kitchen, she noticed that Mack looked solemn. "What is it?" she said.

"I must have been mad," he said.

"How can you say that?" she protested. "Lennox disobeyed a direct order from me!"

"He's a vengeful man. I shouldn't have humiliated him."

"How can he take revenge on you?"

"Easily. He's the overseer."

"I won't allow it," Lizzie said decisively.

"You can't watch over me all day."

"Curse it." She could not allow Mack to suffer for what he had done.

"I'd run away if I knew where to go. Have you ever seen a map of Virginia?"

"Don't run away." She frowned, thinking, then she was struck by an idea. "I know what to do—you can work in the house."

He smiled. "I'd love to. I might not be much of a butler, though."

"No, no—not a servant. You could be in charge of repairs. I have to have the nursery painted and fixed up."

He looked suspicious. "Do you really mean it?"

"Of course!"

"It would be . . . just wonderful to get away from Lennox."

"Then you shall."

"You can't possibly understand what good news this is."

"For me, too—I'll feel safer with you close by. I'm frightened of Lennox."

"With reason."

"You'll have to have a new shirt and a waistcoat, and house shoes." She would enjoy dressing him in good clothes.

"Such luxury," he said, grinning.

"That's settled," she said decisively. "You can start right away."

*

The house slaves were a little grumpy about the party at first. They looked down on the field hands. Sarah, in particular, resented having to cook for "trash that eats hominy and corn pone." But Lizzie mocked their snobbery and jollied them along, and in the end they entered into the spirit of it.

At sundown on Saturday the kitchen staff were cooking up a banquet. Pepper Jones, the banjo player, had arrived drunk at midday. McAsh had made him drink gallons of tea then put him to sleep in an outhouse, and he was now sober again. His instrument had four catgut strings stretched over a gourd, and the sound as he tuned it was halfway between a piano and a drum.

As she went around the yard checking on the preparations Lizzie felt excited. She was looking forward to the celebration. She would not join in the jollity, of course: she had to play Lady Bountiful, serene and aloof. But she would enjoy watching other people let their hair down.

When darkness fell all was ready. A new barrel of cider had been tapped; several fat hams were sizzling over open fires; hundreds of sweet potatoes were cooking in cauldrons of boiling water; and long four-pound loaves of white bread stood waiting to be sliced.

Lizzie paced up and down impatiently, waiting for the slaves to come in from the fields. She hoped they would sing. She had sometimes heard them from a distance, singing plaintive laments or rhythmic work songs, but they always stopped when one of the masters came near.

As the moon rose, the old women came up from the quarters with the babies on their hips and the toddlers trailing behind. They did not know where the field hands were: they fed them in the morning then did not see them until the end of the day.

The hands knew they were to come up to the house tonight. Lizzie had told Kobe to make sure everyone understood, and he was always reliable. She had been too busy to go out into the fields, but she supposed they must have been working at the farthermost reaches of the plantation, and so were taking a long time to return. She hoped the sweet potatoes would not overcook and turn to mush.

Time went by and no one appeared. When it had been dark for an hour she admitted to herself that something had gone wrong. With anger mounting in her breast she summoned McAsh and said: "Get Lennox up here."

It took almost an hour, but eventually McAsh returned with Lennox, who had obviously started his evening's drinking already. By this time Lizzie was furious. "Where are the field hands?" she demanded. "They should be here!"

"Ah, yes," Lennox said, speaking slowly and deliberately. "That was not possible today."

His insolence warned her that he had found some foolproof way to frustrate her plans. "What the devil do you mean, not possible?" she said.

"They've been cutting wood for barrels on Stafford Park." Stafford Park was ten miles upriver. "There's a few days' work to be done so we made camp. The hands will stay there, with Kobe, until we finish."

"You didn't have to cut wood today."

"No time like the present."

He had done it to defy her. It was enough to make her scream. But until Jay came home there was nothing she could do.

Lennox looked at the food on the trestle tables. "Pity, really," he said, barely concealing his glee. He reached out with a dirty hand and tore a piece of ham off a joint.

Without thinking, Lizzie picked up a long-handled carving fork and stabbed the back of his hand, saying: "Put that down!"

He squealed in pain and dropped the meat.

Lizzie pulled the prongs of the fork out of his hand.

He roared with pain again. "You mad cow!" he yelled.

"Get out of here, and stay out of my sight until my husband comes home," Lizzie said.

He stared furiously at her, as if he were about to attack her, for a long moment. Then he clamped his bleeding hand under his armpit and hurried away.

Lizzie felt tears spring to her eyes. Not wanting the staff to see her cry, she turned and ran into the house. As soon as she was alone in the drawing room she began to sob with frustration. She felt wretched and alone.

After a minute she heard the door open. Mack's voice said: "I'm sorry."

His sympathy made her cry fresh tears. A moment later she felt his arms around her. It was deeply comforting. She laid her head on his shoulder and cried and cried. He stroked her hair and kissed her tears. Slowly her sobs became quieter and her grief eased. She wished he could hold her like this all night.

Then she realized what she was doing.

She pulled away from him in horror. She was a married woman, and six months pregnant, and she had let a servant kiss her! "What am I thinking about?" she said unbelievingly.

"You're not thinking," he said.

"I am now," she said. "Go away!"

Looking sad, he turned and left the room.

29

ON THE DAY AFTER LIZZIE'S FAILED PARTY, MACK HEARD NEWS OF Cora.

It was Sunday, and he went into Fredericksburg wearing his new clothes. He needed to free his mind of thoughts of Lizzie Jamisson, her springy black hair and her soft cheeks and her salt tears. Pepper Jones, who had stayed in the slave quarters overnight, went with him, carrying his banjo.

Pepper was a thin, energetic man about fifty years old. His fluent English indicated he had been in America for many years. Mack asked him: "How did you come to be free?"

"Born free," he replied. "My ma was white, although it don't show. My daddy was a runaway, recaptured before I was born—I never saw him."

Whenever he got the chance Mack asked questions about running away. "Is it right what Kobe says, that all runaways get caught?"

Pepper laughed. "Hell, no. Most get caught, but most are stupid— that's how come they were captured in the first place."

"So, if you're not stupid . . . ?"

He shrugged. "It ain't easy. As soon as you run away, the master puts an advertisement in the newspaper, giving your description and the clothes you were wearing."

Clothes were so costly that it would be difficult for runaways to change. "But you could keep out of sight."

"Got to eat, though. That means you need a job, if you stay inside the colonies, and any man that's going to employ you has probably read about you in the newspaper."

"These planters really have things worked out."

"It's not surprising. All the plantations are worked by slaves, convicts and indentured servants. If they didn't have a system for catching runaways, the planters would have starved a long time ago."

Mack was thoughtful. "But you said 'if you stay inside the colonies.' What do you mean by that?"

"West of here is the mountains, and on the other side of the mountains, the wilderness. No newspapers there. No plantations either. No sheriffs, no judges, no hangmen."

"How big is the territory?"

"I don't know. Some say it stretches for hundreds of miles before you come to the sea again, but I never met anyone who's been there."

Mack had talked about the wilderness with many people, but Pepper was the first he felt inclined to rely on. Others retailed what were obviously fantastic stories in place of hard facts: Pepper at least admitted that he did not know everything. As always, Mack found it exciting to talk about. "Surely a man could disappear over the mountains and never be found!"

"That's the truth. Also, he could be scalped by Indians and killed by mountain lions. More likely he could starve to death."

"How do you know?"

"I've met pioneers who came back. They break their backs for a few years, turning a perfectly good piece of land into a useless patch of mud, then they quit."

"But some succeed?"

"Must do, I guess, otherwise there wouldn't be no such place as America."

"West of here, you said," Mack mused. "How far are the mountains?"

"About a hundred miles, they say."

"So close!"

"It's farther than you think."

*

They were offered a ride by one of Colonel Thumson's slaves who was driving a cart into town. Slaves and convicts always gave one another rides on the roads of Virginia.

The town was busy: Sunday was the day the field hands from the plantations round about came in to go to church or get drunk or both. Some of the convicts looked down on the slaves, but Mack considered he had no reason to feel superior. Consequently he had many friends and acquaintances, and people hailed him at every corner.

They went to Whitey Jones's ordinary. Whitey was so called because of his coloring, a mixture of black and white; and he sold liquor to blacks even though it was against the law. He could converse equally well in the pidgin spoken by the majority of slaves or the Virginian dialect of the American born. His tavern was a low-ceilinged room smelling of wood smoke, full of blacks and poor whites playing cards and drinking. Mack had no money, but Pepper Jones had been paid by Lizzie and he bought Mack a quart of ale.

Mack enjoyed the beer, a rare treat nowadays. While they were drinking Pepper said: "Hey, Whitey, have you ever run into anyone who crossed the mountains?"

"Sure have," Whitey said. "There was a trapper in here one time, said it was the best hunting he ever saw, over there. Seems a whole gang of them goes over there every year, and comes back loaded down with pelts."

Mack said: "Did he tell you what route he took?"

"Seems to me he said there was a pass called the Cumberland Gap."

"Cumberland Gap," Mack repeated.

Whitey said: "Say, Mack, weren't you asking after a white girl called Cora?"

Mack's heart leaped. "Yes—have you heard tell of her?"

"Seen her—so I know why you're crazy for her." He rolled his eyes.

"Is she a pretty girl, Mack?" Pepper teased.

"Prettier than you, Pepper. Come on, Whitey, where did you see her?"

"Down by the river. She was wearing a green coat and carrying a basket, and she was getting the ferry over to Falmouth."

Mack smiled. The coat, and the fact that she was taking the ferry instead of wading across the ford, indicated that she had landed on her feet again. She must have been sold to someone kind. "How did you know who she was?"

"The ferryman called her by name."

"She must be living on the Falmouth side of the river—that's why I didn't hear of her when first I asked around Fredericksburg."

"Well, you've heard of her now."

Mack swallowed the rest of his beer. "And I'm going to find her. Whitey, you're a friend. Pepper, thanks for the beer."

"Good luck!"

Mack went out of town. Fredericksburg had been built just below the fall line of the Rappahannock River, at the limit of navigation. Oceangoing ships could come this far, but less than a mile away the river became rocky, and nothing but a flatboat could negotiate it. Mack walked to the point where the water was shallow enough to wade across.

He was full of excitement. Who had bought Cora? How was she living? And did she know what had become of Peg? If only he could locate the two of them, and fulfill his promise, he could make serious plans to escape. He had been suppressing his yearning for freedom while he asked after Cora and Peg, but Pepper's talk of the wilderness beyond the mountains had brought it all back, and he longed to run away. He daydreamed about walking away from the plantation at nightfall, heading west, never again to work for an overseer with a whip.

He looked forward eagerly to seeing Cora. She probably would not be working today: perhaps she could walk out with him. They might go somewhere secluded. As he thought about kissing her, he suffered a pang of guilt. He had woken up this morning thinking about kissing Lizzie Jamisson, and now he was having the same thoughts about Cora. But he was foolish to feel guilty about Lizzie: she was another man's wife, and there was no future for him with her. All the same his excitement was tinged with discomfort.

Falmouth was a smaller version of Fredericksburg: it had the same wharves, warehouses, taverns and painted wood-frame homes. Mack could probably have called at every residence in a couple of hours. But of course Cora might live out of town.

He went into the first tavern he came across and spoke to the proprietor. "I'm looking for a young woman called Cora Higgins."

"Cora? She lives in the white house on the next corner, you'll probably see three cats sleeping on the porch."

Mack's luck was in today. "Thank you!"

The man took a watch from his waistcoat pocket and glanced at it. "But she won't be there now, she'll be in church."

"I've seen the church. I'll go there."

Cora had never been a churchgoer, but perhaps her owner forced her to go, Mack thought as he went outside. He crossed the street and walked two blocks to the little wooden church.

The service had ended and the congregation were coming out, all in their Sunday best, shaking hands and chattering.

Mack saw Cora right away.

He smiled broadly when he saw her. She certainly had been lucky. The starved, filthy woman he had left on the *Rosebud* might have been a different person. Cora was her old self: clear skin, glossy hair, rounded figure. She was as well dressed as ever, in a dark brown coat and a wool skirt, and she wore good boots. He was suddenly glad he had the new shirt and waistcoat Lizzie had given him.

Cora was talking animatedly to an old woman with a cane. She broke off her conversation as he approached her. "Mack!" she said delightedly. "This is a miracle!"

He opened his arms to embrace her but she held out a hand to shake, and he guessed she did not want to make an exhibition outside the church. He took her hand in both of his and said: "You look wonderful." She smelled good, too: not the spicy, woody perfume she had favored in London, but a lighter, floral smell that was more ladylike.

"What happened to you?" she said, withdrawing her hand. "Who bought you?"

"I'm on the Jamisson plantation—and Lennox is the overseer."

"Did he hit your face?"

Mack touched the sore place where Lennox had slashed him. "Yes, but I took his whip from him and broke it in half."

She smiled. "That's Mack—always in trouble."

"It is. Have you any news of Peg?"

"She was taken off by the soul drivers, Bates and Makepiece."

Mack's heart sank. "Damn. It's going to be hard to find her."

"I always ask after her but I've never heard anything."

"And who bought you? Somebody kind, by the look of you!"

As he spoke a plump, richly dressed man in his fifties came up. Cora said: "Here he is: Alexander Rowley, the tobacco broker."

"He obviously treats you well!" Mack murmured.

Rowley shook hands with the old woman and said a word to her, then turned to Mack.

Cora said: "This is Malachi McAsh, an old friend of mine from London. Mack, this is Mr. Rowley—my husband."

Mack stared, speechless.

Rowley put a proprietorial arm around Cora's shoulders and at the same time shook Mack's hand. "How do you do, McAsh?" he said, and without another word he swept Cora away.

*

Why not? Mack thought as he trudged along the road back to the Jamisson plantation. Cora had not known whether she would ever see him again. She had obviously been bought by Rowley and had made him fall in love with her. It must have been something of a scandal for a merchant to marry a convict woman, even in a little colonial town such as Falmouth. However, sexual attraction was more powerful than social rules in the end, and Mack could easily imagine how Rowley had been seduced. It may have been difficult to persuade people like the old lady with the cane to accept Cora as a respectable wife, but Cora had the nerve for anything, and she had obviously carried it off. Good for her. She would probably have Rowley's babies.

He found excuses for her, but all the same he was disappointed. In a moment of panic she had made him promise to search for her; but she had forgotten him as soon as she got the chance of an easy life.

It was strange: he had had two lovers, Annie and Cora, and both had married someone else. Cora went to bed every night with a fat tobacco broker twice her age, and Annie was pregnant with Jimmy Lee's child. He wondered if he would ever have a normal family life with a wife and children.

He gave himself a shake. He could have had that if he had really wanted it. But he had refused to settle down and accept what the world offered him. He wanted more.

He wanted to be free.

30

J AY WENT TO WILLIAMSBURG WITH HIGH HOPES.

He had been dismayed to learn of the sympathies of his neighbors—they were all liberal Whigs, not a conservative Tory among them—but he felt sure that in the colonial capital he would find men loyal to the king, men who would welcome him as a valuable ally and promote his political career.

Williamsburg was small but grand. The main street, Duke of Gloucester Street, was a mile long and a hundred feet broad. The Capitol was at one end and the College of William and Mary at the other—two stately brick buildings whose English-style architecture gave Jay a reassuring feeling of the might of the monarchy. There was a theater and several shops, with craftsmen making silver candlesticks and mahogany dining tables. In Purdie & Dixon's printing office Jay bought the *Virginia Gazette,* a newspaper full of advertisements for runaway slaves.

The wealthy planters who made up the colony's ruling elite resided on their estates, but they crowded into Williamsburg when the legislature was in session in the Capitol building, and consequently the town was full of inns with rooms to let. Jay moved into the Raleigh Tavern, a low white clapboard building with bedrooms in the attic.

He left his card and a note at the palace, but he had to wait three days for an appointment with the new governor, the baron de Botetourt. When finally he got his invitation it was not for a personal audience, as he had expected, but for a reception with fifty other guests. Clearly the governor had yet to realize that Jay was an important ally in a hostile environment.

The palace was at the end of a long drive that ran north from the midpoint of Duke of Gloucester Street. It was another English-looking brick building, with tall chimneys and dormer windows in the roof, like a country house. The imposing entrance hall was decorated with knives, pistols and muskets arranged in elaborate patterns, as if to emphasize the military might of the king.

Unfortunately Botetourt was the very opposite of what Jay had hoped for. Virginia needed a tough, austere governor who would strike fear into the hearts of mutinous colonists, but Botetourt turned out to be a fat, friendly man with the air of a prosperous wine merchant welcoming his customers to a tasting.

Jay watched him greeting his guests in the long ballroom. The man had no idea what subversive plots might be hatching in the minds of the planters.

Bill Delahaye was there and shook hands with Jay. "What do you think of our new governor?"

"I'm not sure he realizes what he's taken on," Jay said.

Delahaye said: "He may be cleverer than he looks."

"I hope so."

"There's a big card game tomorrow night, Jamisson—would you like me to introduce you?"

Jay had not spent an evening gambling since he had left London. "Certainly."

In the supper room beyond the ballroom, wine and cakes were served. Delahaye introduced Jay to several other men. A stout, prosperous-looking man of about fifty said: "Jamisson? Of the Edinburgh Jamissons?" His tone was a little hostile.

The face had a vaguely familiar cast, although Jay was sure he had never met the man before. "The family seat is Castle Jamisson in Fife," Jay replied.

"The castle that used to belong to William McClyde?"

"Indeed." Jay realized the man reminded him of Robert: he had the same light eyes and determined mouth. "I'm afraid I didn't hear your name. . . ."

"I'm Hamish Drome. That castle should have been mine."

Jay was startled. Drome was the family name of Robert's mother, Olive. "So you're the long-lost relative who went to Virginia!"

"And you must be the son of George and Olive."

"No, that's my half-brother, Robert. Olive died and my father remarried. I'm the younger son."

"Ah. And Robert has pushed you out of the nest, just as his mother did me."

There was an insolent undertone to Drome's remarks, but Jay was intrigued by what the man was implying. He recalled the drunken revelations made by Peter McKay at the wedding. "I've heard it said that Olive forged the will."

"Aye—and she murdered Uncle William, too."

"What?"

"No question. William wasn't sick. He was a hypochondriac, he just loved to think he was ill. He should have lived to a ripe old age. But six weeks after Olive arrived he had changed his will and died. Evil woman."

"Ha." Jay felt a strange kind of satisfaction. The sacrosanct Olive, whose portrait hung in the place of honor in the hall of Jamisson Castle, was a murderess who should have been hanged. Jay had always resented the way she was spoken of in reverent tones, and now he welcomed gleefully the news that she had been a blackhearted villain. "Didn't you get anything?" he asked Drome.

"Not an acre. I came out here with six dozen pairs of Shetland wool stockings, and now I'm the biggest haberdasher in Virginia. But I never wrote home. I was afraid Olive would somehow take this from me too."

"But how could she?"

"I don't know. Just superstition, perhaps. I'm glad to hear she's dead. But it seems the son is like her."

"I always thought of him as being like my father. He's insatiably greedy, whoever he takes after."

"If I were you I wouldn't let him know my address."

"He's going to inherit all of my father's business enterprises—I can't imagine he'll want my little plantation too."

"Don't be too sure," Drome said; but Jay thought he was being overdramatic.

Jay did not get Governor Botetourt to himself until the end of the party, when the guests were leaving by the garden entrance. He took the governor's sleeve and said in a low voice: "I want you to know that I'm completely loyal to you and to the Crown."

"Splendid, splendid," Botetourt said loudly. "So good of you to say so."

"I've recently arrived here, and I've been scandalized by the attitudes of the most prominent men in the colony—scandalized. Whenever you're ready to stamp out treachery and crush disloyal opposition, I'm on your side."

Botetourt looked hard at him, taking him seriously at last, and Jay perceived that there was a shrewd politician behind the affable exterior. "How kind—but let's hope that not too much stamping and crushing will be required. I find that persuasion and negotiation are so much better—the effects last longer, don't you know. Major Wilkinson— good-bye! Mrs. Wilkinson—so good of you to come."

Persuasion and negotiation, Jay thought as he passed out into the garden. Botetourt had fallen into a nest of vipers and he wanted to negotiate with them. Jay said to Delahaye: "I wonder how long it will take him to grasp the realities out here."

"I think he understands already," Delahaye said. "He just doesn't believe in baring his teeth before he's ready to bite."

Sure enough, next day the amiable new governor dissolved the general assembly.

✳

Matthew Murchman lived in a green-painted clapboard house next to the bookshop on Duke of Gloucester Street. He did business in the front parlor, surrounded by law books and papers. He was a small, nervous gray squirrel of a man, darting about the room to retrieve a paper from one pile and hide it in another.

Jay signed the papers mortgaging the plantation. He was disappointed at the amount of the loan: only four hundred pounds sterling. "I was lucky to get so much," Murchman twittered. "With tobacco doing so badly I'm not sure the place could be sold for that."

"Who is the lender?" Jay asked.

"A syndicate, Captain Jamisson. That's how these things work nowadays. Are there any liabilities you would like me to settle immediately?"

Jay had brought with him a sheaf of bills, all the debts he had run up since he had arrived in Virginia almost three months ago. He handed them over to Murchman, who glanced through them quickly and said: "About a hundred pounds here. I'll give you notes for all these before you leave town. And let me know if you buy anything while you're here."

"I probably will," Jay said. "A Mr. Smythe is selling a carriage with a beautiful pair of gray horses. And I need two or three slaves."

"I'll let it be known that you're in funds with me."

Jay did not quite like the idea of borrowing so much money and leaving it all in the lawyer's hands. "Let me have a hundred pounds in gold," he said. "There's a card game at the Raleigh tonight."

"Certainly, Captain Jamisson. It's your money!"

*

There was not much left of the four hundred pounds when Jay arrived back at the plantation in his new equipage. He had lost at cards, he had bought four slave girls, and he had failed to beat down Mr. Smythe's price for the carriage and horses.

However, he had cleared all his debts. He would simply get credit from local merchants as he had before. His first tobacco crop would be ready for sale soon after Christmas, and he would pay his bills from the proceeds.

He was apprehensive of what Lizzie might say about the carriage, but to his relief she hardly mentioned it. She obviously had something else on her mind that she was bursting to tell him.

As always, she was most attractive when animated: her dark eyes flashed and her skin glowed pink. However, he no longer felt a surge of desire every time he saw her. Since she had become pregnant he had felt diffident. He imagined it was bad for the baby if the mother had sexual intercourse during pregnancy. But that was not his real reason. Lizzie's being a mother somehow put him off. He did not like the thought of mothers having sexual lusts. Anyway, it was rapidly becoming impracticable: the bulge she carried in front of her was getting too big.

As soon as he had kissed her she said: "Bill Sowerby has left."

"Really?" Jay was surprised. The man had gone without his wages. "Good thing we've got Lennox to take over."

"I think Lennox drove him away. Apparently Sowerby had lost a lot of money to him at cards."

That made sense. "Lennox is a good card player."

"Lennox wants to be overseer here."

They were standing on the front portico, and at that moment Lennox came around the side of the house. With his usual lack of grace he did not welcome Jay back. Instead he said: "There's a consignment of salt cod in barrels just arrived."

"I ordered it," Lizzie said. "It's for the field hands."

Jay was annoyed. "Why do you want to feed them fish?"

"Colonel Thumson says they work better. He gives his slaves salt fish every day and meat once a week."

"Colonel Thumson is richer than I am. Send the stuff back, Lennox."

"They're going to have to work hard this winter, Jay," Lizzie protested. "We have to clear all the woodland in Pond Copse ready for planting with tobacco next spring."

Lennox said quickly: "That isn't necessary. There's plenty of life left in the fields, with good manuring."

"You can't manure forever," Lizzie rejoined. "Colonel Thumson clears land every winter."

Jay realized this was an argument the two of them had been through before.

Lennox said: "We don't have enough hands. Even with the men from the *Rosebud,* we can only just manage to plant the fields we have. Colonel Thumson has more slaves than us."

"That's because he makes more money—due to better methods," Lizzie said triumphantly.

Lennox sneered: "Women just don't understand these things."

Lizzie snapped: "Leave us, please, Mr. Lennox—immediately."

Lennox looked angry but he went away.

"You must get rid of him, Jay," she said.

"I don't see why—"

"It's not just that he's brutal. Frightening people is the only thing he's good at. He can't understand farming and he doesn't know anything about tobacco—and the worst of it is he's not interested in learning."

"He knows how to get the hands working hard."

"There's no point in driving them hard if they're doing the wrong work!"

"You've suddenly become an expert on tobacco."

"Jay, I grew up on a big estate and I saw it go bankrupt—not through the laziness of peasants, but because my father died and my mother couldn't cope with managing land. Now I see you making all the familiar errors—staying away too long, mistaking harshness for discipline, letting someone else make strategic decisions. You wouldn't run a regiment this way!"

"You don't know anything about running a regiment."

"And you don't know anything about running a farm!"

Jay was getting angry but he held it in. "So what are you asking me to do?"

"Dismiss Lennox."

"But who would take over?"

"We could do it together."

"I don't want to be a farmer!"

"Then let me do it."

Jay nodded. "I thought as much."

"What do you mean by that?"

"All this is just so that you can be in charge, isn't it?"

He was afraid she would explode, but instead she went quiet. "Is that what you really think?"

"As a matter of fact, it is."

"I'm trying to save you. You're headed for disaster, I'm fighting to prevent it, and you think I just want to order people around. If that's what you think of me, why the devil did you marry me?"

He did not like her to use strong language: it was too masculine. "In those days you used to be pretty," he said.

Her eyes flashed fire, but she did not speak. Instead she turned around and walked into the house.

Jay breathed a sigh of relief. It was not often he got the better of her.

After a moment he followed her in. He was surprised to see McAsh in the hall, dressed in a waistcoat and indoor shoes, putting a new pane of glass in a window. What the devil was he doing in the house?

"Lizzie!" Jay called. He went into the drawing room and found her there. "Lizzie, I just saw McAsh in the hall."

"I've put him in charge of maintenance. He's been painting the nursery."

"I don't want that man in my house."

Her reaction took him by surprise. "Then you'll just have to suffer it!" she blazed.

"Well—"

"I will not be alone here while Lennox is on the estate. I absolutely refuse, do you understand?"

"All right—"

"If McAsh goes, I go too!" She stormed out of the room.

"All right!" he said to the door as it slammed. He was not going to fight a war over one damned convict. If she wanted the man to paint the nursery so be it.

On the sideboard he saw an unopened letter addressed to him. He picked it up and recognized his mother's handwriting. He sat down by the window and opened it.

> *7, Grosvenor Square*
> *London*
> *September 15th, 1768*

> *My dear son,*
> *The new coal pit at High Glen has been restored after the accident, and coal mining has recommenced.*

Jay smiled. His mother could be very businesslike.

> *Robert has spent several weeks there, consolidating the two estates and arranging for them to be run as one property.*
>
> *I told your father that you should have a royalty on the coal, as the land is yours. His reply was that he is paying the interest on the mortgages. However, I'm afraid the deciding factor was the way you took the best convicts from the* Rosebud. *Your father was furious and so was Robert.*

Jay felt foolish and angry. He had thought he could take those men with impunity. He should have known better than to underestimate his father.

> *I will keep nagging your father over this. In time I'm sure he will give in.*

"Bless you, Mother," said Jay. She was still working hard in his interests even though he was so far away he might never see her again.

Having dealt with important matters she went on to write about herself, relatives and friends, and London social life. Then at the end she returned to business.

> *Robert has now gone to Barbados. I'm not sure why. My instincts tell me he is plotting against you. I can't imagine how he could do you harm but he is resourceful and ruthless. Be always on your guard, my son.*
>
> *Your loving mother,*
> *Alicia Jamisson*

Jay put the letter down thoughtfully. He had the deepest respect for his mother's intuition but all the same he thought she was being overly fearful. Barbados was a long way away. And even if Robert came to Virginia, there was nothing he could do to harm Jay now—was there?

31

IN THE OLD NURSERY WING, MACK FOUND A MAP.

He had redecorated two of the three rooms and he was clearing out the schoolroom. It was the end of the afternoon and he would start work properly tomorrow. There was a chest full of moldy books and empty ink bottles, and he sorted through the contents, wondering what was worth saving. The map was there, folded carefully in a leather case. He opened it up and studied it.

It was a map of Virginia.

At first he wanted to jump for joy, but his elation faded as he realized he could not make head or tail of it.

The names puzzled him until he understood they were in a foreign language—he guessed French. Virginia was spelled "Virginie," the territory to the northeast was labeled "Partie de New Jersey," and everything west of the mountains was called Louisiane, although that part of the map was otherwise blank.

Slowly he began to understand it better. Thin lines were rivers, thicker lines were the borders between one colony and the next, and the very thick lines were mountain ranges. He pored over it, fascinated and thrilled: this was his passport to freedom.

He discovered that the Rappahannock was one of several rivers running across Virginia from the mountains in the west to the Bay of Chesapeake in the east. He found Fredericksburg on the south bank of the Rappahannock. There was no way to tell distances, but Pepper

Jones had said it was a hundred miles to the mountains. If the map was right, it was the same distance again to the other side of the range. But there was no indication of a route across.

He felt a mixture of exhilaration and frustration. He knew where he was, at last, but the map seemed to say there was no escape.

The mountain range narrowed to the south, and Mack studied that part, tracing rivers to their source, looking for a way through. Far to the south he came across what looked like a pass, where the Cumberland River rose.

He remembered Whitey talking about the Cumberland Gap.

That was it: that was the way out.

It was a long journey. Mack guessed it must be four hundred miles, as far as from Edinburgh to London. *That* journey took two weeks by stagecoach, longer for a man with one horse. And it would take even longer on the rough roads and hunting trails of Virginia.

But on the far side of those mountains a man could be free.

He folded the map carefully and restored it to its case, then went on with his work. He would look at it again.

If only he could find Peg, he thought as he swept the room. He had to know whether she was all right before he ran away. If she was happy he would leave her, but if she had a cruel owner he would have to take her with him.

It became too dark to work.

He left the nursery and went down the stairs. He took his old fur cloak off a hook by the back door and wrapped it around him: it was cold outside. As he went out a knot of excited slaves came toward him. In the middle of the group was Kobe, and he was carrying a woman: after a moment Mack recognized Bess, the young slave girl who had fainted in the field a few weeks ago. Her eyes were closed and there was blood on her smock. The girl was accident prone.

Mack held the door open then followed Kobe inside. The Jamissons would be in the dining room, finishing their afternoon dinner. "Put her in the drawing room and I'll fetch Mrs. Jamisson," he said.

"The drawing room?" Kobe said dubiously.

It was the only room where the fire was lit, apart from the

dining room. "Trust me—it's what Mrs. Jamisson would prefer," Mack said.

Kobe nodded.

Mack knocked on the dining room door and entered.

Lizzie and Jay were sitting at a small round table, their faces lit by a candelabra in the center. Lizzie looked plump and beautiful in a low-necked gown that revealed the swell of her breasts then spread like a tent over her bulging abdomen. She was eating raisins while Jay cracked nuts. Mildred, a tall maid with perfect tobacco-colored skin, was pouring wine for Jay. A fire blazed in the hearth. It was a tranquil domestic scene and for a moment Mack was taken aback to be reminded so forcefully that they were man and wife.

Then he looked again. Jay was sitting at an angle to the table, his body averted from Lizzie: he was looking out of the window, watching night fall over the river. Lizzie was turned the other way, looking at Mildred as she poured. Neither Jay nor Lizzie was smiling. They might have been strangers in a tavern, forced to share a table but having no interest in one another.

Jay saw Mack and said: "What the devil do you want?"

Mack addressed Lizzie. "Bess has had an accident—Kobe's put her in the drawing room."

"I'll come at once," Lizzie said, pushing back her chair.

Jay said: "Don't let her bleed on that yellow silk upholstery!"

Mack held the door and followed Lizzie out.

Kobe was lighting candles. Lizzie bent over the injured girl. Bess's dark skin had gone paler and her lips were bloodless. Her eyes were closed and her breathing seemed shallow. "What happened?" said Lizzie.

"She cut herself," Kobe answered. He was still panting from the exertion of carrying her. "She was hacking at a rope with a machete. The blade slipped off the rope and sliced her belly."

Mack winced. He watched as Lizzie enlarged the tear in Bess's smock and gazed at the wound beneath. It looked bad. There was a lot of blood and the cut seemed deep.

"Go to the kitchen, one of you, and get me some clean rags and a bowl of warm water."

Mack admired her decisiveness. "I'll do it," he said.

He hurried to the outhouse kitchen. Sarah and Mildred were washing up the dinner dishes. Sarah, sweating as always, said: "Is she all right?"

"I don't know. Mrs. Jamisson asked for clean rags and warm water."

Sarah passed him a bowl. "Here, take some water off the fire. I'll get you the rags."

A few moments later he was back in the drawing room. Lizzie had cut away Bess's dress around the wound. Now she dipped a rag in the water and washed the skin. As the wound became more clearly visible it looked worse. Mack feared she might have damaged her internal organs.

Lizzie felt the same. "I can't deal with this," she said. "She needs a doctor."

Jay came into the room, took one look, and paled.

Lizzie said to him: "I'll have to send for Dr. Finch."

"As you wish," he said. "I'm going to the Ferry House—there's a cockfight." He went out.

Good riddance, Mack thought contemptuously.

Lizzie looked at Kobe and Mack. "One of you has to ride into Fredericksburg in the dark."

Kobe said: "Mack ain't much of a horseman. I'll go."

"He's right," Mack admitted. "I could drive the buggy, but it's slower."

"That settles it," Lizzie said. "Don't be rash, Kobe, but go as fast as you can—this girl could die."

＊

Fredericksburg was ten miles away, but Kobe knew the road, and he was back two hours later.

When he walked into the drawing room his face was like thunder. Mack had never seen him so angry.

"Where's the doctor?" Lizzie said.

"Dr. Finch won't come out at this time of night for no nigger girl," said Kobe in a shaky voice.

"Curse the damn fool," Lizzie said furiously.

They all looked at Bess. Her skin was beaded with perspiration and her breathing had become ragged. Now and again she moaned, but she did not open her eyes. The yellow silk sofa was red with her blood. She was obviously dying.

"We can't stand here and do nothing," Lizzie said. "She could be saved!"

Kobe said: "I don't think she has long to live."

"If the doctor won't come, we'll just have to take her to him," Lizzie said. "We'll put her in the buggy."

Mack said: "It's not good to move her."

"If we don't she'll die anyway!" Lizzie shouted.

"All right, all right. I'll get the buggy out."

"Kobe, take the mattress from my bed and put it in the back for her to lie on. And some blankets."

Mack hurried to the stables. The stable boys had all gone to the quarters but it did not take him long to put Stripe, the pony, in the traces. He got a taper from the kitchen fire and lit the carriage lamps on the buggy. When he pulled around to the front Kobe was waiting.

While Kobe arranged the bedding Mack went into the house. Lizzie was putting on her coat. "Are you coming?" Mack said.

"Yes."

"Do you think you should, in your condition?"

"I'm afraid that damned doctor will refuse to treat her if I don't."

Mack knew better than to argue with her in this mood. He picked Bess up gently and carried her outside. He laid her carefully on the mattress and Kobe covered her with the blankets. Lizzie climbed up and settled herself beside Bess, cradling the girl's head in her arms.

Mack got up in front and picked up the reins. Three people was a lot for the pony to haul so Kobe gave the buggy a shove to get it started. Mack drove down to the road and turned toward Fredericksburg.

There was no moon, but starlight enabled him to see where he was going. The trail was rocky and rutted, and the buggy bounced along. Mack was worried about jolting Bess, but Lizzie kept saying: "Go faster! Go faster!" The road wound along the riverbank, through rough woodland and the fringes of plantations just like the Jamisson place.

They saw nobody: people did not travel after dark if they could help it.

With Lizzie's urging Mack made good speed and they reached Fredericksburg around suppertime. There were people on the streets and lights in the houses. He drew up the buggy outside Dr. Finch's home. Lizzie went to the door while Mack wrapped Bess in the blankets and carefully lifted her up. She was unconscious but alive.

The door was opened by Mrs. Finch, a mousy woman in her forties. She showed Lizzie into the parlor and Mack followed with Bess. The doctor, a thickset man with a bullying manner, looked distinctly guilty when he realized he had forced a pregnant woman to drive through the night to bring him a patient. He covered his embarrassment by bustling about and giving his wife abrupt orders.

When he had looked at the wound he asked Lizzie to make herself comfortable in the other room. Mack went with her and Mrs. Finch stayed to help her husband.

The remains of a supper were on the table. Lizzie eased herself gingerly into a chair. "What's the matter?" Mack said.

"That ride has given me the most awful backache. Do you think Bess will be all right?"

"I don't know. She's not very robust."

A maid came in and offered Lizzie tea and cake, and Lizzie accepted. The maid looked Mack up and down, identified him as a servant, and said: "If you want some tea you can come in the kitchen."

"I need to see to the horse first," he said.

He went outside and led the pony around to Dr. Finch's stable, where he gave it water and some grain; then he waited in the kitchen. The house was small, and he could hear the doctor and his wife talking as they worked. The maid, a middle-aged black woman, cleared the dining room and brought out Lizzie's teacup. Mack decided it was stupid for him to sit in the kitchen and Lizzie in the dining room, so he went and sat with her, despite the frowns of the maid. Lizzie looked pale, and he resolved to get her home as soon as possible.

At last Dr. Finch came in, drying his hands. "It's a nasty wound but I believe I have done everything possible," he said. "I've stopped the bleeding, sewn up the gash and given her a drink. She's young and she will heal."

"Thank goodness," Lizzie said.

The doctor nodded. "I'm sure she's a valuable slave. She shouldn't travel far tonight. She can stay here and sleep in my maid's quarters, and you can send for her tomorrow or the day after. When the wound closes I'll take out the stitches—she should do no heavy work until then."

"Of course."

"Have you had supper, Mrs. Jamisson? May I offer you something?"

"No, thank you, I'd just like to get home and go to bed."

Mack said: "I'll bring the buggy around to the front."

A few minutes later they were on their way. Lizzie rode up front while they were in the town, but as soon as they passed the last house she lay down on the mattress.

Mack drove slowly, and this time there were no impatient sounds from behind him. When they had been traveling for about half an hour he said: "Are you asleep?"

There was no reply, and he assumed she was.

He glanced behind him from time to time. She was restless, shifting her position and muttering in her sleep.

They were driving along a deserted stretch two or three miles from the plantation when the stillness of the night was shattered by a scream.

It was Lizzie.

"What? What?" Mack called frantically as he hauled on the reins. Before the pony had stopped he was clambering into the back.

"Oh, Mack, it hurts!" she cried.

He put his arm around her shoulders and raised her a little. "What is it? Where does it hurt?"

"Oh, God, I think the baby is coming."

"But it's not due. . . ."

"Another two months."

Mack knew little about such things but he guessed that the birth had been brought on by the stress of the medical emergency or the bumpy ride to Fredericksburg—or both.

"How long have we got?"

She groaned long and loud, then answered him. "Not long."

"I thought it took hours."

"I don't know. I think the backache I had was labor pain. Maybe the baby has been on its way all this time."

"Shall I drive on? We'll be there in a quarter of an hour."

"Too long. Stay where you are and hold me."

Mack realized the mattress was wet and sticky. "What's soaked the mattress?"

"My waters broke, I think. I wish my mother was here."

Mack thought it was blood on the mattress but he did not say so.

She groaned again. When the pain passed she shivered. Mack covered her with his fur. "You can have your cloak back," he said, and she smiled briefly before the next spasm took her.

When she could speak again she said: "You must take the baby when it comes out."

"All right," he said, but he was not sure what she meant.

"Get down between my legs," she said.

He knelt at her feet and pushed up her skirts. Her underdrawers were soaked. Mack had undressed only two women, Annie and Cora, and neither of them had owned a pair of underdrawers, so he was not sure how they fastened, but he fumbled them off somehow. Lizzie lifted her legs and put her feet up against his shoulders to brace herself.

He stared at the patch of thick dark hair between her legs, and he was seized by a feeling of panic. How could a baby come through there? He had no idea how it happened. Then he told himself to be calm: this took place a thousand times a day all over the world. He did not need to understand it. The baby would come without his help.

"I'm frightened," Lizzie said during a brief respite.

"I'll look after you," he said, and he stroked her legs, the only part of her he could reach.

The baby came very quickly.

Mack could not see much in the starlight, but as Lizzie gave a mighty groan something began to emerge from inside her. Mack put two trembling hands down there and felt a warm, slippery object pushing its way out. A moment later the baby's head was in his hands.

Lizzie seemed to rest for a few moments, then start again. He held the head with one hand and put the other under the tiny shoulders as they came into the world. A moment later the rest of the baby slid out.

He held it and stared at it: the closed eyes, the dark hair of its head, the miniature limbs. "It's a girl," he said.

"She must cry!" Lizzie said urgently.

Mack had heard of smacking a newborn baby to make it breathe. It was hard to do, but he knew he must. He turned her over in his hand and gave her bottom a sharp slap.

Nothing happened.

As he held the tiny chest in the palm of his big hand he realized something was dreadfully wrong. He could not feel a heartbeat.

Lizzie struggled to sit upright. "Give her to me!" she said.

Mack handed the baby over.

She took the baby and stared into her face. She put her lips to the baby's as if kissing her, and then she blew into her mouth.

Mack willed the child to gasp air into her lungs and cry, but nothing happened.

"She's dead," Lizzie said. She held the baby to her bosom and drew the fur cloak around the naked body. "My baby's dead." She began to weep.

Mack put his arms around them both and held them while Lizzie cried her heart out.

32

FTER HER BABY GIRL WAS BORN DEAD, LIZZIE LIVED IN A WORLD OF gray colors, silent people, rain and mist. She let the household staff do as they pleased, realizing vaguely after a while that Mack had taken charge of them. She no longer patrolled the plantation every day: she left the tobacco fields to Lennox. Sometimes she visited Mrs. Thumson or Suzy Delahaye, for they were willing to talk about the baby as long as she liked; but she did not go to parties or balls. Every Sunday she attended church in Fredericksburg, and after the service she spent an hour or two in the graveyard, standing and looking at the tiny tombstone, thinking about what might have been.

She was quite sure it was all her fault. She had continued to ride horses until she was four or five months pregnant; she had not rested as much as people said she should; and she had ridden ten miles in the buggy, urging Mack to go faster and faster, on the night the baby was stillborn.

She was angry with Jay for being away from home that night; with Dr. Finch for refusing to come out for a slave girl; and with Mack for doing her bidding and driving fast. But most of all she was angry with herself. She loathed and despised herself for being an inadequate mother-to-be, for her impulsiveness and impatience and inability to listen to advice. If I were not like this, she thought, if I were a normal person, sensible and reasonable and cautious, I would have a little baby girl now.

She could not talk to Jay about it. At first he had been angry. He had railed at Lizzie, vowed to shoot Dr. Finch and threatened to have Mack flogged; but his rage had evaporated when he learned the baby had been a girl, and now he acted as if Lizzie had never been pregnant.

For a while she talked to Mack. The birth had brought them very close. He had wrapped her in his cloak and held her knees and tenderly handled the poor baby. At first he was a great comfort to her, but after a few weeks she sensed him becoming impatient. It was not his baby, she thought, and he could not truly share her grief. Nobody could. So she withdrew into herself.

One day three months after the birth she went to the nursery wing, still gleaming with fresh paint, and sat alone. She imagined a little girl there in a cradle, gurgling happily or crying to be fed, dressed in pretty white frocks and tiny knitted boots, suckling at her nipple or being bathed in a bowl. The vision was so intense that tears filled her eyes and rolled down her face, although she made no sound.

Mack came in while she was like that. Some debris had fallen down the chimney during a storm and he knelt at the fireplace and began to clear it up. He did not comment on her tears.

"I'm so unhappy," she said.

He did not pause in his work. "This will not do you any good," he replied in a hard voice.

"I expected more sympathy from you," she said miserably.

"You can't spend your life sitting in the nursery crying. Everyone dies sooner or later. The rest have to live on."

"I don't really want to. What have I got to live for?"

"Don't be so damned pathetic, Lizzie—it's not your nature."

She was shocked. No one had spoken unkindly to her since the stillbirth. What right did Mack have to make her even more unhappy? "You ought not to talk to me like that," she said.

He surprised her by rounding on her. Dropping his brush, he grabbed her by both arms and pulled her up out of her chair. "Don't tell me about my rights," he said.

He was so angry she was afraid he would do violence to her. "Leave me alone!"

"Too many people are leaving you alone," he said, but he put her down.

"What am I supposed to do?" she said.

"Anything you like. Get a ship back home and go and live with your mother in Aberdeen. Have a love affair with Colonel Thumson. Run away to the frontier with some ne'er-do-well." He paused and looked hard at her. "Or—make up your mind to be a wife to Jay, and have another baby."

That surprised her. "I thought . . ."

"What did you think?"

"Nothing." She had known for some time that he was at least half in love with her. After the failed party for the field hands he had touched her tenderly and stroked her in a way that could only be loving. He had kissed the hot tears on her face. There was more than mere pity in his embrace.

And there was more in her response than the need for sympathy. She had clung to his hard body and savored the touch of his lips on her skin, and that was not just because she felt sorry for herself.

But all those feelings had faded since the baby. Her heart was empty. She had no passions, just regrets.

She felt ashamed and embarrassed to have had such desires. The lascivious wife who tried to seduce the bonny young footman was a stock character in comic novels.

Mack was not just a bonny footman, of course. She had gradually come to realize that he was the most remarkable man she had ever met. He was arrogant and opinionated too, she knew. His idea of his own importance was ludicrously inflated, and it led him into mischief. But she could not could help admiring the way he stood up to tyrannical authority, from the Scottish coal field to the plantations of Virginia. And when he got into trouble it was often because he stuck up for someone else.

But Jay was her husband. He was weak and foolish, and he had lied to her, but she had married him and she had to be faithful to him.

Mack was still staring at her. She wondered what was going through his mind. She thought he was referring to himself when he said "run away to the frontier with some ne'er-do-well."

Mack reached out tentatively and stroked her cheek. Lizzie closed her eyes. If her mother could see this she would know exactly what to say. *You married Jay and you promised to be loyal to him. Are you a woman or a child? A woman keeps her word when it's difficult, not just when it's easy. That's what promising is all about.*

And here she was letting another man stroke her cheek. She opened her eyes and looked at Mack for a long moment. There was yearning in his green eyes. She hardened her heart. A sudden impulse seized her and she slapped his face as hard as she could.

It was like slapping a rock. He did not move. But his expression changed. She had not hurt his face but she had wounded his heart. He looked so shocked and dismayed that she felt an overpowering urge to apologize and embrace him. She resisted it with all her might. In a shaky voice she said: "Don't you dare touch me!"

He said nothing, but stared at her, horrified and wounded. She could not look at his hurt expression any longer, so she stood up and walked out of the room.

✳

He had said, "Make up your mind to be a wife to Jay, and have another baby." She thought hard about that for a day. The idea of having Jay in her bed had become unpleasant to her, but it was her duty as a wife. If she refused that duty she did not deserve a husband.

That afternoon she took a bath. This was a complicated business involving a tin tub in the bedroom and five or six strong girls running upstairs from the kitchen with pitchers of hot water. When that was done she put on fresh clothing before going downstairs for supper.

It was a cold winter's evening and the fire roared in the hearth. Lizzie drank some wine and tried to chatter gaily to Jay the way she used to before they were married. He did not respond. However, that was to be expected, she thought, when she had been poor company for so long.

After the meal was over she said: "It's been three months since the baby. I'm all right now."

"What do you mean?"

"My body is back to normal." She was not going to give him the details. Her breasts had stopped leaking milk a few days after the stillbirth. She had bled a little every day for much longer, but that too had ended. "I mean, my tummy will never be quite as flat again, but . . . in other ways I've healed."

He still did not understand. "Why are you telling me this?"

Trying to keep the exasperation out of her voice she said: "We can make love again, that's what I'm saying."

He grunted and lit his pipe.

It was not the reaction a woman might have hoped for.

"Will you come to my room tonight?" she persisted.

He looked annoyed. "It's the man that's supposed to make these suggestions," he said irritably.

She stood up. "I just wanted you to know that I'm ready," she said. Feeling hurt, she went up to her room.

Mildred came up to help her undress. As she took off her petticoats she said, in a voice as casual as she could manage: "Has Mr. Jamisson gone to bed?"

"No, I don't believe he has."

"Is he still downstairs?"

"I think he went out."

Lizzie looked at the maid's pretty face. There was something puzzling in her expression. "Mildred, are you hiding something from me?"

Mildred was young—about eighteen—and she had no talent for deceit. She averted her eyes. "No, Mrs. Jamisson."

Lizzie was sure she was lying. But why?

Mildred began to brush Lizzie's hair. Lizzie thought about where Jay had gone. He often went out after supper. Sometimes he said he was going to a card game or a cockfight; sometimes he said nothing at all. She assumed vaguely he was going to drink rum in taverns with other men. But if that were all there was to it, Mildred would say so. Now Lizzie thought of an alternative.

Did her husband have another woman?

✳

A week later he still had not come to her room.

She became obsessed with the idea that he was having an affair. The only person she could think of was Suzy Delahaye. She was young and pretty, and her husband was always going away—like many Virginians he was obsessed with horse races and would travel two days to see one. Was Jay sneaking out of the house after supper and riding over to the Delahaye place and getting into bed with Suzy?

She told herself she was being fanciful, but the thought would not go away.

On the seventh night she looked out of her bedroom window and saw the flicker of a candle lamp moving across the dark lawn.

She decided to follow.

It was cold and dark, but she did not delay to dress. She picked up a shawl and drew it around her shoulders as she ran down the stairs.

She slipped out of the house. The two deerhounds, who slept on the porch, looked up at her curiously. "Come, Roy, come, Rex!" she said. She ran across the grass, following the spark of the lantern, with the dogs at her heels. Soon the light disappeared into the woods, but by then she was close enough to discern that Jay—if it was he—had taken the path that led to the tobacco sheds and the overseer's quarters.

Perhaps Lennox had a horse saddled ready for Jay to ride to the Delahaye place. Lennox was deep in this somehow, Lizzie felt: that man was involved whenever Jay went wrong.

She did not see the lantern again, but she found the cottages easily. There were two. Lennox occupied one. The other had been Sowerby's and was now vacant.

But there was someone inside it.

The windows were shuttered against the cold, but light shone through the cracks.

Lizzie paused, hoping that her heart would slow down, but it was fear, not exertion, that made it beat so fast. She was scared of what she would see inside. The idea of Jay taking Suzy Delahaye in his arms the way he had embraced Lizzie, and kissing her with the lips Lizzie had kissed, made her sick with rage. She even thought about turning back. But not knowing would be the worst of all.

She tried the door. It was not locked. She opened it and went inside.

The house had two rooms. The kitchen, at the front, was empty, but she could hear a low voice coming from the bedroom at the back. Were they in bed already? She tiptoed to the door, grasped the handle, took a deep breath, and flung it open.

Suzy Delahaye was not in the room.

Jay was. He lay on the bed in his shirt and breeches, barefoot and coatless.

At the end of the bed stood a slave.

Lizzie did not know the girl's name: she was one of the four Jay had bought in Williamsburg. She was about Lizzie's age, slim and very beautiful, with soft brown eyes. She was completely naked, and Lizzie could see her proud brown-tipped breasts and the tightly curled black hair at her groin.

As Lizzie stared, the girl threw her a look that Lizzie would never forget: a haughty, contemptuous, triumphant look. You may be the mistress of the house, the look said, but he comes to my bed every night, not yours.

Jay's voice came to her as if from a great distance: "Lizzie, oh my God!"

She turned her face to him and saw him flinch at her look. But his fear gave her no satisfaction: she had known for a long time that he was weak.

She found her voice. "Go to hell, Jay," she said quietly, and she turned and left the room.

*

She went to her room, got her keys from the drawer, then went down to the gun room.

Her Griffin rifles were in the rack with Jay's guns, but she left them and picked up a pair of pocket pistols in a leather case. Checking the contents of the case she found a full powder horn, plenty of linen wadding, and some spare flints, but no balls. She searched the room but there was no shot, just a small stack of lead ingots. She took one of the ingots and a bullet mold—a small tool like a pair of pincers—then she left the room, relocking the door.

In the kitchen, Sarah and Mildred stared at her with big frightened eyes as she walked in carrying the pistol case under her arm. Without speaking she went to the cupboard and took out a stout knife and a small, heavy iron saucepan with a spout. Then she went to her bedroom and locked the door.

She built up the fire until it blazed so hot she could not stay near it for more than a few seconds. Then she put the lead ingot in the pan and the pan on the fire.

She remembered Jay coming home from Williamsburg with four young girl slaves. She had asked why he had not bought men, and he said girls were cheaper and more obedient. At the time she had thought no more about it: she had been more concerned about the extravagance of his new carriage. Now, bitterly, she understood.

There was a knock at the door and Jay's voice said: "Lizzie?" The handle was turned and the door tried. Finding it locked he said: "Lizzie—will you let me in?"

She ignored him. At the moment he was cowed and guilty. Later he would find a way to convince himself he had done nothing wrong, and then he would become angry, but for the moment he was harmless.

He knocked and called for a minute or so then gave up and went away.

When the lead was melted she took the pan off the fire. Moving quickly, she poured a little lead into the mold through a nozzle. Inside the head of the tool was a spherical cavity that now filled with molten lead. She plunged the mold into the bowl of water on her washstand, to cool and harden the lead. When she squeezed together the arms of the tool, the head came open and a neat round bullet fell out. She picked it up. It was perfect except for a little tail formed by the lead that had remained in the nozzle. She trimmed the tail with the kitchen knife.

She carried on making shot until all the lead was used up. Then she loaded both pistols and placed them beside her bed. She checked the lock on the door.

Then she went to bed.

33

MACK HATED LIZZIE FOR THAT SLAP. EVERY TIME HE THOUGHT OF IT he felt enraged. She gave him false signals then punished him when he responded. She was a bitch, he told himself; a heartless upper-class flirt who toyed with his feelings.

But he knew it was not true, and after a while he changed his view. Reflection led him to realize that she was at the mercy of conflicting emotions. She was attracted to him, but she was married to someone else. She had a well-developed sense of duty, and she felt scared because it was being undermined. In desperation she tried to put an end to the dilemma by quarreling with him.

He had longed to tell her that her loyalty to Jay was misplaced. All the slaves had known for months that Jay was spending his nights in a cottage with Felia, a beautiful and willing girl from Senegal. But he had felt sure Lizzie would find out for herself sooner or later, and sure enough she had, two nights ago. Her reaction had been characteristically extreme: she had locked her bedroom door and armed herself with pistols.

How long would she keep that up? How would it all end? "Run away to the frontier with some ne'er-do-well," he had said, thinking of himself. But she had not responded to the suggestion. Of course it would never occur to her to spend her life with Mack. No doubt she liked him; he had been more than a servant to her; he had delivered her baby; and she enjoyed it when he embraced her. But all that was a long way from leaving her husband and running off with him.

He was lying restlessly in his bed before daybreak, turning these things over in his mind, when he heard a horse whinny softly outside.

Who could it be at this time of night? Frowning, he slipped off his bunk and went to the cabin door in his breeches and shirt.

The air outside was cold and he shivered when he opened the door. It was a misty morning with a fine rain, but dawn was breaking and he could see, in the silver light, two women entering the compound, one leading a pony.

A moment later he recognized the taller woman as Cora. Why had she ridden through the night to come here? Bad news seemed likely.

Then he recognized the other one.

"Peg!" he cried delightedly.

She saw him and came running to him. She had grown up, he thought: she was inches taller and a different shape. But her face was the same and she threw herself into his arms. "Mack!" she said. "Oh, Mack, I've been so frightened!"

"I thought I'd never see you again," he said. "What happened?"

Cora answered his question. "She's in trouble. She was bought by a hill farmer called Burgo Marler. He tried to rape her and she stabbed him with a kitchen knife."

"Poor Peg," said Mack, and he hugged her. "Is the man dead?"

Peg nodded.

Cora said: "The story has been in the *Virginia Gazette* and now every sheriff in the colony is looking for Peg."

Mack was aghast. If Peg were caught she would certainly be hanged.

The other slaves were woken by their conversation. Some of the convicts came out and recognized Peg and Cora, and there were happy reunions.

Mack said to Peg: "How did you get to Fredericksburg?"

"Walked," she said with a laconic touch of her old defiant personality. "I knew I had to go east and find the Rappahannock River. I traveled in the dark and got directions from people who are out at night—slaves, runaways, army deserters, Indians."

Cora said: "I hid her in my house for a few days—my husband's in Williamsburg on business. But then I heard that the local sheriff was about to raid everyone who was on the *Rosebud.*"

"But that means he'll come here!" Mack said.

"Yes—he's not far behind me."

"What?"

"I'm pretty sure he's on his way now—he was mustering a search party when I left town."

"So why did you bring her here?"

Cora's face hardened. "Because she's your problem. I've got a rich husband and a nice house and my own pew in the church, and I don't want the sheriff to find a murderer in my damn stable loft!"

The other convicts muttered their disapproval. Mack stared at her in dismay. He had once thought of spending his life with this woman. "By God, you're hard-hearted," he said angrily.

"I saved her, didn't I?" Cora said indignantly. "Now I've got to save myself!"

Peg said: "Thank you for everything, Cora. You did save me."

Kobe had been watching the proceedings silently. Now Mack turned to him automatically to discuss the problem. "We could hide her over at the Thumson place," he said.

"That's all right, so long as the sheriff doesn't search there too," Kobe said.

"Damn. I never thought of that." Where could she hide? "They'll search every inch of the quarters, the stables, the tobacco sheds . . ."

Cora said: "Have you fucked Lizzie Jamisson yet?"

Mack was taken aback by the question. "What do you mean, 'yet'? Of course I haven't."

"Don't act stupid. I bet she wants you to."

Mack resented Cora's unromantic attitude but he could not act innocent. "What if she does?"

"Would she hide Peg—for your sake?"

Mack was not sure. How can I even ask the question? he thought. He could not love a woman who would refuse to protect a child in this situation. Yet there was a doubt in his mind as to whether Lizzie would agree to do it. For some reason this made him feel angry. "She might do it out of the kindness of her heart," he said pointedly.

"She might. But selfish lust is a more reliable motive."

Mack heard dogs barking. It sounded like the deerhounds on the porch of the big house. What had disquieted them? Then there was an answering bark from down by the river.

"Strange dogs in the neighborhood," Kobe said. "That's what disturbed Roy and Rex."

"Could it be the search party already?" Mack said with heightened anxiety.

"I think so," said Kobe.

"I was hoping for time to figure out a plan!"

Cora turned away and mounted her pony. "I'm getting out of here before I'm seen." She walked the pony out of the compound. "Good luck," she called softly. Then she disappeared into the misty woods like a ghostly messenger.

Mack turned to Peg. "We're running out of time. Come with me to the house. It's our best chance."

She looked scared. "I'll do whatever you say."

Kobe said: "I'll go and see who the visitors are. If it's the search party, I'll try to slow them down."

Peg held Mack's hand as they hurried through the cold fields and across the damp lawns in the gray light. The dogs came loping down from the porch to meet them. Roy licked Mack's hand and Rex sniffed curiously at Peg, but they made no noise.

Doors were never locked here, and Mack led Peg in through the back entrance. They crept up the stairs. Mack looked out of the landing window and saw, in the black-and-white tones of dawn, five or six men and some dogs coming up from the direction of the river. As he watched, the party split: two men headed for the house and the rest turned toward the slave quarters with the dogs.

Mack went to Lizzie's bedroom door. Don't let me down now, he thought. He tried the door.

It was locked.

He tapped gently, fearful of waking Jay in the next room.

Nothing happened.

He tapped harder.

He heard soft footsteps, then Lizzie's voice came clearly through the door: "Who's there?"

"Hush! It's Mack!" he whispered.

"What the devil are you doing?"

"It's not what you think—open the door!"

He heard a key turn, and the door opened. In the gloom he could hardly see her. She turned back into the room, and he stepped inside, drawing Peg behind him. The room was in darkness.

Her footsteps crossed the room and a blind was raised. In the pale light he saw her, wearing some kind of dressing gown, looking deliciously tousled. "Explain yourself, fast," she said. "And it had better be good." Then she saw Peg, and her attitude changed. "You're not alone."

"Peg Knapp," he said.

"I remember," Lizzie said. "How are you, Peggy?"

"I'm in trouble again," Peg said.

Mack explained. "She was sold to a hill farmer who tried to rape her."

"Oh, dear God."

"She killed the man."

"You poor child," Lizzie said. She put her arms around Peg. "You poor child."

"The sheriff is looking for her. He's outside now, searching the slave quarters." Mack looked at Peg's thin face and saw in his mind the gallows in Fredericksburg. "We have to hide her!" he said.

Lizzie said: "You just leave the sheriff to me."

"What do you mean?" Mack said. He got nervous when she tried to take charge.

"I'll explain to him that Peg was defending herself against rape."

When Lizzie was sure of something she often imagined that no one could disagree with her. It was a vexing trait. Mack shook his head impatiently. "That's no good, Lizzie. The sheriff will say the court has to decide whether she's guilty, not you."

"Then she can stay here until her trial."

Lizzie's ideas were so maddeningly airy that Mack had to force himself to speak calmly and reasonably. "You can't stop a sheriff arresting someone accused of murder, no matter what you think of the rights and wrongs of the case."

"Perhaps she should just stand trial. If she's innocent they can't convict her—"

"Lizzie, be realistic!" Mack said in exasperation. "What Virginian court is going to acquit a convict who kills her owner? They're all terrified of being attacked by their slaves. Even if they believe her story they'll hang her, just to frighten the rest."

She looked angry, and she was about to make some retort when Peg started to cry. That made Lizzie hesitate. She bit her lip then said: "What do you think we should do?"

One of the dogs growled outside, and Mack heard the voice of a man talking to it and calming it. "I want you to hide Peg in here while they search the place," he said to Lizzie. "Will you do it?"

He watched her face. If you say no, he thought, I'm in love with the wrong woman.

"Of course I'll do it," she said. "What do you think I am?"

He smiled happily, flooded with relief. He loved her so much he had to fight back tears. He swallowed hard. "I think you're wonderful," he said huskily.

They had been talking in low voices, and now Mack heard a sound from Jay's bedroom on the other side of the wall. He had a lot more to do before Peg was safe. "I must get out of here," he said. "Good luck!" He left.

He stepped across the landing and ran lightly down the stairs. As he reached the hall he thought he heard Jay's bedroom door open, but he did not look back.

He stopped in the hall and took a deep breath. I'm a house servant here and I have no idea what the sheriff might want, he told himself. He pasted a polite smile to his face and opened the door.

Two men were on the porch. They wore the dress of prosperous Virginians: riding boots, long waistcoats and three-cornered hats. Both carried pistols in leather cases with shoulder straps. They smelled of rum: they had been fortifying themselves against the cold night air.

Mack stood squarely in the doorway, to discourage them from entering the house. "Good morning, gentlemen," he said. He found his heart was beating fast. He struggled to keep his voice relaxed and calm. "This looks like a search party."

The taller of the two said: "I'm the sheriff of Spotsylvania County, and I'm looking for a girl by the name of Peggy Knapp."

"I saw the dogs. Have you sent them down to the slave quarters?"

"Yes."

"Good thinking, Sheriff. That way you'll catch the niggers asleep and they won't be able to conceal the fugitive."

"I'm glad you approve," the sheriff said with a touch of sarcasm. "We'll just step inside."

A convict had no choice when given orders by a free man, and Mack had to stand aside and let them into the hall. He still hoped they would not think it necessary to search the house.

"How come you're up?" the sheriff said with a hint of suspicion in his voice. "We expected to have to wake everyone."

"I'm an early riser."

The man grunted noncommittally. "Is your master at home?"

"Yes."

"Take us to him."

Mack did not want them to go upstairs—they would be uncomfortably close to Peg. "I believe I heard Mr. Jamisson moving around," he said. "Shall I ask him to come down?"

"No—I don't want to put him to the trouble of getting dressed."

Mack cursed under his breath. Evidently the sheriff was determined to take everyone by surprise if possible. But he could not argue. He said, "This way, please," and led them up the stairs.

He knocked on Jay's door. A moment later Jay opened it, wearing a wrap over his nightshirt. "What the devil is all this?" he said irritably.

"I'm Sheriff Abraham Barton, Mr. Jamisson. I apologize for disturbing you, but we're searching for the murderer of Burgo Marler. Does the name Peggy Knapp mean anything to you?"

Jay looked hard at Mack. "It certainly does. The girl was always a thief and I'm not surprised she's turned into a killer. Have you asked McAsh here if he knows where she is?"

Barton looked at Mack in surprise. "So you're McAsh! You didn't mention it."

"You didn't ask," Mack said.

Barton was not satisfied with that. "Did you know I was coming here this morning?"

"No."

Jay said suspiciously: "Then why are you up so early?"

"When I worked in your father's coal mine I used to start at two o'clock in the morning. Now I always wake early."

"I've never noticed."

"You're never up."

"Less of your damned insolence."

Barton said to Mack: "When did you last see Peggy Knapp?"

"When I disembarked from the *Rosebud* half a year ago."

The sheriff turned back to Jay. "The niggers may be concealing her. We've brought dogs."

Jay waved a generous hand. "Go ahead and do whatever you need to."

"We should search the house, too."

Mack caught his breath. He had been hoping they would not think that necessary.

Jay frowned. "It's not likely the child is in here."

"Still, for the sake of thoroughness . . ."

Jay hesitated, and Mack hoped he would get on his high horse and tell the sheriff to go to hell. But after a moment he shrugged and said: "Of course."

Mack's heart sank.

Jay went on: "There's only my wife and me in residence. The rest of the place is empty. But search everywhere, by all means. I'll leave you to it." He closed his door.

Barton said to Mack: "Which is Mrs. Jamisson's room?"

Mack swallowed. "Next door." He stepped along the landing and knocked gently. With his heart in his mouth he said: "Mrs. Jamisson? Are you awake?"

There was a pause, then Lizzie opened the door. Feigning sleepiness, she said: "What on earth do you want at this hour?"

"The sheriff is looking for a fugitive."

Lizzie opened the door wide. "Well, I haven't got one in here."

Mack looked into the room, wondering where Peg was hiding.

Barton said: "May we step inside for a moment?"

There was an almost imperceptible flash of fear in Lizzie's eyes, and Mack wondered whether Barton had seen it. Lizzie shrugged with a semblance of apathy and said: "Feel free."

The two men stepped inside, looking awkward. Lizzie let her dressing gown sag open a little, as if by accident. Mack could not help looking at the way the nightdress draped her rounded breasts. The other two men reacted with the same reflex. Lizzie looked the sheriff in the eye and he turned away guiltily. She was deliberately making them feel uncomfortable so that they would search hastily.

The sheriff lay on the floor and looked under the bed while his assistant opened the wardrobe. Lizzie sat on the bed. With a hasty gesture she picked up a corner of the bedspread and tugged it. Mack glimpsed a small, dirty foot for a split second before it was covered up.

Peg was in the bed.

She was so thin that she hardly made a bulge in the piled-up covers.

The sheriff opened a blanket chest and the other man looked behind a screen. There were not many places to check. Would they pull the covers off the bed?

The same thought must have gone through Lizzie's mind, for she said, "Now, if you're done, I'm going back to sleep," and she got into bed.

Barton looked hard at Lizzie and the bed. Did he have the nerve to demand that Lizzie get out again? But he did not really think the master and mistress of the house were concealing the murderess—he was searching the place only to be comfortable about eliminating the possibility. After a moment's hesitation he said: "Thank you, Mrs. Jamisson. We're sorry to have disturbed your rest. We'll carry on and search the slave quarters."

Mack felt weak with relief. He held the door for them, hiding his jubilation.

"Good luck," Lizzie said. "And, Sheriff—when you've finished your work, bring your men back here to the house and have some breakfast!"

34

L IZZIE STAYED IN HER ROOM WHILE THE MEN AND DOGS SEARCHED THE plantation. She and Peg talked in low voices, and Peg told her the story of her life. Lizzie was horrified and shaken. Peg was just a girl, thin and pretty and cheeky. Lizzie's dead baby had been a girl.

They exchanged dreams. Lizzie revealed that she wanted to live out of doors and wear men's clothing and spend all day on horseback with a gun. Peg took a folded and worn sheet of paper from inside her chemise. It was a hand-colored picture showing a father, a mother and a child standing outside a pretty cottage in the country. "I always wanted to be the little girl in the picture," she said. "But now sometimes I want to be the mother."

At the usual time Sarah, the cook, came to the room with Lizzie's breakfast on a tray. Peg hid under the bedclothes at her knock, but the woman walked in and said to Lizzie: "I know all about Peggy, so don't you worry."

Peg came out again and Lizzie said bemusedly: "Who *doesn't* know?"

"Mr. Jamisson and Mr. Lennox."

Lizzie shared her breakfast with Peg. The child shoveled down grilled ham and scrambled eggs as if she had not eaten for a month.

The search party left as she was finishing. Lizzie and Peg went to the window and watched the men cross the lawn and make their way down to the river. They were disappointed and subdued, walking with slumped shoulders, and the dogs, picking up the mood, trailed obediently behind.

They watched the men out of sight, then Lizzie sighed with relief and said: "You're safe."

They hugged happily. Peg was painfully bony, and Lizzie felt a surge of maternal feeling for the poor child.

Peg said: "I'm always safe with Mack."

"You'll have to stay in this room until we're sure Jay and Lennox are out of the way."

"Aren't you worried that Mr. Jamisson will come in?" Peg asked.

"No, he never comes in here."

Peg looked puzzled but she did not ask any more questions. Instead she said: "When I'm older I'm going to marry Mack."

Lizzie had the strangest feeling that she was being warned off.

*

Mack sat in the old nursery—where he could be sure he would not be disturbed—going through his survival kit. He had a stolen ball of twine and six hooks, made for him by the blacksmith Cass, so that he could catch fish. He had a tin cup and plate of the kind given to slaves. There was a tinder box so he could light fires and an iron pan to cook his food. He had an ax and a heavy knife he had purloined while the slaves were felling trees and making barrels.

At the bottom of the bag, wrapped in a scrap of linen, was a key to the gun room. His last act before leaving would be to steal a rifle and ammunition.

Also in the canvas bag were his copy of *Robinson Crusoe* and the iron collar he had brought from Scotland. He picked up the collar, remembering how he had broken it in the smithy the night he had escaped from Heugh. He recalled how he had danced a jig of freedom in the moonlight. More than a year later he still was not free. But he had not given up.

Peg's return had removed the last obstacle preventing him running away from Mockjack Hall. She had moved into the slave quarters and slept in a hut of single girls. They would all keep her secret. They would always protect one of their own. It was not the first time a fugitive had been hidden in the quarters: any runaway could get a bowl of hominy and a hard bed for the night at every plantation in Virginia.

During the day she roamed the woods, keeping out of sight until darkness fell. Then she returned to the quarters to eat with the hands. Mack knew this could not go on for long. Soon boredom would make her careless and she would be caught. But she would not have to live that way for many days.

Mack's skin tingled with anticipation. Cora was married, Peg was saved, and the map had shown him where he had to go. Freedom was his heart's desire. As soon as they chose, he and Peg could simply walk away from the plantation at the end of the day's work. By dawn they could be thirty miles away. They would hide during the hours of daylight then go on at night. Like all runaways, they would beg food at the slave quarters of the nearest plantation every morning and evening.

Unlike most runaways, Mack would not try to get a job as soon as he had gone a hundred miles. That was how they were always caught. He was going farther away. His destination was the wilderness beyond the mountains. There he would be free.

But Peg had been back a week, and he was still at Mockjack Hall.

He stared at his map and his fishhooks and his tinder box. He was a step away from freedom, but he could not take that step.

He had fallen in love with Lizzie, and he could not bear to leave her.

*

Lizzie stood naked in front of the cheval glass in her bedroom, looking at her body.

She had told Jay she was back to normal after the pregnancy, but the truth was that she would never be quite the same. Her breasts had gone back to their previous size, but they were not as firm, and they seemed to hang a little lower on her chest. Her tummy would never return to normal, she now realized: the slight bulge and the slackness of the skin were with her forever. She had faint silvery lines where her skin had stretched. They had faded, but not completely, and she had a feeling they would always be there. Down below, the place where the baby came out was also different. It had once been so tight that she could hardly get her finger in. That, too, had stretched.

She wondered if this was why Jay no longer wanted her. He had not seen her naked body since the birth but perhaps he knew what it was like, or guessed, and found it disgusting. Felia, his slave girl, had obviously never had a baby. Her body was still perfect. Jay would make her pregnant, sooner or later. But then he might drop her the way he had dropped Lizzie, and take up with yet another woman. Was that how he wanted to live his life? Were all men like that? Lizzie wished she could ask her mother.

She was being treated as something used up, no good anymore, like a worn pair of shoes or a cracked plate. That made her angry. The baby who had grown inside her and made her belly bulge and stretched her vagina was Jay's child. He had no right to reject her afterward. She sighed. It was pointless to get angry with him. She had chosen him and she had been a fool.

She wondered if anyone would ever find this body attractive again. She missed the feeling of a man's hands running over her flesh as if he could never get enough. She wanted someone to kiss her tenderly and squeeze her breasts and press his fingers into her. She could not bear the thought that it would never happen again.

She took a deep breath, pulling in her stomach and sticking out her chest. There—that was almost how she had looked before the pregnancy. She weighed her breasts, then touched the hair between her legs, and toyed with the button of desire.

The door opened.

✳

Mack had to repair a broken tile in the fireplace in Lizzie's room. He had said to Mildred: "Is Mrs. Jamisson up yet?"

Mildred had replied: "Just gone over to the stables." She must have thought he said *Mister* Jamisson.

All of that went through his mind in a split second. Then he thought of nothing but Lizzie.

She was achingly beautiful. As she stood in front of the mirror he could see her body from both sides. Her back was to him, and his hands itched to stroke the curve of her hips. In the mirror he could see the swell of her round breasts and the soft pink nipples. The hair at her groin matched the wild dark curls of her head.

He stood there speechless. He knew he should mutter an apology and get out fast, but his feet seemed clamped to the floor.

She turned to him. Her face was troubled, and he wondered why. Unclothed, she seemed vulnerable, almost afraid.

At last he found his voice. "Oh, but you're beautiful," he whispered.

Her face changed, as if a question had been answered.

"Close the door," she said.

He pushed the door behind him and crossed the room in three strides. A moment later she was in his arms. He crushed her naked body to him, feeling her soft breasts against his chest. He kissed her lips and her mouth opened to him immediately. His tongue found hers and he gloried in the wetness and hunger of her kiss. As he got hard she pulled his hips to her and rubbed herself against him.

He broke away, panting, afraid he would come right away. She tugged at his waistcoat and his shirt, trying to get beneath the clothes to his skin. He threw the waistcoat aside and pulled the shirt over his head. She bent her head and put her mouth to his nipple. Her lips closed over it in a kiss, then she licked it with the tip of her tongue, and finally she bit it lightly with her neat front teeth. The pain was exquisite and he gasped with pleasure.

"Now do it to me," she said. She arched her back, offering her breast to his mouth. He lifted her breast in his hand and kissed the nipple. It was hard with desire. He savored the moment.

"Not so gently," she whispered.

He sucked fiercely, then bit her as she had bitten him. He heard her sharp intake of breath. He was afraid of hurting her soft body but she said: "Harder, I want it to hurt," and he bit down. "Yes," she said, and she pulled his head to her so that his face squashed her breast.

He stopped because he was afraid he would draw blood. When he straightened up she bent to his waist, tugged on the string that held up his breeches, and pulled them down. His penis sprang free. She took it in both hands and rubbed it against her soft cheeks and kissed it. The pleasure was overwhelming and once again Mack broke away from her, not wanting it to end too soon.

He looked at the bed.

"Not there," Lizzie said. "Here." She lay back on the rug in front of the mirror.

He knelt between her legs, feasting his eyes.

"Now, quickly," she said.

He lay on top of her, resting his weight on his elbows, and she guided him inside. He gazed at her lovely face. Her cheeks were flushed and her mouth was slightly open, showing moist lips and small teeth. Her eyes were wide, staring at him as he moved above her. "Mack," she moaned. "Oh, Mack." Her body moved with his and her fingers dug hard into the muscles of his back.

He kissed her and moved gently, but once again she wanted more. She took his lower lip between her teeth and bit down. He tasted blood. "Go faster!" she said frantically, and her desperation took him over and he moved faster, pushing inside her almost brutally, and she said: "Yes, like that!" She closed her eyes, giving herself up to the sensation, and then she cried out. He put his hand over her mouth to quiet her, and she bit his finger hard. She pulled his hips to hers as hard as she could and twisted beneath him, her cries muffled by his hand, her hips rising to his again and again until at last she stopped and sank back, exhausted.

He kissed her eyes and her nose and her chin, still moving gently inside her. When her breathing eased and she opened her eyes she said: "Look in the mirror."

He looked up at the cheval glass and saw another Mack on top of another Lizzie, their bodies joined at the hip. He watched his penis move in and out of her body. "It looks nice," she whispered.

He looked at her. How dark her eyes were, almost black. "Do you love me?" he said.

"Oh, Mack, how could you ask?" Tears came to her eyes. "Of course I do. I love you, I love you."

And then, at last, he came.

*

When the first of the tobacco crop was at last ready for sale, Lennox took four hogsheads into Fredericksburg on a flatboat. Jay waited impatiently for him to come back. He was eager to know what price the tobacco would fetch.

He would not get cash for it: that was not the way the market worked. Lennox would take the tobacco to a public warehouse where the official inspector would issue a certificate saying it was "merchantable." Such certificates, known as tobacco notes, were used as money throughout Virginia. In time the last holder of the note would redeem it by handing it to a ship's captain in exchange for money or, more likely, goods imported from Britain. The captain would then take the note to the public warehouse and exchange it for tobacco.

Meanwhile Jay would use the note to pay his most pressing debts. The smithy had been quiet for a month because they had no iron to make tools and horseshoes.

Fortunately Lizzie had not noticed that they were broke. After the baby was born dead she had lived in a daze for three months. Then, when she caught him with Felia, she had become furiously silent.

Today she was different again. She looked happier and she seemed almost friendly. "What's the news?" she asked him at dinner.

"Trouble in Massachusetts," he replied. "There's a group of hotheads called the Sons of Liberty—they've even had the nerve to send money to that damned fellow John Wilkes in London."

"I'm surprised they even know who he is."

"They think he stands for freedom. Meanwhile, the customs commissioners are afraid to set foot in Boston. They've taken refuge aboard HMS *Romney*."

"It sounds as if the colonists are ready to rebel."

Jay shook his head. "They just need a dose of the medicine we gave the coal heavers—a taste of rifle fire and a few good hangings."

Lizzie shuddered and asked no more questions.

They finished the meal in silence. While Jay was lighting his pipe, Lennox came in.

Jay could see that he had been drinking, as well as doing business, in Fredericksburg. "Is all well, Lennox?"

"Not exactly," Lennox said in his habitual insolent tone.

Lizzie said impatiently: "What's happened?"

Lennox answered without looking at her. "Our tobacco has been burned, that's what's happened."

"Burned!" said Jay.

"How?" said Lizzie.

"By the inspector. Burned as trash. Not merchantable."

Jay had a sickening feeling in the pit of his stomach. He swallowed and said: "I didn't know they could do that."

Lizzie said: "What was wrong with it?"

Lennox looked uncharacteristically flustered. For a moment he said nothing.

"Come on, out with it," Lizzie said angrily.

"They say it's cowpen," Lennox said at last.

"I knew it!" Lizzie said.

Jay had no idea what they were talking about. "What do you mean, 'cowpen'? What's that?"

Lizzie said coldly: "It means cattle have been penned on the land where the crop was grown. When land is overmanured the tobacco acquires a strong, unpleasant flavor."

Jay said angrily: "Who are these inspectors who have the right to burn my crop?"

"They're appointed by the House of Burgesses," Lizzie told him.

"It's outrageous!"

"They have to maintain the quality of Virginia tobacco."

"I'll go to law over this."

Lizzie said: "Jay, instead of going to law, why don't you just run your plantation properly? You can grow perfectly good tobacco here if only you take care."

"I don't need a woman to tell me how to manage my affairs!" he shouted.

Lizzie looked at Lennox. "You don't need a fool to do it, either," she said.

A terrible thought struck Jay. "How much of our crop was grown this way?"

Lennox said nothing.

"Well?" Jay persisted.

Lizzie said: "All of it."

Then Jay understood that he was ruined.

The plantation was mortgaged, he was in debt up to his ears, and the entire tobacco crop was valueless.

Suddenly he found he could hardly breathe. His throat seemed constricted. He opened his mouth like a fish but he could get no air.

At last he drew breath, like a drowning man coming to the surface for the last time.

"God help me," he said, and he buried his face in his hands.

*

That night he knocked on Lizzie's bedroom door.

She was sitting by the fire in her nightdress, thinking about Mack. She was ecstatically happy. She loved him and he loved her. But what were they going to do? She stared into the flames. She tried to be practical, but all the time her mind drifted into remembering how they had made love here on the rug in front of the cheval glass. She wanted to do it again.

The knock startled her. She jumped out of her chair and stared at the locked door.

The handle rattled but she had locked the door every night since she had caught Jay with Felia. Jay's voice came: "Lizzie—open this door!"

She said nothing.

"I'm going to Williamsburg early in the morning to try to borrow more money," he said. "I want to see you before I go."

Still she said nothing.

"I know you're in there, now open up!" He sounded a little drunk.

A moment later there was a thud as if he had thrown his shoulder against the door. She knew that would not achieve anything: the hinges were brass and the bolt was heavy.

She heard his footsteps recede, but she guessed he had not yet given up, and she was right. Three or four minutes later he came back and said: "If you don't open the door I'm going to break it down."

There was a bang as something crashed into the door. Lizzie guessed he had fetched an ax. Another crash split the woodwork and she saw the blade come through.

Lizzie began to feel scared. She wished Mack were nearby, but he was down in the slave quarters, sleeping on a hard bunk. She had to take care of herself.

Feeling shaky, she went to her bedside table and picked up her pistols.

Jay continued to attack the door, his ax smashing into the woodwork with a series of deafening crashes, splintering the timber and causing the walls of the wood-frame house to tremble. Lizzie checked the loading of the pistols. With an unsteady hand she poured a little gunpowder into the priming pan of each. She released the safety catches on the flintlocks and cocked them both.

I don't care now, she thought fatalistically. What will be, will be.

The door flew open and Jay burst in, red faced and panting. With the ax in his hand he stepped toward Lizzie.

She stretched out her left arm and fired a shot over his head.

In the confined space the bang was like a cannon. Jay stopped and held up his hands in a defensive gesture, looking scared.

"You know how straight I can shoot," she said to him. "But I've only got one shot left, so the next will go into your heart." As she spoke she could hardly believe she was tough enough to say such violent words to the man whose body she had loved. She wanted to cry, but she gritted her teeth and stared unflinchingly at him.

"You cold bitch," he said.

It was a clever barb. Coldness was what she accused herself of. Slowly she lowered the pistol. Of course she would not shoot him. "What do you want?" she said.

He dropped the ax. "To bed you one time before I leave," he said.

She felt sick. The image of Mack came into her mind. No one but he could make love to her now. The thought of doing it with Jay was horrifying.

Jay grasped her pistols by the barrels and she let him take them away. He uncocked the one she had not fired then dropped both.

She stared at him in horror. She could not believe this was going to happen.

He came close and punched her in the stomach.

She let out a cry of shock and pain, and doubled up.

"Never point a gun at me again!" he yelled.

He punched her face and she fell to the floor.

He kicked her head and she passed out.

35

ALL THE NEXT MORNING LIZZIE LAY IN BED WITH A HEADACHE SO severe she could barely speak.

Sarah came in with breakfast, looking frightened. Lizzie sipped some tea then closed her eyes again.

When the cook came to take the tray away Lizzie said: "Is Mr. Jamisson gone?"

"Yes, madam. He left for Williamsburg at first light. Mr. Lennox gone with him."

Lizzie felt a little better.

A few minutes later Mack burst into the room. He stood beside her bed and stared at her, shaking with rage. He reached out and felt her face with trembling fingers. Although her bruises were tender, his touch was light, and he did not hurt her; in fact she found it comforting. She took his hand and kissed his palm. They sat together for a long time, not speaking. Lizzie's pain began to ease. After a while she fell asleep. When she woke up he had gone.

In the afternoon Mildred came in and opened the blinds. Lizzie sat up while Mildred combed her hair. Then Mack came in with Dr. Finch.

"I didn't send for you," Lizzie said.

Mack said: "I fetched him."

For some reason Lizzie felt ashamed of what had happened to her, and she wished Mack had not gone for the doctor. "What makes you think I'm sick?"

"You spent the morning in bed."

"I might just be lazy."

"And I might be the governor of Virginia."

She relented and smiled. He cared for her, and that made her happy. "I'm grateful," she said.

The doctor said: "I was told you had a headache."

"I'm not ill, though," she replied. What the hell, she thought, why not tell the truth? "My head hurts because my husband kicked it."

"Hmm." Finch looked embarrassed. "How's your vision—blurred?"

"No."

He put his hands on her temples and probed gently with his fingers. "Do you feel confused?"

"Love and marriage confuse me, but not because my head's damaged. Ouch!"

"Is that where the blow landed?"

"Yes, damn it."

"You're lucky to have so much curly hair. It cushioned the impact. Any nausea?"

"Only when I think about my husband." She realized she was sounding brittle. "But that's no concern of yours, Doctor."

"I'll give you a drug to ease the pain. Don't get too fond of it, it's habit-forming. Send for me again if you have any trouble with your eyesight."

When he had gone Mack sat on the edge of the bed and held her hand. After a while he said: "If you don't want him to kick your head you should leave him."

She tried to think of a reason why she should stay. Her husband did not love her. They had no children and it seemed they never would. Their home was almost certainly forfeit. There was nothing to keep her.

"I wouldn't know where to go," she said.

"I would." His face showed profound emotion. "I'm going to run away."

Her heart missed a beat. She could not bear the thought of losing him.

"Peg will go with me," he added.

Lizzie stared at him, saying nothing.

"Come with us," he said.

There—it was out. He had hinted at it before—"Run away with some ne'er-do-well," he had said—but now he was not hinting. She wanted to say "Yes, yes, today, now!" But she held back. She felt frightened. "Where will you go?" she said.

He took from his pocket a leather case and unfolded a map. "About a hundred miles west of here is a long mountain range. It starts way up in Pennsylvania and goes farther south than anyone knows. It's high, too. But people say there's a pass, called the Cumberland Gap, down here, where the Cumberland River rises. Beyond the mountains is wilderness. They say there aren't even any Indians there, because the Sioux and the Cherokee have been fighting over it for generations and neither side can get the upper hand long enough to settle."

She began to feel excited. "How would you get there?"

"Peg and I would walk. I'd head west from here to the foothills. Pepper Jones says there's a trail that runs southwest, roughly parallel with the mountain range. I'd follow that to the Holston River, here on the map. Then strike out into the mountains."

"And . . . if you were not alone?"

"If you come with me we can take a wagon and more supplies: tools, seed, and food. I won't be a runaway then, I'll be a servant, traveling with his mistress and her maid. In that case I'd go south to Richmond then west to Staunton. It's longer, but Pepper says the roads are better. Pepper could be wrong but it's the best information I've got."

She felt scared and thrilled. "And once you reach the mountains?"

He smiled. "We'll look for a valley with fish in the stream and deer in the woods, and perhaps a pair of eagles nesting in the highest trees. And there we'll build a house."

✳

Lizzie packed blankets, woolen stockings, scissors, needles and thread. As she worked, her feelings seesawed from elation to terror. She was deliriously happy at the thought of running away with Mack.

She imagined them riding through the wooded country side by side and sleeping together in a blanket under the trees. Then she thought of the hazards. They would have to kill their food day by day; build a house; plant corn; doctor their horses. The Indians might be hostile. There could be desperadoes roaming the territory. What if they got snowed in? They could starve to death!

Glancing out of her bedroom window she saw the buggy from MacLaine's tavern in Fredericksburg. There was luggage on the back and a single figure on the passenger seat. The driver, an old drunk called Simmins, had obviously come to the wrong plantation. She went down to redirect him.

But when she stepped out onto the porch she recognized the passenger.

It was Jay's mother, Alicia.

She was wearing black.

"Lady Jamisson!" Lizzie said in horror. "You should be in London!"

"Hello, Lizzie," said her mother-in-law. "Sir George is dead."

*

"Heart failure," she said a few minutes later, sitting in the drawing room with a cup of tea. "He collapsed at his place of business. They brought him to Grosvenor Square but he died on the way."

There was no sob in her voice, no hint of tears in her eyes, as she spoke of the death of her husband.

Lizzie remembered the young Alicia as pretty, rather than beautiful, and now there was little remaining of her youthful allure. She was just a middle-aged woman who had come to the end of a disappointing marriage. Lizzie pitied her. I'll never be like her, she vowed. "Do you miss him?" she said hesitantly.

Alicia gave her a sharp look. "I married wealth and position, and that's what I got. Olive was the only woman he loved, and he never let me forget it. I don't ask for sympathy! I brought it on myself, and so I bore it for twenty-four years. But don't ask me to mourn him. All I feel is a sense of release."

"That's dreadful," Lizzie whispered. Such a fate had been in the cards for her, she thought with a shiver of dread. But she was not going to accept it. She was going to escape. However, she would have to be wary of Alicia.

"Where's Jay?" said Alicia.

"He's gone to Williamsburg to try to borrow money."

"The plantation hasn't prospered, then."

"Our tobacco crop was condemned."

The shadow of sadness crossed Alicia's face. Lizzie realized that Jay was a disappointment to his mother, just as he was to his wife—though Alicia would never admit it.

"I suppose you're wondering what's in Sir George's will," Alicia said.

The will had not crossed Lizzie's mind. "Did he have much to bequeath? I thought the business was in trouble."

"It was saved by the coal from High Glen. He died a very rich man."

Lizzie wondered whether he had left anything to Alicia. If not she might expect to live with her son and daughter-in-law. "Did Sir George provide for you?"

"Oh, yes—my portion was settled before we married, I'm happy to say."

"And Robert has inherited everything else?"

"That's what we all expected. But my husband left a quarter of his wealth to be divided among any legitimate grandchildren alive within a year of his death. So your little baby is rich. When am I going to see him, or her? Which did you have?"

Alicia had obviously left London before Jay's letter arrived. "A little girl," Lizzie said.

"How nice. She's going to be a rich woman."

"She was born dead."

Alicia offered no sympathy. "Hell," she swore. "You must be sure to have another, quickly."

✳

Mack had loaded the wagon with seed, tools, rope, nails, cornmeal and salt. He had opened the gun room with Lizzie's key and taken all the rifles and ammunition. He had also loaded a plowshare. When they reached their destination he would convert the wagon into a plow.

He would put four mares in the traces, he decided, and take two stallions in addition, so that they could breed. Jay Jamisson would be furious at the theft of his precious horses: he would mind that more than the loss of Lizzie, Mack felt sure.

While he was roping down the supplies, Lizzie came out.

"Who's your visitor?" he asked her.

"Jay's mother, Alicia."

"Good God! I didn't know she was coming."

"Nor did I."

Mack frowned. Alicia was no threat to his plans but her husband might be. "Is Sir George coming?"

"He's dead."

That was a relief. "Praise be. The world is well rid of him."

"Can we still leave?"

"I don't see why not. Alicia can't stop us."

"What if she goes to the sheriff and says we've run away and stolen all this?" She indicated the pile of supplies on the wagon.

"Remember our story. You're going to visit a cousin who has just started to farm in North Carolina. You're taking gifts."

"Even though we're bankrupt."

"Virginians are famous for being generous when they can't afford it."

Lizzie nodded. "I'll make sure Colonel Thumson and Suzy Delahaye hear of my plans."

"Tell them that your mother-in-law disapproves and she may try to make trouble for you."

"Good idea. The sheriff won't want to get involved in a family quarrel." She paused. The look on her face made his heart race. Hesitantly she said: "When . . . when shall we leave?"

He smiled. "Before first light. I'll have the wagon taken down to the quarters tonight, so that we won't make much noise as we go. By the time Alicia wakes up we'll be gone."

She squeezed his arm quickly then hurried back into the house.

＊

Mack came to Lizzie's bed that night.

She was lying awake, full of fear and excitement, thinking of the adventure that would begin in the morning, when he came silently into the room. He kissed her lips, threw off his clothes, and slipped into bed beside her.

They made love, then lay talking in low voices about tomorrow, then made love again. As dawn approached Mack drifted into a doze, but Lizzie stayed awake, looking at his features in the firelight, thinking of the journey in space and time that had brought them from High Glen all the way to this bed.

Soon he stirred. They kissed again, a long, contented kiss, then they got up.

Mack went to the stables while Lizzie got ready. Her heart raced as she dressed. She pinned up her hair and put on breeches, riding boots, a shirt and a waistcoat. She packed a dress she could quickly slip on if she needed to revert to being a wealthy woman. She was frightened of the journey they were about to take, but she had no qualms about Mack. She felt so close to him that she would trust him with her life.

When he came for her she was sitting at the window in her coat and three-cornered hat. He smiled to see her in her favorite clothes. They held hands and tiptoed down the stairs and out of the house.

The wagon was waiting down by the road, out of sight. Peg was already sitting on the seat, wrapped in a blanket. Jimmy, the stable boy, had put four horses in harness and roped two more to the back. All the slaves were there to say good-bye. Lizzie kissed Mildred and Sarah, and Mack shook hands with Kobe and Cass. Bess, the field hand who had been injured on the night Lizzie lost her baby, threw her arms around Lizzie and sobbed. They all stood silent in the starlight and watched as Mack and Lizzie climbed on the wagon.

Mack cracked the reins and said: "Hup! Walk on!"

The horses took the strain, the wagon jerked and they moved off.

At the road Mack turned the horses in the direction of Fredericksburg. Lizzie looked back. The field hands were standing in complete silence, waving.

A moment later they were gone from sight.

Lizzie looked ahead. In the distance, dawn was breaking.

36

M ATTHEW MURCHMAN WAS OUT OF TOWN WHEN JAY AND LENNOX
reached Williamsburg. He might be back tomorrow, his
servant said. Jay scribbled a note saying he needed to borrow
more money and would like to see the lawyer at his earliest
convenience. He left the office in a bad temper. His affairs were in a
complete mess and he was impatient to do something about it.

Next day, forced to kill time, he went along to the red-and-gray-brick
Capitol building. Dissolved by the governor last year, the assembly had
reconvened after an election. The Hall of Burgesses was a modest, dark
room with rows of benches on either side and a kind of sentry box for
the speaker in the middle. Jay and a handful of other observers stood at
the back, behind a rail.

He swiftly realized that the colony's politics were in turmoil.
Virginia, the oldest English settlement on the continent, seemed ready
to defy its rightful king.

The burgesses were discussing the latest threat from Westminster:
the British Parliament was claiming that anyone accused of treason
could be forced to return to London to stand trial, under a statute that
dated back to Henry VIII.

Feelings ran high in the room. Jay watched in disgust as one
respectable landowner after another stood up and attacked the king. In
the end they passed a resolution saying that the treason statute went
contrary to the British subject's right to trial by a jury of his peers.

They went on to the usual gripes about paying taxes while having no voice in the Westminster Parliament. "No taxation without representation" was their parrot cry. This time, however, they went farther than usual, and affirmed their right to cooperate with other colonial assemblies in opposition to royal demands.

Jay felt sure the governor could not let that pass, and he was right. Just before dinnertime, when the burgesses were discussing a lesser local topic, the sergeant-at-arms interrupted the proceedings to call out: "Mr. Speaker, a message from the governor."

He handed a sheet of paper to the clerk, who read it and said: "Mr. Speaker, the governor commands the immediate attendance of your House in the council chamber."

Now they're in trouble, Jay thought with relish.

He followed the burgesses as they trooped up the stairs and through the passage. The spectators stood in the hall outside the council chamber and looked through the open doors. Governor Botetourt, the living embodiment of the iron fist in the velvet glove, sat at the head of an oval table. He spoke very briefly. "I have heard of your resolves," he said. "You have made it my duty to dissolve you. You are dissolved accordingly."

There was a stunned silence.

"That will be all," he said impatiently.

Jay concealed his glee as the burgesses slowly filed out of the chamber. They collected their papers downstairs and drifted into the courtyard.

Jay made his way to the Raleigh Tavern and sat in the bar. He ordered his midday meal and flirted with a barmaid who was falling in love with him. As he waited he was surprised to see many of the burgesses go past, heading for one of the larger rooms in the rear. He wondered if they were plotting further treason.

When he had eaten he went to investigate.

As he had guessed, the burgesses were holding a debate. They made no attempt to hide their sedition. They were blindly convinced of the rightness of their cause, and that gave them a kind of mad self-confidence. Don't they understand, Jay asked himself, that they're inviting the wrath of one of the world's great monarchies? Do they suppose they can get away with this in the end? Don't they realize that the might of the British army will sooner or later wipe them all out?

They did not, evidently, and so arrogant were they that no one protested when Jay took a seat at the back of the room, although many there knew he was loyal to the Crown.

One of the hotheads was speaking, and Jay recognized George Washington, a former army officer who had made a lot of money in land speculation. He was not much of an orator, but there was a steely determination about him that struck Jay forcibly.

Washington had a plan. In the northern colonies, he said, leading men had formed associations whose members agreed not to import British goods. If Virginians really wanted to put pressure on the London government they should do the same.

If ever I heard a treasonable speech, Jay thought angrily, that was it.

His father's enterprise would suffer further if Washington got his way. As well as convicts, Sir George shipped cargoes of tea, furniture, rope, machinery and a host of luxuries and manufactures that the colonists could not produce themselves. His trade with the North was already down to a fraction of its former worth—that was why the business had been in crisis a year ago.

Not everyone agreed with Washington. Some burgesses pointed out that the northern colonies had more industry and could make many essentials for themselves, whereas the South depended more on imports. What will we do, they said, without sewing thread or cloth?

Washington said there might be exceptions, and the assembly began to get down to details. Someone proposed a ban on slaughtering lambs, to increase the local production of wool. Before long Washington suggested a small committee to thrash out the technicalities. The proposal was passed and the committee members were chosen.

Jay left the room in disgust. As he passed through the hall Lennox approached him with a message. It was from Murchman. He was back in town, he had read Mr. Jamisson's note, and he would be honored to receive Mr. Jamisson at nine o'clock in the morning.

*

The political crisis had distracted Jay briefly, but now his personal troubles came back to him and kept him awake all night. At times he blamed his father for giving him a plantation that could not make money. Then he would curse Lennox for overmanuring the fields instead of clearing new land. He wondered if his tobacco crop had in fact been perfectly all right, and the Virginian inspectors had burned it just to punish him for his loyalty to the English king. As he tossed and turned in the narrow bed, he even began to think Lizzie might have willed the stillborn child to spite him.

He got to Murchman's house early. This was his only chance. No matter where the fault lay, he had failed to make the plantation profitable. If he could not borrow more money his creditors would foreclose the mortgage and he would be homeless as well as penniless.

Murchman seemed nervous. "I've arranged for your creditor to come and meet you," he said.

"Creditor? You told me it was a syndicate."

"Ah, yes—a minor deception, I'm sorry. The individual wanted to remain anonymous."

"So why has he decided to reveal himself now?"

"I . . . I couldn't say."

"Well, I suppose he must be planning to lend me the money I need—otherwise why bother to meet me?"

"I daresay you're right—he hasn't confided in me."

Jay heard a knock at the front door and low voices as someone was admitted.

"Who is he, anyway?"

"I think I'll let him introduce himself."

The door opened and in walked Jay's brother, Robert.

Jay leaped to his feet, astonished. "You!" he said. "When did you get here?"

"A few days ago," Robert said.

Jay held out his hand and Robert shook it briefly. It was almost a year since Jay had seen him last, and Robert was getting more and more like their father: beefy, scowling, curt. "So it was you who loaned me the money?" Jay said.

"It was Father," Robert said.

"Thank God! I was afraid I might not be able to borrow more from a stranger."

"But Father's not your creditor anymore," Robert said. "He's dead."

"Dead?" Jay sat down again abruptly. The shock was profound. Father was not yet fifty. "How . . . ?"

"Heart failure."

Jay felt as if a support had been pulled away from beneath him. His father had treated him badly, but he had always been there, consistent and seemingly indestructible. Suddenly the world had become a more insecure place. Although he was already sitting down Jay wanted to lean on something.

He looked again at his brother. There was an expression of vindictive triumph on Robert's face. Why was he pleased? "There's something else," Jay said. "What are you looking so damned smug about?"

"I'm your creditor now," Robert said.

Jay saw what was coming. He felt as if he had been punched in the stomach. "You swine," he whispered.

Robert nodded. "I'm foreclosing on your mortgage. The tobacco plantation is mine. I've done the same with High Glen: bought up the mortgages and foreclosed. That belongs to me now."

Jay could hardly speak. "You must have planned this," he said with a struggle.

Robert nodded.

Jay fought back tears. "You and Father. . . ."

"Yes."

"I've been ruined by my own family."

"You've been ruined by yourself. You're lazy and foolish and weak."

Jay ignored his insults. All he could think of was that his own father had plotted his downfall. He remembered how the letter from Murchman had come just a few days after his arrival in Virginia. Father must have written in advance, ordering the lawyer to offer a mortgage.

He had anticipated that the plantation would get into difficulties and he had planned to take it back from Jay. His father was dead but had sent this message of rejection from beyond the grave.

Jay stood up slowly, with a painful effort, like an old man. Robert stood silent, looking scornful and haughty. Murchman had the grace to act guilty. With an embarrassed look on his face he hurried to the door and held it for Jay. Slowly Jay walked through the hall and out into the muddy street.

✳

Jay was drunk by dinnertime.

He was so drunk that even Mandy, the barmaid who was falling in love with him, appeared to lose interest. That evening he passed out in the bar of the Raleigh. Lennox must have put him to bed, for he woke up in his room the following morning.

He thought of killing himself. He had nothing to live for: no home, no future, no children. He would never amount to anything in Virginia now that he had gone bankrupt, and he could not bear to go back to Britain. His wife hated him and even Felia now belonged to his brother. The only question was whether to put a bullet into his head or drink himself to death.

He was drinking brandy again at eleven o'clock in the morning when his mother walked into the bar.

When he saw her he thought perhaps he was already going mad. He stood up and stared at her, frightened. Reading his mind, as always, she said: "No, I'm not a ghost." She kissed him and sat down.

When he recovered his composure he said: "How did you find me?"

"I went to Fredericksburg and they told me you were here. Prepare yourself for a shock. Your father's dead."

"I know."

That surprised her. "How?"

"Robert is here."

"Why?"

Jay told her the story and explained that Robert was now the owner of both the plantation and High Glen.

"I was afraid the two of them were planning something like that," she said bitterly.

"I'm ruined," he said. "I was thinking of killing myself."

Her eyes widened. "Then Robert didn't tell you what was in your father's will."

Suddenly Jay saw a gleam of hope. "Did he leave me something?"

"Not you, no. Your child."

Jay's heart sank again. "The child was stillborn."

"A quarter of the estate goes to any grandchildren of your father born within a year of his death. If there are no grandchildren after a year, Robert gets everything."

"A quarter? That's a fortune!"

"All you have to do is make Lizzie pregnant again."

Jay managed a grin. "Well, I know how to do that, anyway."

"Don't be so sure. She's run away with that coal miner."

"What?"

"She left, with McAsh."

"Good God! She's left me? And gone off with a convict?" It was deeply humiliating. Jay looked away. "I'll never live this down. Good God."

"That child is with them, Peg Knapp. They took a wagon and six of your horses and enough supplies to start several farms."

"Damned thieves!" He felt outraged and helpless. "Couldn't you stop them?"

"I tried the sheriff—but Lizzie had been clever. She gave out a story that she was taking gifts to a cousin in North Carolina. The neighbors told the sheriff I was just a cantankerous mother-in-law trying to stir up trouble."

"They all hate me because I'm loyal to the king." The seesaw of hope and despair became too much for Jay and he sank into lethargy. "It's no good," he said. "Fate is against me."

"Don't give up yet!"

Mandy, the barmaid, interrupted to ask Alicia what she would like. She ordered tea. Mandy smiled coquettishly at Jay.

"I could have a child with another woman," he said as Mandy went away.

Alicia looked scornfully at the barmaid's wiggling rear and said: "No good. The grandchild has to be legitimate."

"Could I divorce Lizzie?"

"No. It requires an act of Parliament and a fortune in money, and anyway we don't have the time. While Lizzie is alive it has to be her."

"I've no idea where she's gone."

"I do."

Jay stared at his mother. Her cleverness never ceased to amaze him. "How do you know?"

"I followed them."

He shook his head in incredulous admiration. "How did you do that?"

"It wasn't difficult. I kept asking people if they had seen a four-horse wagon with a man, a woman and a child. There's not so much traffic that people forget."

"Where did they go?"

"They came south to Richmond. There they took a road called Three Notch Trail and headed west, toward the mountains. I turned east and came here. If you leave this morning you'll be only three days behind them."

Jay thought about it. He hated the idea of chasing after a runaway wife: it made him look such a fool. But it was his only chance of inheriting. And a quarter of Father's estate was a huge fortune.

What would he do when he caught up with her? "What if Lizzie won't come back?" he said.

His mother's face set in grim lines of determination. "There is one other possibility, of course," she said. She looked at Mandy then turned her cool gaze back on Jay. "You could make another woman pregnant, and marry her, and inherit—if Lizzie suddenly died."

He stared at his mother for a long moment.

She went on: "They're headed for the wilderness, beyond the law. Anything can happen out there: there are no sheriffs, no coroners. Sudden death is normal and no one questions it."

Jay swallowed dryly and reached for his drink. His mother put her hand on the glass to prevent him. "No more," she said. "You have to get started."

Reluctantly he withdrew his hand.

"Take Lennox with you," she advised. "If worse comes to worst, and you can't persuade or force Lizzie to come back with you—he will know how to manage it."

Jay nodded. "Very well," he said. "I'll do it."

37

T HE ANCIENT BUFFALO-HUNTING TRACK KNOWN AS THREE NOTCH Trail went due west for mile after mile across the rolling Virginia landscape. It ran parallel to the James River, as Lizzie could see from Mack's map. The road crossed an endless series of ridges and valleys formed by the hundreds of creeks that trickled south into the James. At first they passed many large estates like the ones around Fredericksburg, but as they went farther west the houses and fields became smaller and the tracts of undeveloped woodland larger.

Lizzie was happy. She was scared and anxious and guilty, but she could not help smiling. She was out of doors, on a horse, beside the man she loved, beginning a great adventure. In her mind she worried about what might happen, but her heart sang.

They pushed the horses hard, for they feared they might be followed. Alicia Jamisson would not sit quietly in Fredericksburg waiting for Jay to come home. She would have sent a message to Williamsburg, or gone there herself, to warn him of what had happened. Were it not for Alicia's news about Sir George's will, Jay might have shrugged his shoulders and let them go. But now he needed his wife to provide the necessary grandchild. He would almost certainly chase after Lizzie.

They had several days' start on him, but he would travel faster, for he had no need of a wagonload of supplies. How would he follow the fugitives' trail? He would have to ask at houses and taverns along the way, and hope that people noticed who went by. There were few travelers on the road and the wagon might well be remembered.

On the third day the countryside became more hilly. Cultivated fields gave way to grazing, and a blue mountain range appeared in the distant haze. As the miles went by the horses became overtired, stumbling on the rough road and stubbornly slowing down. On uphill stretches Mack, Lizzie and Peg got off the wagon and walked to lighten the load, but it was not enough. The beasts' heads drooped, their pace slowed further, and they became unresponsive to the whip.

"What's the matter with them?" Mack asked anxiously.

"We have to give them better food," she replied. "They're existing on what they can graze at night. For work like this, pulling a wagon all day, horses need oats."

"I should have brought some," Mack said regretfully. "I never thought of it—I don't know much about horses."

That afternoon they reached Charlottesville, a new settlement growing up where Three Notch Trail crossed the north-south Seminole Trail, an old Indian route. The town was laid out in parallel streets rising up the hill from the road, but most of the lots were undeveloped and there were only a dozen or so houses. Lizzie saw a courthouse with a whipping post outside and a tavern identified by an inn sign with a crude painting of a swan. "We could get oats here," she said.

"Let's not stop," Mack said. "I don't want people to remember us."

Lizzie understood his thinking. The crossroads would present Jay with a problem. He would have to find out whether the runaways had turned south or continued west. If they called attention to themselves by stopping at the tavern for supplies they would make his task easier. The horses would just have to suffer a little longer.

A few miles beyond Charlottesville they stopped where the road was crossed by a barely visible track. Mack built a fire and Peg cooked hominy. There were undoubtedly fish in the streams and deer in the woods, but the fugitives had no time for hunting and fishing, so they ate mush. There was no taste to it, Lizzie found, and the glutinous texture was disgusting. She forced herself to eat a few spoonfuls, but she was nauseated and threw the rest away. She felt ashamed that her field hands had eaten this every day.

While Mack washed their bowls in a stream Lizzie hobbled the horses so that they could graze at night but not run away. Then the three of them wrapped themselves in blankets and lay under the wagon, side by side. Lizzie winced as she lay down, and Mack said: "What's the matter?"

"My back hurts," she said.

"You're used to a feather bed."

"I'd rather lie on the cold ground with you than sleep alone in a feather bed."

They did not make love, with Peg beside them, but when they thought she was asleep they talked, in low murmurs, of all the things they had been through together.

"When I pulled you out of that river, and rubbed you dry with my petticoat," Lizzie said. "You remember."

"Of course. How could I forget?"

"I dried your back, and then when you turned around . . ." She hesitated, suddenly shy. "You had got . . . excited."

"Very. I was so exhausted I could hardly stand, but even then I wanted to make love to you."

"I'd never seen a man like that before. I found it so thrilling. I dreamed about it afterward. I'm embarrassed to remember how much I liked it."

"You've changed so much. You used to be so arrogant."

Lizzie laughed softly. "I think the same about you!"

"I was arrogant?"

"Of course! Standing up in church and reading a letter out to the laird!"

"I suppose I was."

"Perhaps we've both changed."

"I'm glad we have." Mack touched her cheek. "I think that was when I fell in love with you—outside the church, when you told me off."

"I loved you for a long time without knowing it. I remember the prizefight. Every blow that landed on you hurt me. I hated to see your beautiful body being damaged. Afterward, when you were still unconscious, I caressed you. I touched your chest. I must have wanted you even then, before I got married. But I didn't admit it to myself."

"I'll tell you when it started for me. Down the pit, when you fell into my arms, and I accidentally felt your breast and realized who you were."

She chuckled. "Did you hold me a bit longer than you really needed to?"

He looked bashful in the firelight. "No. But afterward I wished I had."

"Now you can hold me as much as you like."

"Yes." He put his arms around her and drew her to him. They lay silent for a long while, and in that position they went to sleep.

✳

Next day they crossed a mountain range by a pass then dropped down into the plain beyond. Lizzie and Peg rode the wagon downhill while Mack ranged ahead on one of the spare horses. Lizzie ached from sleeping on the ground, and she was beginning to feel the lack of good food. But she would have to get used to it: they had a long way to go. She gritted her teeth and thought of the future.

She could tell that Peg had something on her mind. Lizzie was fond of Peg. Whenever she looked at the girl she thought of the baby who had died. Peg had once been a tiny baby, loved by her mother. For the sake of that mother, Lizzie would love and care for Peg.

"What's troubling you?" Lizzie asked her.

"These hill farms remind me of Burgo Marler's place."

It must be dreadful, Lizzie thought, to have murdered someone; but she felt there was something else, and before long Peg came out with it. "Why did you decide to run away with us?"

It was hard to find a simple answer to that question. Lizzie thought about it and eventually replied: "Mainly because my husband doesn't love me anymore, I suppose." Something in Peg's expression made her add: "You seem to wish I had stayed at home."

"Well, you can't eat our food and you don't like sleeping on the ground, and if we didn't have you we wouldn't have the wagon and we could go faster."

"I'll get used to the conditions. And the supplies on the wagon will make it a lot easier for us to set up home in the wilderness."

Peg still looked sulky, and Lizzie guessed there was more to come. Sure enough, after a silence Peg said: "You're in love with Mack, aren't you?"

"Of course!"

"But you've only just got rid of your husband—isn't it a bit soon?"

Lizzie winced. She herself felt this was true, in moments of self-doubt; but it was galling to hear the criticism from a child. "My husband hasn't touched me for six months—how long do you think I should wait?"

"Mack loves me."

This was becoming complicated. "He loves us both, I think," Lizzie said. "But in different ways."

Peg shook her head. "He loves me. I know it."

"He's been like a father to you. And I'll try to be like a mother, if you'll let me."

"No!" Peg said angrily. "That's not how it's going to be!"

Lizzie was at a loss to know what to say to her. Looking ahead, she saw a shallow river with a low wooden building beside it. Obviously the road crossed the river by a ford just here, and the building was a tavern used by travelers. Mack was tying his horse to a tree outside the building.

She pulled up the wagon. A big, roughly dressed man came out wearing buckskin trousers, no shirt, and a battered three-cornered hat. "We need to buy oats for our horses," Mack said.

The man replied with a question. "You folks going to rest your team and step inside and take a drink?"

Suddenly Lizzie felt a tankard of beer was the most desirable thing on earth. She had brought money from Mockjack Hall—not much, but enough for essential purchases on the journey. "Yes," she said decisively, and she swung down from the wagon.

"I'm Barney Tobold—they call me Baz," said the tavern keeper. He looked quizzically at Lizzie. She was wearing men's clothing, but she had not completed the disguise and her face was obviously female. However, he made no comment but led the way inside.

When her eyes adjusted to the gloom Lizzie saw that the tavern was one bare earth-floored room with two benches and a counter, and a few wooden tankards on a shelf. Baz reached for a rum barrel, but she forestalled him, saying: "No rum—just beer, please."

"I'll take rum," Peg said eagerly.

"Not if I'm paying, you won't," Lizzie contradicted her. "Beer for her too, please, Baz."

He poured beer from a cask into wooden mugs. Mack came in with his map in his hand and said: "What river is this?"

"We call it South River."

"Once you cross over, where does the road lead to?"

"A town called Staunton, about twenty miles away. After that there's not much: a few trails, some frontier forts, then real mountains, that nobody's ever crossed. Where are you people headed, anyway?"

Mack hesitated so Lizzie answered: "I'm on my way to visit a cousin."

"In Staunton?"

Lizzie was flustered by the question. "Uh . . . near there."

"Is that so? What name?"

She said the first name that came into her head. "Angus . . . Angus James."

Baz frowned. "That's funny. I thought I knew everyone in Staunton, but I don't recognize that name."

Lizzie improvised. "It may be that his farm is some way from the town—I've never been there."

The sound of hoofbeats came from outside. Lizzie thought of Jay. Could he have caught up with them so soon? The sound made Mack uneasy too, and he said: "If we want to make Staunton by nightfall . . ."

"We don't have time to linger," Lizzie finished. She emptied her tankard.

"You've hardly wet your throats," Baz said. "Drink another cup."

"No," Lizzie said decisively. She took out her pocketbook. "Let me pay you."

Two men walked in, blinking in the dim light. They appeared to be local people: both were dressed in buckskin trousers and homemade boots. Out of the corner of her eye Lizzie saw Peg give a start, then turn her back on the newcomers, as if she did not want them to see her face.

One of them spoke cheerily. "Hello, strangers!" He was an ugly man with a broken nose and one closed eye. "I'm Chris Dobbs, known as Deadeye Dobbo. A pleasure to meet you. What news from the East? Them burgesses still spending our taxes on new palaces and fancy dinners? Let me buy you a drink. Rum all round, please, Baz."

"We're leaving," Lizzie said. "Thanks all the same."

Dobbo looked more closely at her and said: "A woman in buckskin pants!"

She ignored him and said: "Good-bye, Baz—and thanks for the information."

Mack went out and Lizzie and Peg moved to the door. Dobbs looked at Peg and registered surprise. "I know you," he said. "I've seen you with Burgo Marler, God rest his soul."

"Never heard of him," Peg said boldly, and walked past.

In the next second the man drew the logical conclusion. "Jesus Christ, you must be the little bitch that killed him!"

"Wait a minute," Lizzie said. She wished Mack had not gone out so quickly. "I don't know what crazy idea you've got into your head, Mr. Dobbs, but Jenny has been a maid in my family since she was ten years old and she's never met anyone called Burgo Marler, let alone killed him."

He was not to be put off so easily. "Her name isn't Jenny, though it's something like that: Betty, or Milly, or Peggy. That's it—she's Peggy Knapp."

Lizzie felt sick with fear.

Dobbs turned to his companion for support. "Ain't it her, now?"

The other man shrugged. "I never saw Burgo's convict more than a time or two, and one little girl looks much the same as another," he said dubiously.

Baz said: "She fits the description in the *Virginia Gazette,* though." He reached under the counter and came up with a musket.

Lizzie's fear went away and she felt angry. "I hope you aren't thinking of threatening me, Barney Tobold," she said, and her voice surprised her by its strength.

He replied: "Maybe you should all stay around while we get a message to the sheriff in Staunton. He feels bad about not catching Burgo's murderer. I know he'll want to check your story."

"I'm not going to wait around while you find out you're mistaken."

He leveled the gun at her. "I think you're going to have to."

"Let me explain something to you. I'm walking out of here with this child, and there's only one thing that you need to know: if you shoot the wife of a wealthy Virginian gentleman, no excuse on earth is going to keep you from the gallows." She put her hands on Peg's shoulders, stepped between her and the gun, and pushed her forward.

Baz cocked the flintlock with a deafening click.

Peg twitched under Lizzie's hands, and Lizzie tightened her grip, sensing the girl wanted to break into a run.

It was three yards to the door but they seemed to take an hour to get there.

No shot rang out.

Lizzie felt sunshine on her face.

She could contain herself no longer. Shoving Peg forward she began to run.

Mack was already in the saddle. Peg jumped up on the seat of the wagon and Lizzie followed.

"What happened?" Mack said. "You look as if you've seen a ghost."

"Let's get out of here!" Lizzie said, snapping the reins. "That one-eyed fellow recognized Peg!" She turned the wagon to the east. If they headed for Staunton they would first have to ford the river, which would take too long, and then they would be riding into the sheriff's arms. They had to go back the way they had come.

Looking over her shoulder she saw the three men in the tavern doorway, Baz still holding the musket. She whipped the horses into a trot.

Baz did not shoot.

A few seconds later they were out of range.

"By God," Lizzie said gratefully. "That was a nasty moment."

The road turned a corner into the woods and they passed out of sight of the tavern. After a while Lizzie slowed the horses to a walk. Mack brought his horse alongside. "We forgot to buy oats," he said.

✳

Mack was relieved to escape but he regretted Lizzie's decision to turn back. They should have forded the river and gone on. Staunton was obviously where Burgo Marler's farm was, but they could have found a side trail around the town, or slipped through at night. However, he did not criticize her, for she had been forced to make an instant decision.

They stopped where they had made camp the night before, at the place where Three Notch Trail was crossed by a side trail. They drove the wagon off the main road and concealed it in the woods: they were now fugitives from justice.

Mack looked at his map and decided they would have to go back to Charlottesville and take the Seminole Trail south. They could turn west again after a day or two without coming within fifty miles of Staunton.

However, in the morning it occurred to Mack that Dobbs might be heading for Charlottesville. He could have passed by their hidden campsite after dark and reached the town ahead of them. He told Lizzie of his worry, and proposed riding into Charlottesville alone to check that the coast was clear. She agreed.

He rode hard and reached the town before sunrise. He slowed his horse to a walk as he approached the first house. The place was quiet: nothing was moving but an old dog scratching itself in the middle of the road. The door of the Swan tavern was open, and smoke came from its chimney. Mack dismounted and tied his horse to a bush, then cautiously approached the tavern.

There was no one in the bar.

Perhaps Dobbs and his sidekick had been heading the other way, toward Staunton.

A mouthwatering smell was coming from somewhere. He went around to the back and saw a middle-aged woman frying bacon. "I need to buy oats," he said.

Without looking up from her work she said: "There's a store opposite the courthouse."

"Thanks. Have you seen Deadeye Dobbs?"

"Who the hell is he?"

"Never mind."

"Would you like some breakfast before you go?"

"No thanks—I wish I had time."

Leaving his horse, he went up the hill to the wooden courthouse. Across the square was a smaller building with a roughly painted sign saying "Seed Merchant." It was locked up, but in an outhouse at the back he found a half-dressed man shaving. "I need to buy oats," he said again.

"And I need a shave."

"I'm not going to wait. Sell me two sacks of oats now or I'll get them at the South River ford."

Grumbling, the man wiped his face and led Mack into the store.

"Any strangers in town?" Mack asked him.

"You," he replied.

It seemed Dobbs had not come here last night.

Mack paid with Lizzie's money and took the two big sacks on his back. When he went outside he heard hooves and looked up to see three horsemen riding in from the east, going fast.

His heart skipped a beat.

"Friends of yours?" said the seed merchant.

"No."

He hurried down the hill. The riders pulled up at the Swan. Mack slowed his pace as he approached and tipped his hat down over his eyes. As they dismounted he studied their faces.

One of them was Jay Jamisson.

Mack cursed under his breath. Jay had almost caught up, thanks to yesterday's trouble at South River.

Luckily Mack had been cautious, and as a result he was forewarned. Now he had to reach his horse and get away without being seen.

Suddenly he realized that "his" horse had been stolen from Jay, and it was roped to a bush not three yards away from where Jay now stood.

Jay loved his horses. If he gave this one a glance he would recognize it as his own. And he would know in a flash that the runaways were nearby.

Mack stepped over a broken fence into an overgrown lot and watched through a screen of bushes. Lennox was with Jay, and there was another man he did not recognize. Lennox tied up his mount next to Mack's, partly masking the stolen horse from Jay's view. Lennox had no love of horses and would not recognize the beast. Jay tied up next to Lennox. *Go inside, go inside!* Mack shouted in his head, but Jay turned and said something to Lennox. Lennox replied, and the other man laughed coarsely. A drop of sweat rolled down Mack's forehead and into his eye, and he blinked it away. When his vision cleared the three were walking into the Swan.

He breathed a sigh of relief. But it was not over yet.

He came out of the bushes, still bent under the weight of two sacks of oats, and walked quickly across the road to the tavern. He transferred the sacks to the horse.

He heard someone behind him.

He did not dare to look around. He put one foot in the stirrup, then a voice said: "Hey—you!"

Slowly, Mack turned. The speaker was the stranger. He took a deep breath and said: "What?"

"We want breakfast."

"See the woman out back." Mack mounted his horse.

"Hey."

"What now?"

"Has a four-horse wagon passed through here with a woman, a girl and a man?"

Mack pretended to think. "Not lately," he said. He kicked his horse and rode off.

He did not dare to look back.

A minute later he had left the town behind.

He was anxious to get back to Lizzie and Peg, but he was forced to go more slowly because of the weight of the oats, and the sun was warm by the time he reached the crossing. He turned off the road and down the side trail to the hidden campsite. "Jay is in Charlottesville," he said as soon as he saw Lizzie.

She paled. "So close!"

"He'll probably follow Three Notch Trail across the mountains later today. But as soon as he reaches the South River ford he'll find out that we turned back. That will put him only a day and a half behind us. We'll have to abandon the wagon."

"And all our supplies!"

"Most of them. We have three spare horses: we can take whatever they will carry." Mack looked along the narrow trail leading south from the camp. "Instead of going back to Charlottesville we could try taking this track south. It probably cuts a corner and meets up with the Seminole Trail a few miles out of town. And it looks passable for horses."

Lizzie was not the type to whine. Her mouth set in a determined line. "All right," she said grimly. "Let's start unloading."

They had to abandon the plowshare, Lizzie's trunk full of warm underwear, and some of the cornmeal, but they managed to keep the guns, the tools and the seed. They roped the pack horses together then mounted up.

By midmorning they were on their way.

38

F OR THREE DAYS THEY FOLLOWED THE PRIMEVAL SEMINOLE TRAIL southwest, through a majestic series of valleys and passes that wound between lush forested mountains. They passed isolated farms, but they saw few people and no towns. They rode three abreast, the pack horses following in a line. Mack became saddle-sore, but despite that he felt exhilarated. The mountains were magnificent, the sun was shining, and he was a free man.

On the morning of the fourth day they breasted a rise and saw, in the valley below, a wide brown river with a series of midstream islands. On the far bank was a cluster of wooden buildings. A broad flat-bottomed ferry boat was tied up at a jetty.

Mack reined in. "My guess is that this is the James River, and that settlement is a place called Lynch's Ferry."

Lizzie guessed what he was thinking. "You want to turn west again."

He nodded. "We've seen almost nobody for three days—Jay will have trouble picking up our scent. But if we cross that ferry we'll meet the ferryman, and it might be hard to avoid the tavern keeper, the storekeeper and all the local busybodies."

"Good thinking," Lizzie said. "If we get off the road here he won't be able to figure out which way we've gone."

Mack looked at his map. "The valley climbs to the northwest and leads to a pass. Beyond the pass we should be able to join the trail that runs southwest from Staunton."

"Good."

Mack smiled at Peg, who was silent and indifferent. "Are you in agreement?" he said, trying to bring her into the decision.

"Whatever you want," she said.

She seemed unhappy, and Mack assumed it was because she was frightened of being caught. She must be tired, too: sometimes he forgot that she was so small. "Cheer up," he said. "We're escaping!" She looked away. He exchanged glances with Lizzie, who made a helpless gesture.

They turned off the trail at an angle and went down through sloping woodland to reach the river half a mile or so upstream from the settlement. Mack thought they probably had not been observed.

A flat track ran west along the bank for several miles. Then it turned away from the river, skirting a range of hills. The going was hard, and they frequently had to dismount and lead the horses up stony rises, but Mack never lost the intoxicating feeling of freedom.

They ended the day beside a fast-running mountain stream. Lizzie shot a small deer that came to drink from a rocky pool. Mack butchered it and made a spit to roast a haunch. Leaving Peg to watch the fire he went to wash his bloodstained hands.

He made his way downstream to where a small waterfall dropped into a deep pool. He knelt on a ledge and washed his hands in the falling water. Then he decided to bathe, and took off all his clothes. He stepped out of his breeches and looked up to see Lizzie.

"Every time I take off my clothes and jump in a river—"

"You find me watching!"

They both laughed.

"Come and bathe with me," he said.

His heart beat faster as she stripped. He gazed lovingly at her body. She stood naked in front of him with a what-the-hell expression on her face. They embraced and kissed.

When they paused for breath he was struck by a foolish notion. He looked down at the deep pool ten feet below and said: "Let's jump."

"No!" she said. Then she said: "All right!"

They held hands, stood at the edge of the shelf, and jumped, laughing helplessly. They hit the water holding hands. Mack went under and let go of Lizzie. When he surfaced he saw her a few feet away, snorting and blowing and laughing at the same time. Together they swam toward the bank until they felt the riverbed below their feet, then they stopped to rest.

Mack drew her to him. With a thrill of excitement he felt her bare thighs against his. He did not want to kiss her now, he wanted to look at her face. He stroked her hips. Her hand closed around his stiff penis, and she looked into his eyes and smiled happily. He felt as if he would explode.

She put her arms around his neck and lifted her legs so that her thighs squeezed his waist. He settled his feet firmly on the riverbed and took her weight. He lifted her a fraction. She wriggled a little and settled on him. He slid inside her as easily as if they had been practicing for years.

After the cold water her flesh was like hot oil on his skin. Suddenly he felt as if he were in a dream. He was making love to Lady Hallim's daughter in a waterfall in Virginia: how could it be real?

She put her tongue in his mouth and he sucked it. She giggled, then her face became serious again, and a look of concentration came over her. She pulled on his neck, lifting herself, then let her body sink down again, repeatedly. She groaned deep in her throat and half closed her eyes. He watched her face, mesmerized.

Out of the corner of his eye he saw something move on the bank. He turned his head and glimpsed a flash of color, then it was gone. Someone had been watching. Had Peg stumbled on them accidentally, or was it a stranger? He knew he should worry, but Lizzie moaned louder, and the thought left his mind. She began to cry out, her thighs squeezed him in a rhythm that went faster and faster, then she crushed her body to his and screamed, and he held her tight and shook with passion until he was drained.

✳

When they returned to the campsite Peg was gone.

Mack had a bad feeling. "I thought I saw someone, down by the pool, when we were making love. It was just a glimpse, and I couldn't even tell whether it was man, woman or child."

"I'm sure it was Peg," Lizzie said. "I think she's run off."

Mack narrowed his eyes. "What makes you so sure?"

"She's jealous of me because you love me."

"What?"

"She loves you, Mack. She told me she was going to marry you. Of course it's just a girlish fantasy, but she doesn't know that. She's been miserable for days, and I think she saw us making love and ran away."

Mack had a dreadful feeling this was true. He imagined how Peg felt and the thought was agonizing. Now that poor child was wandering alone in the mountains at night. "Oh, God, what are we going to do?" he said.

"Look for her."

"Aye." Mack shook himself. "At least she hasn't taken a horse. She can't have gone far. We'll search together. Let's make torches. She's probably gone back the way we came. We'll find her asleep under a bush, I'll bet."

*

They searched all night.

They backtracked for hours, shining their lights into the woods on either side of the winding trail. Then they returned to their camp, made new torches, and followed the stream up the mountainside, scrambling over rocks. There was no sign of her.

At dawn they ate some of the venison haunch, loaded their supplies on the horses, and went on.

It was possible she had gone west, and Mack hoped they would stumble on her on the track, but all that morning they walked without finding her.

At midday they came upon another trail. It was just a dirt road, but it was wider than a wagon and there were hoof marks in the mud. It ran from northeast to southwest, and in the distance beyond it they could see a range of majestic mountains rising into the blue sky.

This was the road they had been searching for, the way to the Cumberland Gap.

With heavy hearts, they turned southwest and rode on.

39

ON THE MORNING OF THE NEXT DAY, JAY JAMISSON WALKED HIS horse down the hill to the James River and looked across the water to the settlement called Lynch's Ferry.

Jay was exhausted, aching and dispirited. He intensely disliked Binns, the ruffian Lennox had hired in Williamsburg. He was weary of bad food, filthy clothes, long days in the saddle and short nights on the hard ground. In the last few days his hopes had gone up and down like the endless hill tracks he was traveling on.

He had been tremendously excited when he reached the South River ford and learned that Lizzie and her partners in crime had been forced to turn back. However, he was puzzled about how they had passed him on the road.

"They turned off the trail somewhere," Deadeye Dobbs had said confidently as they sat in the tavern beside the river. Dobbs had seen the three fugitives the previous day and had recognized Peg Knapp as the missing convict who had killed Burgo Marler.

Jay supposed he must be right. "But did they go north or south?" he said worriedly.

"If you're running from the law, south is the direction you need— away from sheriffs and courthouses and magistrates."

Jay was not so certain. There might be lots of places in the thirteen colonies where an apparently respectable family group—husband, wife and maidservant—could quietly settle down and effectively disappear. But Dobbs's guess seemed more likely.

He told Dobbs, as he told everyone, that he would pay a reward of fifty English pounds to anyone who arrested the fugitives. The money—enough to buy a small farm out here—had come from his mother. When they parted, Dobbs crossed the ford and went west, toward Staunton. Jay hoped he would spread the word about the reward. If the fugitives managed somehow to give Jay the slip they might yet be caught by others.

Jay returned to Charlottesville, expecting to find that Lizzie had passed through Charlottesville and turned south. However, the wagon had not been seen again. Jay could only guess they had somehow bypassed Charlottesville and found another route to the southbound Seminole Trail. Gambling on that assumption, he had led his gang along the trail. But the countryside was becoming lonelier, and they met no one who recalled seeing a man, a woman and a young girl on the road.

However, he had high hopes of getting some information here at Lynch's Ferry.

They reached the bank and shouted across the fast-moving river. A figure emerged from a building and got into a boat. A rope was stretched from one bank to the other, and the ferry was attached to the rope in an ingenious way so that the pressure of the river's flow drove the boat across the river. When it reached the near bank Jay and his companions led their horses aboard. The ferryman adjusted the ropes and the boat began to move back across.

The man had the dark clothes and sober manner of a Quaker. Jay paid him and began to question him as they crossed the river. "We're looking for a group of three people: a young woman, a Scotsman of about the same age, and a young girl of fourteen. Have they been through here?"

The man shook his head.

Jay's heart sank. He wondered if he was on the wrong track entirely. "Could someone have passed through here without you seeing them?"

The man took his time replying. Eventually he said: "He'd have to be a heck of a good swimmer."

"Suppose they crossed the river somewhere else?"

There was another pause, and he said: "Then they didn't pass through here."

Binns snickered, and Lennox silenced him with a malevolent glare.

Jay looked out over the river and cursed under his breath. She had not been seen for six days. She had slipped away from him somehow. She could be anywhere. She could be in Pennsylvania. She could have returned to the East and be on a ship heading for London. He had lost her. She had outwitted him and cheated him of his inheritance. If ever I see her again, by God I'll shoot her in the head, he thought.

In fact he did not know what he would do if he caught her. He worried at the question constantly as he rode the uneven trails. He knew she would not willingly come back to him. He would have to bring her home bound hand and foot. She might not yield to him even after that: he would probably have to rape her. The thought excited him strangely. On the trail he was disturbed by lascivious memories: the two of them caressing in the attic of the empty Chapel Street house with their mothers outside; Lizzie bouncing on their bed, naked and shameless; making love with Lizzie on top, squirming and moaning. But when she was pregnant, how would he make her stay? Could he lock her away until she gave birth?

Everything would be much simpler if she died. It was not unlikely: she and McAsh would surely put up a fight. Jay did not think he could murder his wife in cold blood. But he could hope she might get killed in a fight. Then he could marry a healthy barmaid, make her pregnant and take ship for London to claim his inheritance.

But that was a happy dream. The reality was that when he finally confronted her he would have to make a decision. Either he took her home alive, giving her ample opportunity to frustrate his plans, or he had to kill her.

How would he dispatch her? He had never killed anyone and had only once used his sword to injure people—at the coal yard riot when he had captured McAsh. Even when he hated Lizzie most he could not imagine plunging a sword into the body he had made love to. He had once trained his rifle on his brother and pulled the trigger. If he had to kill Lizzie it might be best to shoot her from a distance, like a deer. But he was not sure he could manage even that.

The ferry reached the other side. Alongside the landing was a substantial wood-frame building with two stories and an attic. Several more well-built houses were neatly ranged on the slope that rose steeply from the river. The place seemed a prosperous small trading community. As they disembarked the ferryman said casually: "There's somebody waiting for you all in the tavern."

"Waiting for us?" said Jay in astonishment. "How did anyone know we were coming?"

The ferryman answered a different question. "Mean-looking fellow with one closed eye."

"Dobbs! How did he get here ahead of us?"

Lennox added: "And why?"

"Ask him," said the ferryman.

The news had lifted Jay's spirits and he was eager to solve the riddle. "You men deal with the horses," he ordered. "I'll go and see Dobbs."

The tavern was the two-story building alongside the ferry dock. He stepped inside and saw Dobbs sitting at a table eating stew from a bowl.

"Dobbs, what the devil are you doing here?"

Dobbs raised his good eye and spoke with his mouth full. "I come to claim that reward, Captain Jamisson."

"What are you talking about?"

"Look over there." He nodded toward the corner.

There, tied to a chair, was Peg Knapp.

Jay stared at her. This was a piece of luck! "Where the hell did she come from?"

"I found her on the road south of Staunton."

Jay frowned. "Which way was she heading?"

"North, toward the town. I was coming out of town, going to Miller's Mill."

"I wonder how she got there."

"I've asked her, but she won't talk."

Jay looked again at the girl and saw bruises on her face. Dobbs had not been gentle with her.

"I'll tell you what I think," Dobbs said. "They came almost this far but they never crossed the river. Instead they turned west. They must have abandoned their wagon somewhere. They went on horseback up the river valley to the Staunton road."

"But you found Peg on her own."

"Yes."

"So you picked her up."

"It wasn't that easy," Dobbs protested. "She ran like the wind, and every time I grabbed her she slipped through my fingers. But I was on a horse and she wasn't, and in the end she tired."

A Quaker woman appeared and asked Jay if he wanted something to eat. He waved her away impatiently: he was too eager to question Dobbs. "But how did you get here ahead of us?"

He grinned. "I came down the river on a raft."

"There must have been a quarrel," Jay said excitedly. "This murdering little bitch left the others and turned north. So the others must have gone south." He frowned. "Where do they imagine they're going?"

"The road leads to Fort Chiswell. Beyond that there's not much in the way of settled land. Farther south there's a place called Wolf Hills, and after that it's Cherokee country. They aren't going to become Cherokee, so I'd guess they'll turn west at Wolf Hills and head up into the hills. Hunters talk about a pass called Cumberland Gap that leads across the mountains, but I've never been there."

"What's on the other side?"

"Wilderness, they say. Good hunting. Kind of a no-man's-land between the Cherokee and the Sioux. They call it the bluegrass country."

Jay saw it now. Lizzie was planning to start a new life in undiscovered country. But she would fail, he thought excitedly. He would catch her and bring her back—dead or alive.

"The child is not worth much on her own," he said to Dobbs. "You have to help us catch the other two, if you want your fifty pounds."

"You want me to be your guide?"

"Yes."

"They're a couple of days ahead of you now, and they can travel fast without the wagon. It's going to take you a week or more to catch up."

"You get the whole fifty pounds if we succeed."

"I hope we can make up the time before they leave the trail and go off into the wilderness."

"Amen to that," said Jay.

40

T EN DAYS AFTER PEG RAN OFF, MACK AND LIZZIE RODE ACROSS A wide, flat plain and reached the mighty Holston River.

Mack was elated. They had crossed numerous streams and creeks but there was no doubt in his mind that this was the one they were looking for. It was much wider than the others, with a long midstream island. "This is it," he said to Lizzie. "This is the edge of civilization."

For several days they had felt almost alone in the world. Yesterday they had seen one white man—a trapper—and three Indians on a distant hill; today, no white men and several groups of Indians. The Indians were neither friendly nor hostile: they kept a distance.

Mack and Lizzie had not passed a cultivated field for a long time. As the farms became fewer, the game had increased: bison, deer, rabbits and millions of edible birds—turkeys, duck, woodcocks and quail. Lizzie shot more than the two of them could eat.

The weather had been kind. Once it had rained, and they had trudged through mud all day and shivered, soaking wet, all night; but the next day the sun had dried them out. They were saddle-sore and bone-tired, but the horses were holding up, fortified by the lush grass that was everywhere and the oats Mack had bought in Charlottesville.

They had seen no sign of Jay, but that did not mean much: Mack had to assume he was still following them.

They watered the horses in the Holston and sat down to rest on the rocky shore. The trail had petered out as they crossed the plain, and beyond the river there was not the faintest sign of a track. To the north the ground rose steadily and in the far distance, perhaps ten miles away, a high ridge rose forbiddingly into the sky. That was where they were headed.

Mack said: "There must be a pass."

"I don't see it," said Lizzie.

"Nor do I."

"If it isn't there . . ."

"We'll look for another one," he said resolutely.

He spoke confidently but at heart he was fearful. They were going into unmapped country. They might be attacked by mountain lions or wild bears. The Indians could turn hostile. At present there was plenty of food for anyone with a rifle, but what would happen in the winter?

He took out his map, though it was proving increasingly inaccurate.

"I wish we'd met someone who knew the way," Lizzie fretted.

"We've met several," he said.

"And each told a different story."

"They all painted the same picture, though," Mack said. "The river valleys slant from northeast to southwest, just as the map shows, and we have to go northwest, at right angles to the rivers, across a series of high ridges."

"The problem will be to find the passes that cut through the mountain ranges."

"We'll just have to zigzag. Wherever we see a pass that could take us north, we go that way. When we come up against a ridge that looks impassable, we turn west and follow the valley, all the time looking out for our next chance to turn north. The passes may not be where this map shows them to be, but they're in there somewhere."

"Well, there's nothing to do now but try," she said.

"If we get into trouble we'll have to retrace our steps and try a different route, that's all."

She smiled. "I'd rather do this than pay calls in Berkeley Square."

He grinned back. She was ready for anything: he loved that about her. "It beats digging for coal, too."

Lizzie's face became solemn again. "I just wish Peg was here."

Mack felt the same way. They had seen no trace of Peg after she had run off. They had hoped they would catch up with her that first day, but it had not happened.

Lizzie had cried all that night: she felt she had lost two children, first her baby and then Peg. They had no idea where she might be or whether she was even alive. They had done all they could to look for her, but that thought was small consolation. After all he and Peg had been through together, he had lost her in the end. Tears came to his eyes whenever he thought about her.

But now he and Lizzie could make love every night, under the stars. It was spring, and the weather was mild. Soon they would build their house and make love indoors. After that they had to store up salt meat and smoked fish for the winter. Meanwhile he would clear a field and plant their seeds. . . .

He got to his feet.

"That was a short rest," Lizzie said as she stood up.

"I'll be happier when we're out of sight of this river," Mack said. "Jay might guess our route thus far—but this is where we shake him off."

Reflexively they both looked back the way they had come. There was no one in sight. But Jay was on that road somewhere, Mack felt sure.

Then he realized they were being watched.

He had seen a movement out of the corner of his eye and now he saw it again. Tensing, he slowly turned his head.

Two Indians were standing just a few yards away.

This was the northern edge of Cherokee country, and they had been seeing the natives at a distance for three days, but none had approached them.

These two were boys about seventeen years old. They had the straight black hair and reddish tan skin characteristic of the original Americans, and wore the deerskin tunic and trousers the new immigrants had copied.

The taller of the two held out a large fish like a salmon. "I want a knife," he said.

Mack guessed the two of them had been fishing in this river. "You want to trade?" Mack said.

The boy smiled. "I want a knife."

Lizzie said: "We don't need a fish, but we could use a guide. I'll bet he knows where the pass is."

That was a good idea. It would be a tremendous relief to know where they were going. Mack said eagerly: "Will you guide us?"

The boy smiled, but it was obvious he did not understand. His companion remained silent and still.

Mack tried again. "Will you be our guide?"

He began to look troubled. "No trade today," he said doubtfully.

Mack sighed in frustration. He said to Lizzie: "He's an enterprising kid who's learned a few English phrases but can't really speak the language." It would be maddening to get lost here just because they could not communicate with the local people.

Lizzie said: "Let me try."

She went to one of the pack horses, opened a leather satchel, and took out a long-bladed knife. It had been made at the forge on the plantation, and the letter "J," for Jamisson, was burned into the wood of the handle. It was crude by comparison with what you could buy in London, but no doubt it was superior to anything the Cherokee could make themselves. She showed it to the boy.

He smiled broadly. "I'll buy that," he said, and reached for it.

Lizzie withdrew it.

The boy offered the fish and she pushed it away. He looked troubled again.

"Look," Lizzie said. She bent over a large stone with a flat surface. Using the point of the knife she began to scratch a picture. First she drew a jagged line. She pointed at the distant mountains, then at the line. "This is the ridge," she said.

Mack could not tell whether the boy understood or not.

Below the ridge she drew two stick figures, then pointed at herself and Mack. "This is us," she said. "Now—watch carefully." She drew a second ridge, then a deep V-shape joining the two. "This is the pass," she said. Finally she put a stick figure in the V. "We need to find the pass," she said, and she looked expectantly at the boy.

Mack held his breath.

"I'll buy that," the boy said, and he offered Lizzie the fish.

Mack groaned.

"Don't lose hope," Lizzie snapped at him. She addressed the Indian again. "This is the ridge. This is us. Here's the pass. We need to find the pass." Then she pointed at him. "You take us to the pass—and you get the knife."

He looked at the mountains, then at the drawing, then at Lizzie. "Pass," he said.

Lizzie pointed at the mountains.

He drew a V-shape in the air, then pointed through it. "Pass," he said again.

"I'll buy that," Lizzie said.

The boy grinned broadly and nodded vigorously.

Mack said: "Do you think he got the message?"

"I don't know." She hesitated, then took her horse's bridle and began to walk on. "Shall we go?" she said to the boy with a gesture of invitation.

He started to walk beside her.

"Hallelujah!" said Mack.

The other Indian came too.

They struck out along the bank of a stream. The horses settled into the steady gait that had brought them five hundred miles in twenty-two days. Gradually the distant ridge loomed larger, but Mack saw no sign of a pass.

The terrain rose remorselessly, but the ground seemed less rough, and the horses went a little faster. Mack realized the boys were following a trail only they could see. Letting the Indians take the lead, they continued to head straight for the ridge.

They went all the way to the foot of the mountain and suddenly turned east then, to Mack's enormous relief, they saw the pass. "Well done, Fish Boy!" he said joyfully.

They forded a river and curved around the mountain to emerge on the far side of the ridge. As the sun went down they found themselves in a narrow valley with a fast-flowing stream about twenty-five feet wide, running northeast. Ahead of them was another ridge. "Let's make camp," Mack said. "In the morning we'll go up the valley and look for another pass."

Mack felt good. They had followed no obvious route, and the pass had been invisible from the riverbank: Jay could not possibly follow them here. He began to believe he had escaped at last.

Lizzie gave the taller boy the knife. "Thank you, Fish Boy," she said.

Mack hoped the Indians would stay with them. They could have all the knives they wanted if they would guide Mack and Lizzie through the mountains. But they turned and went back the way they had come, the taller of the two still carrying his fish.

A few moments later they had disappeared into the twilight.

41

JAY WAS CONVINCED THEY WOULD CATCH LIZZIE TODAY. HE KEPT UP A fast pace, driving the horses hard. "They can't be far ahead," he kept saying.

However, there was still no sign of the fugitives when he reached the Holston River at dusk. He was angry. "We can't go on in the dark," he said as his men watered their horses. "I thought we would have caught them by now."

"We're not far behind, calm down," Lennox said testily. As the group traveled farther from civilization he became more insolent.

Dobbs put in: "But we can't tell which way they went from here. There's no trail across the mountains—any fool that wants to go has to find his own route."

They hobbled the horses and tied Peg to a tree while Lennox prepared hominy for supper. It had been four days since they had seen a tavern, and Jay was sick of eating the mush he fed his slaves, but it was now too dark to shoot game.

They were all blistered and exhausted. Binns had dropped out at Fort Chiswell, and now Dobbs was losing heart. "I should give up and go back," he said. "It ain't worth fifty pounds to get lost in the mountains and die."

Jay did not want him to go: he was the only one with any local knowledge. "But we haven't caught up with my wife yet," Jay said.

"I don't care about your wife."

"Give it one more day. Everyone says the way across the mountains is north of here. Let's see if we can find the pass. We may catch her tomorrow."

"And we may waste our damn time."

Lennox spooned the lumpy porridge into bowls. Dobbs untied Peg's hands long enough for her to eat, then tied her up again and threw a blanket over her. No one cared much for her well-being, but Dobbs wanted to take her to the Staunton sheriff: he seemed to think he would be admired for capturing her.

Lennox got out a bottle of rum. They wrapped themselves in their blankets and passed the bottle and made desultory conversation. The hours went by and the moon rose. Jay dozed fitfully. At some point he opened his eyes and saw a strange face at the edge of the circle of firelight.

He was so scared he could not make a sound. It was a peculiar face, young but alien, and he realized after a few moments that it belonged to an Indian.

The face was smiling, but not at Jay. Jay followed the gaze and saw that it was focused on Peg. She was making faces at the Indian, and after a minute Jay figured that she was trying to get him to untie her.

Jay lay dead still and watched.

There were two Indians, he saw. They were young boys.

One of them stepped silently into the circle. He was carrying a big fish. He put it gently down on the ground, then drew a knife and bent over Peg.

Lennox was as quick as a snake. Jay hardly saw what happened. There was a blur of movement and Lennox had the boy in an armlock. The knife fell to the ground. Peg gave a cry of disappointment.

The second Indian vanished.

Jay stood up. "What have we here?"

Dobbs rubbed his eyes and stared. "Just an Indian boy, trying to rob us. We should hang him as a lesson to the others."

"Not yet," said Lennox. "He may have seen the people we're after."

That thought lifted Jay's hopes. He stood in front of the boy. "Say something, savage."

Lennox twisted the boy's arm harder. He cried out and protested in his own language. "Speak English," Lennox barked.

"Listen to me," Jay said loudly. "Have you seen two people, a man and a woman, on this road?"

"No trade today," the boy said.

"He does speak English!" Dobbs said.

"I don't think he can tell us anything, though," Jay said dispiritedly.

"Oh, yes he can," Lennox said. "Hold him for me, Dobbo." Dobbs took over and Lennox picked up the knife the Indian had dropped. "Look at this. It's one of ours—it has the letter 'J' burned into the handle."

Jay looked. It was true. The knife had been made at his plantation! "Why, then he must have met Lizzie!"

Lennox said: "Exactly."

Jay felt hopeful again.

Lennox held the knife in front of the Indian's eyes and said: "Which way did they go, boy?"

He struggled, but Dobbs held him tight. "No trade today," he said in a terrified voice.

Lennox took the boy's left hand. He hooked the point of the knife under the nail of the index finger. "Which way?" he said, and he pulled out the nail.

The boy and Peg screamed at the same time.

"Stop it!" Peg yelled. "Leave him alone!"

Lennox pulled out another fingernail. The boy began to sob.

"Which way to the pass?" Lennox said.

"Pass," the boy said, and with a bleeding hand he pointed north.

Jay gave a sigh of satisfaction. "You can take us there," he said.

42

MACK DREAMED HE WAS WADING ACROSS A RIVER TO A PLACE called Freedom. The water was cold, the river bottom was uneven and there was a strong current. He kept striding forward but the bank never got any closer, and the river became deeper with every stride. All the same he knew that if he could just keep going he would eventually get there. But the water got deeper and deeper, and eventually it closed over his head.

Gasping for breath, he woke up.

He heard one of the horses whinny.

"Something's disturbed them," he said. There was no reply. He turned over and saw that Lizzie was not beside him.

Perhaps she had gone to answer a call of nature behind a bush, but he had a bad feeling. He rolled quickly out of his blanket and stood up.

The sky was streaked with gray and he could see the four mares and two stallions, all standing still, as if they had heard other horses in the distance. Someone was coming.

"Lizzie!" he called.

Then Jay stepped from behind a tree with a rifle pointed at Mack's heart.

Mack froze.

A moment later Sidney Lennox appeared with a pistol in each hand.

Mack stood there helpless. Despair engulfed him like the river in his dream. He had not escaped after all: they had caught him.

But where was Lizzie?

The one-eyed man from South River ford, Deadeye Dobbs, rode up, also carrying a rifle, with Peg on another horse beside him, her feet tied together under the horse's belly so she could not get off. She did not seem to be injured, but she looked suicidally miserable and Mack knew she blamed herself for this. Fish Boy was walking alongside Dobbs's horse, tied by a long rope to Dobbs's saddle. He must have led them here. His hands were covered with blood. For a moment Mack was mystified: the boy had shown no sign of injury before. Then he realized that he had been tortured. He felt a wave of disgust for Jay and Lennox.

Jay was staring at the blankets on the ground. It was obvious that Mack and Lizzie had been sleeping together. "You filthy pig," he said, his face working with rage. "Where's my wife?" He reversed his rifle and swung the butt at Mack's head, hitting him a bone-crunching blow to the side of the face. Mack staggered and fell. "Where is she, you coal-mining animal, where's my wife?"

Mack tasted blood. "I don't know."

"If you don't know I might as well have the satisfaction of shooting you through the head!"

Mack realized Jay meant it. Sweat broke out all over him. He felt the impulse to beg for his life but he clamped his teeth together.

Peg screamed: "No—don't shoot—please!"

Jay pointed the rifle at Mack's head. His voice rose to a hysterical pitch. "This is for all the times you've defied me!" he screamed.

Mack looked into his face and saw murder in his eyes.

*

Lizzie lay belly down on a grassy tuft behind a rock, with her rifle in her hand, waiting.

She had picked her spot the night before, after inspecting the riverbank and seeing the footprints and droppings of deer. As the light strengthened she watched, lying dead still, waiting for the animals to come to drink.

Her skill with a rifle was going to keep them alive, she reckoned. Mack could build a house and clear fields and sow seed, but it would be at least a year before they could grow enough to last them through a winter. However, there were three big sacks of salt among their supplies. Lizzie had often sat in the kitchen of High Glen House watching Jeannie, the cook, salting hams and haunches of venison in big barrels. She knew how to smoke fish, too. They would need plenty: the way she and Mack were behaving, there would be three to feed before a year passed. She smiled happily.

There was a movement in the trees. A moment later a young deer came out of the woods and stepped daintily to the water's edge. Bending its head, it stuck out its tongue and began to drink.

Lizzie cocked the flintlock of her rifle silently.

Before she could aim, another deer followed the first, and within a few moments there were twelve or fifteen of them. If all the wilderness is like this, Lizzie thought, we'll grow fat!

She did not want a big deer. The horses were fully loaded and could not carry spare meat, and anyway the younger animals were more tender. She picked her target and took aim, pointing the rifle at its shoulder just over the heart. She breathed evenly and made herself still, the way she had learned back in Scotland.

As always, she suffered a moment of regret for the beautiful animal she was about to destroy.

Then she pulled the trigger.

✳

The shot came from farther up the valley, two or three hundred yards away.

Jay froze, his gun still pointed at Mack.

The horses started, but the shot was too distant to give them a serious scare.

Dobbs brought his mount under control then drawled: "If you shoot now, Jamisson, you'll warn her and she could get away."

Jay hesitated, then slowly lowered his gun.

Mack sagged with relief.

Jay said: "I'll go after her. The rest of you stay here."

Mack realized that if only he could warn her, she might yet escape. He almost wished Jay had shot him. It might have saved Lizzie.

Jay left the clearing and headed upstream, gun held ready.

I have to make one of them fire, Mack realized.

There was an easy way to do that: run away.

But what if I'm hit?

I don't care, I'd rather die than be recaptured.

Before caution could weaken his resolve he broke into a run.

There was a moment of stunned silence before anyone realized what was happening.

Then Peg screamed.

Mack ran for the trees, expecting a bullet to slam into his back.

There was a bang, followed by another.

He felt nothing. The shots had missed him.

Before more shots came he stopped in his tracks and raised his hands in the air.

He had done it. He had given Lizzie her warning.

He turned slowly, keeping his hands up. It's up to you now, Lizzie, he thought. Good luck, my love.

*

Jay stopped when he heard shooting. It had come from behind him. It was not Lizzie who had fired, but someone back in the clearing. He waited, but there was no more gunfire.

What did it mean? McAsh could hardly have got hold of a weapon and loaded it. Anyway, the man was a coal miner: he knew nothing of guns. Jay guessed that Lennox or Dobbs had shot McAsh.

Whatever the truth, the all-important task was to capture Lizzie.

Unfortunately, the shooting had warned her.

He knew his wife. What would she do?

Patience and caution were foreign to her. She rarely hesitated. She reacted quickly and decisively. By now she would be running this way.

She would be almost back in the clearing before she thought to slow down and look ahead and make a plan.

He found a spot where he could see clearly for thirty or forty yards along the bank of the stream. He hid himself in the bushes. Then he cocked the flintlock of his rifle.

Indecision struck him like a sudden pain. What would he do when she came into his sights? If he shot her all his troubles would be over. He tried to pretend he was hunting deer. He would aim for the heart, just below the shoulder, for a clean kill.

She came into view.

She was half walking and half running, stumbling along the uneven riverbank. She was wearing men's clothing again, but he could see her bosom heaving with exertion. She carried two rifles under her arm.

He aimed at her heart, but he saw her naked, straddling him on the bed in the Chapel Street house, her breasts quivering as they made love; and he could not shoot.

When she was ten yards away he stepped out of the undergrowth.

She stopped in her tracks and gave a cry of horror.

"Hello, darling," he said.

She gave him a look of hatred. "Why couldn't you just let me go?" she said. "You don't love me!"

"No, but I need a grandchild," he said.

She looked scornful. "I'd rather die."

"That's the alternative," he said.

✳

There was a moment of chaos after Lennox fired his pistols at Mack.

The horses were frightened by the close-range shooting. Peg's ran away. She stayed on, tied as she was, and hauled on the reins with her bound hands, but she could not stop it and they disappeared into the trees. Dobbs's horse was bucking and he fought to bring it under control. Lennox began hastily to reload his weapons.

That was when Fish Boy made his move.

He ran at Dobbs's horse, jumped on behind him, and wrestled Dobbs out of the saddle.

With a burst of exhilaration Mack realized he was not yet beaten.

Lennox dropped his pistols and ran to the rescue.

Mack stuck out a foot and tripped Lennox.

Dobbs fell off his horse, but one ankle got tangled in the rope by which Fish Boy was tied to the saddle. The horse, now terrified, bolted. Fish Boy clung to its neck for dear life. It ran out of sight, dragging Dobbs along the ground after it.

With savage glee Mack turned to face Lennox. Only the two of them were left in the clearing. At last it had come to a fistfight between them. I'll kill him, Mack thought.

Lennox rolled over and came up with a knife in his hand.

He lunged at Mack. Mack dodged, then kicked Lennox's kneecap and danced out of range.

Limping, Lennox came at him. This time he feinted with the knife, let Mack dodge the wrong way, then struck again. Mack felt a sharp pain in his left side. He swung with his right fist and hit Lennox a mighty blow to the side of the head. Lennox blinked and raised the knife.

Mack backed away. He was younger and stronger than Lennox, but Lennox probably had much experience of knife fights. With a stab of panic he realized that close combat was not the way to defeat a man with a knife. He had to change his tactics.

Mack turned and ran a few yards, looking for a weapon. His eye lit on a rock about the size of his fist. He stooped and picked it up and turned.

Lennox rushed him.

Mack threw the rock. It hit Lennox squarely in the center of the forehead, and Mack gave a shout of triumph. Lennox stumbled, dazed. Mack had to make the most of his advantage. Now was the moment to disarm Lennox. Mack kicked out and connected with Lennox's right elbow.

Lennox dropped the knife and gave a cry of dismay.

Mack had him.

He hit Lennox on the chin with all his might. The blow hurt his hand but gave him deep satisfaction. Lennox backed away, fear in his eyes, but Mack was after him fast. He punched Lennox in the belly, then hit him on each side of the head. Dazed and terrified, Lennox staggered. He was finished, but Mack could not stop. He wanted to kill the man. He grabbed Lennox by the hair, pulled his head down, and kneed him in the face. Lennox screamed and blood spurted from his nose. He fell to his knees, coughed, and vomited. Mack was about to hit him again when he heard Jay's voice say: "Stop or I'll kill her."

Lizzie walked into the clearing and Jay followed, holding his rifle to the back of her head.

Mack stared, paralyzed. He could see that Jay's rifle was cocked. If Jay even stumbled, the gun would blow her head off. Mack turned away from Lennox and moved toward Jay. He was still possessed by savagery. "You've only got one shot," he snarled at Jay. "If you shoot Lizzie, I'll kill you."

"Then perhaps I should shoot you," Jay said.

"Yes," Mack said madly, moving toward him. "Shoot me."

Jay swung the rifle.

Mack felt a wild jubilation: the gun was no longer pointed at Lizzie. He walked steadily toward Jay.

Jay took careful aim at Mack.

There was a strange noise, and suddenly a narrow cylinder of wood was sticking out of Jay's cheek.

Jay screamed in pain and dropped the rifle. It went off with a bang and the ball flew past Mack's head.

Jay had been shot in the face with an arrow.

Mack felt his knees go weak.

The noise came again, and a second arrow pierced Jay's neck.

He fell to the ground.

Into the clearing came Fish Boy, his friend, and Peg, followed by five or six Indian men, all carrying bows.

Mack began to shake with relief. He guessed that when Jay captured Fish Boy, the other Indian had gone for help. The rescue party must have met up with the runaway horses. He did not know what had happened to Dobbs, but one of the Indians was wearing Dobbs's boots.

Lizzie stood over Jay, staring at him, her hand covering her mouth.

Mack went over and put his arms around her. He looked down at the man on the ground. Blood was pouring from his mouth. The arrow had opened a vein in his neck.

"He's dying," Lizzie said shakily.

Mack nodded.

Fish Boy pointed at Lennox, who was still kneeling. The other Indians seized him, threw him flat and held him down. There was some conversation between Fish Boy and the oldest of the others. Fish Boy kept showing his fingers. They looked as if the nails had been pulled out, and Mack guessed that was how Lennox had tortured the boy.

The older Indian drew a hatchet from his belt. With a swift, powerful motion he cut off Lennox's right hand at the wrist.

Mack said: "By Jesus."

Blood gushed from the stump and Lennox fainted.

The man picked up the severed hand and, with a formal air, presented it to Fish Boy.

He took it solemnly. Then he turned around and hurled it away. It flew up into the air and over the trees, to fall somewhere in the woods.

There was a murmur of approval from the Indians.

"A hand for a hand," Mack said quietly.

"God forgive them," said Lizzie.

But they had not finished. They picked up the bleeding Lennox and placed him under a tree. They tied a rope to his ankle, looped the rope over a bough of the tree, and raised him until he was hanging upside-down. Blood pumped from his severed wrist and pooled on the ground beneath him. The Indians stood around, looking at the grisly sight. It seemed they were going to watch Lennox die. They reminded Mack of the crowd at a London hanging.

Peg came up to them and said: "We ought to do something about the Indian boy's fingers."

Lizzie looked away from her dying husband.

Peg said: "Have you got something to bandage his hand?"

Lizzie blinked and nodded. "I've got some ointment, and a handkerchief we can use for a bandage. I'll see to it."

"No," Peg said firmly. "Let me do it."

"If you wish." Lizzie found a jar of ointment and a silk handkerchief and gave them to Peg.

Peg detached Fish Boy from the group around the tree. Although she did not speak his language, she seemed to be able to communicate with him. She led him down to the stream and began to bathe his wounds.

"Mack," said Lizzie.

He turned to her. She was crying.

"Jay is dead," she said.

Mack looked at him. He was completely white. The bleeding had stopped and he was motionless. Mack bent and felt for a heartbeat. There was none.

"I loved him once," Lizzie said.

"I know."

"I want to bury him."

Mack got a spade from their kit. While the Indians watched Lennox bleed to death, Mack dug a shallow grave. He and Lizzie lifted Jay's body and placed it in the hole. Lizzie bent down and gingerly withdrew the arrows from the corpse. Mack shoveled soil over the body and Lizzie began to cover the grave with stones.

Suddenly Mack wanted to get away from this place of blood.

He rounded up the horses. There were now ten: the six from the plantation, plus the four Jay and his gang had brought. Mack was struck by the peculiar thought that he was rich. He owned ten horses. He began to load the supplies.

The Indians stirred. Lennox seemed to be dead. They left the tree and came over to where Mack was loading the horses. The oldest man spoke to Mack. Mack did not understand a word, but the tone was formal. He guessed the man was saying that justice had been done.

They were ready to go.

Fish Boy and Peg came up from the waterside together. Mack looked at the boy's hand: Peg had made a nice job of the bandage.

Fish Boy said something, and there followed an exchange in the Indian language that sounded quite angry. At last all the Indians but Fish Boy walked away.

"Is he staying?" Mack asked Peg.

She shrugged.

The other Indians went eastward, along the river valley toward the setting sun, and soon disappeared into the woods.

Mack got on his horse. Fish Boy unroped a spare horse from the line and mounted it. He went ahead. Peg rode beside him. Mack and Lizzie followed.

"Do you think Fish Boy is going to guide us?" Mack said to Lizzie.

"It looks like it."

"But he hasn't asked a price of any kind."

"No."

"I wonder what he wants."

Lizzie looked at the two young people riding side by side. "Can't you guess?" she said.

"Oh!" said Mack. "You think he's in love with her?"

"I think he wants to spend a little more time with her."

"Well, well." Mack became thoughtful.

As they headed west, along the river valley, the sun came up behind them, throwing their shadows on the land ahead.

✳

It was a broad valley, beyond the highest range but still in the mountains. There was a fast-moving stream of pure cold water bubbling along the valley floor, teeming with fish. The hillsides were densely forested and alive with game. On the highest ridge, a pair of golden eagles came and went, bringing food to the nest for their young.

"It reminds me of home," said Lizzie.

"Then we'll call it High Glen," Mack replied.

They unloaded the horses in the flattest part of the valley bottom, where they would build a house and clear a field. They camped on a patch of dry turf beneath a wide-spreading tree.

Peg and Fish Boy were rummaging through a sack, looking for a saw, when Peg found the broken iron collar. She pulled it out and stared quizzically at it. She looked uncomprehendingly at the letters: she had never learned to read. "Why did you bring this?" she said.

Mack exchanged glances with Lizzie. They were both recalling the scene by the river in the old High Glen, back in Scotland, when Lizzie had asked Mack the same question.

Now he gave Peg the same answer, but this time there was no bitterness in his voice, only hope. "Never to forget," he said with a smile. "Never."

ACKNOWLEDGMENTS

For invaluable help with this book I thank the following:

My editors, Suzanne Baboneau and Ann Patty;

Researchers Nicholas Courtney and Daniel Starer;

Historians Anne Goldgar and Thad Tate;

Ramsey Dow and John Brown-Wright of Longannet Colliery;

Lawrence Lambert of the Scottish Mining Museum;

Gordon and Dorothy Grant of Glen Lyon;

Scottish MPs Gordon Brown, Martin O'Neill, and the late John Smith;

Ann Duncombe;

Colin Tett;

Barbara Follett, Emanuele Follett, Katya Follett and Kim Turner;

And, as always, Al Zuckerman.